Nevada Barr studrnia,
and spent sever⋅⋅⋅⋅⋅⋅⋅⋅⋅⋅⋅⋅⋅⋅⋅⋅⋅⋅⋅⋅⋅⋅⋅eatre
worlds. At thirty⋅⋅⋅⋅⋅⋅⋅⋅⋅⋅⋅⋅⋅⋅⋅⋅⋅⋅⋅⋅⋅⋅ange
and became a ⋅⋅⋅⋅⋅⋅⋅⋅⋅⋅⋅⋅⋅⋅⋅⋅⋅⋅⋅⋅⋅⋅⋅⋅⋅⋅⋅ has
worked on Isle Royale in Lake Superior, at Guadalupe
Mountains in Texas, Mesa Verde in Colorado and is now
a ranger at Natchez Trace Parkway in Mississippi.

Track of the Cat introduced park ranger sleuth Anna
Pigeon and won the Agatha and Anthony Awards for the
Best First Mystery Novel of the Year. *A Superior Death*,
Mountain of Bones and *Firestorm* also feature Anna
Pigeon and are available from Headline.

'I have never read a better mystery debut. It clearly ought
to stand as one of the best mystery novels of the year'
USA Today

'Outstanding evocations of creatures and climate . . .
Distinctly different from standard crime fare. Informed,
intelligent, altogether excellent'   *Literary Review*

'An eventful, characterful story with a slam-bang
denouement, all set in a wilderness environment Barr
knows, loves and describes with poetic passion'
Los Angeles Times

'Brilliant nature writing with a beautifully crafted mystery
as a bonus'   Sara Paretsky

Also by Nevada Barr

Track of the Cat
A Superior Death
Mountain of Bones
Firestorm

Endangered Species

Nevada Barr

HEADLINE

First published in Great Britain in 1997
by HEADLINE BOOK PUBLISHING

10 9 8 7 6 5 4 3 2 1

ISBN 0 7472 5531 8

Printed and bound in Great Britain by
Mackays of Chatham PLC, Chatham, Kent

HEADLINE BOOK PUBLISHING
A division of Hodder Headline PLC
338 Euston Road
London NW1 3BH

For Chris Pepe,
who makes me look good
and does it with such unfailing charm
I'm allowed to believe it's all my own cleverness

ACKNOWLEDGMENTS

Special thanks to Gary Barr,
Mary Barr, J.D. Lee and Newton Sikes

Special thanks to Gary Barr,
Mary Barr, J. D. Lee,
and Newton Sikes

1

BLACK AND BLOOD-WARM, water slammed into Anna's back, rushing over her shoulders and down the front of her shirt. Closing her eyes against the salt sting, she clung to the turtle's carapace and concentrated on keeping her footing as the wave dragged against her legs, sucked the sand from beneath her sneakers.

The loggerhead wouldn't be washed unwillingly back into the Atlantic. There was little the turtle couldn't handle in the sea. It was land, that unfamiliar and ever-changing universe, that had baffled her. For miles she'd swum from God knew where to lay her eggs on the beach of Cumberland Island, one of the Golden Isles off the coast of Georgia. In her tiny brain—or perhaps her great heart—instinct had programmed a map with such precision that out of thousands of miles of coastline she'd found her way back to this narrow ribbon of sand.

Anna ducked as another wave broke across her shoulders, and

embraced the animal hard against her. The ripples of the logger-head's armored back, nearly a yard across, dug into her cheek where flesh thinned over bone. She could feel the powerful scrape of the creature's back flipper against the sodden fabric of her trousered thigh.

Water flooded around her, warmer on the back of her neck than the mild summer air, and Anna wondered how turtles thought, how this turtle thought. On the chart that instinct tattooed on her soul, was there a picture? In whatever passed for a loggerhead's mind's eye, had she seen, remembered the flat welcoming beaches?

"Sorry, old girl," Anna muttered as she heaved against several hundred pounds of sea beast. A capricious tide had trenched out a four-foot-high sand and shell escarpment along fifty yards of ocean front. A week ago the sand had been flat; two weeks hence it would be again. Tonight it was proving impassable. Still, with the eternal patience that seemed endemic to turtles, rocks, and other long-lived, slow-moving creatures, the loggerhead had beached herself and started her trek inland.

Loggerheads coming ashore north and south of the ephemeral cliff were making their appointed rounds. Between drenchings, Anna could hear the delighted cries of park rangers, volunteers, and researchers celebrating the renewed cycle of this threatened species.

Over the past hour, since she'd been drafted into the turtle-midwifing business, Anna had received a crash course in the repro-ductive habits of the loggerhead. In an ideal world, they made their way up onto the beach, above high tide, dug a nest, laid the eggs, and buried them. Their role in the universe completed, they re-turned to the sea, and, it was presumed, never looked back until four or five years rolled by and they again felt the urge to come home to nest.

The turtle Anna danced with in the crashing surf could not

negotiate the sand cliff and was exhausting herself with the effort. Too tired to fight any longer, she was giving up.

"Dear Lord, she's laying. Give me your hat," came an exasperated cry near Anna's ear. The words were carried on a gust of foul-smelling air. For an instant Anna thought she'd shoved her face too near the east end of the westbound turtle. When she realized it was Marty Schlessinger's breath, she began to believe the rumors that the biologist ate roadkill.

The Atlantic drew back and the full weight of the loggerhead was laid again in Anna's and Marty's arms. "Don't hurt her," the biologist warned as Anna felt the little muscles in her sacroiliac stretch and complain.

"Fat chance," she grumbled, but she braced herself, forearms on thighs, shoulder against shell, and held on.

In a sudden peace left behind by the receding waters, the moon pushed over an inky horizon to paint a path in silver over the ocean and onto the back of turtle under Anna's chin.

By the clear light she could see Marty Schlessinger's face inches from her own. Fifty years were etched in the lines of determination carved on either side of an uncompromising mouth. Long hair, worn in pigtails like an aging Pippi Longstocking's, fell in white ropes across the loggerhead's shell.

The returning ocean forced Anna to her knees. Her thigh was wedged against the turtle's carapace, the animal's flipper hard against the outside of her leg.

"Hat, hat, hat," Schlessinger growled.

Anna snatched off her baseball cap and poked it into the biologist's groping fingers.

"Hold her," Schlessinger ordered.

"Christ!" Anna breathed as the other woman relinquished her grip on the turtle to gather the eggs.

Unlike many sea turtles, the loggerhead's egg-laying machinery was recessed beneath the rear of its shell, and Anna could not see the eggs. By the ecstatic chirps percolating from the biologist, she guessed the laying was a success.

"No!" Schlessinger cried suddenly. Such was the pain in her voice that Anna was unpleasantly reminded that the coast of Georgia was the breeding grounds for the great white shark.

"What?" she demanded.

"Lost a baby."

Anna was relieved but had the good sense to keep quiet. Schlessinger would consider the loss of a ranger's leg somewhat less heartrending than that of an embryonic loggerhead.

Minutes ticked by. Waves banged at Anna's back, tried to buckle her knees. Sand gritted between her teeth and salt sealed her eyes. The muscles in her arms and shoulders had progressed from ache, to jelly, to constant torturous throb. All sense of glamour and adventure was long since gone.

"This is getting to be work," she grunted.

"Quiet," Marty said.

Anna wedged her knee more firmly under the loggerhead's shell and began counting back from one hundred. When she reached zero, she decided, Marty and the little loggers were on their own.

Zero came and went and still she held on. Numbers blurred. "I'm losing it," she said.

"No. Not yet."

Various retorts bottled up behind Anna's teeth but she lacked breath to voice them.

A wave rushed between her knees, buoyed up the turtle, and gave her shoulders some respite. When the water receded and the weight settled again, she cried out.

"Hold her still," Schlessinger snapped.

Anna tried. "In my next life I'm going to be bigger," she hissed.

"Quiet," Schlessinger said again. Then: "Okay. I guess that's the lot. Let her down. Gently. Gently."

Anna couldn't unlock any part of her body. "Can't," she said finally.

"Oh for Christ sake." With the next wave Schlessinger eased the weight of the turtle from the tripod Anna had made of her body. "At least you can hold these." The biologist proffered Anna her National Park Service cap. It was full of leathery orbs a little larger than golf balls. "Careful," she warned as Anna stretched stiff arms to receive them. "I counted."

There was no mistaking the threat. Marty knew how many eggs were there. Should one turn up missing on Anna's watch, there would be hell to pay.

She held the cap between her hands as if it were the Holy Grail.

Cooing, the biologist turned the massive turtle back toward the sea and watched her shining shell till the ocean took her. "Fun's over," she said curtly. "Time to get to work."

Oddly, Anna felt invigorated. The magic of the turtle eggs she carried was seeping into her tired bones. The glory of the logger-head's fight and her part in it filled her with a sense of accomplishment that diminished the ache in her back and legs. Slopping sand and water with every step, she squished up the darkened beach after Marty Schlessinger.

Just above the high-tide line Schlessinger stopped, locked folded arms across her chest, and surveyed the dunes between the water and the tangle of oak and palmetto that choked the interior of the island.

A three-quarter moon, free now of the sea, cast its light over the sand. Each twig and blade of grass was etched on one side with unnatural clarity, and on the other plunged into impenetrable shadow. The jungle beyond was lightless, a jagged wall of pine and live oak silhouetted against a faint glow from the mainland.

"This'll do," Schlessinger said, and dropping on all fours, began to dig like a dog after a particularly tasty bone. Sand, first dry, then clumped and wet, sprayed out between her legs and over Anna's shoe tops.

A shovel would have expedited the process. Anna didn't know if Schlessinger was unprepared, a purist, or a fanatic. She suspected the latter two.

On Cumberland Island just over a week and already Anna knew all about the marine biologist. To be more precise, she knew all the gossip. Tonight was the first time she'd actually laid eyes on the woman, though the first day she'd arrived the tarpaper shack Schlessinger called home had been pointed out along with other island landmarks.

The residents of Cumberland granted Marty Schlessinger the status usually reserved for witches and mad scientists. In her mid-fifties, she lived in a ramshackle house she'd inherited when widowed by a crash some fifteen years before.

Schlessinger's bizarre reputation was not unearned. In her wake headless turtle carcasses and the mutilated corpses of animals killed on the island's rudimentary road system turned up with nauseating regularity.

The loggerheads, Anna knew from watching, washed up on the beach with all parts intact. Shrimpers plied their trade offshore. Turtles were caught in the nets and drowned. Schlessinger retrieved the skulls and brains, Anna guessed, for dissection and study.

The butchered roadkill was a little harder to explain. Maybe Schlessinger did eat it. Behind her house Anna had noticed a hog pen. Maybe they were the beneficiaries.

Rumors of varying morbidity and credibility dwindled down from these two provocative habits. The rumor Anna dearly hoped was true was that Schlessinger ate blood-fat ticks from the carcasses of the animals. "Pops 'em like M and M's," Guy Marshall, her crew boss on this venture, had assured her. That was something she wanted to see. The poetic justice of it tickled her.

Eccentricity made Schlessinger well suited to Cumberland Island National Seashore. Once a vacation home for the very rich, Cumberland had been privately owned until the 1970s. In the past fifty years most of the flashier millionaires had moved to more fashionable addresses, leaving only a handful of moneyed and powerful families behind, but the ghost of those glory days remained in the crumbling mansions and burned-out relics.

In the early 1970s, eighteen thousand acres of the twenty-thousand acre island was deeded over to the federal government to be preserved as a national park. Those who were less than charitable suggested the land had been given to the NPS more to keep the riffraff from buying up parcels the rich were tired of paying taxes on than to "conserve the scenery and the natural and historic objects and the wildlife therein . . ."

Those selfsame cynics also intimated that the fire crew, of which Anna was part, had been bivouacked on Cumberland to soothe the nerves of those privileged few with the ear and purse strings of various congressmen.

Cumberland was in the midst of a drought. The palmetto that carpeted much of the island would burn hot and fast if ever ignited. It could be argued that the natural areas would benefit from such a cleansing by fire. But the palmetto grew up to some very influential doorsteps.

Whatever the politics, firefighters from the National Park Service had been housed on the island in a presuppression capacity for the past ten weeks. Twelve hours a day, seven days a week, over the course of their three-week rotations, they wandered around racking up overtime in heavy boots and two derelict pumper trucks on the off chance something would happen.

So far the sum total of excitement had been the ongoing chemical warfare with Cumberland's voracious tick population and the discovery in an inland slough of fourteen baby alligators still living at home with an impressive mom the locals called Maggie-Mary. Maggie hadn't been seen in so many years, apocrypha added more to her length and girth than the mere passage of time could have managed.

And, tonight, the loggerheads. According to Marty they nested May through August. Usually they came up on the beaches at night, usually at high tide. The eggs incubated for eight weeks; then the little hatchlings clawed their way out of their protective graves and, with luck and the fierce intercession of Marty Schlessinger, found their way to the Atlantic Ocean.

Each new nest was recorded, protected, and timed. The next hatching was due in nine days. In a rare unguarded moment Marty had divulged this bit of information and Anna had pounced on it. When the baby loggerheads made their dangerous dash for the sea she wanted to be in the turtle vanguard.

"Eggs!" came a curt demand and Anna was snapped out of her brown study. She dropped to one knee and presented Marty with the cap in an unconsciously courtly gesture.

One by one the biologist lifted out the treasure of turtle eggs and settled them into the sand. When they had been arranged to her liking, 147 eggs in all, she ordered Anna to stand back. With great care she refilled the hole and gently tamped it down. To Anna's amazement the woman then collapsed, elbows and knees on the ground, and began flailing her forearms and shins in frenzied arcs.

After half a minute of this she stood and dusted the sand from her trousers, looking as sane as anyone. "Loggerheads aren't particular," she explained. "They scuff over the areas with their flippers but don't seem to feel a need to disguise the nest carefully."

Marty handed Anna back the ball cap and she absentmindedly pulled it on her head. An unpleasant trickle of water and turtle slime crawled beneath her collar.

Up and down the beach, easily visible against the pale sand, the great shapes of the loggerheads moved with startling agility back toward the sea. Dark clusters of humanity, self-appointed guardian angels, cheered.

"Quiet!" Marty growled.

"Does the noise bother the turtles?" Anna asked.

"Of course it does," the biologist snapped.

As near as Anna could tell, anything less serious than a shark with a bullhorn went largely ignored by these phlegmatic amphibians. She cheered with the others, but silently lest she set Schlessinger off.

"Want to come back to the fire dorm for a beer?" Anna asked on impulse.

"Never touch the stuff," Schlessinger replied.

"Me neither," Anna said, to see if it still felt like a lie.

"Recovering alcoholic?"

Anna said nothing.

"That's BS," the biologist declared. "I don't drink because I don't need it."

Any warm fuzzy feelings the turtles had engendered in Anna evaporated.

Marty Schlessinger turned and stalked toward the black curtain of inland foliage. Anna fell in step beside her, simply because they were headed for the same place. On their daily circuits of the island the firefighters customarily drove the trucks down the beach in one direction, and kept to the dirt lanes on the island's interior on the other. In deference to the turtles, all night travels were confined to the inland roads. One such track ended in a sandy spur a quarter-mile north of where the egg laying was concentrated.

Volunteers, rangers, and the rest of fire crew had started back in the direction of the parked vehicles as Anna and Marty reached their destination. Schlessinger began rearranging boxes, a broom, and two new-looking shovels on the back of a battered all-terrain vehicle she used to get around the island.

An obnoxious, if infectious, hooting laugh cut through the lesser sounds and was answered by what Anna could only describe as a snarl, or as close to a snarl as a beast without claws and fangs can come.

"That man's on my Better Off Dead list," Marty Schlessinger said. "Mitch Hanson has no more business here than Hitler at a bar mitzvah."

"Maybe he likes turtles," Anna said, just to see what kind of reaction she'd get.

Schlessinger snorted and Anna was impressed at the range and accuracy of her animal sounds. "Hah," Marty said as if translating. "Maybe he thought we were serving Jack Daniel's." She stabbed her shovel into the sand. The handle quivered like the shaft of a harpoon.

For several seconds Anna watched as the biologist slammed around pieces of equipment. Wet white braids smacked against her bare arms and she made little plosive noises as if she was carrying on a heated conversation with herself.

Anna lounged against the fender of one of the rusting green trucks they'd inherited from the crew they had replaced. Along with the salt scent of the sea and the fecund perfume of the jungle, a faint sickly-sweet odor made it to her nostrils.

Her flashlight lay on the seat of the truck. She retrieved it and combed the ground with its yellowing beam till she found what she was looking for. Pushed partially off the road several yards from the rear wheels of Marty Schlessinger's ATV was the carcass of a young raccoon. From the looks of it, it hadn't been dead long. Scavengers had yet to disembowel it. Whether it had been struck by a vehicle or had died of natural causes, Anna couldn't tell. She played the light over the little corpse invitingly but Schlessinger didn't give it so much as a glance.

The others approached. Schlessinger fired up her four-wheeler and gutted the night with the noise of her departure.

Anna sighed and clicked off the light. Evidently Marty wasn't going to eat so much as a tick tonight. She shrugged in the darkness. It was always good to have something to look forward to.

2

GUY MARSHALL, a man in his late forties with a chiseled face, no hair to speak of, and the body of a rodeo cowboy—lean and strong and stove up in one knee—walked in from the beach. The moon reflected off his pate, casting a deep shadow over his eyes.

Anna and the rest of the crew had dressed for the occasion in light-weight clothing and tennis shoes. Marshall wore regulation firefighting regalia: lemon-yellow shirt, olive drab pants of fire-retardant NoMex, and heavy lug-soled, lace-up, leather boots. He'd been wearing them for so many years he probably thought they were comfortable.

Marshall was crew boss in charge of the abbreviated presup-pression crew: Anna and three men, one from Gulf Islands, one from Cape Hatteras, and one from the Natchez Trace Parkway. Fire crews were drawn from a well of red-carded rangers—those with the training who could also pass the physical. The call went out to the national parks. District rangers let go whoever they could best spare—or whoever had a favor coming or whined the loudest. Fire details, especially one as cushy as presuppression on Cumberland Island, were much sought after. Twenty-one twelve-hour days with time and a half for overtime plus per diem rounded out one's paycheck nicely.

The crew boss threw one leg across the seat of the ATV he'd claimed for his own and shot a thin stream of tobacco juice into the sand. In the moonlight it looked like an ink blot on white paper.

A seal balancing a ball on its nose, Anna thought, looking at the impromptu Rorschach. She made a mental note to ask her sister when next she called what sort of incipient madness that might indicate.

Laughter wafted up from the beach; the throaty laugh of the interpretive ranger who lived on the island, echoed by the barklike guffaw of a member of fire crew and the booming hoot that had so incensed Marty Schlessinger.

"They're all crazier'n bedbugs," Guy said without rancor, and ejected another stream of tobacco juice neatly over the handlebars. "Watching a bunch of turtles bury eggs has got 'em all lit up like the Fourth of July. I'd hate to see 'em in a hen yard. They'd think they died and went to heaven. Takes all kinds, I guess. Look at museum curators. The Park Service's got a whole passel of 'em. What do they do? Sit around and watch old shit get older."

"We could have stayed back at the dorm and watched *Under Siege Two*," Anna reminded him. On the island there were only two available videos, *Under Siege II* and *Fire Weather: A Meteorologist's View*.

"Like I always say, turtles is damn good entertainment," Guy drawled.

What was left of Marshall's hair was steel-gray and cropped close in a horseshoe that extended from ear to ear just above his collar. He pulled a comb from his hip pocket and carefully ran it through the back and sides. "Reliving my glory days," he said when he caught Anna watching.

For a minute or two they waited without speaking as the others made their way across the dunes. Flashlights had been summarily banned by Schlessinger. Light disoriented the turtles—not only when they came ashore to nest but when the babies hatched. Theory had it that when turtles as a species were young, man had not yet discovered fire, let alone electricity. Temperature dictated that the hatchlings emerge from their sand incubators at night. Instinct told them to creep toward the lights on the horizon, the stars over the sea that would be home.

With electric lights and beachfront condos, baby turtles were often confused, crawling inland toward the false stars and dying.

At present the moon made flashlights unnecessary and Anna reveled in the gentle southern night. Ten p.m. and it was still over eighty degrees. Even with the drought, the air was humid. Anna's hair curled and her fingernails grew. After so long in the high desert of southern Colorado's Mesa Verde National Park, she felt like a raisin turning back into a grape.

Near the ocean there was always a slight breeze—enough to cool the sweat and make the air feel alive. Overhead it played through the tinder-dry leaves of the live oaks, producing a delicate clatter, a sweet counterpoint to the throbbing shush of waves against the shore.

The open space between the tree line and the sea suited Anna. As in the wide country of the Southwest, the eye could roll out to the distance, the soul expand into the great spaces. Back in the dense woods she didn't breathe as easily. There the air scarcely moved and the clatter was like as not ticks dropping from the vegetation in search of new homes with better-stocked larders.

Like the hero in a drawing room comedy, Dijon Smith entered laughing. "Oooeee, I wish I had balls the size of a ghost crab's," he said. "Those little suckers aren't afraid of anything." Anna knew what he meant. The little crustaceans, the biggest not more than ten inches from claw to claw, would stand on their back legs and challenge the ton-and-a-half pumper trucks as they drove down the beach.

Dijon's dark skin soaked up the moonlight till he looked a shadow of himself. In a cliché Anna would never give voice to, all she could see were the whites of his eyes and his flashing teeth.

At twenty-two, Dijon was the baby of the bunch by nearly ten years and complained good-naturedly about being stuck in the retirement home for aging firefighters. Under the spreading branches of a live oak, Smith jumped up, caught hold of a limb, and began chinning himself with an irritating effortlessness.

"That's knocking ticks down on you," Guy warned.

"Shit! No lie?" Dijon dropped and began brushing off his shoulders and arms. "Don't tell me that, man. I hate those little mother—" A glance at Anna. "Buggers."

"They can sense your body heat like heat-seeking missiles," the crew boss said. "You shake their tree and they drop on you."

"Ticks." Dijon shuddered and did a little dance designed either to dislodge insects or get a laugh. With Dijon Smith it was hard to tell. Bending over at the waist, he fluttered his fingers through his close-cropped hair.

"Don't flick them on me," Anna griped, and jumped back. So convincing was the performance, she half believed he was acrawl with bloodsucking monsters.

Marshall slumped back on the ATV, feet over the handlebars,

back against his day pack. Guy could get comfortable anywhere; a highly desirable attribute in a wildland firefighter. "Get your eggs all laid?" he asked.

"I haven't gotten anything laid since we came to Cumbersome Isle," Dijon returned. "Even those turtles are starting to look good. I've got to get out of here. I need sex and pizza. This sand and surf and tick shit is driving me out of my"—again the look at Anna—"frigging mind."

Anna smiled in the dark. Misplaced as it was, she appreciated the sentiment and cleaned up her language around Smith to keep her credit good.

Al Magnus, Rick Spencer, Mitch Hanson, and Lynette Wagner washed up from the beach on a gust of chatter. Headlights and engine noise sliced the night as Anna buckled herself onto the bench seat of the pumper truck. Hanson had driven his government vehicle; Lynette rode with Dijon and Rick in a second truck as decrepit as the one Anna shared with Al.

Magnus was a short stocky man somewhere in his thirties but exuding the ageless maturity of the devoted family man. While the ATV and the truck growled into the night, Al scraped out the bowl of his pipe, then banged it against the side of the truck. The smell of sea air and stale tobacco radiated from his clothing and the cab began to feel as homey as a country living room.

"No sense eating dust," he explained. He tamped fresh tobacco in the bowl.

"Who's that Mitch Hanson guy?" Anna asked in idle curiosity. "Marty seemed deeply aggrieved that he not only had the temerity to exist but the unmitigated gall to do it in her vicinity."

Al finished the tamping and went through the lengthy ritual of lighting his pipe before he answered. An addiction to pipe tobacco gave the user an unearned air of deep and considered wisdom. When the pipe was drawing properly, he said: "Mitch isn't a bad sort. He's a dozer operator with maintenance. Keeps the roads passable. An over-the-hill party boy. Double dipper. He's pretty much retired twice but's still on the payroll. Maybe that's what's getting to Marty."

Anna nodded in the dark. Scattered throughout government services were retired military men pulling a full pension and a salary. Those who worked inspired jealousy. Those who coasted, hatred and contempt.

Evidently Hanson was in the latter category. Anna had seen him grading the inland lanes. Or, now that she thought about it, she'd seen his bulldozer. Either he was nowhere around or he was lounging in the shade gossiping with the locals. He looked to be fifty or thereabout. His belly confirmed the aging-party-animal motif; thirty extra pounds rounded out his face and middle.

The sight and sounds of the other vehicles faded. Al turned the key and fired up the engine. Inland the lanes were narrow, the palmetto close and thick. Stiff fingers of vegetation skritched along the sides of the truck. Despite the muggy heat, Anna rolled her window up. Without light she couldn't defend herself against the whip of the fronds.

The road was washboarded and hosted deep ruts where streams carried rainfall from the interior. These seeming obstacles had no effect on Magnus and he roared along at a bone-rattling thirty miles per hour. In the beams of the headlights the lane unfurled, a twisting white ribbon through a tunnel of green. It put Anna in mind of Mr. Toad's Wild Ride in Disneyland. She cinched her seat belt as tight as it would go and braced both feet against the dashboard.

"How'd you make out with Marty Schlessinger?" Al bawled over the racket of the truck. "Did she ask you to dinner?"

"Nope. I asked her over but she wasn't in the mood to go slumming."

"Too bad. Jimmy gave me a list of questions I'm supposed to ask her." Jimmy was Al's eight-year-old son. They talked almost every night. In a small office building about a mile from the dorm was a telephone fire crew had access to. Anna and Al were the only members who seemed to have anyone to call. Most evenings they flipped a coin to see who went first.

Among Park Service nomads there were two mind-sets: those who threw themselves wholeheartedly into each new adventure, sleeping with whoever presented, eating what was set before them, and drinking deep from each intoxicating cup they came across; and those with a strong tether to home—a cord more often than not made of telephone wire. Age was a dividing factor—the young were liberal, having as yet acquired nothing worth conserving—but the newly single and dedicated bachelors swelled those ranks.

The clatter of rusting metal drowned out even Al's basso profundo and Anna settled into a favorite pastime: watching the world go by. Spotlit into unnaturally bright colors, the jungle flickered past in patterns of green and black. This was a dry jungle with a fragile grip on land. Soil was thin and sandy, the island prey to hurricanes that could flatten it or divide it in two with a sudden waterway. Plants grew with the voracious disregard of the condemned, springing from the rough ground in impenetrable thickets to fight for light and air beneath oaks broad-shouldered enough to have weathered a century of storms.

Occasionally the glancing blow of the high beams would stun a night creature. Two baby raccoons, postcard-perfect, hung halfway up a palm tree. Al passed in a thunderous cloud of dust without ever seeing them. Anna hoped the quake of their passage wouldn't dislodge the kits. A sow and three piglets dashed for cover beneath the palmetto fronds. Three deer grazed in a meadow in the center of the island where a Beechcraft on loan for drug interdiction was tied down at the end of a dirt strip.

There were few meadows maintained on the island. This was

one of the largest. Even more than in daylight, Anna felt the relief of coming out into the open after so long a time closed beneath the dusty canopy of vegetation.

Moonlight turned the deer to shadows, the dry grass to textured marble. Unlike the feral pigs, deer on Cumberland were not hunted. These looked up as the truck ground past but didn't leave off chewing.

Beside the meadow, tucked behind a cottage that could have lured Hansel and Gretel to their deaths, was Stafford, one of the derelict mansions. Built by Andrew Carnegie for his daughter, it had been a place of carriages and candlelight and southern hospitality. This fine old house, like a dowager duchess fallen on evil times, now fought just to keep body and soul together.

Within were wooden staircases, sconces, parquet floors, coffered ceilings—craftmen's work that, if artisans could still be found, would cost a fortune to replicate. All was threatened by time and mildew. The Park Service scrambled for funds to battle the decay and drafted plans to bring back the grandeur, but for now it sat empty and vulnerable, roofline sagging, foundation crumbling.

Several of these magnificent hulks dotted the island. Anna had wandered through most of them, a pleasant break in the monotony. Nostalgia, memories of lives never lived but only imagined, dwelt in the silent dust-filled halls, the moldering books left on the shelves, the broken furniture stashed in enormous cellars; in a moth-eaten fur abandoned in an upstairs nursery. There was something fascinating in the flotsam of the past, once valued things discarded when their owners moved on.

When they reached the south end of the island, the road unraveled into poorly marked byways leading to various NPS facilities. Al negotiated unerringly through the knot and turned at last onto the street where they stayed. Several houses and two barracks were scattered beneath oak trees on the east side of the road. A garage and storage barn were on the right. Further down this minuscule Main Street the maintenance buildings clustered. The structures were all of wood, scoured to vintage softness by the ocean winds. Wherever metal touched—door hinges, nailheads, window locks— streaks of burnt orange attested to the constant rust.

At eleven at night all was dark and deserted but for the house that quartered fire crew. The screened-in porch was aglow from lights spilling out the open door. Behind the ubiquitous row of boots, banned from the interior by Guy in an attempt to slow the migration of the dunes from outside to in, Anna could see people lounging in metal folding chairs. The spark of a cigarette butt traced a slow arc to someone's mouth.

Lynette Wagner, Cumberland's GS-4 interpretive ranger, stood in the doorway, yellow light turning the brown frizz of a shoulder-length perm to red. Her laughter bobbed on top of the hum of conversation. Two shadows hovered near her, Dijon and Rick no doubt. Lynette always had boys dancing attendance. She was not yet thirty, single, and good-enough looking, but it was more than just her physical charms. Somehow she'd managed to strike the perfect balance between being one of the boys and being one of the girls. A tomboy with a strong maternal instinct; the combination drew men like flies. Everything they could want: mother, buddy, and lover rolled into one.

For all Anna could tell, it was genuine—Lynette to the core— and she found it as attractive as the men did though probably not for the same reasons.

The chairs were occupied by Cumberland's district ranger and his alarmingly pregnant wife. The district ranger, Todd Belfore, spent much of each day with fire crew. He'd only been on the island five months and already he was bored. Mostly he grumbled about being in charge of law enforcement where enforcing law wasn't allowed. Word had come down that the wealthy denizens of Cumberland were "not accustomed to interference." Tourists were fair game but they were disappointingly well behaved.

Anna had met Tabby, his wife, only once before. The woman was so big with child that when Anna first laid eyes on her, she'd made a mental note to review her emergency childbirth procedures. Mrs. Belfore was a small-boned woman, pale and blond and clingy. There weren't many moments when she wasn't clutching some part of her husband's anatomy. In a pinch even a sleeve or shirttail sufficed. Tonight she seemed particularly in need of reassurance. She held his right forearm in a death grip, his hand palm up on her lap like a dead white spider. Under the circumstances Anna didn't hold Tabby's neediness against her but she hadn't found much to say to the woman either.

Lynette said something indecipherable and Rick laughed too loud and too long.

"Party. Party," Al said neutrally. Anna couldn't tell if he was being sarcastic or merely observant.

She dug in her pocket for a coin. "Heads or tails?"

"The phone's all your'n, Ms. Pigeon," he replied. "If Jimmy's not in bed by now, he should be."

Anna traded up, leaving the pumper truck for Guy's ATV. When he'd claimed the four-wheeler the crew boss made noises about convenience and flexibility, but he was fooling no one. He took it because it was fun. And he was entitled. No one begrudged him.

On the all-terrain vehicle the night swirled around Anna, dried the sweat in her hair. Even the noise of its little engine didn't detract. Over the short trip to the office she passed four armadillos rooting alongside the road. The weird little beasts delighted her. Since coming to the island she'd spent a good chunk of time stalking them. The animals were nearsighted and not terribly bright. Rick, who hailed from the Natchez Trace Parkway in southern Mississippi and claimed to be an armadillo expert, told her if she could sneak up and touch one, catch it by surprise, it would spring straight up in the air a couple of feet. Anna didn't know if he was pulling her leg or not. She didn't much care. It was something to do.

The office housing the telephone was on the inland waterway between the coast of Georgia and Cumberland Island. Just to the south was a one-room museum and a covered bridge that led to the boat-docking area. One light shone like a star on the waters where the houseboat Mitch Hanson shared with his wife was docked. Trees had been cut away to protect the structures from wildfire and windfall. In this man-made meadow a herd of twenty or thirty small island deer grazed.

Anna pulled into the dirt parking lot, switched off the ATV, and let the silence settle before she went to the door.

Inside she took a Baby Ruth from the cupboard in the kitchenette and left fifty cents in a coffee cup set aside for that purpose. Blissful in solitude, she sat in the chief ranger's chair and put her feet on his desk, the better to savor her candy and her telephone call.

3

MOLLY PICKED UP on the second ring. At the sound of her sister's gruff "Hello" Anna felt muscles relax that she hadn't known were tensed.

"Am I interrupting anything?" she asked.

"Nope. Letterman's a bust tonight." There was a sound of stretching at the tail end of Molly's sentence and Anna suspected she was reaching for an ashtray. The nicotine bone's connected to the phone bone, her sister had once told her and Anna wondered if her calls were cutting years off Molly's life.

"Why do you do that?" she asked irritably.

"Because it's politically incorrect, noxious, and potentially lethal," Molly replied, unperturbed. "Are you still a castaway?"

"Still. Three weeks is a lot longer when you're wearing fire boots."

Molly cackled. "Time and a half?"

"The big bucks," Anna said. "Pays my phone bills."

"You know, I would call you if you were ever anywhere real. Two nights in a row. To what do I owe the honor? I thought it was Frederick's turn."

"I'm playing hard-to-get."

"Hah."

"I wanted to talk," Anna said seriously. "And not have to be nice."

"Or witty or charming," Molly added. She wasn't being sarcastic; she understood the burden of maintaining one's good behavior for any length of time.

For the past year Anna had been carrying on a long-distance love affair with Frederick Stanton, an FBI agent she'd worked with on a couple of homicides. They'd fallen "in love"—for lack of a better phrase—over their third corpse.

There had been an intoxicating night, an awkward breakfast, and a breathless goodbye. Then letters, letters and phone calls, eleven months' worth. Soon, Anna knew, she would have to leave this comfortable limbo and deal with Frederick on a more flesh-and-blood basis: shoes under the bed, dual vacations, mutual friends.

He was beginning to talk about the future, urging her to come to Chicago.

Anna wasn't sure she cared for that. Conversations about the future always seemed to pivot on how much one was willing to sacrifice in the here and now.

When she'd married Zach—in what now seemed a past as distant and distorted as King Arthur's court or the Ice Age—life had been simple. She had nothing. Zach had nothing. No home, no pets, no jobs. Merging was easy. They commingled their paperback books, bought a pretty good mattress, borrowed money to make their security deposit, and started a future with all the forethought of a blue jay planting an acorn.

Endangered Species

For seven years it grew and flourished; then Zach had been killed. To look ahead became too lonely, and out of self-preservation Anna had started living each day as it came. Now it was habit.

She carried his ashes from park to park, promising herself one day she would pour them—and the dreams of her early twenties—to the four winds to scatter. The time had never seemed right. Before leaving Mesa Verde for Cumberland Island, she'd even gone so far as to take the ash tin from her underwear drawer and pry loose the lid. She'd gotten them no further than the coffee table.

Now there was Frederick, and with him, baggage, his and hers: jobs, geography, his kids, Anna's cat, his bird, houses. After years of kicking around amid the mouse droppings and leaky faucets of National Park Service housing, Anna had finally landed a plum: a house of native stone with a tiny tower bedroom that overlooked the green mesas of southern Colorado. During the past year she'd noted an odd tingling sensation in the soles of her feet and thought perhaps she was beginning to put down a few tentative roots.

Not a good time to be calling Atlas and breaking out the bubble wrap.

"Come to think of it," Anna said, meaning Frederick, boys, and the conjugal life in general, "I don't even want to talk about it." Instead, she told Molly of the turtles and Marty Schlessinger. After ten minutes it dawned on her she was doing all the talking and she shut up, letting the line cool, waiting to see if Molly needed to talk.

Nothing but the sucking sound of a Camel drawn straight into dying lungs came over the wire. Molly had been a psychiatrist for over twenty years. Listening had become a habit, as had keeping herself to herself. Born, Anna suspected, from knowing how easily one's words, however carefully couched, could expose weakness. "What have you been up to?" she coaxed.

Another second or two ticked by and Anna's antennae went up.

Silence could mean nothing; aggravated silence was a *clue*. Psychiatry wasn't the only profession taught to listen for weakness.

"What?" Anna demanded.

"Another death threat." Molly laughed. Annoyance, edginess, defensiveness, and maybe a small thread of fear wove through the short patch of sound.

Momentarily Anna was stunned as both ends of the statement smacked into her. "Another," she said flatly, and was pleased that her voice lacked any trace of warmth. Molly sensed warmth as cannily as the Cumberland Island ticks. In seconds she could worm herself into it and evade the conversational thrust.

"It's only the second," Molly defended herself. She was trying to shrug it off. Anna could see her as clearly as if she stood on the other side of the chief ranger's desk. This close to bedtime she would be wearing a sweat suit—the expensive embroidered kind never meant to be sweated in—probably in lavender, crimson, or pink. On her feet, big feet for so small a woman, would be fuzzy white ankle socks with tiger stripes on them. The day's mascara would have migrated down to form smudges beneath her lower lashes, and her short, thick, gray-streaked hair would be worked into a frenzy of curls from fingers being constantly thrust through it.

Molly saw herself as piano wire: strong, sharp, unbreakable. When she was encased in Dior suits, high heels, and a wall full of formidable diplomas and awards, this probably wasn't too far off the mark. In downy pink PJs and tiger paws, she looked tiny and vulnerable. Wet, she wouldn't weigh more than 110 pounds.

Anna closed her eyes and wished for a glass of Mondavi red, room temperature; a large glass with a sturdy stem filled too close to the top for polite society. Reluctantly she let the image go. "You'd better tell me the whole story," she said. "If you leave any parts out it'll give me bad dreams."

"What about Al?" Molly had grown accustomed to Anna's phone-sharing dilemmas.

"He lost the coin toss. You may begin."

There was a pause, tense and poised, the kind divers make on the high board as the strategies of their controlled fall coalesce into their muscles.

"Part of it is me being dramatic, no doubt. Believe it or not, death threats are fairly common—macroscopically speaking. We get our share: husbands whose wives decided to divorce them after getting therapy, patients who spent a ton of money and are still crazy as bedbugs. Mostly threats are like obscene phone calls—the kick is in the words and the shock. No follow-up is called for." A long slow inhalation followed. Anna pictured the smoke trickling up through her sister's fingers as, cigarette in hand, she raked back her curls.

For the first time she envied Molly her addiction. At least she still had her drug. Dirty and deadly as it was, nobody woke up facedown on a car seat with no recollection of the last eight hours because they'd smoked one too many cigarettes.

"What was different about this threat?" Anna asked.

"For one, it was a woman. Very rare. Very. Not for women to scream, 'I'm going to kill you,' et cetera, but for a serious telephone death threat it's quite unusual. And two, it didn't sound as if she'd made any attempt to disguise her voice. She sounded stressed, repressed, and decidedly clear."

"What did she say?"

"Hang on." A series of clicks serrated the silence, then a sweet, low-pitched voice, almost a vibrato from underlying emotion, said: "You deserve to die. Not just your kind, you personally. It will be my pleasure to do the honors. My plate is rather full right now but rest assured I will pencil you in as soon as there's an opening."

"Could you hear it?" Molly again.

"You taped the threat?" Anna was impressed. Her sister was a cool customer.

"No. She left it on my answering machine."

Anna laughed in spite of herself. "I'm surprised she didn't fax it. God. The consummate businesswoman. 'Pencil you in'?"

Molly laughed with her and when the laughter wore out they were both scared.

"Too weird," Anna said. "A practical joke?"

Molly shook her head. Anna could tell from the wavering shush of smoky breath blown across the receiver. "I've listened to it umpteen times and can't make heads or tails of it. Do you think I should call the police?"

Molly never asked for advice. Flattery and alarm vied for space in Anna's heart. "Yes. By all means. If it turns out to be nothing, terrific."

"Do you think they'd take me seriously?"

"You're rich, white, pushing fifty, and well connected."

"Of course." Again Molly laughed. Hers was an evil-sounding chuckle that Anna loved. The sort of chortle Dorothy might have heard shortly before all hell broke loose in the land of Oz. "For a moment there, I was ten years old again, freckled and redheaded and afraid of crying wolf. I'm a grown-up, by God!" Molly said.

"Save the tape," Anna cautioned.

"Done. Two copies. One in a safe-deposit."

"What was the first threat like?"

"A note came in the mail. It was on expensive stationery and written in calligraphy—the kind that was all the rage for fancy Earth Day party invitations a few years back. Kind of a walk-in-Broccoli-Forest feel to it. You're on hold again."

A moment later the phone clattered back to Molly's ear. "Still there?"

"Still here."

"Okay—and for the comfort of your little cop mind I want you to know I'm holding this with sterile tweezers while I read it.

"It's very formal, like the call. 'Dr. Pigeon: There is apparently no end to the damage you do. Stupidity? Greed? Or just old-fashioned evil? You need to be dead and I need to do it. Please reflect on this. I wish you to be as uncomfortable as is humanly possible, should you be, after all, human.' "

Holding the mouthpiece of the phone away from her face so as not to be munching the Baby Ruth in her sister's ear, Anna let the words soak in. The note was strangely dispassionate, hatred grown cold, held close in the mind till a warped but compelling logic grew up around it.

"I suppose you've gone through your patient list to see if anybody might carry a grudge?"

"More than once. Contrary to Hollywood's febrile depictions, a psychiatrist's life is not fraught with serial killers. Killers of any kind are rare. Killers who seek help are virtually nonexistent. Except for my prison work—and that's mostly drug rehab and depression—my patients are wealthy neurotics. I handle maybe fifteen psychotics at any given time on hospital and prison rounds. Of the few that are not incarcerated, four are men and the other is a homeless person, a bag lady. She has trouble stringing sentences together and eats out of garbage cans. Hardly the type for fancy stationery."

"The ones in lockup, they could call you or mail a letter, couldn't they?" Anna asked.

"I suppose. It doesn't feel right but I'll give it some thought. It's possible. These people are crazy, not stupid."

Muted voices distracted Anna. "Just a sec," she said, and held the phone to her chest the better to listen. The office building, like the crew quarters, was closed up tight to seal in the air-conditioning. Though grateful for a respite from the Georgia heat,

Anna hated being cut off from the summer, the sounds of the night, frogs and crickets. Snuggling up in winter was different. Winter didn't sing to her the way summer did.

Molly temporarily forgotten, she set the receiver on the desk and forced open the window. The voices became clearer: human distraught, tearful. "Doggone it," she whispered to herself.

"Molly?"

"I'm here."

"There's some kind of altercation outside. I'd shine it on—not my park and all that—but it sounds like a woman's crying. Probably nothing but you never know."

"Go check." Relief permeated Molly's voice. She was relieved to have the spotlight off of her. The threats upset her. That, more than the fear of personal violence, was what was bothering her.

God forbid the great psychiatrist should not be controlling some small aspect of life, Anna thought and smiled. "I'm calling you back," she said.

"Not tonight."

"Tomorrow then."

"Same time, same station." A click and the line went dead. "Goodbye" wasn't in Molly's vocabulary. Anna was unoffended, she'd grown used to it a lifetime ago. Molly had walked her to her first day of school in Mrs. White's first-grade class. Outside the door she handed Anna the paper sack with the lunch their mother had made, then sat her down on a low bench under a row of coat hooks. Anna was six, Molly fourteen.

"Pay attention," Molly had said. "I'm going to want details." She turned and walked away without a backward look. Anna hadn't felt abandoned; not then, not ever. She knew whatever happened, Molly would be back to hear the details.

4

SUCKING THE LAST of the Baby Ruth from her fillings, Anna stepped onto the concrete stoop at the office's back door. Weeping ebbed and flowed like the waves of an incoming tide, each sob breaking higher than the last.

A fan of the night, Anna had made her phone call without switching on the lights. After the indoor dark, her night vision was keen, and moonlight washed gently over the landscape. Across the field, where the deer had stopped grazing to listen with more curiosity than alarm, a pickup truck idled, its headlights plowing yellow-white furrows in the dust of the lane.

Two figures stood beside the truck, one so close to the front bumper that her dress was caught by the headlight and showed bright red, the only scrap of true color in the nightscape. The other, a man Anna guessed from the timbre of his mutterings, was trying to grab the woman's shoulders and being batted away on each attempt.

Fifty yards separated Anna from the couple. She walked quietly, keeping to the grass-covered berm between the wheel ruts. It didn't cross her mind to return to the office to call for backup or alert Cumberland's law enforcement ranger. Family squabbles in national parks were as ordinary as parking tickets, though considerably more volatile. As she closed the distance it occurred to her that she'd grown dangerously complacent and it would behoove her to cultivate a healthy sense of fear in the not too distant future.

"You would leave me," the woman cried clearly, and lurched back into the glare of the headlight. It was then Anna saw the swollen belly and knew her for Tabby Belfore, the district ranger's wife.

The man stepped forward, reaching for Tabby.

"Hey, Todd!" Anna yelled, hoping if violence was in the offing to avert it. "You guys need any help?"

She was close enough now to see their faces. Annoyance mixed with sheepishness. Tabby blotted at her eyes with her fingertips; a woman concerned about makeup damage. There were no signs of high drama, just the usual earmarks of a spat.

Because of training and a natural distrust of people, Anna checked Tabby for any signs of abuse. "Having engine trouble?" she asked easily.

Todd Belfore was a small man, five foot three or four and not more than 140 pounds, but muscular and self-assured. "Nope. We were having a fight," he said with disarming candor. "Tabby's smarter than me. I had to stop driving and concentrate if I had any hope of winning."

Tabby laughed. It didn't sound forced, so Anna joined her. After that there was nothing else to say and the Belfores stood looking foolish, both sets of eyes flitting everywhere to avoid making contact with Anna's.

"We'd better be getting on home," Tabby said finally.

Todd got back into the truck so fast he cracked his head against the frame. "No harm done. Hard as a rock." He laughed again, alone this time.

"Guess we better be going." Tabby backed away from Anna, heading toward the passenger side. She didn't seem afraid or anxious. Reassured, Anna watched them drive away to be swallowed up by the oak woods.

The district ranger and his wife lived in an upstairs apartment in the Plum Orchard mansion. At one time the mansion had been open for the public to tour but funds had failed and it was now closed to visitors. Tabby probably felt isolated. From their brief acquaintance she didn't strike Anna as a woman of great inner resources.

As she walked back to the ATV an old Doris Day movie she hadn't watched in years floated into her mind: *Midnight Lace*. Day played an heiress, married and rich. She shopped, she looked terrific, she mixed martinis and had them waiting when Rex Harrison returned from a hard day at the office. And she was compellingly, endearingly helpless in an era when the helplessness of grown women was accepted, admired—at least in fiction.

Mrs. Belfore had some of Day's blond vulnerability. People found themselves wanting to look after her. In *Midnight Lace* there was an attraction even for Anna. It would be delicious to sink back into frailty and let the battles be fought around you.

As she fired up the ATV, she allowed herself a brief fantasy of giving in, giving up, giving over; absolute trust and, so, absolute dependence. Appealing, but only momentarily. To the victor go the spoils. It wasn't healthy to align oneself with the spoils.

Back in the air-conditioned sanctity of her upstairs bedroom, Anna stretched naked on her yellow fire-issue sleeping bag. A room and a bed of her own; a rare luxury on a fire assignment. "God bless sexism," she said to the spirits above the raked ceiling. As crew boss, Guy had claimed one bedroom. He'd assigned her another as the only female. The remaining three crew members shared the third. As in every crew since the first group of Cro-Magnons banded together to stomp out the first grass fire, there was a magnificent nose, a man who snored with the resonance of a dull chain saw cutting through hardwood. On this crew Rick did the honors.

Through two closed doors it was dulled to a comfortable rumble. A little imagination could mutate it into a purr and Anna liked to pretend Piedmont, her orange tiger cat, was curled up beside her. Cats were such excellent soporifics.

Folding her hands behind her head, she stretched till her ankles cracked. She had a lot to think about. Besides, she was too lazy to go to sleep. It would mean getting up and crossing seven feet of hardwood floor to switch off the light.

How serious was the threat against her sister? she wondered. For Molly to mention it at all indicated some concern. On a couple of occasions there had been those who wished Anna ill. Oddly, before the fear and outrage set in, her feelings were hurt; a childish sense of, How could anyone dislike *me*? Anna had felt that from Molly. For a healer it must be worse.

In law enforcement, emergency response, firefighting—the things rangers were involved with—a great deal of one's time was spent sitting around waiting for something bad to happen. When boredom set in, it was inevitable that one sort of hoped something bad would happen. No malice intended, just something interesting to do. A psychiatrist dedicated her life to ameliorating the impact of those bad happenings. It would hurt to be the object of deadly hatred even if you knew the polysyllabic name for the syndrome.

Molly would get over the insult—probably by morning. Despite her vocation, Anna's sister was remarkably sane. The threats were the tangible aspect of the greater evil of hatred and possibly madness. How real the actual danger was, Anna couldn't fathom. The note and the message were so pedestrian. There was a hollow bureaucratic ring to them. Impersonal to the point of cruelty. Anna remembered her fifth-grade teacher, Mr. White, telling her that hatred wasn't the worst of emotions. If one hated one still cared. Indifference was the most inhuman.

Anna could picture the author of the threats calmly penciling "Kill Dr. Pigeon" on her calendar between "Meet with client rep" and "Get facial."

Tomorrow night she would test Al Magnus's patience. She'd call both Molly and Frederick. Surely sleeping with an FBI agent earned a girl some perks.

As had every day since Anna arrived on the island, Thursday dawned hot and humid, the overnight low scarcely dipping below eighty. Inland the heat was intensified by the clack of cicadas and the intermittent drone of the drug interdiction plane making its sweep of the woodlands. By nine a.m. it was ninety-three degrees.

On the shore a sea breeze made it livable. Anna and Rick patrolled the beach. Al and Dijon were condemned to the suffocating interior till they switched in midafternoon.

Shore duty pleased Anna because of the air and the ever-changing patterns of water and shell and sand. Sky mosaics, painted by clouds, had yet to begin for the day. Cumberland sat beneath an inverted bowl of burnished and burning blue.

At intervals were solitary fishermen, their folding chairs plunked down where the last lick of surf could wash over their toes, cooler and fishing rod in serene attendance. Creels were set several yards from the main encampments, an island phenomenon that had been in place for many years. Legend had it the alligator they called Maggie-Mary would crawl down from the inland dunes, moving as quietly as a ghost for all her great and scaly length, and rob them of their catch. The creels were set apart lest she inadvertently rob them of a leg or a hand in the process.

Rick was happy with beach patrol because of the nude sunbathers. It never ceased to amaze Anna that in America naked was such a big deal. In parks all across the country naked sunbathers, skinny-dippers, and topless hikers were warned and cited and occasionally arrested under any statute that was handy, from Disturbing the Peace to Disorderly Conduct.

The only ticket Anna thought fit this trumped-up crime was Interfering with Agency Functions. It certainly interfered with Rick's and Dijon's. Dijon, Anna forgave—maybe because she liked him, but mostly because he was twenty-two. Dogs bark, cats sharpen their claws, boys ogle and pant. Rick—in his mid-thirties, married, Baptist, and a born-again redneck transplanted from Massachusetts to southern Mississippi—Anna was less tolerant of. He condemned while he leered and it was hard to tell which activity gave him the greater thrill.

This morning Anna was driving, Rick riding shotgun. For the past twenty minutes he'd been working himself into a lather over abortion rights. Rush Limbaugh and G. Gordon Liddy were his much quoted experts on the subject. Anna was attempting a Zen-like state and failing miserably. The heat, the boredom, and Rick were a combination that would have gotten Gandhi's loincloth in a bundle.

She kept her equilibrium by a base but satisfying amusement. Each time Rick raised his binoculars to inventory an unsuspecting sunbather's assets, Anna steered the truck toward the nearest hillock or water-cut in the beach. So far she'd scored two "Fucks" and one "Dammit, Anna."

If people did harbor the inner child psychologists had brought into vogue, hers needed a good spanking, Anna thought, as she turned the wheel to take better advantage of a trench the retreating tide had left behind.

"Shit," Rick growled as the binoculars banged against the soft tissue around his eyes. "You drive like a girl." He too was bored and hot, but if he'd hoped to get a rise out of Anna he was disappointed.

"Don't I though," she said as she adjusted her mental scoreboard: Anna 4, Rick 0.

"I'll drive," he said.

That suited her. Flocks of pelicans were skimming the ocean, flying between the chocolate-colored waves like bombers down narrow canyons. What seabirds lacked in color, they more than made up for in grace and complexity. Anna never tired of watching the many ways they interacted with the sea. Besides, torturing Rick was beginning to pall. He'd never caught on to the game: fish in a barrel, no challenge.

She let the truck roll to a stop and switched off the ignition.

Rick was a big man, thick through the chest, shoulders, and head. His face was a perfect oval. Clustered in the center were a dark mustache, two close-set eyes, and a nondescript nose. The eyes had the puffy look of a perennial hangover, though as near as Anna could tell, he suffered more from allergies than alcoholism. His hair was almost black and clipped so short that the crown of his head, where he was balding, had a peculiar look of having been sanded.

Like every man Anna had ever known, Rick had to spend a minute or two performing some inscrutable ritual before he could get out of a parked vehicle. She slid from the seat and crouched in a scrap of shade afforded by the truck to watch the silt-laden waves break into buttery foam. She'd never spent much time by the sea. Even the waters of Lake Superior had scared her. The Atlantic both scared and fascinated. In its own way the shore was as harsh an environment as the high deserts of Colorado and Texas. The constancy of the August heat, the sand and salt and wind—by day's end human strength was abraded away.

The crunch of boots let her know Rick had uprooted. Over the protest of creaking joints she pushed herself up. It was still early and the sun was at her back as she walked around the truck's tailgate. To the west the green foliage showed dark behind shimmering white dunes. Clouds were just beginning to build, as they did every day, making a promise of rain they never kept. One of the clouds drooped, an uncharacteristic gray. Anna cupped her hands around the brim of her ball cap to cut the glare.

"Hey, Rick." He walked up beside her and she pointed.

"Smoke?"

"Looks like it."

"Hallelujah! Hazard pay!" With a cowboy's "Yee-hah!" he leaped two yards and threw himself behind the wheel.

Anna was galvanized as well. Lethargy, heat, the myriad aches and pains of hours spent patrolling over rough ground in a truck with wasted shocks were banished.

Rick laughed as he cinched down his seat belt. Firefighters, like fire horses, stamped and snorted at the first sniff of smoke. Anna felt the excitement but hers was tempered with the tragic memories of the Jackknife fire the summer before. Like the sea, fire was elemental. It would be many years before she would again underestimate its power. Or its indifference to human life.

5

RICK DROVE like a madman, dropping from gear to gear, revving the tired engine as if more gas could give it a new lease on life. Bouncing like a bean in a tin cup, Anna fought to buckle her seat belt. Between them, ricocheting from thigh to thigh across the vinyl, the portable radio crackled for attention. Finally secured, Anna caught it as it skittered toward the floor, and thumbed down the mike. "This is Pigeon. Yes. We see it. We're about three quarters the way to the north end of the island due east of the smoke. Maybe two miles."

The truck nosed over a lip of water-sculpted sand and Anna's chin smacked into the King radio. Anna 4, Rick 1, she thought as she grabbed at the armrest for stability. Over the airwaves Dijon added to the racket. He and Al were on the southernmost tip of the island near Dungeness, about ten miles from the smoke. They wouldn't reach the fire for at least twenty minutes. The frustration in Dijon's voice made Anna smile. "Don't put it out till we get there," were his parting words.

Anna looked at the fanatic grin on Rick's face and laughed. They would try their damnedest to kill it before the others arrived. It was part of the game, the competition, the testosterone follies. She loved it.

"Yee-hah!" she mimicked Rick, shouting over the engine. "Are we having fun yet?"

Guarding the woodlands from the Atlantic was a rampart of dunes running the length of Cumberland. Near the tips of the island, where they were always being rearranged by the tides, the dunes were only four or five feet high. In the center they climbed to forty and fifty feet, great slow-moving waves of fine white earth.

In several places along the oceanfront weathered wooden boardwalks snaked out from the jungle and across the barrier of dunes providing access to the beach. For Anna, these, more than the crumbling mansions, symbolized the island's heyday, a time when it glittered with wealthy holidaymakers escaping the confines of the cities.

Vehicle access was less nostalgic. Roads had been hacked into the relatively dependable floor of the forest, but egress over the dunes was always chancy. Anna braced herself as Rick gunned the engine, building momentum to carry the heavy truck up through soft and sliding sand. Speed increased, the truck shuddered and screamed. Near the crest of the dune, when Anna thought surely Rick was going to roll the top-heavy pumper, he forced another few horses into the carburetor and they plowed through the peak of the shifting mountain.

"Well done!" Anna yelled as they fishtailed down the far side. Rick had his shortcomings but timidity was not among them. More than once Anna had gotten hopelessly stuck by chickening out and letting off the gas too soon.

Endangered Species

From the vantage point provided by forty-five feet of altitude, she concentrated on the smoke, the tag end of road protruding from the greenery, the sun. Once the trees swallowed them, all sense of direction would be gone. Until they were right on top of the fire they would be unable to see—or probably even smell—the smoke.

Judging from the size of the gray smudge, the fire was still small, probably less than a tenth of an acre. The pumper truck carried two hundred gallons of water and a hundred feet of hard hose line. There was virtually no wind. Barring unforeseen circumstances, she and Rick should be able to at least contain the blaze until the others arrived.

Cushioning her chin with her finger lest Rick score another point, Anna raised the King and put in a call to Guy Marshall. He was on the western edge of the island, six miles from the burn. Though he was careful not to say, Anna guessed he was at Lynette's. The interpreter had a cozy little cabin in the woods near the salt marshes that she shared with the fattest dog Anna had ever seen. Lynette insisted the beast was a weimaraner, but Anna had never seen one wider than it was long. Personally, she suspected the dog's mother of mating with one of the island's feral pigs.

Oak leaves closed overhead, forming a tunnel of plant material. What light penetrated had a green and dusty hue as if viewed through old bottle glass. Unlike in the northern forests Anna had known on Isle Royale, the colored light didn't lend a watery feel. On Cumberland, shade provided no respite from heat, crushing humidity no relief from drought.

Fifty yards ahead the white tongue of sandy soil marking the lane forked. "Stay left," Anna ordered. Rick wrestled the truck over the berm between the tracks without slowing. If there was any oncoming traffic Anna hoped it weighed significantly less than they did.

Dividing her attention between the odometer and the ceiling of trees, she counted off the seconds. Forest canopy refused even a glimpse of the sky. Only hope and habit kept her looking. When she estimated they had traveled about two and a half miles, she told Rick to stop. With no asphalt to screech his tires on, he made do with skidding on the washboarded road till the truck shuddered to a halt in a cloud of dust.

Anna started to say something rude but she could tell he was expecting it, so she forbore comment. "This is my best guess," she said as residual quivers from the wild ride left her entrails. "To the east of this road and a half-mile in either direction."

"Not much to go on," Rick said.

She couldn't argue with him. There was an illusion that fire was easy to find. Smoke, flames, crackling, popping, Bambi and Thumper fleeing in its path. This wasn't true with smaller fires burning in deep or heavy fuels. At Mesa Verde more than one fire crew had wandered around lost within fifty yards of a fire until the helicopter came and planted itself over the burn, hovering till they got there.

"I don't suppose that drug plane could help us out?" Anna wondered aloud.

"No ground-to-air," Rick said, tapping the radio.

She knew that. She was just wishing. She radioed Guy to say they'd arrived somewhere in the vicinity of the fire; then, with less than their former enthusiasm, they climbed from the truck.

Anna rummaged behind the seat until she laid hands on a can of insect repellent. The stuff was almost pure DEET, guaranteed to rot the central nervous system if one was exposed to it over long periods of time. A primitive loathing of all bloodsucking creatures squelched environmental and health concerns, and she doused her boots and trouser cuffs. Rick took the can and repeated the exercise. When they were both thoroughly toxic they stood absolutely still, heads tilted back, nostrils flaring like stallions scenting for danger.

Endangered Species

Dust, DEET, and sweat were the only odors Anna could discern. Rustling stirred the duff somewhere beneath the tangle of brush but there was no way of knowing whether it was fire, rattlesnake, or raccoon.

Both sides of the lane were shoulder-deep in undergrowth. Without air to tickle their fancies, the bladelike palmetto leaves hung limp. Above them, pine and oak mixed to form a gray-green dome. The graceful twisting branches of the live oaks were furred with what looked to be dead brown plants. Resurrection fern, Anna had been told. With the first rains these apparently dead ferns would unfurl and turn green overnight.

"Walk the road a ways?" Rick suggested.

"May as well. Maybe we'll get lucky." Anna took a shovel and a Pulaski—the Janus-faced firefighting tool, axe on one side and hoe on the other—from the back of the truck. By virtue of his broad back, Rick inherited the piss pump, a five-gallon rubber water bladder rigged to be worn as a backpack with a hand-operated pump.

"No lightning," Rick said. "What do you figure started it?"

"Kids?" Anna offered.

"Dirtbags."

Rick's dirtbag category covered so many suspects, Anna chose not to reply and they trudged back the way they'd come, both too engrossed to waste energy on words. Being cut off from the sky demoralized Anna. Being closed in under the greenery like a flea on a Saint Bernard's back made her cranky. "A good burn would do this place a world of good," she grumbled. "Open it up some."

Rick said nothing. He'd stopped in the middle of the road, his head back, his eyes wide and unseeing as if he heard voices, the kind that tell people to walk into a McDonald's and open fire. "Smell it?" he asked.

Anna joined him in concentrated catatonia. After a moment she shook her head.

"Out there. It's gotta be." Rick turned abruptly and pushed eastward through the underbrush. Ten inches shorter than he, Anna flinched as the fronds slashed back against her face. She dropped back a pace and pulled the plastic goggles down from her hard hat to protect her eyes.

Within twenty feet the thicket petered out. Well-spaced trees formed the pillars of a cathedral-sized clearing. Underfoot, leaves and needles smothered lesser growth, carpeting the ground in red-gold. Along the short side of the rough rectangle, where the organ might stand were this indeed a church, was an old hog pen from the days when all-out attempts to rid the island of pigs had been in force. Around the pen the ground had been dug up in a belt ten feet wide and twice that long where modern-day pigs rooted their contempt of the old order. Of the many exotic species let loose on park lands, one could argue that pigs were the most destructive. Maybe because, like people, they were smart and adapted well.

In the center of the clearing Rick and Anna reenacted their idiot/savant tableau. "I smell it now," Anna said, breathing in the unmistakable scent of smoke. "But I can't tell from where."

Rick snuffled in a professional manner; a connoisseur sipping the air. Evidently he hit on something, because he strode purposefully toward the pigsty. On faith, Anna followed.

Palmetto took them in its claustrophobic embrace, wrapping them in dust and webs. One of Cumberland's celebrated residents was the Golden Orb spider, renowned for its enormous webs, some large enough and strong enough to ensnare small birds. The lady herself was famous not only for her ability to mend this impressive net but for her size. Tip to tail she could measure up to two inches, her long and many legs tufted with fur.

Anna repressed a shudder. All the really hellacious spiders would be scraped off by Rick's bulky frame. At least that's what she told herself.

Again the underbrush thinned, bushes growing far enough apart that she and Rick could walk between them. Anna pulled her goggles down around her neck and squeegeed the sweat from her forehead with the flat of her hand. A scrap of turquoise caught her eye. Cumberland's forest, unlike Michigan's and Walt Disney's, was not filled with flowers. At least not in August. Nature exploited a palette of grays, tans, and greens, saving blue for sky and sea.

Mentally, Anna chalked the bit of color up to garbage. Though beautiful, Cumberland was not pristine. People had used her for their own ends since before the Spanish had landed in the 1500s.

Rick was pushing on. Anna ran to catch up. A second scrap of blue wedged head-high in the trunk of a pine tree jarred her brain from its single-minded pursuit of the fire. Above the blue material was a gash so fresh that sap oozed down, marking the tree with dark tracks on the bark.

"Rick!" Anna hollered.

He stopped and looked back, impatience clear on his face.

"What color was that drug interdiction plane that was buzzing around?"

Impatience hardened into annoyance. "How the hell should I know?"

Anna pointed to the damaged tree, the bit of painted metal.

"Shit," Rick said. "That would do it."

Understanding pulled the scales from Anna's eyes and suddenly she saw the myriad clues her busy brain had overlooked. The tops of the bushes were broken in places. A section of cable her mind had written off as litter, a scar in the tree beyond where the blue flagged the path. As these pieces fell into place she became aware of a faint roaring, a hum like that of a vacuum cleaner in another room: palmetto burning hot.

Twenty yards further on, heat hit them in a shimmering curtain. With it came the muted crackle of fire snapping the bones of the undergrowth. A wall of bushes six feet high and alive with flame blocked their way. Beyond the burning thicket, Anna could see the top of a small pine beginning to sprout blossoms of fire. Except for that, the trees had not yet caught.

She trotted parallel to the burn. Customarily she and Rick would have made a quick assessment and begun scraping line in the duff, clearing away the combustible fuels to stop the fire spreading, at least along the ground. With the plane crash, human life was factored in and the saving of property became secondary.

Anna talked on the radio as she ran, telling Guy of the new twist. After she'd signed off she heard him radioing headquarters. There was no reply. Next he tried Lynette. As the interpreter took over dispatching duties, Anna tuned their chatter out and turned all of her attention to breaching the flames separating them from the downed plane.

In less than a minute she was around the screen of palmetto and into a clearing scattered with young pines. The aircraft, a twin-engine prop plane, had rolled over onto its back and nosed into the ground. The belly of the airplane was painted white and looked vulnerable, like the underside of a landed fish. Wheels, popped loose from their housing, pawed at the air. Part of the left wing was crumpled beneath the fuselage, the metal curled and wrinkling. That was where the fire burned hottest and Anna guessed an in-board fuel tank had exploded on impact or shortly thereafter. Half of the right wing was sheared off, the engine thrust skyward in an angry metal fist. Left behind in the rush to demolition, the severed tips of the wings lay a distance from the aircraft. A stump of the tail remained, elevators hanging from torn cables.

From what Anna could see beneath and beyond the wings, the cabin was partially crushed, shards of Plexiglas squeezed out from the metal frames in the cockpit. It looked as if the airplane had cut through the canopy at an angle, left wing pointed toward the earth.

When it struck, the force had driven the cabin into the ground, shattering the windows and smashing in the roof.

Fire poured from the lower engine and was taken up by the palmetto. Orange claws curved around the cabin, bubbling the paint and melting the broken windows.

The intensity of the heat and the knowledge that the plane's second fuel tank had yet to explode paralyzed Anna. In her mind, as it had a year ago below Banyon Ridge, the fire mushroomed out from the trees in a storm of destruction. Terror roared through her insides, wiping her clean of morality, ethics, courage, and thought. Dropping the Pulaski, she turned to run.

Rick had come up behind her. Blindly, she smacked into him and lost her balance.

"Watch where you're going," he growled, knocking her unceremoniously back onto her feet.

The jolt snatched her back from the coniferous forests of northern California and the nightmare that only nine of them had survived. Breath was coming fast and her knees were shaking so bad she couldn't move, but the cowardly retreat had been aborted; honor and face were intact. Though she'd never tell him, Rick had done her a great service.

Fighting to retain her equilibrium, she retrieved her Pulaski. "Okay, okay," she said, as much to herself as to him. Somebody needed to take charge but Anna still had the shakes. She'd locked her knees but her insides twanged like cheap guitar strings. It was all she could do to tie one thought to another.

"Piss pump to the passenger side. The right," Rick said, filling the void. "Maybe somebody's alive. The fire's circling back through the brush. You take it."

Relieved, Anna nodded but didn't move. "Cut the fuels away before the fire gets to the plane," Rick spelled out for her, and gave her the shove she needed. Her first steps were stumbling, her legs still wanting to run. Movement burned away the residual fear and she began to function.

Lest panic again blindside her, Anna attacked the flames with a fury that, once the adrenaline subsided, would leave her with a strained back and a hyperextended elbow. Sweat fell like salt rain to turn to vapor on the superheated ground. Escaping from her hard hat, tendrils of hair singed and curled.

Ignited by the explosion, fire had burned out from the downed aircraft, cutting an angry swathe through the palmetto. Like a ravening beast, appetite unslaked, it doubled back from the point of origin and ran greedily toward the unburned tail of the aircraft.

In a dead-heat race with the flames, Anna chopped line, clearing to bare soil a path a yard and a half wide between the burn and the plane.

In the cabin were the dead or the dying. She suppressed that knowledge in her need to complete the physical task at hand. Dimly, she was aware of paint crackling, the groan of metal shifting and the snap of rubber and plastics, but her world had narrowed to the one tentacle of the dragon she had been sent to hack off. The writhing of the rest could be dealt with later.

The thicket wasn't more than fifteen feet wide at the point where the plane had nosed in. Unless the shrubs ignited the live oaks, the fire would slow to a creep when it hit the duff beyond the underbrush. It wasn't long before Anna succeeded in separating the plane from the fire. With her primary task accomplished, the scope of her world opened somewhat and she turned back to the mangled aircraft.

On the passenger side of the inverted fuselage, Rick stood in the angle where the wing stub met the cabin, squirting water on the metal. Not six inches from his fanny was a fuel tank, the only one remaining attached to the main part of the wreckage that had yet to explode.

Endangered Species

A thin line of smoke, rising straight up in the still air, caught Anna's eye. Beneath the duff, creeping almost unseen, fire from the palmetto was crawling through the leaf litter toward the fuel tank. Anna abandoned the secured left flank of the plane and, in a controlled frenzy of hoeing, began clearing away burning debris. Acrid smoke was sucked through the bandanna tied across the lower half of her face. Mucus ran from her nose and she breathed as sparingly as exertion would allow.

A shovel appeared in her peripheral vision. Dijon and Al had arrived. Dijon joined Anna and began throwing dirt on the trail of flame, broken free of the litter now and snaking toward the wing. Al manned a second piss pump, aiming his stream onto the metal cowling of the engine itself. Guy Marshall must have arrived at roughly the same time as the other two. When Anna looked past Al, he was there, Pulaski in hand.

It was good to be among friends.

Through the bite of the smoke Anna became aware of the odor of gasoline. At that moment she heard Guy shouting "Fall back! Fall back!"

Fire had circled around Dijon and met up with a trickle of high octane fuel soaking through the mat of needles and leaves that had yet to be scraped away. Flame burned narrow and high with the intensity of a lit fuse.

"Fall back!" Guy shouted again.

Dijon threw a spadeful of dirt at the back of Rick's legs to get his attention. "Back," he and Anna yelled in unison; then they turned and ran.

6

THE EXPLOSION, when it came, was not so much heard as felt. A heavy and unseen hand slammed into Anna's back, lifting her off her feet. Time slowed, a break in the space-time continuum, and, for that instant, it was as if she hung suspended in the air. To her right she could see Dijon, hands outstretched like a young black Superman, hanging in space. His face was set, determined, as if he flew toward a brick wall intending to smash through.

Anna noticed her left hand stretched in front of her clutching the Pulaski. Afraid she'd fall on one of the blades, she let it go. There was time, in that stopwatch moment, to see her fingers uncurl from the handle and the two-edged tool fall away.

Time caught up with itself. Dijon, the trees blurred and Anna hurtled to the ground. The forest floor scraped the goggles from her face, shoved prickling needles down the collar of her shirt and dust up her nose. Something plowed into her booted feet and she thought a chunk of burning metal had crippled her till it began clawing its way up and she knew it was Rick.

"Everybody okay? Are you okay, Anna?" An obnoxious finger rapped against the plastic of her hard hat. She rolled one eye clear of the dirt to see Guy standing over her.

"I'm not done falling," she complained.

"Learn to bounce," he said unsympathetically. He was on to Rick and Dijon as Anna pushed herself warily to her knees, not yet sure everything still worked.

"Up and at 'em," Marshall said.

Dijon, disgustingly young and resilient, was already on his feet and running back toward the plane. Rick had made it to his knees. Lest she be last, Anna dragged herself up before Al Magnus cleared the ground, and followed Guy and the others back toward the line.

The explosion had extinguished more fire than it set. Within minutes Rick and Dijon had the flames contained. Though it still burned it was no longer in danger of spreading.

The task of salvaging what they could from the plane's cabin fell to Anna and Guy. The blast had torn most of the remaining stub off the right wing, leaving a black stain on the side of the aircraft just below, or—as the fuselage was inverted—now above where the passenger sat. Anna crouched down to assess the best way of getting at the cockpit. Behind her she could hear Guy on the radio.

The downed plane was a twin-engine Beechcraft owned and operated by a man named Slattery Hammond. Hammond worked as a freelance drug interdiction and/or resource management plane, hiring his services out to various government agencies. Cumberland Island National Seashore was sharing him with the United States Forest Service in an effort to curb the marijuana-growing industry along the coast.

Hammond had flown off the island that morning to make a low-level sweep of St. Simons, Jekyll Island, and Cumberland, looking for contraband crops. Norman Hull, Cumberland's chief ranger, was slated to accompany him.

Lynette's voice, deepened now by professional responsibility, came on to say a medevac helicopter had been requested from Jacksonville, Florida. Lynette was attempting to contact the district ranger, Todd Belfore, to meet the medevac unit and lead them to the burn as soon as she had an estimated time of arrival.

Wheels were turning, the Incident Command System was gearing up. Soon Anna, Guy, Dijon, Al, and Rick would settle back into their relatively insignificant cog roles as the Interagency Incident Command machine took over. There was great comfort in that. Nothing, not even the U.S. military, could mobilize as quickly and efficiently.

After this last transmission Guy replaced his radio on his belt. "The pilot wasn't alone. Chief Ranger Hull was with him. There'll be two . . . ah . . . men in there," he said. The hesitation took place as he stopped himself from saying "bodies." The explosion of the gas tank destroyed any shred of hope they might have had that anyone in the airplane still lived, but they had to operate as if lives could be salvaged. The concept of giving up too soon was abhorrent.

What was left of the wing and the fuselage formed a smoldering and unstable tent of ruined metal. Leaf litter smoked beneath the wreckage. Using the blunt side of the Pulaski, Anna scraped the smoldering material into a blackened heap behind her, then, on hands and knees, crawled under the amputated stub of wing. Paint had been burned off the door, and the Plexiglas in the side window melted in black sticky tears that crept down the denuded metal. At Anna's request, Guy turned the paltry stream from his rapidly depleting water pack onto the door handle. When it had cooled enough so that it wouldn't immediately burn through the leather of her gloves, she gave it a pull. Much to her surprise, it worked. The door opened half an inch, then stuck fast, the top mired in a mess of smoking rubber and crushed metal. "We're going to have to pry it out," she said.

"Hang on. I'll get the guys and we'll lift this thing so you can get at it."

The melted window was almost at ground level. Bending down in the attitude of a long-adrift sailor kissing the earth, Anna peered into the cabin. Energies released from the force of the crash, then the onslaught of the fire had wreaked havoc inside. A nauseating odor that Anna knew to be roasting human flesh and hair was overlaid with the pungent sting of gases created when many petroleum products were melted down into their component parts.

Clothing, upholstery, seat belts—all had been reduced to cinders. The people they'd held in place had fallen down, crumpled with the rest of the trash on the ruined instrument panel. Without stronger light and a better angle Anna couldn't tell where organic matter ended and inorganic began.

Emergency medical training taught her to seek the carotid artery to separate the living from the dead. In this tangled mass she saw a blackened tube shape that was very possibly what was left of the passenger's neck, but she couldn't bring herself to remove her glove and press her bare hand in through the melt of flesh.

Straightening up, she sat back on her heels in the relatively fresh air a foot or two from the plane. While Guy organized the crew she stared at the canopy of leaves beyond the burn, her brain in neutral. Inside the Beechcraft there was no life, she was sure of it. Training, courage, adrenaline—all the necessary ingredients for heroics—were of no use. Now she hoped only to disturb as little as possible and keep her breakfast down.

"On three. Ready, Anna? Anna!"

She jerked her chin up at the repetition of her name.

"Sorry to wake you," Guy said. "You want to pry that door off when we lift?"

"Sure thing." Anna dropped back to her knees. She squirmed down under the remnant of wing and forced the blade of her Pulaski between the door and the main body of the plane, then braced herself to use the Pulaski handle as a lever. "Ready," she said.

"On three."

Guy counted down, and as the bulk of the aircraft was lifted from the scorched earth, Anna dug her heels in and pulled back. Brittle creaks heralded the breakage of fused hinges. The door popped open, swinging out in a crippled arc. The last shred of metal let go and it fell away from the fuselage.

"Okay," Anna said. "High enough."

She heard scraping as the men wedged a log or limb under the wing stub and the faintest of groans as they let the weight settle on the prop.

With the door removed she could better see the carnage within. The body furthest from her had burned black but for the right ear, horribly pink and lifelike in a nest of hair singed into a likeness of wire. On the left arm, much of the flesh from elbow to knuckle was charred and falling away in strips, but a single square of red-and-blue-plaid fabric remained over a chunk of tissue that, from the ruin of a watch, Anna guessed was the pilot's wrist.

Curled around the dead pilot, as if his had been the first to burn loose from the seat belt, was the body of the passenger. It was burned beyond recognition, beyond human. It was crisp and sere and, Anna knew from experience, would crumble if she touched it.

Guy folded down and crawled beneath the plane. Through the smoke and sweat and stench, Anna caught a whiff of cologne and was immeasurably touched by it. Overwrought, she told herself, but the humanity in the gesture struck a chord somewhere in the vicinity of her heart.

"Done deal," Guy said as he looked inside the cabin. "Get out of here, Anna. We're finished. Fire's out."

Anna crawled backward, rump first into the open air. As soon as she was clear, Guy followed.

"Dead?" Dijon asked.

He was so young Anna guessed he'd not seen much death, and she watched closely to see how he was taking it. Between the black of his skin and the gray of the ash it was hard to tell. His voice sounded matter-of-fact but he'd probably put forth some effort to make sure it would before he'd opened his mouth.

"Crispy Critters?" Rick asked, a little too jovially.

Al worked to get his pipe going and said nothing.

The three radios they carried among the five of them crackled to life. Guy responded and they stood in a half-circle, their backs to the dead men, listening.

A helicopter had been dispatched with two paramedics. They were on final to land at St. Marys to pick up the chief ranger, Norman Hull.

It took a few seconds for the name to register. "Hull?" Guy echoed stupidly.

"Norman Hull, Chief Ranger," Lynette repeated clearly.

"I thought he was our second dead guy," Anna said.

The radio took stage again, this time a male voice scratching through the ether from air to ground issuing orders.

"Apparently not," Guy said.

7

IN UNSPOKEN ACCORD, the five of them retired to the unburned edge of the clearing, sat down in the dirt, and began uncapping water bottles. Rick was putting on a bit of a show, dredging up black humor to ward off shock. Dijon bought into it, but Anna noticed the only one eating lunch was Al.

Every day he had the same thing, two PB&Js on white bread. "Want half?" he offered when he caught Anna's eye. She took the proffered sandwich. In her yellow pack was a peanut butter and honey sandwich of her own. Later maybe she'd return the favor. At the moment there was something reassuring in the breaking of bread with another.

"Health food again?" Rick jibed. His hand rested on his belt. Anna suspected he was secretly fondling his "six-pack," the ridged stomach muscles that adorned the covers of bodybuilding magazines.

"Ambrosia," Al said, unperturbed.

"I bet your kid loves it when you cook," Dijon put in.

"As a matter of fact, he's wild about my cooking." A dab of strawberry jelly quivered momentarily on Al's cheek. Before he wiped it away Anna's ever-active brain had likened it to blood, guts, and half-cooked flesh. The childhood song "great green gobs of greasy, grimy gopher guts floating in the pink lemonade" made its tinny music in the recesses of her memory and she smiled.

Guy shoveled gorp into his mouth and talked expertly around the mash. Paramedics would not be needed. A coroner would. The radio vied with the thump of a helicopter and the growl of an ATV. The cavalry was arriving.

Anna leaned back against a young oak and poured water into her dehydrated body. Al smoked. Guy, Rick, and Dijon wandered back into the fray. By ones and twos it seemed most of the island was trickling in to see the wreck. The green and gray of NPS uniforms predominated and Anna had little doubt she had been introduced to some of them, but she wasn't good with names and faces. The only person she recognized was Mitch Hanson. His thinning gray hair was slicked over his forehead with sweat and hair spray. Bright blue eyes sparkled under sparse brows and he seemed of good cheer; a sweaty grubby Saint Nick only sporadically remembering to look somber as befitted the occasion.

Everyone else talked in low voices, looked frequently into the nonexistent distance, and milled around purposefully. The pattern was familiar; nobody wanted to take charge. Anna took another long drink of water and closed her eyes.

When she opened them again, order had been restored. A glance at Al's watch told her she'd only dozed for a quarter of an hour but the difference was marked. Norman Hull, Cumberland's chief ranger, had arrived on scene. Hull was tall, long-legged and long-necked. A receding hairline provided him with an impressive brow that ended in a frizz of graying brown curls. Pale blue eyes blinked from behind thick lenses and his rubbery face was in constant motion as he directed the operation.

Yellow police tape had gone up around the aircraft. Photographs were being taken and every third person was talking on a cellular phone or a radio.

An ATV arrived with a plump middle-aged man in madras shorts and a crushed fishing cap. From the unhesitating beeline he made toward the corpses, Anna guessed he was the coroner. He and Hull crouched on the far side of the aircraft, near the broken passenger door.

All Anna could see of them was their feet beneath the remnants of the wing. Death was certain; the coroner needed only to give a look and a signature to make it legal. They were probably looking for identification on the second corpse. She didn't envy them the task.

Tired of floating around the edges of things, Dijon came back and flopped onto the ground. "They going to leave those guys or what?" he asked.

"I doubt it," Anna said. "They'll put them in body bags and take them to the morgue. Since they didn't die under a doctor's care they've got to be autopsied. Besides, if they left them here it wouldn't look good. Though the critters would get a good supper out of the deal."

"Already cooked." Dijon licked his lips. "If you like your meat well done."

Anna laughed at the sheer ghoulishness of it and because she could tell that with his macabre joke Dijon had shocked himself. The mental picture arrived half a second behind his words and he looked suddenly nauseated.

Guy separated himself from a knot of men gathered around the nose of the airplane and walked back toward the crew. "Looks like they figured out who the second man was," he said as he dug through his yellow pack. Sweat glittered in beads on his bald pate. For an instant Anna thought they were blisters from second-degree burns and felt her stomach lurch. Guy pulled a blue handkerchief from the pack and mopped his head and neck. "Face and hands were pretty much gone but the chief ranger found a brass belt buckle and what's left of a nine-millimeter handgun. And he found the guy's badge. Looks like he was a ranger. They've radioed in the numbers on the back of the badge but nobody's waiting on pins and needles—they only got one law enforcement ranger on Cumberland."

"Todd Belfore," Al said.

Guy nodded.

"That kinda takes the fun out of it," Rick said.

Guy settled into the dirt and lay back, using his pack as a head-rest. Al puffed absently on a dead pipe. Dijon couldn't take the stillness and leaped up to join Rick gossiping with an extraneous maintenance worker.

Dead strangers evoked a smorgasbord of the lesser emotions and served as marvelous educational tools, warnings, and veiled threats. When an acquaintance was killed it was closer to home; one knew some of the threads that tied the deceased to a common humanity. Without enough real connection to grieve, one was left in an uncomfortable place between curiosity and embarrassment.

Chief Ranger Hull crossed the clearing, wiping his hands carefully on a clean white pocket hanky. Scenting a shift in the action, Rick and Dijon drifted back to the rest of the crew.

Hull stopped near Guy's feet and the crew boss sat up as a sign of respect. "Mr. Marshall here has probably already told you the pilot was Slattery Hammond. He was flying drug interdiction for us and the Department of Forestry." Hull never looked up from his hands while he talked, but continued to rub meticulously between each finger with the square of cotton. His face worked maniacally, the eyebrows rising as if in sudden surprise, then dropping, his mouth stretching as if he were trying to scrape something from his rabbity teeth by moving his lips over them. For the first time Anna saw the facial gestures for what they were; not emotion but uncontrolled tics or nervous spasms, worse now that he was under pressure. "We're pretty sure the second man was our district ranger, Todd Belfore. Mr. Marshall said he'd spent time with you, so I realize this is bad news for you as well as us."

Finally Norman Hull pocketed the handkerchief and Anna breathed a sigh of relief. Till it stopped she'd not realized how much his Pontius Pilate routine was getting on her nerves.

"It will be worst for Mrs. Belfore—Tabby. As you are probably aware she is . . . ah . . . with child. Very much so." Despite the god-awful circumstances, his old-world delicacy elicited a mental smile from the part of Anna's brain that eschewed modern cynicism. "I would greatly appreciate it, Mr. Marshall—Guy—if you wouldn't mind lending me this young lady. I feel Mrs. Belfore would be more comfortable if there was another woman present."

Panic rose in Anna's chest. "Where's Lynette?" she demanded cravenly.

"Lynette's gone over to the mainland," Hull said. He sounded offended, as if he had offered Anna a great honor. In a way he had.

"Sorry," Anna said. "Caught me off guard. Sure, I'll come. Damn." She levered herself up from the duff but she could tell she'd not been quick enough. Disapproval flickered through the busy machinations of the chief ranger's face.

Shouldering her pack, she followed him docilely from the oak woods. A shiny blue Ford pickup truck waited for them in the dust of the lane. That Hull managed to keep it glossy through sand and salt and drought spoke reams about the man.

Anna buckled herself in and the chief ranger drove south. The closer they came to Plum Orchard, the slower the truck moved.

Hull was dreading this as much as she was. Anna took comfort in that. Regardless of her gender she didn't doubt he'd do the actual breaking of the news. He was chief ranger. They were paid for that sort of thing and most took their responsibilities to heart. Stewardship extended to all the animals in the park, even the two-legged variety.

Plum Orchard was a gracious old Georgian Revival–style mansion built in 1898 by Andrew Carnegie for his son. In the grand tradition, it rose three stories with arched floor-to-ceiling windows along the ground floor and four fine strong pillars supporting a gabled porch roof two stories high. A railed veranda ran around three sides. Several additional porches were tucked into odd angles. One, near the back, still boasted a wide swinging bench that Anna liked to catnap on when they were involved in the tedious process of filling rubber stock tanks with well water.

Two of these tanks marred the expanse of front lawn. With the continuing drought the crew kept them full so that should fire break out, helicopters could fill their drop buckets. The island was surrounded by water but so delicate was the chemistry of life that to use salt water to quench inland fires would damage the ecological balance.

Beyond the tanks, ancient oaks, furred in resurrection ferns and dripping veils of Spanish moss, dotted the grounds. Two stately palms, grown taller than the house, stood sentinel at the front entrance. Behind the house was the inland waterway that separated the island from the mainland and the town of St. Marys.

Ranger Hull followed the graveled drive around to the back of the house and switched off the ignition. He and Anna had not exchanged a single word since they'd left the burn site. The bang of a screen door rattled down from the upstairs apartment and they exchanged guilty glances.

"Waiting isn't going to make it any easier," he said, and pulled the handle on his door. Anna noticed he didn't actually push it open till he satisfied himself that she was going to do the same. Her earlier cowardice had not gone unnoticed. To redeem herself, she stepped smartly from the truck and walked around the tailgate.

Wooden stairs, added in recent years as a fire escape and to provide private access to the apartment, led up to the second floor. Tabby Belfore had come onto the small landing outside the screen door. The sun was behind her, shining through the thin fabric of her summer dress and her fine blond hair. The dress was pale yellow and sheer, very much like her hair. Backlit, the clothing appeared burned away, only a halo left surrounding her narrow shoulders and swollen belly. To Anna she was beautiful, reminiscent of a stunning painting she'd once seen by Gustav Klimt of a pregnant nude veiled in crimped auburn hair. Anna found herself running up the steep steps, suddenly afraid Tabby would fall.

"You're Anna, aren't you?" Tabby began, knowing the answer but feeling the need to make hostess noises.

"Yes. Fire crew." Anna had reached the top and, standing between Tabby and the stairs, felt both relieved and foolish. Chief Ranger Hull pushed up behind her and she was glad to turn the situation over to him.

"May we step inside, Mrs. Belfore?" Hull asked courteously.

All was not well and Tabby sensed it. Her delicate face closed like a poppy at sundown. Wordlessly she backed into the hallway between the stairs and the kitchen. A gentleman, Norman Hull held the door and Anna was forced to enter next.

Tabby closed both hands on her skirt, crumpling the fabric above her knees. She continued to back away till a kitchen chair stopped her.

"Why don't we sit?" Anna said gently.

Obediently, Tabby lowered herself onto the seat. She looked for all the world like a waif expecting to be beaten. Her eyes were downcast, her fingers clutching convulsively, her shoulders pinched up around her ears as if to ward off a blow.

She didn't ask a single question.

"We have some rather bad news," Hull said. Anna willed him to kneel, bend down, anything to close the gulf between Tabby Belfore and himself. Though the kitchen was small, the space loomed like a gulf and Anna could imagine Mrs. Belfore pitching face forward into it. Quietly she slipped behind the chair, sat on her heels and rested her elbows on her knees, forming human arms to the straight-backed chair that held Tabby. The girl seemed unaware Anna was not part of the furniture. Her fingers loosed the flimsy dress and closed around Anna's wrist.

Still she didn't look up and she didn't ask for the news.

"Todd has been killed in an airplane crash," Hull said evenly. "We are terribly sorry for your loss. If there's—"

Tabby's head jerked up, her mouth slightly open; a quick look at the chief ranger, away, and again the look. A classic double take so out of place, the beginnings of a laugh were startled out of Anna's throat. The laughter went on and for an instant Anna thought she'd gone off her rocker, but it was Tabby who was laughing. Anna got ready to grab the girl if she had to.

Abruptly, the laughter stopped. "No. Not Todd," Tabby said. "That's not funny."

Norman Hull slowly turned his Stetson around, running the brim through his fingers. His face was working overtime: the eyebrows up, a sudden grimace. Despite the tic, concern was clear in his eyes. "The drug interdiction plane crashed and the pilot was killed," Hull began again. This time Tabby was nodding as if she understood, as if she was taking the information in.

"Todd was with him. We're pretty sure he didn't feel anything. Death was instantaneous."

Tabby sat stone-still. Anna shifted her weight. Her right leg was going to sleep. Hull looked at her for help or corroboration but she merely shrugged. Tabby had heard. There was nothing to do but wait.

"Todd wasn't with him," Tabby said finally. Neither Anna nor Norman Hull replied. Tabby looked from one to the other, the emotions on her face as readable as those of a very young child: disbelief, rage, fear. And something else. The last one, Anna couldn't read. It was how she imagined a woman's face would look if her heart suddenly imploded and she had the misfortune to go on living.

Another few seconds passed. Anna started to get to her feet. Tabby began screaming, raw gouts of desperation. Reaching up, she raked her fingers down her cheeks. The nails had been bitten to the quick but the force of the clawing left angry welts.

Anna turned to Hull. "Get that helicopter. Get her out of here. To a hospital."

The chief ranger nodded, put his Stetson square on his head, and left the kitchen. Anna could hear his boots clattering down the wooden stairs to the truck where he'd left his radio.

Tabby's screams sawed out with the regularity of breath. Anna caught hold of her hands but the fingers remained stiff and curled as if she were still tearing at her face. Twice Anna begged her to stop. The screams went on and the moment Anna loosed her hands the rending of the flesh began again.

"Come on, come on, take it easy, we'll get you through this." Anna was murmuring the words she'd murmured to a hundred shaken and injured people over the years. She scarcely heard her own voice.

A coffee cup sat on the drainboard, an inch of cold coffee scummed with milk in it. Anna dumped it and refilled it with cold water. In a sudden snapping movement she threw it in Tabby's face.

Abruptly the screaming stopped. Tabby's hands transformed back into something resembling human appendages. Spluttering like one nearly drowned, she wiped the water from the front of her dress.

"You can't do this," Anna said quietly. "Much as you want to, you can't fall apart now."

Tabby smoothed her hands over her belly. The water made the fabric of the dress adhere to her skin and Anna could see a pulsing movement as if a tiny hand or foot pounded the ceiling for quiet.

"Oh my God," Tabby said. "Oh my dear God." She didn't cease to weep but the tears came silently, mixing with the water Anna had thrown, dripping off her jaws and down the bodice of her dress.

Anna pulled up a second chair and sat knee to knee with Tabby, ready to catch her if she fell.

They were still sitting like that when the helicopter came.

8

NAKED, ANNA STOOD on the shore. Warm wavelets licked at her bare toes like friendly puppies. There was just enough breeze so she could feel the air moving across her skin. Dusk had come and gone and the cloak of night gave her privacy for this ultimate freedom. She marveled at how different life was without clothes on; better—at least until it grew cold or buggy. For modern Victorians—a culture that kept nudity in darkened movie theaters linked always with sex and more often than not with violence—to be outdoors and naked was exhilarating, wild, dangerous.

Particularly for a woman alone.

Anna pushed that thought aside. It was media-borne and not usually true. Fear sold ad space and so television and the newspapers mainlined it.

For a long ways out the ocean was shallow, and she walked sixty yards before the water came to her waist. Stars overhead, stars on the water, she sank down and let the sea lift her. The rubber bands that held her braids had been cut and the insistent pulse of the ocean unraveled her smoke-matted hair. Something, seaweed maybe, slunk past her left leg, touching the back of her knee. She added sharks to the list of things she refused to think about. Fear was a burglar, breaking into one's mind, stealing away peace. Mentally she bolted her doors and drifted with the night.

The fire was out, the bodies bagged; yellow police tape cordoned off the crash site. Though Anna had never worked a plane wreck before, the dead and dying were not strangers to her. The twisting roads of Mesa Verde National Park and the straight fast highway through the southern edge of the Guadalupe Mountains had claimed their share of motorists. There had even been a man burned to death in a wildfire she'd worked in California. But he'd been totally consumed, reduced to elemental ash.

What was troubling Anna was the pilot's right ear. That pink, human ear nestled in the carnage. The image would take a while to fade. Weeks would pass before the sight of a shrimp in a nest of fettuccine or a dried apricot among the peanuts was rendered harmless.

Lowering her feet to the sandy bottom, Anna spread her legs and leaned into the sleepy surf, reveling in the sensual thrill of water against her skin. The moon crept misshapen over the horizon, spilling its light across the Atlantic. Twining it through her fingers, Anna wove strands of gold into the dark salt water, enjoying the mindless play.

After the fire had been declared out and the brass and the medics and the machinery had ferried each other back to the mainland, Guy had gathered the crew together.

"Bear with me now, I've had the training but this is the first time I've had to use it," he'd said as he stood in front of the house that served as the fire dorm. His face was blacked from soot. Kept clean by his hard hat, his head gleamed in the growing dusk. Propping one foot on the stump of a tree cut nearly level with the ground, he rocked slowly, thinking.

Legs dangling like children, Anna and Dijon sat side by side on the tailgate of the pumper truck. Rick leaned against a fender and Al sat on one of the coolers, methodically packing his pipe.

A southern evening trickled in from the east, filling the cracks between the shadows with soothing darkness. Drought had knocked the mosquitoes to their knees and only an occasional bloodthirsty whine pierced the tranquillity. Stars had yet to shine and the sky was colorless with the abdication of the sun.

Air-conditioning, sofas, lights, window screens—all were less than twenty feet away but no one thought to move the meeting indoors. For the five of them, tailgates and trucks were familiar ground, closer to home than strange quarters.

"You've all heard of critical-incident stress management?" Guy asked, looking around for a neutral spot where he could aim a stream of tobacco juice. "Anybody ever been through a session?" Everybody but Dijon raised a hand. "Good. Then help me out. You pretty much know the drill. Anybody want to go first?"

Ten seconds ticked by; then Rick said: "It's a crock of shit, if you ask me."

Anna felt a stab of anger on Guy's behalf but the crew boss took Rick's words in stride, recognizing them for what they signified: discomfort. This new touchy-feely stuff had yet to be embraced by some of the rank and file.

Hands on hips, Guy stared upward a moment; a man collecting his thoughts. "Then why don't you just kind of be here in case somebody needs you to listen, okay, Rick?" he said at last. "We won't be doing group hugs or nothing."

Rick was nailed in by that. No face lost. Nothing to bluster against. He propped an elbow on the edge of the truck bed and tried to look superior.

Anna understood the impulse. She didn't want to talk about her feelings either. Maybe nobody else shared them. Maybe they weren't good enough. Maybe it was nobody's damn business. Maybe they were inappropriate; that was the fear that silenced most people.

Goaded by fear of fear, Anna decided to go first. "I was afraid the widow was going to drop that baby right then and there."

Nods all around. Nobody outraged. It was just a thought. Anna felt a little bad for referring to Tabby Belfore as "the widow." Just distancing herself, she guessed.

Half a minute crept by, tension stretching the seconds till Anna swore she could feel herself aging, but she was damned if she was going to go first twice.

"Hanson bothered me," Dijon blurted out.

"Yeah? Why?" Anna knew that Guy, ever diligent to his duties as crew boss, was trying to coax. He was following the book. But being born a booted, hard-hatted man, there was a lack of conviction. Like a good soldier he followed orders, even those he didn't thoroughly comprehend.

It didn't matter. Dijon answered anyway and that was what counted, the talking. "He was so fucking 'Ho, ho, ho.'" Dijon had forgotten to clean up his language in front of a lady. He must have been upset. "Then he'd go all fakey, undertaker-sad."

"Maybe he didn't know what else to do," Al said.

"He's a dirtbag," Rick said.

More silence followed, less strained this time. Night was flowing from the east. The anonymity bestowed by darkness eased their minds.

"I don't figure anybody was still alive by the time we got there," Dijon said tentatively. The hope in his voice seemed to crystallize all their thoughts. Finding dead bodies—even fresh ones—was one thing, but to be there, helpless witness to the migration of souls, was something else entirely.

Transmuted from gold to silver, the moon had shrunk to the size of a dime. The dunes were white with its light. Silhouetted against the sands, a small herd of horses walked north in single file: a stallion— even at this distance Anna could see impressive equipment drooping nearly to his hocks—five mares, and two foals. The Cumberland horses; the herd numbered close to three hundred animals. For decades they'd run wild on the island. They were part of the lore, part of the allure, part of the history. And a dilemma for the NPS. The fragile dune and interdune structures hadn't evolved to cope with equine depredation. Hardened hooves of these exotic beasts destroyed the delicate plant life that held the sand in place. Their enormous appetites grazed down the vegetation between dune and forest, and the sand was migrating inland, smothering the freshwater lakes.

It would be political suicide to kill them and economic folly to deport them. Blessedly uninvolved in higher management, Anna chose to float on the tide and enjoy them.

Not for the first time the scene in the Belfores' kitchen played through her mind. Tabby's reaction had bothered Anna at the time. In retrospect it seemed even stranger and she wondered if Tabby had slipped a cog under the strain.

In her years as a park ranger, Anna had delivered her share of bad news. People took the hit in a lot of ways. The storm of grief had been expected. The denial wasn't out of place. Tabby's sudden laughter, though jarring, hadn't been particularly alarming. Comedy of the absurd was based on the fact that what startles may very well get a laugh.

Lazily, Anna looked toward shore. The horses were gone. So was the ATV she'd borrowed to come to the beach. A jolt of adrenaline disturbed her calm till she spotted it where she'd left it. A strong current, scarcely felt in so large a body of water, was carrying her north, parallel to the island.

The beach was devoid of humanity but not of life. Minute skittering, too far away for Anna to identify, attested to abundant activity. Ghost crabs probably; maybe even baby loggerhead turtles from an earlier laying, though she doubted it. Marty Schlessinger would have been in attendance had that been the case. And, too, the nests tended to be further north, east of where the drug interdiction plane went in.

Anna's thoughts had come full circle, back to the accident and its aftermath. Back to Tabby Belfore's kitchen. She recommenced playing "What's wrong with this picture?" In a moment she hit on it. It wasn't the surprise, the laughter, or the denial, but that they had come late—a split second too late. Tabby had been waiting for bad news, just not the bad news she got.

What, if anything, that portended, Anna wasn't sure.

Rolling over onto her belly, she let the waves carry her shoreward till her fingers touched bottom. The deliciously wicked and wonderful sensation enveloped her again as she wandered nude down the shoreline, turning now and again to watch the moon fill her watery footprints with silver.

9

FREDERICK SAT staring at the old black rotary phone. A corner of the coffee table was cleared of the ubiquitous slither of magazines to accommodate it. In the bedroom of his small Chicago apartment dwelt all the FBI agent's high-tech communications equipment: fax, modem, answering machine, Touch-Tone cordless. But when he really wanted to talk, he came to the rotary. It had heft and substance. He could press the round receiver to his ear and shut out the world, whisper into the cupped mouthpiece and feel close to the other end of the line.

Staring at the lump of plastic, still warm from Anna's call, he was dismayed to think how much of his life—social, family, business, and love—was conducted over the phone.

Danny and Taters fluttered down from the magazines stacked on the mantel over a fireplace broadcasting the soulless life of a television on mute. The budgerigars, one blue, one green, pecked around the base of the telephone. Frederick had the bachelor's habit of dining in front of the TV and there was usually a tidbit to be had about this time of the evening.

Danny, the blue budgie, had Anna Pigeon to thank for Taters. When Frederick had become enamored of Anna he'd taken pity on Danny's isolation and bought him a ladyfriend. The girl at the pet shop, still in high school and no more a judge of bird gender than Frederick, had lost her fifty-fifty gamble. Still it was a happy ending. The birds were close as brothers.

Making squeaky noises with his lips, Frederick put out his finger. Danny hopped aboard and looked at him with one bright eye. Piedmont, Anna's tomcat, would devour his feathered friends if ever he got the chance. Frederick hoped that wasn't a metaphor for his relationship with the little ranger.

He smiled at the word. It never crossed Anna's mind that she was little. Probably she'd be offended if he suggested it. He had learned to be careful around her. If he picked up one end of a piano she'd run around to lift the other. One day she was going to hurt herself. One day she was going to get herself killed.

Frederick sat with that thought for a moment. Danny flew to the top of his head and scratched a cascade of baby-fine hair over his forehead. It tickled the bridge of his nose. Time for a haircut. Absently he shoved it and an agitated budgie back.

Life without Anna, at least tethered to his heart by phone line, was not unthinkable. Unfortunately, at forty-five with twenty-three years in law enforcement, there was very little left that was unthinkable. But living alone had grown tiresome, the long-distance relationship a lonely and irritating compromise. "I wish Anna liked the city," he said to the bird on his head. "Or I liked dirt and bugs and thousands of square miles of nothing."

Anna had said she was going for a swim. Frederick thought of her firm body slipping through the sea and felt a pleasant stirring.

"Guess it's time to earn my keep," he said to the little green bird hopping along the edge of the table.

A pair of heavy plastic half-glasses, the cheap kind from the grocery store, lay near the phone. Frederick pushed them halfway up his long nose with a practiced movement and studied the numbers he'd written on the back of July's electric bill.

In the year he'd been with Anna her sister, Molly, had taken on superhuman proportions. He'd never met or spoken with her but he didn't doubt she knew everything about him, from how he voted in the last election to the size of his penis. Once a man started sleeping with a woman, he was a fool to think he had any secrets left.

Cradling the telephone to his ear, he dialed. He hadn't much of an idea what he could say or do. Death threats were vague unpredictable things and could mean anything from a desire for power over someone to an actual warning. The motive was always to harass but the degree of real danger was on a sliding scale. Too often the procedures TV had taught the public to believe in as standard magic—DNA, fingerprints, paper type, handwriting—couldn't be applied. Career criminals, those citizens who tended to have their fingerprints on record, weren't much given to letter writing. Computers had done away with the idiosyncrasies of the old typewriters, and most grades of paper were sold by the tens of millions of sheets.

He would listen, make suggestions, earn some Brownie points, and maybe something clever would come to him. Adolescent as it was, Frederick admitted to a fantasy of rescuing Anna's sister from fiends most foul. It would look great on his résumé.

"Hello," snapped over the line, and he was alarmed to find Molly home. A message on a machine would have been the easy way out.

"This is Frederick Stanton of the FBI," he said stiffly, then rolled his eyes at himself.

"This is Dr. Pigeon," returned a cool voice.

Title to title, they waited.

"I just called to see if my introduction was truly pompous or if I should work on it," Frederick said. Molly laughed and he was relieved. The laugh itself was an infectious cackle suitable for the kidnapper of Toto and other strong women in history.

It died away and a black void of phone silence crawled into Frederick's ear. Having initiated the contact, he was obliged to go first. "Anna asked me to call. She's worried about the threats you've been getting."

There was a sharp intake of breath that he took for outrage till he remembered Molly was a smoker. As a young man he'd smoked. Caffeine and telephones still brought on the occasional urge. "Why don't you give me your read on it? I'm not sure what, if anything, I can do to help. Maybe just allay Anna's fears." He couldn't remember ever having used the word "allay" in a sentence. He realized he wanted to impress Molly Pigeon.

Another indrawn breath, then Molly said: "Much as I hate to admit it, this one's got me twitchy." Like Anna's, the psychiatrist's voice was deep, but there was a distinct difference. Molly sounded as if she weighed each word, passing judgment on its deservedness before allowing it utterance. Frederick suspected Molly would be even harder to know than Anna. Rather than being put off, he found it challenging.

"I've had death threats before—I imagine you have, too."

Frederick nodded, then remembered to accompany it with the appropriate listening sound.

"This one—or maybe I should say these, I've heard from her three times now—have a different feel to them. They're very cold. Very concise. More as if she has been assigned to . . . to do this job, rather than a frothing-at-the-mouth hatred."

Frederick waited till he was sure she'd finished then he asked: "Why do you think it's a woman?"

"I know it's a woman," Molly said. "The choice of words, the handwriting, the stationery, the voice on my message machine, all were female."

"Could you be fooled?"

A moment's silence, then: "Yes."

Frederick admired an answer devoid of excuses. Anybody could be fooled anytime. Professionals had a harder time admitting that than most. His opinion of Molly went up a notch. Till that instant he'd not realized how prepared he was to dislike her. Defensive, he told himself. Anna had talked so much about her sister, he'd felt intimidated.

He asked Molly all the questions Anna had asked and then drummed his fingers on the coffee table, hoping for a constructive thought. Molly waited without nervous chatter and he almost forgot she was there.

"Okay," he said finally. "What we've got is basically nothing, so I'm not going to tell you to call the police. At this point it would be a waste of time."

"Good," Molly said, but Frederick wasn't listening, he was following his train of thought.

"What I can do in my exalted position as an FBI guy—" He almost added, "and your sister's boyfriend," but the absurdity of the word derailed the thought. "What I can do," Frederick pushed on, "is set the computers to computing. Find out if there's any history of this particular pattern. If you've got the names and dates of birth of anybody you think might be involved, I can run them for criminal histories. If there are fingerprints on the note, I can run them and see if we get a hit. All this will probably lead nowhere but it's standard operating procedure. It'll at least clear the decks a little. If you like, I've got some things you can do."

"Let me get a pen," Molly said, and: "Shoot."

"These threats usually come on the tail end of some event,

something fairly recent. *The Count of Monte Cristo* notwithstanding, most folks don't carry a grudge that long."

"Attention deficit disorder," Molly said, and Frederick laughed.

"Write down any event surrounding you—maybe you were only peripherally involved—that might generate an impulse for revenge. Go back, say, six months, no more. Vary your routines: when you go out, how you get to work, where you eat lunch. Don't be predictable. Pay attention to anyone you see more than once when there's no reason to—maybe on the subway and later at a restaurant. That sort of thing."

"Damn," Molly said. "Now I'm getting scared."

"Scared is good," Frederick told her.

"Trust your paranoia?"

"What scares Anna?" he asked apropos of nothing, and was startled at the suddenly voiced thought.

"Everything that shouldn't and nothing that should."

Loyalty to Anna seeming at odds with the need to know her better, Frederick was debating whether to ask Molly to elaborate. After a moment's pause she took the decision from him. He could hear caution in her voice and knew he was being trusted. Afraid to break the gossamer thread of her approval, he listened with the mouthpiece held away from his face lest a stray noise distract her.

"After Anna's husband, Zach, was killed she went into a black depression and stayed there for close to a year. During that time she was not sane. We didn't lock her up, but I came close a time or two. She tried to kill herself. Not cries for help so much as to take her mind off worse things, if you can imagine. Anyway . . ."

Molly drew out the word and Frederick could hear the conversation was about to come to a close. He let the breath he'd not realized he was holding escape.

"Anyway, she came out of it, but somewhere along the line she lost something."

"Survival instinct?" Frederick hazarded a guess.

"I don't know. I'm working on it. I've got to run. Have you anything else?"

Frederick had barely voiced his "No" before the line went dead.

Clearing the bird droppings off his calendar, he took it from beneath the phone. Business put him in Baltimore on Friday. If Molly was amenable, he'd stop over in New York on the way home.

Meeting the mythical sister, he mocked himself, but the thought excited him.

10

AT FIVE A.M. Anna slunk downstairs to reap the rewards of coffee beans sown the night before. Their quarters were blessed with a state-of-the-art automatic coffee maker and each evening she made it her business to load it and set the timer. In order to maintain the charade that they were indispensable, all fire crews on this presuppression assignment worked six a.m. to six p.m.; a lot of hot, slow hours to fill with ever-vigilant boredom. Coffee gave her a reason to get out of bed.

Eschewing the idea of community cooking, each member of this crew had decided to fend for himself and, burrowing through the refrigerator in search of heavy cream for her coffee, Anna could catalogue her fellows by what they ate: Vegetables and peanut butter for Al. Kraft macaroni and cheese, made in vats and eaten for days—Dijon. The beer and red meat were Rick's. A jar of Miracle Whip, three loaves of Wonder bread, and an assortment of cold cuts served Guy for breakfast, lunch, and dinner. He'd had a wife cooking for him so long that when he was away from the home fires he counted on the kindness of strangers' wives or ate sandwiches.

Despite careful concealment, the cream carton felt suspiciously light. Them what mocked luxury were the first to pilfer, Anna thought ungenerously.

"Nice pajamas."

She turned to see Guy. Nearly always the second pilgrim to worship at the coffee shrine, he was dressed in NoMex and two pairs of socks. If not for the self-imposed sand regulation, Anna didn't doubt he would have been laced into his heavy lug-soled fire boots.

"Do you sleep in fire clothes?" she asked.

"These ain't clothes," Guy told her as he poured himself a cup of coffee and another for her. "I just had myself tattooed green and yellow a couple of years back. Saves time."

"I believe it. You're baggy and wrinkled enough."

Insults exchanged, they sat down together at an oversized Formica-topped table surrounded by metal folding chairs. Both stared contentedly at nothing, waiting for the caffeine to burn away the night's vapors. In her blue-and-white-striped PJs Anna felt mildly self-conscious but didn't intend to be cowed by it. Nobody on a fire wore pajamas. It simply wasn't done. Not manly, she suspected. One slept in one's clothes, underpants, or nothing. When men were being men in a man's world they didn't allow for lounging attire. It spoiled the ambiance. Usually Anna bowed to fashion from necessity. On a real fire there was little space for nonessentials. But this was presuppression. They lived in a house, slept in beds, and kept regular hours.

Without realizing she did it, she shot the cuffs of her pajamas and sat up a tad straighter.

Halfway down his first cup, Guy became coherent. "Had a long talk with Norman Hull last night while you were dancing with the fishes. They got an aviation investigator they borrowed from the Forest Service flying down from Washington today."

"Why?"

"They always do if there's a fatality. Aviation safety stuff. You never work an airplane crash before?"

Anna shook her head.

"Me neither. I found one in the back country once but it was a kazillion years old before I got there. Just bones. Hull wants to borrow a couple of you guys to help out, seeing as Todd's dead and they got nobody else. I'm giving him you and Rick."

"What if we get a fire?"

"We should be so lucky."

Inaction was wearing on everyone's nerves, along with the ticks, the heat, and Rick's snoring.

The new assignment came like a reprieve, a day out of school, and Anna was careful not to gloat. Rick had no such qualms and by the time they got the call to meet Hull and the aviation safety inspector at the dock, the rest of the crew were glad to see the last of them.

Eight in the morning and already it was hot. Heat stayed through the nights but air-conditioning gave a false sense of weather. It jarred Anna to sweat in the early-morning light. In the mountains the sun dictated the temperature. On Cumberland heat radiated from the soil, the trees, the air itself.

Rick leaned on the fender of the pumper truck and Anna sat on the hood. Firefighters were seldom found standing unaided. Too many years leaning on shovels.

A small green-and-white inboard puttered across the glassy water of the channel between Cumberland and the coast. Near land the water was brown, a rich-looking soup. Grasses waved in saltwater marshes along the shallows housing an abundance of life that never failed to amaze Anna. Life was everywhere, even in the high desert, if one had the patience to look and to wait. In this warm sea, life crawled and hopped and flapped over every available space. Patience was not required.

The NPS boat docked and its human cargo crawled, hopped, and flapped out onto the wooden dock. Hull trotted down from the office to welcome them. His scarecrow figure, all angles and planes, topped by the flat-brimmed Smokey Bear hat, dominated the three lesser beings dressed in the pale green uniform of the United States Forest Service.

"Shall we make ourselves useful?" Anna asked.

"Why not." Rick levered himself away from the fender.

A long white barn, open at both ends, reminiscent of a New England covered bridge, spanned the area from solid ground to the floating docks where the boat was moored. Hull and the three visiting dignitaries seemed capable of handling the luggage, so Anna and Rick stopped in the shade and waited.

Two squat men, their faces deep in the shadow of their green ball caps, came first carrying the bulk of the luggage. Norman Hull walked behind them, crabbing his steps to match those of his companion.

Anna narrowed her eyes against the ubiquitous glare. The Forest Service officer with Hull was a woman. White hair, cut short and curling in such casual perfection it had to be natural, caught the sun like the down on a dandelion. Anna guessed she was five foot three or four, but that could have been an illusion; she stood ramrod-straight, shoulders back, like a retired military man. The bearing created a sense of height and authority.

The woman's eyes were hidden behind dark aviator glasses. The lower half of her face was wrinkled and sagged at the jawline. Anna put her age somewhere between fifty-five and sixty-five.

"Yikes!" Rick said. "Get a load of Grandma."

Anna oinked a couple of times, granting his status as a sexist pig, and he laughed.

"Maybe she'll bake us cookies," he said.

Somehow Anna doubted that.

The two carriers of heavy objects stepped under the covered quay and grunted with surprise as Anna and Rick materialized from the shadows. Hull and the white-haired woman were close behind. The chief ranger stopped to make the introductions. Shorty Powell, a blunt mustachioed man in his forties, was the fixed-wing specialist. Wayne Pitt, the second man, was of an age with Powell and close to the same build but carried his weight around his middle. He was the maintenance specialist. A dark, incredibly curly beard obscured much of his face.

The woman, Alice Utterback, was the chief investigator. "Mrs. Utterback," Hull introduced them, "this is Anna Pigeon and Rick . . ."

"Spencer," Rick filled in for him.

"Alice," the woman said.

When Anna shook her hand it was warm and dry, the grip firm. The fingers were wrinkled, the knuckle of her pinky knobbed by arthritis or an old break. Though her eyes were hidden behind the dark lenses and Anna couldn't see them, she felt them. Rick, herself, the truck, were all quickly assessed and filed. What the verdict was, Anna couldn't guess. Alice Utterback's face gave nothing away. She didn't smile much, Anna noted. A distinctly unfeminine trait. Women—girls—were taught to smile under any and all circumstances. Probably the human equivalent of the little dog showing the big dog its throat as a sign of submission. Alice Utterback was evidently a big dog.

"Your quarters aren't much," Norman Hull apologized as the procession started up again, moving toward the waiting trucks. "We've opened up an old VIP dorm but it's in pretty bad shape."

Anna quashed an urge to offer her room to the older woman. Giving in to generous impulses usually left her grouchy by day's end. And Alice Utterback looked like she was accustomed to fending for herself.

"It'll be fine," Utterback said.

"Do you want to settle in? Freshen up?" Hull asked, old-world manners taking precedence over new-order political correctness.

"I'm pretty darn fresh," Alice told him, and smiled for the first time. Her teeth were yellow and crooked but not displeasing. They suited the weathered face. "Shorty and Wayne will let me know if I go beyond fresh and start getting ripe."

"We try and stay downwind," Shorty said, and Alice laughed.

"Let's get to it then," Hull suggested.

Wreckage was strewn over two hundred yards; bits of the shattered Beechcraft marked the way like trail signs. Rick was set to flagging the points of impact and the final resting place of the airplane much as he would have in a routine traffic accident investigation. Measurements would be made, fixed points—landmarks the accident investigators hoped were permanent—established so that the crash could be plotted on paper for the report and, if need be, reconstructed later should questions arise.

The fixed-wing expert, the man Alice called Shorty, took Chief Ranger Hull and a 35mm camera and began a detailed recording of all that Rick flagged and measured.

Wayne, Alice's maintenance specialist, wandered around with a magnetic compass, and pencils stored absurdly in the thatch of his beard. At least three had been poked into the tangled curls, as a woman might stick them in her bun. It put Anna in mind of a half-remembered fairy tale about a man with birds nesting in his whiskers.

Alice gave Anna the chore of secretary. Clipboard in hand, she followed the older woman around jotting down notes. There'd been a time when Anna was younger and easily offended that she would have taken umbrage at being cast in the traditional female role. In the intervening years she'd lived through enough bureaucracy to know secretaries not only were the glue in the mix, holding the cumbersome aspects of government together, but frequently were the only ones in possession of all the facts. In one form or another— letter, fax, phone call, or gossip—all information passed over their desks.

And, too, there wasn't much heavy lifting, so Anna was content to be Utterback's Girl Friday.

Alice Utterback crawled beneath the remaining shreds of the blasted wing on the passenger side of the Beechcraft. A black cord was around her neck, both ends disappearing into her shirt pocket. Pulling on the cord, she dragged out a small powerful Maglite and began tracing the beam methodically over the instrument panel.

Clutching the clipboard to her chest, Anna frog-walked in as close as she could get and watched the proceedings. The ghosts had been hauled off along with the corpses and she was glad. Despite the macabre remnants of humanity—a burned button, what could have been blood or oil spattered beneath the instrument panel in the one unburned portion of the floorboards—the cockpit was cleansed of emotion. Now it was just a puzzle and Anna was enjoying watching the chief investigator gather together the pieces.

"Norman Hull said two killed," Alice remarked without stopping her work.

"Yes, ma'am," Anna said.

"Pilot was a private contractor?"

"Slattery Hammond." Anna filled in the name.

Alice clicked the Maglite off and rocked back on her heels. "Slattery Hammond. Why am I not surprised?"

Anna waited. The question was rhetorical and with Alice Utterback somehow one wasn't tempted to pry.

"I flew with him once or twice when I worked in Region Six—in Washington State," Utterback volunteered. "He was a hotshot. Or thought he was. One of those fellas you've got to get to know quick because they aren't going to live all that long. Too bad they usually manage to take someone with them when they go. The passenger was the district ranger here?"

"Todd Belfore."

Alice switched her light back on and returned her focus to the instrument panel. "Norman said he left a widow."

"She's in a hospital in St. Marys. Or was yesterday. She's seriously pregnant."

"That's a pity," Alice said, and: "Write this down." Speaking slowly, undoubtedly accustomed to giving dictation to people not trained in shorthand, she listed the readings on the instruments: "Gas valve is on the auxiliary tanks, landing gear is up, altimeter looks about right, throttles . . . too damaged to tell."

In her best Catholic school hand, Anna wrote down every word.

"Does this tell you anything?" she asked.

"Not much," Alice admitted. "But you never know. We may turn up something."

Shorty came over then and they cleared out, leaving him room to photograph the interior of the plane.

Utterback strolled around in what appeared to be an aimless fashion. Hands shoved deep in her pockets, she scuffed through the duff, gazed at the trees, the sky, whistling soundlessly. Finally she stopped, pinched her underlip in a thoughtful way, and stared intently at the ground.

"What?" Anna asked after a minute.

"I think I'm getting a cold sore," Alice said abstractedly. "I hate those doggone things." She plucked a little longer at the offending lip, then said: "Write this down. Put it in parentheses so I'll know it's just me guestimating and not God's honest truth.

"It looks like Hammond was flying too low and too slow. For some reason the airplane rolled sharply to the left and flew nose down. He hadn't left himself any maneuvering room and stacked it, inverted, nose down."

"Got something, Alice?" Wayne called.

"Nothing to take to the bank."

Again Utterback wandered off. Scribbling, Anna tagged along.

"Inboards blew?" Alice asked. "There's two on each wing, one close in, one further out—inboards and outboards," she said before Anna was forced to expose her ignorance. "Did the ones close in explode?"

"Yes, ma'am. The left tank exploded on impact and the right shortly after we arrived."

Alice was nodding; it tallied with what she'd seen. "Got the severed wingtips mapped?" she hollered at Rick and Shorty.

"Right yes. Left no," the Forest Service man called back.

Alice resumed her soundless whistling and meandered toward the aircraft's right wing. It lay forty yards north of the fuselage and was still, to some extent, intact. The outboard tank inside the wing had not been ruptured. Cables and lines snaked out to shredded ends like the sinews and ligaments of a severed limb. Leaf litter, plowed up on impact, covered the leading edge. The trailing edge was a foot off the ground, lending an aspect of movement and speed to the derelict wing.

The sun had climbed past meridian. Anna's stomach was beginning to growl tentatively for lunch. Down in the live oaks there wasn't the faintest breath of air and the temperature was near a hundred degrees. Sweat ringed the men's armpits, staining their shirts all the way to the belt line. Rivulets trickled down Anna's neck and back, doing an excellent job of mimicking the sensation of little tick feet burrowing down for a snack.

Alice was completely untouched: her weathered skin was dry and powdery-looking, her white hair lying in neat waves. Twice she circled the wingtip. Anna stood aside, pen poised, trying to look intelligent. "Could he have run out of gas?" she ventured.

"Could've," Alice said. "Always take a look." She crouched down by the trailing edge and removed the gas cap. "Hey, Shorty," she called. "I need to take a peek in the outboard tank. Got a match?"

Familiar laughter at a standard joke filtered back to them as Utterback poked the beam of her Maglite into the recesses of the gas tank.

"Nearly half full. Write that down," she said. "Right auxiliary a quarter full—make it a quarter."

Dutifully Anna scratched out the word "half," feeling a mild resentment that her so-far perfect notes were now besmirched.

"My, my, what have we here?" Alice took off her glasses and pushed her eyeball up to the tank's opening. "Some sort of foreign object."

Anna resisted the childish urge to say, "Let me see! Let me see!"

Shorty had come up behind them. "Let me see," he demanded, and Anna was jealous.

"Looky." Alice handed him the Maglite. "Way in the back. Kind of an amoeba thing."

"Quit with the fifty-cent words," Shorty grunted as he squatted to look.

After some discussion as to the nature of the alien item, Anna was dispatched to find something with which to fish it out. "Maybe a coat hanger," was Alice Utterback's unhelpful suggestion.

Lest she miss out on anything, Anna jogged to where the

pumper truck was parked on the road. Amid the collected garbage behind the seat was a length of welding rod. Feeling mildly heroic, she carried her prize back to the accident site.

"Perfect," Alice said, and Anna was rewarded for her zeal.

Five minutes' careful maneuvering produced a plastic bag, the sort the grocery stores provide by the roll in the produce section.

With great care, Alice laid it out on the wing. The excitement had attracted the others and the six of them stood around staring at it.

"Got stuck in by accident?" Shorty offered, then argued with himself. "Not likely. Too big. You'd have to poke it down on purpose."

"Could have been there for years," Wayne suggested. He was the mechanic and that gave his opinion weight. "I've found stranger stuff. Once I found a used condom in the tail of an old J-three Cub. The bag might have fallen in when the tank was being manufactured and got sealed up."

"How long will plastic last in hundred-octane solution?" Alice asked.

Nobody knew.

"You know what to do for your next science project," she said. "Bag it and send it to the National Transportation Safety Board lab. Maybe there was something in it."

"Sugar," Anna said. The parks were well enough versed in the methods of monkey wrenchers for her to take a stab at the obvious. Sugar in the gas tank was the oldest of tricks, almost a cliché, but very effective.

"Why not just pour the sugar in? Why stuff in the whole bag?" Alice asked.

"Good measure?"

Everyone ignored Anna.

"Would it cause the aircraft to malfunction and crash, Mrs. Utterback?" the chief ranger asked. Hull always sounded stilted, and Anna began to wonder if English was his second language.

"It'd wreck the engine," Alice said, "but it shouldn't cause a crash like this. Photograph it. Bag it," she said again, and lost interest. Speculations were of little import. When the facts came back from the lab the issue would be reopened.

With a purpose that was a mystery to all, Alice stomped off, Anna in tow, and set up camp at the ruin of the left wing where it rested a dozen yards from its fellow.

The left outboard fuel tank was ruptured, the gasoline all leaked away, but Alice wouldn't leave it alone. While the others continued with their mapping and data collection she and Anna sifted through the litter around the ruined wing. Twice Anna asked what they were looking for. Twice she was told: "Just looking."

Near sundown, as the men were packing their equipment to leave, Alice Utterback muttered, "Bingo," and, "Eureka." Buried in the leaf litter seven feet from the ruptured tank, she'd found what she was searching for: a second plastic bag.

"Somebody was up to something," she said. "But I'll be jiggered if I know what."

11

IN THE FLATLANDS of east Georgia the sun set in slow motion. Twilight filtered down like fine dust, a gray drift over the brash colors of summer. Anna drove, Alice Utterback riding shotgun. There was no place they had to be and Anna idled along at twenty miles per hour enjoying herself. After a day of following Alice it felt good simply to sit. Utterback never seemed to tire and while the others took breaks for a cigarette, a drink, a bull session, the two of them had worked.

Even now the chief investigator was not truly relaxed. The plastic sacks they'd found in the Beechcraft's outboard fuel tanks rested in sealed evidence bags on the truck's dashboard. Ignoring the kaleidoscope of green and gold spinning past the windows, Alice stared at the bags and Anna fancied she could hear the well-oiled gears of the older woman's brain whirring.

"Clearly the bags were stuck in the tanks on purpose," Alice said after a while, talking more to herself than to Anna. "Though to what purpose I can't imagine. There's just no good reason. Hammond might've stuck them there to smuggle something but it'd be a pretty feeble attempt. If they had anything in them you'd have a heck of a time fishing them out and if they didn't, what's the point?"

"Could they gum up the works somehow?" Anna asked. "Like sand or throwing a wooden shoe in the machinery?"

"Sabotage?" Alice echoed. "Not really. I mean I suppose they could float around in there, maybe settle over the fuel outlet and stop it up. But the odds of both of them doing it at the same time and staying put long enough to cut off the gas are pretty slim. Something sure as heck stacked that Beechcraft though. Hammond was a boob but he wasn't a bad pilot. Still, short of some kind of interference, Hammond shouldn't have plowed in like he did. The Beechcraft is a forgiving little airplane. Under most conditions it'll see you home—or at least to a flat spot. If somebody wanted to kill him, there are better ways."

"Would anybody want to kill Slattery Hammond?" Anna asked.

"Oh sure. He was one of those guys that always had something going. A bit of a schemer. And he was flying drug interdiction. That wouldn't endear him in some circles."

"You think he was onto something?"

"I doubt it. Those guys play hardball. I can't see a dope dealer stuffing sandwich bags in a fuel tank—not unless Slattery was about to bust up a ring of ten-year-olds. What was that fella's name with him? Belfore? Maybe he'd got on the wrong side of somebody."

"He wasn't even supposed to be in the plane," Anna said. "The chief ranger was scheduled for that flight."

"Maybe somebody knew he and Hull switched."

A memory surfaced in Anna's mind: Tabby in a red dress, partially lit by the glow of a headlight, crying: "You would leave me!" as her husband grabbed at her.

"Maybe," Anna conceded. "Or maybe somebody was after Norman."

"Moot point anyway. These bags just don't hold water as murder weapons. We'll learn more tomorrow." Alice wiped the evidence off the dashboard into a leather briefcase, effectively closing the investigation for the day.

"Watch it!" she yelled suddenly, and Anna slammed on the brakes. On the dirt, stopping the tires had little effect on forward movement and they skidded ahead. Two vehicles, both lightweight trucks, one the chief ranger's, the other borrowed from maintenance to carry Wayne and Shorty, were stopped in the middle of the road. Neither had taillights or flashers showing. Even as Anna cursed them she knew she'd never mention it; she too was driving blind. Evening had crept upon them so imperceptibly, she'd not realized how dark it had grown.

Several feet short of Norman Hull's rear bumper the truck shuddered to a stop. Half a moment later a choking cloud of fine white dust engulfed them.

Feeling righteous, if belatedly so, Anna switched on the truck's lights to avoid waylaying another unwary motorist. The headlights raked the side of the blue pickup truck and, as the dust cleared, picked out a group of men huddled beyond it to the side of the road.

"Hit a deer," Anna said as she opened the door.

It wasn't a deer, it was a beautiful young man from Austria. And he hadn't been hit by a car, he'd been shot.

As Anna and Alice approached, the knot of men untied itself. Rick spoke first. "Anna, get your butt over here and take a look at this guy's leg."

Anna did as she was told. The young Austrian sat on a berm of white dirt and shell that Mitch Hanson had dredged from the south end of the island to resurface the inland roads. In the uncertain light he looked terribly pale. His hair, pulled back in a ponytail, was a harsh contrast in dark brown. He was probably not more than twenty-five, but pain and exhaustion pulled taut the skin of his face and he looked considerably older.

Beside him was a young Indian woman—American, not East Indian—as strikingly beautiful as her companion. She was slight and dark, her face made up of clear planes and sculpted curves. Eyes and hair were close to true black. From her small, perfect ears hung stylized bear fetishes in turquoise saddled with silver.

She had both hands pressed over her mouth as if to keep from screaming or vomiting. The instant Alice and Anna entered the circle the hands fluttered apart and she began trying to talk.

What she had been holding in was gasps. Even as her hands flew through the air trying to tell her story, words were gusted out incoherently. She was panting, as if she'd just run the hundred-yard dash.

"Sorry," she finally managed. "I can't breathe. The thing—the bullet—got Guenther in the leg. I've been carrying him for miles."

"Dragging," the Austrian said in perfect English, accented just enough to make even a middle-aged ranger's heart skip a beat.

Dragging was probably closer to the mark from the look of them. Guenther was a good-sized man, six feet, maybe 175 pounds. The woman was slight of frame and slender. "What's your name?" Anna asked her.

"Shawna."

"Breathe, Shawna." To Guenther, Anna said: "I'm Anna Pigeon. I'm an emergency medical technician. Can I look at your leg?"

Wayne or Shorty had gone back to the truck and turned on the headlamps. The hard, unilateral light obscured utterly what was in shadow and ruthlessly illuminated all else.

Feeling a need to explain why nothing had been done prior to her arrival, Rick said: "We got here maybe a minute before you."

Anna grunted her acceptance of that as she shined Alice Utterback's Maglite behind the Austrian's knee.

Both hikers were dressed in shorts, heavy boots, and knee-high socks. Guenther's left leg below the knee was swathed in layers of fabric obviously cannibalized from out of their packs. T-shirts of various colors made up the bulk of it.

"It hasn't bled through," Anna said. "How long ago did it happen?" Guenther and Shawna looked at one another. Time had clearly ceased to be a measurable linear entity.

"Four hours?" Shawna guessed.

"An hour?" Guenther offered.

"A while," Anna compromised. They were satisfied with that. "I doubt there's much I can do you haven't already done," she went on. "You're still up and talking. I'd say the two of you did a dynamite job. I'm not going to mess with the dressing—all it would do is start the bleeding again. When we get you to a doctor, he can take it off."

"I was planning to take the boat to the mainland later," Hull said. He and his wife and their thirteen-year-old daughter lived in St. Marys, a small town just across the estuary from Cumberland. "We'll go ahead and leave now. I'll drive you to the hospital there."

"Sooner is better," Anna agreed.

"Anna, if you will get the young lady's statement en route, I would appreciate it," Hull said, and began issuing instructions for the loading and transport of the injured man.

Guenther was settled in the back of the chief ranger's pickup on a pad of blankets. Wayne rode beside him to keep him company and to keep an eye on him.

Shawna tucked herself in the cab of the pumper truck between Anna and Alice. "I love him," she said wearily as she buckled herself in, "but he can sure be a pain in the ass. I hope the doctors give him drugs. He needs mellowing out big-time."

She'd regained breath and equilibrium. As Anna fell in line, the last in their little convoy, she asked again what happened.

"Turnabout's fair play," Alice said, and assuming the role of secretary, pulled a legal pad out of her briefcase to take notes.

"I don't really know what happened," Shawna told them after a moment's deliberation. "We'd been camping at Lake Whitney for a couple of days." Whitney was one of the lovely freshwater lakes being threatened by the encroaching dunes. Because of the delicacy of the island's ecosystem, camping there was highly illegal, but Anna let it pass. She wanted the story told without interruptions.

"We broke camp and were cutting cross-country. I don't know how long we'd been walking—we were more or less lost but that was the idea. We knew we couldn't get too lost on a little island. Eventually you're bound to stumble across something that will set you straight. We were pushing through a thick bushy place. Guenther was ahead of me a little ways. There was this huge explosion, then Guenther was down on the ground grabbing his leg and yelling."

"Whereabouts were you?" Anna asked.

Shawna shook her head. "I can't even guess. We'd been wandering, you know, looking at things. Then I was pretty freaked. And carrying Guenther was no picnic. Somewhere between the lake and where you found us. I'm sorry." Shawna was panting again, as if the telling were as strenuous as the doing.

"That's okay. Did you see anyone?" Anna asked.

"Nobody."

"Did you hear anything, like somebody running or talking?"

"Nothing. Just the bang, then nothing." Shawna leaned forward, elbows on knees, and rubbed her face hard with both hands.

"You must be pretty pooped," Alice said kindly.

"That's not the half of it," Shawna replied.

For several minutes they rode in silence. Anna struggled with the urge to press the girl for more information and the desire to leave her in peace. Information won.

"Describe the wound to me," she said. A slight sniff emanated from Alice Utterback's direction and Anna assumed it was disapproval. "In detail," she added, just to be contrary.

Shawna thought for a few moments and Anna realized she gave the girl's answers more credence than she might have because they were so well considered. In one so young, this methodical habit of the mind was unexpected.

"It bled a lot so I can't tell you exactly. It was a mess and we just wanted to wrap it up before he lost too much blood. Both of us have first aid. We teach skiing in the winter and you have to. It looked like a gouge, a furrow, like the bullet came through the back of his leg sideways and just plowed this trough in his calf."

Guns in national parks were strictly forbidden but that didn't mean they weren't there. As they were in much of America, guns were abundant in the parks. Poachers carried them, criminals, researchers dealing with potentially dangerous animals, citizens feeling the need for self-protection, law enforcement officers. Short of strip-searching every visitor and, on Cumberland Island, every resident, there was no way of keeping them outside park boundaries.

"How big was the furrow?" Anna asked.

"Huge. The Grand Canyon. Maybe three inches wide and an inch or two deep. Seriously. A big chunk of his calf was gone, like a big old bite had been taken out of it."

Alice reached behind Shawna, still bent nearly double over her knees, her face in her hands, and tapped Anna on the shoulder. When she had Anna's attention she pointed to the girl. Tears were pouring through her fingers, falling in great dollops, making mud in the dust on her thighs. Anna had never seen anyone cry like that; buckets.

"If you keep on you'll dehydrate yourself," she said. Alice must have given her a dirty look. Anna felt a slight tingling on the right side of her neck. "It'll be okay," she added lamely.

"What if he's crippled?" Shawna whispered.

Anna had no answer to that. For two beautiful young people living by the strength and grace of their bodies, it was hard to think of a more bitter blow. Anna hoped Alice would jump in with something wise and motherly, but she didn't.

As they emerged from the woods into the clearing that heralded the offices and dock, an ATV roared out of the darkness, its headlight bouncing with each rut. The lane was too narrow for cars to pass safely and Anna eased the truck over to let the smaller vehicle by.

The ATV pulled up alongside and stopped. Marty Schlessinger, her white braids frayed by the wind, glared at them through the truck's open window. Anna was unoffended. Schlessinger glared at everyone, not so much a message of malice, Anna thought, as a habit of looking deeply at phenomena, studying the creatures of the planet.

"What's all the ruckus?" the biologist demanded. "Hull's rampaging around like a scarecrow in a windstorm. You find something at the crash?"

Anna shook her head, wishing Marty would turn off the ATV's engine rather than shouting over the considerable din. "A kid got shot in the leg. We found him up the road. Norman's taking him and his girlfriend over to St. Marys. The kid's going to be okay," she added, more for Shawna's benefit than the biologist's.

The darkness had deepened, but because Marty was so close, Anna could read her face. The information registered with a look of mild surprise and confusion. Her eyes narrowed and she drew down her brows and the corners of her mouth. Something clicked in her mind, Anna could see it in the sudden opening of her face.

"I heard the shots," Marty declared. "And I can just about tell you where."

Anna didn't believe her. It was too pat, too aggressive. And Shawna said there'd been but a single shot. "When?" Anna asked.

Schlessinger looked blank. "When what?"

She was stalling for time. "When did you hear the shots?"

Shawna pulled her face free of her hands. "We think it was about—"

"Not now," Anna snapped. "When did you hear the shots, Marty? And how many were there? Best guess."

Marty gave Anna a long slow look and this time there was malice in it. "I can't recall," she said evenly, gunned the ATV, and was gone, leaving them to roll their windows up hastily to shut out her dust.

The line for the phone was longer than usual—Alice taking precedence with a series of business calls. Anna went next. Neither Frederick nor Molly was home. Feeling bereft, she left snippy messages on their machines and joined Alice Utterback on the concrete stoop to wait while Al called his family.

The air was warm and soft and black. Moonrise wouldn't be for several hours and the low wattage of stars couldn't burn through the moist air. Alice was sitting on the concrete, legs crossed tailor fashion, apparently at ease alone in the dark. Anna curled down beside her, unconsciously aping the other woman's pose.

"Soaking in the silence," Alice said after a moment.

Anna felt no need to respond and they sat in quiet companionship for several minutes. Cumberland's stillness was impressive; a living silence deepened by the gentle stirrings of night creatures, minute cracklings and scuffling not diluted with so much as a breath of a breeze.

Unfortunately this cloak of peace was not adequate to sedate

Anna's busy mind. "If the wound was as deep as Shawna said, it had to be a forty-five-caliber bullet or maybe a shotgun slug. My money'd be on a slug. A forty-five would tear the flesh, not just blow it away."

Since Anna was obviously waiting, Alice replied. "Shawna might have exaggerated. She was rattled."

"Might have," Anna said, but she didn't think so. Answers so carefully thought through were more than likely fairly accurate. "We'll probably never know. Whoever did it is long gone by now. Shoot, we don't even know exactly where it happened. Statements will be taken, et cetera, but nobody'll even go look. It'd be a waste of time. Look for what?"

"Poachers?" Alice offered. In her voice Anna could hear that weary acceptance of the necessity for conversation. The considerate thing to do would have been to leave her to her reverie but Anna was in a mood to chat.

"Poachers don't lean toward handguns," she said. "And there's no game on this island big enough to require a shotgun slug. Even the pigs are just pigs, not wild boars or anything."

"Mmmm," Alice murmured noncommittally.

Anna continued to ignore the other woman's desire to enjoy the lush Georgia night. "People do strange things. Especially hunters. I could see somebody hunting pigs with a shotgun. Not a sportsman—as if outsmarting a pig was a challenging sport—but somebody who liked the killing."

"Now there's a cheery thought."

"When I lived in Texas, hunters there had what they called a sound shot, as in, 'I didn't see anything but I got in a sound shot.' Meaning they'd heard something in the brush and just blasted away at it. Maybe Guenther was shot by a hunter of that ilk—the poacher never even knew he hit anything. Let alone a person."

"Shawna said Guenther yelled."

"Okay. A deaf, quiet Texas pig poacher with a shotgun."

Alice said nothing and Anna turned the unlikely possibilities over in her mind. Unwelcome thoughts of Molly, of the threats, of Frederick and the future hummed like bees in a jar but she chose not to let them out. Working on the leg wound puzzle was an excellent distraction.

"A shotgun's an up-close and personal kind of a weapon," she said, and heard a tiny sigh of exasperation escape her companion. "It's hard to shoot with any accuracy at more than fifteen yards or so."

Al pushed out through the office door and Alice jumped up with an unflattering alacrity. "It's way past my bedtime," she declared, and led the way to the truck.

Before noon the following day the mystery of the plastic bags and Guenther's assailant was pushed from everyone's mind. The six of them—Alice, Anna, Rick, Wayne, Shorty, and Norman Hull—were at the site of the airplane wreck finishing up the investigation.

Wayne, the maintenance specialist, had spent the morning following all the control linkages from the cockpit to the controls themselves: cables, rods, hinges, attach bolts. It was standard procedure and this time it bore fruit.

Alice Utterback understood the mechanic's findings immediately. Due to their technical nature, Wayne dragged out pen and paper and mapped out the sequence of events for the chief ranger. Anna hovered over Wayne's left shoulder soaking up information.

The flaps—moveable portions on the trailing edge of the wings—were used to slow the plane or to increase lift. They were operated by control rods running from the fuselage out the wing and to the flaps themselves. From the sketch Wayne was drawing it looked very mechanical. The pilot pushed a lever, the flap motor turned, an actuator arm twisted, pushing rods out, and the flaps were forced down. Anna was surprised it wasn't more high-tech, with electronic goodies and computer confusions.

The control rods were bolted to the flap motor arms in the belly of the airplane. When Wayne tracked them in from the wings, he discovered the bolt fastening the right rod was missing and the rod and actuator arm were separated.

Without that bolt in place, when the pilot activated the flaps only the left one would extend. The left wing would elevate suddenly and the plane would roll sharply to the right. Flying low and slow as they surmised Hammond had been, there would be no room to recover. He'd have corkscrewed right into the ground.

Wayne finished his lecture and they all continued to stand around staring at his rude sketch as if more information would be forthcoming.

"Could it be an accident?" Hull asked finally. His voice was ripe with hope. Accidents, acts of God, required less paperwork than felonies.

"Yup," Wayne replied. "Some brain-dead mechanic might've forgotten to replace the bolt, or replaced it but neglected to put a nut on it. Maybe he did the nut and left off the cotter pin that secures it. It's not likely the nut vibrated off but I suppose it could happen. We'll need to get hold of Hammond's aircraft logbooks, see when it was last in the shop, who the mechanic was. This isn't something that could just toodle along unnoticed. It'd have to have happened between his last flight and this one."

"I don't think his logbooks were in the airplane," Alice said. "Maybe they were—reduced to ash. Usually maintenance logs are kept separate from the airplane for exactly that reason. The papers in the glove box weren't bound and there wasn't any sign of a flight bag."

"We'll check his house," Hull said.

"Could anybody else get at the actuator arm?" Anna asked. Norman Hull gave her a look of irritation. There were enough cans of worms around without her prying open another.

"Anybody," Wayne said. "There's a little metal plate in the plane's belly. Take out six screws and, bingo, you're there. You would have to know a little about airplanes and it'd help to know the pilot. Some use flaps a lot, some don't. A flap-using pilot probably would have tripped this little booby trap fairly early on and maybe not have got himself killed. But my money's on the mechanic. Incompetence is more common than murder."

"Whatever the case," Hull said, "this information is confidential. On a need-to-know basis." He looked directly at Anna and Rick. "There is nobody you know who fits this description. Are there any questions?"

There were none. Pecking order was established. Anna and Rick were merely migrant workers. For some reason Hull wanted them to remember that.

12

ALICE UTTERBACK had all the answers the Beechcraft's remains would afford. The police tape was taken down, the equipment packed, the Cumberland Island maintenance division alerted to start the cleanup. Rick was released back to the fire crew and Anna dispatched to the maintenance shop to pick up a key to Hammond's place so she could get his logbooks for Alice.

The pilot had been renting park housing on the island for the duration of his assignment. After a modest amount of gossip was proffered in exchange for the key, the maintenance man gave Anna directions. Hammond's house was about one third of the way north between the dock and Plum Orchard. In that two-mile stretch, there were a number of homes of both park personnel and island inhabitants who still retained the right to live there.

With the dense screen of oak and palmetto, only thin dusty tributaries to the main road hinted at the existence of these dwell-

ings. Some of the drives were marked with the name of the home-
owner, some with the name of the road, and some not at all.

Hammond's house was in the last category and Anna enjoyed a
good bit of sight-seeing before she finally found it tucked back in
the trees. Slated for demolition as soon as time and funds were
allotted, the house had been allowed to deteriorate into earth tones.
The unpainted board siding had weathered to a velvety gray and
fallen leaves and pine needles drifted up to the foundation and over
the low porch slab. Several of the windows had lost their screens
and the flotsam of a series of renters littered the bare yard: an old
stovepipe, the skeleton of a kitchen chair, rusted coffee cans. Anna
parked the truck beside a shed housing an unidentifiable piece of
machinery and sat for a moment letting the heat coalesce around
her.

Feral pigs had rooted a crooked trench to an old watering trough
set under a live oak. Gray beards of Spanish moss hung to the
ground. If any sound existed beyond the green enclosure, it was
absorbed by the foliage. On this tiny populated island Anna felt
more isolated than she had miles into the backcountry of west
Texas.

"Logbooks," she said to motivate herself, and climbed from the
truck.

Hammond's door was unlocked. Perhaps in an urban setting
that might have tripped some alarm, but Anna took little note. In
the parks, people were lax about security. It was one of the joys of
living there.

Inside, the place had the bleak look of the itinerant bachelor.
Seedy brown light leaked through old paper shades pulled all the
way down. If there was an air conditioner, Hammond hadn't left it
on. The temperature was easily above a hundred degrees and the
place smelled like old gym socks. A scarred Formica table held the
remains of several meals mixed in among newspapers, magazines,

and junk mail. Against a wall between the two blinded windows was a couch faded from use and sunlight. Its once orange and brown plaid had mellowed to a less offensive hue. More newspapers, underpants, and a single dirty sneaker were scattered over it to casual effect. No curtains softened the windows, no rugs rescued the blue speckled linoleum floors, no pictures graced the walls. An old metal office desk had been shoved against the wall where the front door banged it every time it opened. Littered with papers and used coffee cups, it looked the most promising.

As Anna closed the door behind her, she was caught by a stealthy sound from the nether regions of the small house. For a moment she froze, listening, then wrote it off to the creaking of an old structure.

Slattery Hammond's bookkeeping habits weren't any better than his housekeeping. She sat at the desk and methodically shuffled through his piles: unpaid bills, envelopes full of snapshots, canceled checks, a postcard from North Cascades in Washington bearing the predictable "Having a wonderful time. Wish you were here," signed "Bonnie."

The Beechcraft was his; Anna found several payments to a West Coast bank on the loan. Any heirs were in for a disappointment however; she also found a bill for the airplane's insurance that was long past due. There were half a dozen snapshots Scotch-taped to the wall. One was of Slattery standing beside his plane.

Having never seen the man at his best, Anna studied it with interest. Hammond was surprisingly good-looking. For some reason—perhaps the name Slattery or maybe his reputation as recounted by Alice Utterback—Anna had pictured him as a greaseball. If he was, his evil ways had yet to leave their stamp on his features. He looked to be in his early thirties, tall and lean, with brown hair that fell over his forehead. His eyes were wide-set and ingenuous, his smile that of a boy.

"Deadly," Anna said, and put the photo back where she'd found it.

Of the other five pictures, four were of a girl of eighteen or twenty playing on a beach and one was a long shot of a pale-haired hiker who struck Anna as vaguely familiar and she wondered if it was someone she'd known. The coincidence wouldn't have surprised her. The Park Service was small and mobile. Rangers from all over crossed paths in training, in transit, and many of them traveled to other parks when they had the time off.

Three drawers yielded up Hammond's checkbook, a .357 Colt revolver, four boxes of ammunition, a stale Marlboro, and a pile of mouse droppings. No logbooks. "Damn," Anna whispered, and pushed her chair back to survey the room for another likely spot. Nothing presented itself. Hammond traveled light.

She wandered into the kitchen but wasn't inspired to touch anything. What dishes Hammond had were crusted with food and piled in the sink. The counters hadn't been wiped for a while and two thin black trails of sugar ants had snaked out to feast on the windfall.

Half the cupboard doors hung open. Anna opened the rest: dust, shotgun shells, more mouse droppings, and three cans of chili. The kitchen drawers produced little more. Steeling herself for Hammond's *Good Housekeeping* coup de grâce, she opened the refrigerator. It wasn't bad. There was nothing in it but beer, ten or fifteen rolls of Kodak film, margarine, and a pair of blunt-nosed scissors, the kind people buy for little kids. For a moment Anna pondered the significance of the scissors, but drew a blank. Undoubtedly this was one secret Slattery had taken with him to the grave.

The freezer was better stocked, holding ice, vodka, and twelve packages wrapped in tinfoil. Anna dutifully unwrapped each one though she could see no reason a pilot would be so paranoid about his logbooks that he would disguise them as food. They contained nothing but chunks of badly butchered meat. Closing the door, she noticed three zip-lock bags on the interior shelf. At first glance they appeared to contain one pork chop or one ham bone each. On close examination she was both disgusted and mystified. Each baggie held one obviously used tampon.

"Oh ish!" she said, using Frederick's favorite expletive.

The bedroom boasted a single bed with a sleeping bag on it, and a beat-up dresser vomiting clothes. Eau de gym socks overlaid the mess. Anna made a cursory search of the dresser, picking through the contents as if they crawled with body lice or crabs, but found nothing of interest.

The closeness in the sealed house, aggravated by the myriad odors of garbage and dirty laundry, was beginning to get to Anna. A feeling of suffocation and tunnel vision built under her sternum and behind her eyes. The bedroom closet was the only place she'd not yet searched. She determined to make short work of it and get out of there.

When she opened the closet door, the room erupted. Hammond's clothes flew out at her as if they had a life of their own. A heavy plaid shirt flapped winglike at her face and she heard herself yelling. Then something struck a jarring blow above her left ear. Inside her skull she felt her brain shift and her body was jolted as if she'd fallen from a great height. A vortex of darkness opened in front of her and she pitched forward into it.

13

NEW YORK CITY always exhilarated Frederick. Despite its size and brawling image, Chicago felt small, clean, and easily escaped. Frederick's vision of Manhattan, locked in by rivers and the sea, was that of an overburdened ship; like photos he'd seen of derelict boats bursting with Haitian refugees. Or maybe a birthday balloon in that anxious limbo between plump and pop, a sense of danger, high stakes.

New York was considered the murder capital of the world. Statistics didn't bear that out; it was just that the city was so condensed. When everyone is packed onto half a dozen avenues, everything becomes public, corpses and dirty laundry included.

Several weeks earlier a couple from Ely, Nevada, in Manhattan for the first time, had found the naked body of a three-year-old stuffed in a Bloomingdale's bag on the hood of their rented

Hyundai. Even in the Big Apple that wasn't the norm, but they'd left for home convinced they'd been to, if not Sodom, then Gomorrah.

The night was warm and he had walked up from the Parker Meridien, where he was staying at great personal expense. The Parker Meridien had the key ingredient in the hotel business: location. For that Frederick shelled out the cash and put up with the insufferable young snob at the registration desk.

Dr. Molly Pigeon had agreed to meet with him at a pub near the corner of Ninth and Fifty-ninth. More, he suspected, out of curiosity to see her little sister's beau than to discuss the death threats. Dr. Pigeon had described the place: near a corner, glassed-in sidewalk seating, window frames painted green. In New York on Ninth Avenue that didn't narrow it down much and Frederick pulled a slip of paper out of his pocket with the pub's name written on it. This was the place.

Standing outside in the dark gave him the edge, and feeling slightly foolish for the professional paranoia of a lifetime, he stepped into shadow and searched through the tables. Back from the windows, by a six-by-six post supporting the pseudo greenhouse, he found her. There wasn't any doubt in his mind that it was Anna's sister. There was a strong familial resemblance. Molly was older and her features more refined—delicate almost. Her face had a look of control Anna's lacked and her lips were fuller, more sensuous, but she was unquestionably a Pigeon. A formidable one. Everything about her breathed power, competence, and control. Her deep purple suit was tailored, her high heels without a scuff, her short manicured nails painted with clear polish. Only two chinks showed in the armor: she was smoking and a nervous habit of running her fingers through her hair had turned an expensive cut into a girlish, bedroom tousle.

My turn next, Frederick thought as he walked through the door. Anticipating her inspection, he stood straighter and tugged the cuffs of his linen sport coat, bought for the occasion, down toward his knuckles. Off-the-rack clothes seldom had sleeves long enough and a government salary didn't allow for tailor-mades. Not with a kid in college. Brushing aside an adolescent fear of appearing uncool, he headed toward Dr. Pigeon's table.

She stood when she saw him. In her eyes there was no judgment and her smile was warm and slightly crooked. The illusion of coldness was dispelled. But not the illusion of control. Her handshake, the invitation to sit, the slight nod that brought a waiter running, all gave Frederick the reassuring feeling that he'd been accepted into a well-ordered universe.

"Scotch, no ice," Frederick said to the waiter.

"The same," Molly said, then cackled. "You and I are going to get along fine." Her eyes were hazel, like Anna's, and deeply crinkled at the corners. Feigned or not, they almost twinkled with interest, as if she eagerly awaited the fascinating story of his life. Frederick could see how she commanded $150 an hour.

"An FBI agent," Molly stated.

Beyond Dr. Pigeon's shoulder, Frederick could see the waiter gossiping with the bartender. He wanted his Scotch. Needed it might be closer to the truth. Meeting Molly had him as nervous as a boy on his first date.

"A psychiatrist," he countered.

Molly laughed again and the sheer ghoulish sound of her odd chortle made him laugh with her.

"Don't you sometimes wish you had an occupation that didn't require comment?" she asked.

The drinks were on their way. Unwittingly, Frederick breathed out his relief. "Yes," he answered honestly. "When I'm tired, I've been known to lie just to avoid a discussion of Ruby Ridge."

"It could be worse." Molly accepted her Scotch. "You could work for the IRS."

Within thirty minutes the last of the ice was broken, the preliminaries were over, and two more Scotches were on their way. To his surprise, Frederick found he was relaxed and enjoying himself. Molly was no longer a legend but flesh and blood, a sophisticated, urbanized Anna, with an openness he missed in her sister.

At the thought of Anna, he reluctantly got down to the supposed business of this meeting. "Did you do your homework?" he asked.

"Indeed I did." Molly pulled a black leather briefcase from beneath the table and plucked a manila folder from an outside pocket.

The folder had a computer-generated label on the top. "DEATH THREATS" was written in block letters. A tiny skull and crossbones adorned one end, a knife dripping red blood the other. "Oh," Molly said, when she caught his glance. "Clip art. New software. I couldn't resist."

Having replaced the briefcase under the table, she opened the folder. The papers were neatly typed, two copies of each, and Frederick marveled at her organization. Anybody that well prepared—for anything—was impressive. Frederick had to shake off a feeling of being second-string, a day late, a dollar short.

"Don't be intimidated by all this bull," Molly said, waving a fine-boned hand over the papers. "Two things: I'm anal-retentive and I like to play around with my computer."

Frederick was not reassured. That she'd read his insecurities so easily was more alarming than her overdeveloped organizational skills. In less than an hour Molly Pigeon was coming to know him better than most did in a year.

"Let's take a look at what you've come up with," he said. He reached for the file and was met by a whiff of tantalizing floral scent. Just enough to make him want to lean closer. He coughed to cover his embarrassment.

Endangered Species

Molly had a complete client list, first names only to maintain privacy. By each name was a brief description of their disorder. Among the medical terms Frederick was amused to find a few good old-fashioned diagnoses: "Cheryl M.—terminal boredom," "Steven P.—pompous ass."

The second page was given the heading "Seriously Ill." Under that she had listed the people she cared for who suffered from debilitating illnesses: paranoia, schizophrenia, bipolar disorders, clinical depression, psychosis.

"Brought these because this is where people seem to want to look first. I didn't know if you'd be the exception. Anyway, I've discounted all of them for one reason or another. Some are locked up, some are too dysfunctional. The rest have problems that simply don't manifest in violence or threats of violence toward others."

Frederick nodded. Those suffering to the point they were committed to a doctor's care usually didn't have the energy or facility to plot complex crimes.

"Here's my cast list," Molly said, and pushed the third sheet across the table. "I really don't think any of these people did it. I'm at a loss, I'm afraid. These are just the people I couldn't rule out altogether."

Those she felt might be responsible for the threatening calls and letters had been highlighted in yellow, and a more detailed diagnosis followed.

"James L." Molly read the first name on the list and Frederick followed along on his printout. "This patient isn't the usual for me. Mostly I've priced myself out of the real world. My clients tend to be wealthy neurotics. This man worked for Packard Electric as a machinist. He's forty-seven years old, white, Vietnam vet. He wanted full disability for posttraumatic stress syndrome from the war. He'd read an article mentioning my name in *Time* magazine and thought my word would carry sufficient weight to get him his early retirement. He put on a decent show, but I thought he was a fraud and said so."

"He didn't take it well?"

"Not him so much as wife number two. A woman twenty years his junior who had plans of her own: two incomes—both his."

Frederick dug a pen out of his inside breast pocket. "Better describe her."

"Early twenties, with the unlikely name of Portia. Small—about Anna's size."

Frederick smiled to himself. Molly was no bigger than Anna but apparently suffered from the same John Wayne complex as her sister.

"Red hair—from a bottle—worn big. Country western singer-big. Good voice till she got angry, then shrill. Regular features but ordinary, even with heavy makeup. She entered data for the same company as her husband. She wanted to quit—she'd married so she wouldn't have to work. When he lost his suit against Packard she got ugly, made some threats."

"What exactly?"

"The usual. You'll get yours, one day you'll be sorry—that sort of thing."

"Any wording like that used in the notes or on the phone messages?"

"No," Molly said, then, after a sip of Scotch and a moment's deliberation added, "Maybe. I seem to remember her suggesting I wasn't human. That theme recurred in one of the phone messages." She laughed. "Maybe I'm not. When Anna and I were kids we got hold of one of those tabloids—I think it was the *Enquirer*. The front-page article was about aliens masquerading as humans and mating with the locals to produce hybrid offspring. The attributes of these half-breeds suited our mom right down to her eyeteeth. We've often speculated that we are a quarter Trafalmagorian on our mother's side."

"That explains a lot," Frederick said. He glanced over the rim of his Scotch and into her eyes. There was unexpected depth there.

Molly smiled and he felt a warmth that unnerved him. He grabbed up the pen, forgotten by his notebook. "Not human. Portia," he said aloud as he scribbled the words down. "I'll need her last name and any other information you've got on her.

"What else?" Frederick asked, needing to stick to business and wondering why.

"Sheila T.—Thomas, Sheila Thomas." Molly read the next name on the list. "She was coming to me for depression and anxiety. According to her, her husband was a jerk. She was having an affair with his brother. I counseled her to take stock of the shortcomings in her marriage and discuss them with her husband. She took this to mean she should tell her husband about her infidelity with his brother. A course of action I think she was leaning toward anyway. Rage, anger, desire to lash out. She told him and he promptly divorced her. Due to the circumstances, she came out on the short end of the stick when it came to the property settlement. Sheila blamed me for the divorce."

"She made threats?"

"A few. Not life-and-death. More along the lines of getting my license revoked, getting me blackballed, hints at connections in high places. I included her because she was literate, well-spoken, a businesswoman, and the two nasty notes she sent me were beautifully written on expensive stationery. And no," she said as Frederick looked up, "I didn't keep them. This all transpired four months ago and I didn't think much of it at the time."

"The last one here is a Nancy B." Frederick read the final name on the short list.

"Bradshaw," Molly said. "Nancy's a real reach but I threw her in because she has a demonstrated capacity for physical violence against things if not people. I only saw her once. She came to me because her life was a shambles. She was drinking too much and having affairs even though she swore she worshiped the ground her sainted husband walked on. I suggested maybe there was at least perceived tarnish on his halo and she was acting out because she was angry with him on some level. She went from zero to sixty in sixty seconds, from sitting in an armchair to stomping around my office throwing books and smashing a lamp. To our mutual benefit, that was our first and last session."

Frederick jotted down a few words to jog his memory, then gathered up the pages Molly had provided and stowed them neatly in his inside breast pocket. What he would ever use them for, he couldn't imagine, but she'd gone to so much trouble he didn't want to seem ungrateful.

For a minute, maybe more, they sat without speaking. The sounds of a city's summer night leaked in around the windowpanes. Sirens in the distance, human conversation muted to wordlessness, traffic. Having lived in cities all his adult life, Frederick found these sounds comforting. The bleak wilderness vistas Anna so loved didn't stir an answering echo in his heart. The sound of wind in the pines wasn't music to him. It struck his ear as the very breath of loneliness.

"How long did Anna live in the city?" he asked.

"Seven years," Molly replied, as if it were a number she kept always in the forefront of her mind.

"Do you think she could ever move back?"

Molly shot him a long look. "I have my doubts," she said at last. "After Zach's death, Anna ran into the wilderness much like an Old Testament prophet seeking her God or a reasonable facsimile thereof. I think she found it. She's doing okay playing at Smokey

Bear. I don't know how she would fare back in an urban environment."

Feeling somehow disloyal talking about Anna, Frederick took a last look at his notes.

"Not much, is there?" Molly voiced his thoughts.

"Not much."

"None of them feels right to me either."

The check came and Frederick paid it, relieved he didn't have to go two falls out of three with Dr. Pigeon for the privilege.

"What about media coverage?" Frederick asked as they were leaving the pub. "That brings out the weirdos."

"A trial. An insanity defense," Molly said after a moment's thought. "That got a bit of coverage. I was the expert witness for the defense. But that was years ago and we won, so they've no cause for complaint. For a while I had people beating down my door to testify for them or somebody they knew, but I won't do it anymore. After the Mack trial I quit."

"Why?"

"There are just too many people who are genuinely insane. No doubt about it, they're mentally ill and they're going to stay mentally ill. I came to the decision that though I pity them deeply, I'm not arrogant enough to believe I can fix them, and I cannot, in good conscience, loose them on society."

"It's not you loosing them, it's the jury."

Molly just laughed. She lifted her hand imperiously, giving Frederick a start. A cab pulled over to the curb. "Can I drop you somewhere?"

Frederick thanked her but wasn't going far enough to warrant a ride.

As the cab was pulling away Molly rolled down the window. "I like you," she said.

Approval. Everybody craved it. Frederick laughed aloud at

himself, then stopped abruptly. The words had meant more to him than simple approval. They'd made his little heart go pitty-pat. "Not good," he whispered to himself as he watched the cab drive away, Molly straight and strong in the back seat, the enormity that was New York City wrapped around her like a well-fitting cloak.

14

ANNA RODE into the conscious world on a tide of nausea that washed up from the vicinity of her bowels, broke in a sour foam, and spewed out her throat.

Gagging, she tried to push herself to her knees and failed. Bile trickled from her lips, unpleasantly warm against her cheek. The sour smell sickened her further but still she couldn't find the strength to lift her face off the linoleum. Somewhere between her will and her muscles there had been a breakdown. Messages were not getting through.

For a minute she lay as one dead, giving in to the inertia. In a brief gust of optimism, it occurred to her that possibly she could open her eyes. The eyes, being in her head—closer, as it were, to the center of power—might work. She paused, gathering her strength, then centered it near the bridge of her nose. With a herculean effort, she raised her eyelids a quarter of an inch.

The vista was not inspiring: dirty blue flooring, a bit of plaid fabric, and a black rubber lozenge. Because it was unexplained, she fixated on the black rubber. For a frustrating eternity identification eluded her. Finally perspective shifted and she saw it for what it was: a thick waffled shoulder pad forming the butt of a twelve-gauge shotgun.

The rubber was probably why she was still alive. Not that being alive struck her as particularly attractive at the moment.

Screwing her courage to the sticking place, she blinked. Each time it grew easier. "Oil can," she croaked absurdly, thinking, like the Tin Man in *The Wizard of Oz*, that all her joints had rusted.

The scratch of her own feeble words cut into her head and pain swelled until it seemed her head must explode or her brains leak out her ears onto the floor. Squeezing her eyes shut only made it worse, adding a sense of vertigo, and she opened them again. Images dripped through the cracks in her brain: searching Hammond's house, opening the closet, the contents falling on her.

Short-term memory was coming back. Perhaps she hadn't sustained any serious brain damage. Between the years of drinking and the occasional blow to the head, she didn't have any little gray cells to spare.

Starting small, she wiggled fingers, then toes, flexed muscles gently. When a modicum of control was restored, she fished her watch out of her pocket and pulled it up as far as the chain would allow. Another staggering effort of will was required to bring the tiny gold numbers into focus: 2:04. She'd not been unconscious long—a few minutes at most. Another good sign.

Pushing herself up, she rolled into a sitting position, her back resting against the wall. Surely her brain had been bruised. Not only did it hurt but the pain went out along all the nerve paths till there was no part of her that didn't throb in sympathy. Anna was groaning, she couldn't help it. She was glad there was no one around to hear.

Like fog lifting, the pain began to recede, traveling back up the synapses till it was at last contained in a burning knot behind her left ear. As the pain localized, Anna was able to think again.

What were the odds that the shotgun had merely tumbled down on her head when she opened the closet? Slim to nonexistent. The gun didn't weigh more than five or ten pounds. The blow that struck her unconscious carried considerably more wallop. It crossed her mind to feel the size of the lump on her skull but she wasn't ready to know that much.

Somebody wanted her out of the way. Maybe permanently.

A spurt of adrenaline sent a shiver through the sweat between her breasts. Breathing deeply, she calmed herself with oxygen and logic. If anyone wanted to kill her, they would have. If they'd thought the deed accomplished, they'd be long gone. If they came back to finish her off, she was too weak to defend herself anyway.

Vomit was drying on her face, the air was unbreathable. She was losing track of where the sweltering airless heat left off and the suffocating ache in her head began. She had to get a drink of water; she had to get out of Hammond's house.

Walking struck her as too ambitious and, her head down like a bone-weary mule's, she crawled on hands and knees out of the bedroom and across the living room. The front door stood wide open. Anna thanked her erstwhile assailant. The effort of opening it would have set off a new spate of sparks in her battered brainpan.

Afraid to stop lest she never get going again, she crawled over the front stoop, down the dirt path, and across twenty feet of duff to where she'd parked the truck. Moving carefully, as if her head were a porcelain egg only precariously balanced on her neck, she pulled herself up and onto the seat of the pumper truck. Her much-needed reward was a quart of warm drinking water from her fire canteen. Some she spilled, some she couldn't keep down, but most of it was soaked up by her dehydrated body.

She hadn't forgotten there was water in Hammond's house. She just didn't want any part of it.

Under her right hand was the King radio. The keys were in the ignition where she'd left them. Anna reviewed her options. She could radio for help. In minutes everyone within hailing distance would swarm down on her. The role of victim would be wrapped around her till she was trussed up like a Christmas turkey. Everyone would have a high old time clucking and caring and bustling her off to St. Marys to the hospital. There they would take her clothes, her boots, and her radio and put one of those wretched little plastic bracelets on her wrist.

"Everybody will be so fucking *jolly*," Anna whispered through dry lips. Motivated by this grisly scenario, she reached up and fingered her head wound. Goose egg was as good a description as any, but soft to the touch like a water balloon and very tender. From the size of it, the mechanism of injury, and the length of time she was out, Anna suspected she'd sustained at least a slight concussion.

So: bundled and trundled ignominiously to the emergency room, diagnosed with a concussion and demobbed. Not just Anna— it didn't work that way. The whole crew would be sent home and a new one dispatched to replace them. This assignment was vacation money for Al's family, seed money for Rick's garage door business.

All in all, Anna decided she'd just as soon have a headache on Cumberland at time and a half than a headache in Mesa Verde for considerably less money.

Letting the pain in her head settle, she stared at the gaping front door of Slattery Hammond's rental. Someone had gotten there before her. That they were up to no good was obvious. Why else hide? It was also fairly obvious they'd been looking for something they either knew or suspected Slattery kept in his house. The something was therefore valuable, incriminating, or embarrassing. She was there for the maintenance logs. She'd not found them, but surely the only one they could incriminate was the so-far apocryphal mechanic.

Drugs? Guns? Used tampons? Kiddy scissors? Pornography? Letters? Cash? That staple in old movies: a cigarette butt with lipstick on it and not Slattery's shade? Anna's head hurt too much to pursue it and she let the thoughts scatter.

Ten minutes saw her sufficiently recovered to try the ignition key and ease the truck gingerly over the bumps between Hammond's and the district office. Movement was good, some basic difference between the quick and dead, confirmation that she was not yet among the latter.

In the dirt parking lot behind the ranger station, she parked in the shade and pulled the side mirror around to see if her looks passed muster. Though she had chosen to hide her little adventure quite literally under her hat, she was disappointed. She looked fine. Physical trauma should produce at least enough blood or bandages to get one some sympathy. Even her color was good. The pallor of shock and the flush of fever evidently canceled each other out.

Hull was in his office, the door open. He welcomed Anna and urged her to sit. For once she was grateful for his formality. Standing had not yet become an occupation she excelled at. And the air-conditioning was heaven.

"Anna?"

She heard him say her name as from a distance and realized she'd allowed herself to sink back in the chair and close her eyes.

"Thinking," she said idiotically. Chief Ranger Hull was too polite to comment.

"Did you find the aircraft logs for Mr. Hammond's Beechcraft?"

Anna started to shake her head, thought better of it and said: "No."

"Mrs. Utterback suggested the logs might be in the mechanic's shop. I'll leave that to her."

"Somebody had been to Hammond's before I got there," Anna told him.

Hull's eyebrows flew up either in inquiry or because of his nervous disorder. His forehead wrinkled far up on his scalp and the eyes behind the thick glasses bulged slightly. It was a face that invited confession but Anna quashed the urge.

"The place had been searched. What, if anything, was taken, I have no way of knowing."

Hull's myopic blue eyes slid off Anna's face and his long thin hands began stirring in the mess of papers on his desk. Poking through the pages as if seeking something vitally important, he asked Anna, "Are you sure?"

"Positive."

That wasn't the answer he was hoping for.

"Is there anyone who knew him well enough to know what he kept in the house?" Anna asked.

"No. Mr. Hammond was what we used to call a lone wolf. No one came to visit him that I recall—we tend to know each other's business on the island. Too well, I sometimes think." The last sentence sounded bitter, unusual in a man as rigidly controlled as Norman Hull.

"Have you heard anything about Tabby Belfore?" Anna changed the subject.

"Yes. That reminds me. She's doing much better. The baby hasn't come and evidently that's causing some—well—*emotional* problems. They can't very well give her tranquilizers in her condition. Unfortunately she's insisting on returning to Cumberland to her apartment. Her doctor is opposed to the idea but he can't forbid it. Mrs. Belfore's agreed to let someone stay with her for a few days."

An alarmed froglike croak escaped Anna's lips. The chief ranger pretended not to notice.

"It's been cleared with Guy," he said without looking up.

Hull wasn't asking her and Anna was unpleasantly reminded that the National Park Service was designed along paramilitary lines. She could say no, but the repercussions wouldn't be worth it.

"Do you have any aspirin?" she asked plaintively, as he pushed a key across the desk. "I've got a whale of a headache."

Hull steered her to Renee, his secretary, and closed his door firmly behind her. As usual Renee's desk was empty. Beyond the Xerox, through an old-fashioned sash window, Anna could see her in the shade of the porch smoking one of her endless cigarettes. The woman was uniquely suited to the pastime. She carried all her weight from the groin up, giving her the shape of a little chimney, and if one squinted and used one's imagination, her overbleached hair could pass for smoke.

Renee was helpful. Rummaging boisterously through her desk drawers, she said: "This has been some week, hasn't it? More excitement than we've had around here in a coon's age. That boy getting his leg shot off, Todd getting killed in that wreck. Mitch was telling me and Louise—Louise is his wife—about how tore up that airplane was. And the bodies all burnt up like. Norm's daughter, Ellen, was at the houseboat. She and Louise are kind of special friends. Both are into gardening, if you'd believe that. And Louise living on a boat. Maybe it's just something to say. Ellen doesn't get on all that well with her mom. Louise kind of fills that bill. Anyway, Mitch is going on about the bodies and all, never thinking. It could've just as easy been Norman, Ellen's daddy. God, then I'd've been out of a job. If you ask me, he ought to send the regional director a case of bourbon. If he hadn't called Norm at the St. Marys office and kept him on the line, he'd've made that flight instead of Todd.

"Nope," Renee said finally. "I could've swore I had some Bufferin in here somewhere but I guess they all got ate up. Sorry." She flopped down in her swivel chair and looked ready to kill a little more time in idle chatter, but Anna didn't feel up to it. She mumbled her thanks and made her escape.

In the break room she stole a Coke, promising the honor system two quarters when she had them. Pressing the cold can against the lump on her skull, she again braved the heat of the August sun.

Feeling like an exile, she cleaned out her room in the fire dorm and drove to Plum Orchard. If Guy wanted the truck back, he could damn well come and get it. Anna resented being sold down the river even as she welcomed the solitude of the Belfores' apartment and the chance to lie down before her head fell off.

The trip up the two flights of stairs took the last of her strength. Abandoning her red fire pack on the first landing, she staggered in the door.

The medicine cabinet was a disappointment. Apparently the Belfores treated only maladies of the ego. A clutter of products promising to restore hair, keep skin young, and grow strong fingernails filled the shelves. No analgesics. Anna sat on the toilet and, head in hands, indulged in a few tears of self-pity.

From a phone in the bedroom she called the Cumberland Island National Seashore Visitors' Center in St. Marys. A cheerful female voice answered. Anna introduced herself and begged this happy soul to send some aspirin over on whichever boat was going to the island next.

It must have been a slow day. The woman kept Anna on the line for five minutes, marveling at the recent tragedy and telling again the story of the regional director's call saving Norman Hull from the jaws of death. There was something in near misses, twists of fate, that rekindled in the human psyche the desire to believe in a grand master plan.

Anna stayed on the line until the voice promised a bottle of Excedrin on a maintenance boat leaving around three-thirty.

Endangered Species

Silence was a balm. To lie down on a bed, exquisite. Had some quiet unobtrusive servant tiptoed in and turned on the air conditioner, Anna would have believed in a kindly God. As it was, she lay in the stifling heat, feeling the trickles of sweat prick under her clothes.

Sleep pressed heavily on her limbs, forcing her eyelids closed. Was she indeed concussed, she knew she mustn't give in to it. Vaguely she remembered that people with head injuries needed to be awakened periodically for the first ten hours. For the life of her she couldn't remember why.

Fending off the sandman's advances, she propped herself up against the pillows and reached again for the bedside phone.

"Mesa Verde National Park."

"Hey, Frieda," she said wearily. "It's Anna."

Frieda was the dispatcher at Mesa Verde, the chief ranger's secretary, and, Anna hoped, a friend.

"What's up?" Frieda asked.

Directness: it was one of the many things for which Anna admired the woman. She gave Frieda a brief account of the airplane crash. She didn't mention the blow to the back of her head. Not because Frieda would tell anyone—Mesa Verde's dispatcher was a safe repository for even the most sensitive information—but because the effort of convincing her she wasn't hurt was too much to contemplate.

"See what you can dig up on Slattery Hammond," Anna said. "He used to work for the Forest Service in Region Six. Each pilot has to be approved by the aviation department yearly. The records ought to be in Redmond or Portland. And could you call me back in half an hour whether you find out anything or not?" Anna was afraid that, left to her own devices, she would sleep too long.

Frieda promised she would. If she thought the request peculiar she kept it to herself. It wasn't in Frieda's job description to do investigative background work but she was good at it and, when other duties weren't pressing, enjoyed it. Frieda had been with the NPS for eighteen years, half her life. Anybody who hadn't slept on her couch, borrowed her car, or mooched a free meal off of her knew someone who had. The dispatcher had connections in odd and useful places.

"Hammond. USFS. Region Six. Got it," Frieda said.

Anna let a sigh escape. "How's Piedmont?" she asked, her pain making her homesick for the comforts of her cat.

"Misses his mom—other than that, good. Bella's taken to coming with me. While I clean the cat box she plays with the cat. As a team, we're unbeatable."

Bella was the seven-year-old daughter of one of the park employees. Anna had fallen in love with the child her first summer at Mesa Verde.

"Good deal," Anna said. "I've got to go." She hung up before the ache in her head deprived her of the power of coherent speech.

Secure in the knowledge that Frieda wouldn't let her sleep to death, Anna let her eyes unfocus and her mind drift. In the narrow and fuzzy field of her vision was the bedroom door standing half open, a lacy pink peignoir hanging from a hook on the back. What looked like a tiny little kid's purse or a giant padlock hung from the doorknob. Because she didn't know what it was, the object aggravated Anna. Above it was a dead bolt and above that a chain lock. A chain lock on an inside door; that wasn't the usual. Taken in the context of the two locks, the unidentified hanging object lost its mystery. Anna had seen them before. They were traveler's intruder alarms, motion detectors. When disturbed they emitted a loud obnoxious noise.

Three security measures on the bedroom door. Jesus, Anna thought, as she slid into a heavy sleep. At least one of the Belfores was sure as hell afraid of something.

15

ANNA WAS UP at four-thirty. At six she was to pick up Dijon at the fire dorm and patrol the north end of the island. Guy had made a special trip to Plum Orchard the evening before to tell her her work with fire crew was in no way alleviated by the nightly baby-sitting chore. The first was her job, the second her duty.

Anna was feeling anything but dutiful. Her temples pounded as if something vaguely equine were trapped in her skull hammering with iron-shod hooves to get out. Her neck was stiff from sleeping on the sofa in the Belfores' living room. Foraging for coffee in the unfamiliar kitchen, she cursed Norman Hull, Guy, Tabby, and whoever had tried to crack her skull.

The logical assumption was that whoever had bashed her over the head was the same individual who sabotaged Slattery's Beechcraft. Frieda's inquiries had turned up some interesting connections. Hammond had a reverse discrimination suit filed against Alice Utterback. Prior to going to the Washington, D.C., office, Alice had been head of aviation for Region Six. She'd passed over Hammond's application three times. All three times she hired a female pilot to fill the position he applied for. When he finally crawled on board in a seasonal capacity, he alleged Alice had discriminated against him in an assortment of petty ways. Anna's favorite was the accusation that Alice had put up a poster of Charles Lindbergh over his picture of Miss November in a hangar in Redmond, Oregon.

Alice certainly had the knowledge to wreck an airplane. And was now in an excellent position to screw up the investigation. Not for a moment did Anna believe that particular scenario. Still, it made her uncomfortable.

Being a woman of wisely maintained cynicism, Frieda had run not only Hammond but all the possible targets of the saboteur through NCIC, the National Criminal Information Center. Hammond, Belfore, and Hull all had clean records.

Anna had not thought to run the chief or district rangers. People with felonies on their records were automatically barred from carrying a law enforcement commission. Frieda knew better and told Anna horror stories of a goodly number who'd slipped through the cracks: convicted murderers wearing the green and gray, representing the NPS to a trusting public.

Through the grapevine, Frieda had also discovered that though Hammond had no record, he'd had some run-ins with the local police in Hope, Canada, the small town outside North Cascades National Park in Washington where some of the park employees kept "city homes." Cops had showed up at his apartment more than once. What about was open for speculation.

Caffeine, a shower, and two Excedrin transformed Anna into something more closely resembling a human being, and at five a.m. she slipped quietly from the Belfores' apartment to greet the day. The sun had not yet deigned to rise but there was promise in the east. Standing on the wooden landing halfway down the fire escape, she absorbed the freedom to be had out of doors.

She had known her head hurt, realized the couch was lumpy. What hadn't occurred to her till she was free of it was the tension and sorrow that permeated every stick of furniture and scrap of fabric that made up the Belfore home. Even before Tabby returned from the mainland, Anna had sensed it. Fear was there in the many locks, in the unguents and creams for maintaining youth; sadness in the pink chiffon dressing gown unsuited for a widow, in the wide bed, lonely for one; in every picture where, against a glorious back-drop of green mountains, a blond woman smiled at a dead man.

Breathing deeply of the soft air, Anna let some of that tension leave her. Her mind sank into the holding warmth of a southern dawn as the first light shamed the stars from the sky. The horrid littles of being human: life, death, birth, love and betrayal, were of no moment to her today. All she had to do was drive a truck and look for smoke. Even with a headache and a bad attitude, she should be able to do that.

As she neared the meadow by Stafford mansion, rusted shocks and rough road were well on the way to undoing her resolve. Early light poured into the clearing. Splashed over the sand-blasted wind-shield it was blinding. A small dark shape—a dog maybe—darted into the glare obscuring the road in front of the truck and Anna slammed on the brakes. She skidded to a stop without any sickening bumps. To her left was the meadow, to her right a wall cemented from sand and shell that separated Stafford and its attendant cottage from the dirt road.

The critter she'd narrowly avoided sending to the promised land was disappearing through a gate in the wall. A glimpse of white tail and spotted rump was all Anna was afforded. Then, like a magical moment in a fairy tale, a face peeked back around the gatepost. A fawn not more than a month old looked up at her with Disney eyes. Anna laughed aloud. Feeling blessed, she watched in stillness, expecting this wilderness apparition to vanish with the usual alacrity of wild things.

This little fellow stayed. He poked his head several inches further around the gate and cocked it to one side. A pink tongue flicked out and wet a black nose.

Like most women her age, Anna had been raised with the animated classics. The good and pure, the Cinderellas and Snow Whites, could sit down and all the gentle creatures of the forest would come and nestle in their skirts. Drawn by this childhood fantasy, one that wouldn't die regardless of the number of squirrels, raccoons, and armadillos that rejected her advances, Anna climbed slowly from the truck.

Leaving it parked in the lane, driver door open, she worked her way toward the fawn. Her voice slid into the upper registers, and even as she cooed sweet nonsense, she wondered what it was about babies, regardless of their species, that made people talk funny.

Head lowered, looking at her through impossibly long lashes, the fawn watched. When Anna was less than six feet from him, she felt a wave of dizziness and realized she'd been holding her breath. She let it escape in a rush and the tiny animal turned and ran, not as if it was afraid, but as if it wanted to play.

Enchanted, Anna followed.

Inside the walls nestled a cottage. Once it had probably been the gatekeeper's quarters. A row of potted plants in the window and a bicycle leaning against the plaster wall attested to more modern inhabitants.

The mansion and grounds had been allowed to deteriorate. Weeds recaptured what had been lawns. Bushes, run wild, tangled up close to the kitchens at the rear of the mansion, much as the curse of thorns had wrapped around Sleeping Beauty's castle.

The mansion itself was not so grand as Plum Orchard, being smaller and boxier, built with the feel of a Mediterranean villa yet retaining an American hardiness to withstand Atlantic storms. There were no vistas dotted with live oaks, but a long rectangular lawn in the process of being reclaimed by nature. Wide steps built to usher visitors up to the front doors were crumbling. Stones loosed by time and weather lay scattered in the weeds.

It was to this doorway the fawn ran, trotting up the stairs to pause beneath the veranda and look back at Anna. Laughing, she ran after, careful to keep her footfalls quiet and her aura benign.

The clatter of hooves gave away the fawn's direction as he scampered down the long porch and around the corner of the house. Seconds later, Anna rounded the same corner. The fawn was nowhere to be seen. Weed-eaten lawn stretched empty in three directions. The northern wing of the mansion, housing the kitchens and servants' quarters, walled off this half of the garden from the entrance gate and cottage.

Nothing moved, not even the crawling heat. For reasons Anna had never been curious enough to ask about, the heat on Cumberland didn't create the shimmering curtains of mirage that heat in the desert did.

At her feet were concrete stairs leading to a cellar door that stood open eight or ten inches. Unless the deer was equipped with turbojets, there was no other place he could have reached and secreted himself in the time he'd been out of her sight. Though she'd never seen a wild animal bolt into a human habitation for safety, she pursued him down the steps. Engrossed in a fairy tale, it didn't even strike her as particularly odd.

The cellar was as big as the house, wings disappearing into the gloom, one north and the other east. Anna found a switch by the door and, without much hope, clicked it on. To her surprise, half a dozen dim bulbs cast an inadequate light. The ceiling was low—she could reach up and touch it with the palm of her hand—and coffered into countless recesses by beams, pipes, and exposed wiring. The floor was of smooth concrete.

Over the years bits and pieces of jumbled lives had made their way into these catacombs. History, a lot of junk, and some convenient storage were tucked away in the shadows. From behind an old coal furnace, with as many arms as a Jules Verne nightmare, peeked a classic baby buggy with huge wheels and a tattered bonnet. Fragments of derelict furniture were piled against the walls.

A bleat, like that of a lamb, caught Anna's attention. Beyond the furnace, in one of the alcoves in the eastern wing, she could just make out the form of the fawn. A bleat: she realized that though she'd seen a goodly number of fawns, she'd never heard one speak. Its voice carried the imperious helplessness of all babies and she smiled. "You gonna run, little buddy?" she said coaxingly.

The fawn vanished, swallowed by shadows. She followed deeper into the labyrinth of cellar. Around an abutment of concrete, amid white PVC pipe lying in unstable piles and plastic containers of fertilizer and herbicides, he was waiting.

Anna folded down onto the floor and there in the artificial dusk of a turn-of-the-century cellar, she got her Snow White dream. The fawn pushed his nose against her, licked her chin, and let her pet the graceful spotted arc of his neck.

So absorbed was she in the magic of the moment that when a perfectly friendly voice said: "Oh there you are," she nearly jumped out of her skin. The fawn skittered away to take shelter behind the stout legs of the intruder.

An elderly woman, probably in her seventies, with tightly permed iron-gray hair and thick glasses framed in blue plastic, blocked what little light leaked from the bulb in the next alcove. In this twilight her skin was ageless but her voice spoke of wear and tear and her body had settled into the comfortable lumps brought on by too many years' exposure to fried chicken and gravity.

"I see you've met Flicka," she said pleasantly, and reached behind her so the fawn could butt his head against the soft of her palm. When Anna said nothing, the woman went on. " 'Flicka.' Pretty silly, I guess, but 'Bambi' seemed too cute. Mona and I aren't very imaginative when it comes to names."

Anna recovered her equilibrium. The abrupt switches from Disney to Stephen King to the real world had taken some adjusting to. Rising from the dust, she said: "Anna Pigeon, fire crew," and stuck out her hand because she couldn't think of anything else appropriate to do.

"Dot," the woman said, and captured the proffered hand, holding on to it as if Anna were a lost child. Short of jerking rudely back, there was little Anna could do but submit. "Mona and I are VIPs—Volunteers in Parks—working on turtle inventory and related subjects. A step up, I must say, from our first assignment."

"What was that?" Anna asked politely, trying to think of a dignified way to get her hand back.

"Cellar inventory. That's when Flicka first came. He got into the habit of playing down here." Dot laughed. "We volunteer for six weeks of sun and fun on the Golden Isles in our golden years and we get stuck with cellar inventory." Despite the words, Dot's good cheer seemed undiminished.

"Maintenance saved us. They decided to use the old place for storage." She waved at the pipes and bottles and Anna's hand escaped. She hid it in her pocket lest it again be snatched. "That ended our troglodyte period," Dot said. "Coffee? It's on."

Meekly, Anna followed her from the cellar, the fawn trotting along at the older woman's heels like a well-trained pup.

Mona, the other half of this marriage—and from the dear and

135

comfortable way the women treated one another, Anna guessed it was a relationship of long standing—was slight and strong, with broad hips and the flat butt that comes with age. Her hair was brown with stark white streaks at the temples. "Bride of Frankenstein," she said, and laughed when Anna complimented her on them. Her face was wrinkled and soft with the agelessness of elves in old drawings. Either her eyesight was keen or she wore contacts; nothing filtered the warmth from eyes as dark and liquid as Flicka's.

Mona and Dot were retired schoolteachers from West Virginia. Summers they volunteered for the National Park Service. They'd worked in Yellowstone, and Hovenweep, Rocky Mountain, and Fort Pulaski. Their tastes were eclectic and their store of knowledge vast and varied. At a rough estimate, Anna guessed between them they had over a century of experience. They were as much national treasures as the parks themselves, and Anna was content to snuggle down in their cluttered kitchen and drink their coffee.

As was inevitable in an island society, the talk turned inward, to the airplane wreck and the ripples it continued to send through the isolated colony.

"I liked Slattery," Mona said, taking Anna by surprise. She'd had the impression everyone hated the man. On reflection, she realized the only person she'd spoken to about Hammond was Alice Utterback and he had a lawsuit filed against her. "Slattery was a real charmer," Mona went on, offering a package of store-bought cinnamon rolls to Anna.

"A man gets extra points for being charming to horrid old women," Dot said.

"Yes indeed. Smacks of genuine good manners. Nothing to gain."

"Unless he's a pervert," Dot said.

"Unless *you're* a pervert," Mona returned pointedly, and Dot was chastened. Precisely for what, Anna had no idea.

"Slattery was an amateur marine biologist. The life cycle of the loggerheads fascinated him. He spent a lot of his spare time poking through the old files," Mona said.

"That's how we got to know him," Dot told Anna. "Poking became our second assignment, right after Morlock duty."

"We're putting all the back files in some sort of order and entering the data on the computer." Mona took up the story.

"A mad dash into the twentieth century," Dot added. "A mere handful of years before it ends."

"Money makes all things possible. Some clever soul got a hundred and twelve grand out of the U.S. government to study the loggerheads. Pays our room and board," Mona said.

"Not board, just room. Maybe board next year. The second half is due come September. Hull wants all the files squeaky-clean and high-tech by Labor Day."

"It'd be easier with assistants," Mona said.

"You just want someone besides me to boss."

"On the rolls but never showed."

"Kids today . . ." Dot clucked.

"A mess. A nightmare," Mona said. "If we didn't possess the patience of Job—"

"And nearly the same number of years on the job—"

"We'd be more or less completely nuts—"

"Instead of incompletely nuts—"

"By now," Mona finished.

Yup, Anna thought, old married couple.

"And Todd was a good enough fellow," Mona said, as if feeling she'd been remiss. "He hadn't much time for a couple of senior citizens."

"Bookworms."

"Computer nerds."

"Schoolteachers."

The two women exchanged comments with such rapidity, many of them fraught with private humor, that Anna was dizzied. She helped herself to a pastry to steady her mind.

"But a dear with his wife," Mona concluded. Both faces grew somber so suddenly and in such concert with one another that only an inhaled crumb and a brief coughing fit rescued Anna from laughter.

"How is Tabby?" Dot asked with what looked to be very real if belated concern.

Anna saw no reason not to tell them. Theoretically everyone was a suspect and appearances could be deceiving, but Dot and Mona struck her as women who had outgrown murder. Mona lit a Virginia Slim and Dot folded her hands attentively as Anna began. Good listeners; Anna bet they'd been excellent teachers.

She told them as much as she knew. Mitch Hanson had dropped Lynette and Tabby off at Plum Orchard around six the evening before, and Anna found herself in the awkward role of playing hostess to the returning owner. Tabby hadn't cared, hadn't seemed to notice. Had Norman Hull's comments, and her own rudimentary knowledge of pharmacology, not come into play, Anna would have thought Tabby was drugged. Her movements were slow, her responses to questions and other stimuli sluggish. Her head moved first, her eyes tracking a second later. Her speech, though not slurred, gave that impression. Tabby would lose interest in what she was saying before the thought was complete and her sentences often dribbled to a stop in the middle.

Crippling depression; it didn't take Anna long to recognize it. After Zach died she'd swum in those dark waters. That had been years ago but she could still remember. Her body remembered: the weight behind the breastbone, the pressure at the base of the skull, the tedious exhausting necessity to breathe in and breathe out, the endless theatrical that demons put on just behind the eyes, making it impossible to focus on the words of those still living.

Overlying this miasma of grief in Tabby was a need for self-destruction only held at bay by the life she carried within her. Damage she could do that would not touch the baby, Tabby welcomed. Making tea, Anna caught her pressing her fingers against the red rings of the electric burner. The flesh was white as ash when Anna snatched them off and held them under the cold water tap.

Later, when Anna thought Tabby was working on a cross-stitch of three goslings traipsing after a bonneted goose, she found the girl was repeatedly plunging the needle into the flesh of her forearm. She was spelling something out with dots of fresh blood. When Anna tried to read it, she smeared the letters and let herself be washed and anointed with Neosporin.

There followed an earnest lecture as Anna told her that everything she did, right down to destructive thoughts and watching the six o'clock news, affected her unborn child. Maybe Anna was telling the truth. Who could know?

Lynette was no help. She only stayed a quarter of an hour, then, refusing a ride from Anna, walked the mile and a half home. Either she had problems of her own or she'd caught Tabby's sadness. The usually bright eyes were lackluster and she scarcely spoke. Anna had little doubt some well-meaning person of the male persuasion with only slightly ulterior motives would turn up to succor the young woman, so she let her go without argument, relieved not to have two zombies in the house.

When Anna had finished her story, Dot said: "Lynette was sweet on Slattery," clearing up at least one of the minor mysteries.

"Was he sweet on her?" Anna unconsciously picked up the other woman's phrasing.

Mona answered. "With Slattery who could tell?"

"He was unilaterally charming," Dot explained. "Pleasant for antiquarian educators but no doubt aggravating for sweet young things."

Anna's radio grumbled, reminding her she wasn't paid to sit around having coffee. After weaseling an invitation to come play with Flicka anytime she wanted, she took her leave.

Driving south, she considered her conversation with the two women. Had Tabby targeted Todd because he "would leave her"? Lynette targeted Hammond for flirting with septuagenarians? Or was the one that got away, Norman Hull, the intended target? Motive was a stumbling block when the identity of the intended victim was up for grabs.

Love was a respectable motive for murder, well represented in fact and fiction, but it wasn't Anna's favorite for this type of crime. Love, the kind that could get one killed, was passionate, immediate, dramatic—at least a majority of the time. In crimes of the heart there was often, quite literally, a smoking gun.

Murder by sabotage or—if Wayne had his way—by incompetence, breathed cold.

In some evil recess of her mind Anna was pleased it had happened on her shift. Presuppression was deadly dull. Taken from a purely heartless point of view, a murder investigation was downright entertaining.

Anna laughed at the wickedness of the thought and was instantly punished by an echo of pain from behind her left ear. Abruptly her mood changed, reality setting in with a vengeance, reminding her to stay alert lest her demise prove amusing to someone else; someone she owed one hell of a headache.

16

ON THE NORTH END of the island were the Cumberland Mountains—hillocks not nearly so majestic as the dunes—left behind when the sea severed the island's tip. Across a causeway, that tip still existed, privately owned. Because it was inaccessible and therefore mysterious, Anna was fantasizing about swimming the narrow channel and exploring it. Of course she never would. There were ten standard firefighting orders. Had there been an eleventh, it might have said that the instant a firefighter left her station there was bound to be a call-out.

"What time is it?" Dijon asked.

"Two minutes later than last time you asked."

They lay side by side on the hood of the truck, their backs against the windshield. Having finished their sack lunches, they'd declared siesta appropriate, and as long as Guy didn't catch them at it, it would be. Neither worried; stealth and all-terrain vehicles were mutually exclusive.

"We could go feed the baby alligators," Dijon suggested.

"I am shocked," Anna said mildly. "Maggie-Mary would get us. Besides, it's against Superintendent's Orders." Feeding wild animals human food was seldom healthy for them, and feeding wild animals that could grow up to feed on you, unwise at the best of times.

"Pissing in the wind," Dijon defended himself.

As oblique as the comment was, Anna understood. Tourists, island dwellers, fishermen—everyone—had hand-fed the little gators since they were hatchlings. Now the babies, all fourteen of them, were a couple of feet long. Whenever a human approached the pool they lived in, they all came crowding around like pigeons in the park. But with pointier teeth.

So far Anna had kept to the moral high ground and not given in to the temptation to feed them, but she watched Rick and Dijon do it and enjoyed the show, which was just as bad. Hypocrite, she reproved herself, but there was no power behind the thought. The day was too warm, the clatter of cicadas too soothing, and the baby gators too much fun to watch for her to get up a strong case against herself.

Her mind wandered off the glittering Atlantic and onto earthier things. Alice Utterback had located the aircraft logs at the office at the St. Marys airport where Hammond had his mechanic work done. They were all in order and up-to-date. The Beechcraft had been given its hundred-hour check two weeks prior to the accident. At that time everything had been in order and signed off on. The mechanic, an older man and a staple in St. Marys, not only had the recommendations of his peers but had no idea who owned the airplane when he worked on it, or who might or might not be flying with Hammond in the future. That left sabotage, intentional and deadly.

"What do you know about either of the guys killed in the crash?" Anna asked. She was aware that she avoided the use of their names. She didn't want to make it personal.

"Sleuthing, eh?" Dijon said in a passable English accent. "Why not. I've been to law enforcement school and I could pass for Denzel Washington."

"In your dreams."

"Most of what I got's from Lynette," Dijon said. "Hearsay. Not admissible. I got an eighty-two on that exam."

"Bully for you."

"Lynette had the hots for Hammond. You'd think the sun rose and set in his pants."

"Wouldn't give you the time of day?"

"You got it. And to resist me you have to admit she must've had it bad."

Anna laughed. "Rick teaching you how to brag?"

"If it's true, it ain't bragging. Lynette seemed kind of down, so me and Rick dropped by her place last night with a couple of six-packs."

Anna's guess that Lynette wouldn't suffer for broad shoulders to cry on had been right on the money.

"Rick and Lynette got pretty smashed—"

"Not you?"

"Me? You kidding? The stuff has no effect on me anymore."

"Anyway . . ." Anna prompted.

"What do you mean *anyway*? You're the one keeps interrupting, lousing up the flow."

"Sorry."

"Could you grovel and beseech me?"

"Not that sorry."

"Anyway," Dijon went on amiably, "it pretty much turned into a pity party, which was okay by me. Women cry, you get to hold 'em. Beats sitting around staring at you old farts all night."

"You have a heart as big as all outdoors," Anna said dryly.

"I do, don't I? She'd met Slattery a few years back—before she got on permanent she was a seasonal up in Alaska somewhere. They went at it hot and heavy, then he started screwing around on her. Lynette didn't say that. 'Betrayed my trust,' is how she put it."

"Screwing around," Anna agreed.

"Hey, you *are* old, aren't you?"

"I've been around the block."

"Before I was born."

Anna let that pass. She couldn't think of an adequate rejoinder. Besides, it was true. "So he comes here and they start up again?"

"Lynette's story is that he'd seen the light, found God, been washed in the blood of the lamb. Lynette's big into Jesus, did you know that?"

"Nope."

"Me neither. She seems so cool."

"Maybe the one doesn't preclude the other," Anna said.

Dijon snorted. "She says Hammond came crawling back on his belly all drippy with true repentance and talking diamond rings and picket fences and having her babies."

A break in the conversation followed that neither of them bothered to fill. The sounds of summer were sufficient to banish silence with quiet.

"He wanted to get laid," Anna said after a minute.

"In a bad way," Dijon concurred. "Nothing against Lynette, but the whole story was just too perfect: hearts and flowers and crap. Guaranteed to make them drop their drawers."

"Are you going to give it a try?"

"Whatever works . . ."

"Maybe Slattery 'betrayed her trust' one too many times," Anna suggested.

"You mean . . . Naw." Dijon pushed himself up off the windshield and stared out across the causeway. After a moment he shook his head. "No. I don't see it." Then: "You think?"

"Take it easy," Anna laughed. "I don't think anything. We're just talking."

Dijon leaned back. "Boy, that would be a twist, wouldn't it? Lynette icing her lover? I like it."

If Dijon had any idea how his innocence showed through a hundred cracks in his armor, he would have been mortified. Anna stored that thought away in case she needed it for self-defense at some later date.

"What else you got?" he asked.

"Not a whole hell of a lot," Anna admitted. "Tabby knocking off Todd?"

"Never happen. That woman couldn't unhook her own bra. Without Todd, she's falling apart."

"What if he was going to run out on her?" Anna told him the story of their midnight contretemps in the meadow.

"Still can't see it," he said, settling his cap more comfortably over his face. "She'd crawl—not kill—if her man was walking out."

"I don't know," Anna said. She was thinking of the burned fingers and the needle punctures. "She's tearing herself up over something."

"Grief."

There was more to it than that, but since she didn't know what, Anna kept the thought to herself. "How about Norman Hull? He was supposed to be on that flight. Maybe he knew better."

Dijon considered that for a while. "No," he said finally. "Too big a pain in the butt to fill Todd's position. Who'd take it? There's diddly-shit to do. You'll have to do better than Hull."

Anna told him about Slattery Hammond's lawsuit against Alice Utterback.

"That's it," he said languidly. "A woman carrying that much brass is unnatural. Ball-busting bitch nails middle-class white guy. I bet it happens all the time." He was trying to get a rise out of Anna, but with his youth and transparency, he only succeeded in being kind of cute.

"Let's go mess with Marty Schlessinger," Anna said suddenly. "She lied to me about hearing the shot that hit that Austrian kid."

"God, I hate it when people lie to me," Dijon said.

"You're in for a miserable life then," Anna told him. "Everybody lies all the time just for the hell of it. By the way, you've got a tick on your neck."

"Jesus Christ!" Dijon yelled, and scrambled from the hood to wrench the side mirror out to where he could examine himself. "Shit. There's no tick."

"See what I mean?"

"Anna, I wish you had balls. Then I'd know what to do with you."

"I do," she said as she fired up the truck's engine. "A whole collection mounted on the wall of my study."

Marty Schlessinger lived in a shack. The house, the hog pens, the outbuildings, stuck out of the forest floor like a rejected set from *The Grapes of Wrath*. If the buildings had ever been painted, sun and salt air had stripped them bare again.

The house was built in the southern tradition Anna had heard referred to as a "shotgun shack." The rooms were arranged in a line, one after the other from front door to back. Presumably, one could fire a shotgun through the entire structure without doing too much damage. The screen on the front door was blasted outward as if someone had tested the theory. Most of the window screens were torn or missing. The shake siding had been broken in several places as if a truck had backed into the house and the damage had never been repaired. Gouts of tar paper flagged the holes.

The hog pen was ten or fifteen feet from the house. Fence and shelter were the same weathered gray. Repairs had been made with whatever came to hand. A rusting dozer blade shored up a stretch of fence line. The door of an automobile, yellow upholstery still clinging to the side, had been used to stop a hole dug beneath the wire.

Being clever creatures, the pigs were sleeping through the heat of the day. Under the rude and crumbling shelter, Anna could see a sow with eight or a dozen piglets, all of whom had fallen asleep suckling. Cumberland Island's pigs were unlike any she'd ever seen. In most ways—eyes and ears and snouts and tails—they were thoroughly swinish, but their markings were odd. Dark hash marks the length of the pig ran down their tawny backs from nape to rump. They weren't the stripes of a zebra but the stylized markings she was used to seeing on the backs of chipmunks. Island life must have made for creative couplings.

Schlessinger's ATV was parked in the remains of a shed adjacent to the sty. The wide door lay on the ground several yards from the building. Long pointed hinges, rusted the color of dried blood, were attached to the wood.

"Looks like she's home," Anna said. "Shall we?"

"What'll we say we're here for?" Dijon asked, suddenly shy.

"Just being neighborly."

"You do the talking," he said, and climbed from the truck. He took a last glance in the side mirror. Still looking for the tick.

The biologist had to know they were there. Not more than a vehicle or two passed her place on any given day. And Anna and

Dijon had waited in their truck the requisite few minutes required when paying calls south of the Mason-Dixon line, but Marty hadn't come out on the porch to greet them. Schlessinger forced everyone to do things the hard way.

Walking several yards apart, Anna and Dijon approached the ratty dwelling as if John Dillinger waited within. Schlessinger had that effect on people.

"You knock," Dijon said. He was whispering.

Anna had to force herself not to follow suit. Rapping on the doorframe, she called: "Hi. Anybody home?"

"Yeah," came a sharp voice. Anna took that as an invitation and pulled the screen open.

Marty's home wasn't air-conditioned and, though her windows were open, the shades were all drawn. The air was close and heavy with innumerable odors, all of them vile: rotting animal parts, formaldehyde, grilled cheese, dirty laundry, coffee, mildew.

Anna covered her nose with her sleeve, then, realizing it was the height of rudeness, lowered it and tried to breathe normally.

Clad in a dingy brassiere and sweatpants cut off above the knee, a bottle of Nestea in one hand, the biologist sat in an overstuffed chair tucked back in a corner. Stuffing showed through on both the arms where the fabric was worn away. She didn't move when Anna and Dijon came in. Her eyes were narrowed against the light. She looked as if she dared either one of them to comment on her wardrobe or her lifestyle.

Blind from the sunlight, Anna saw everything, including the half-naked biologist, as mud brown. The house was kept worse than the pigsty. Every surface was covered in chunks of shell or bone. Papers littered the floor and were piled haphazardly among books and magazines. Trays and dissecting equipment, smelling as if they'd not been cleaned since the last adventure in marine pathology, were pushed to one side of a wooden table just outside the cooking area. Through a wide arch was a bedroom, also furnished in Early Junkyard, and the back door.

Schlessinger had her feet propped on a lobster trap with two one-by-twelves nailed across it. Open and unopened mail was piled on this makeshift coffee table. More spilled from the shelves of an unstable bookcase next to the front door.

"Hey, Marty," Anna said pleasantly.

Undone by the brassiere and the aging flesh it failed to adequately conceal, Dijon mumbled something and became instantly engrossed in reading the spines of the books.

"Are you lost?" Schlessinger asked. Her attitude was the only cool spot on the island. Sweat was starting and Anna felt it crawling through her hair.

"No. Just on patrol and thought we'd drop by."

Schlessinger took a swig of her tea and said nothing.

Anna's eyes were adjusting to the dimness. Marty's face was pale. Her blue eyes looked unnaturally large because the pupils had shrunk to pinpoints. Her feet, elevated on the coffee table, tapped the air rapidly as if keeping time to a hot jazz beat in her brain. Hostility radiated from her. She didn't seem frightened or nervous, just swelled with ambient anger, like a pit bull looking for somebody to chew on.

Clearly this wasn't going to be passed off as a social call. Interest piqued, Anna began her questions with a feeling akin to excitement. Maybe cops smelled emotional violence the way fire horses scented smoke: pulses quickened, hooves stamped to be in on the chase.

"We had a few minutes," Anna began, as if Marty had welcomed them with open arms, "and I thought I'd pop by and see if you remembered any more about those shots you heard."

"Shots?" Marty echoed, and Anna believed she'd genuinely forgotten. Then the biologist's face hardened with returning memory and she said, "What shots?" like a bad actor.

Anna outlined the roadside report Marty had given, just as if Schlessinger's question had been an honest one.

"That's not how I remember it," Marty said when Anna had finished. "I asked you if you had heard anything. You weren't listening." She took her feet from the lobster trap and leaned forward, elbows on knees. Tufts of white hair curled from her armpits. Without even wanting a peek, Anna was afforded full view of generous cleavage, all deep brown. Marty tanned in the nude. Schlessinger's eyes followed Anna's to her own chest, apparently noticing for the first time that she was only half dressed. The realization left her unmoved.

"Now that's settled, maybe you should get back to work. That's what you're here for, aren't you? Work? Or is that concept too complex for government employees?" The pale eyes fixed on Anna's face. Uneasiness began somewhere in the vicinity of her heart and was pumped out along her arteries like poison.

"Yeah," Anna said, rising from the edge of the chair where she'd perched. "Thanks for your time. We'd better get—"

"Hey," Dijon interrupted. "I used these things all through college. No wonder I got C's."

Both women had forgotten Dijon. While they conducted their tête-à-tête he'd continued his perusal of Schlessinger's bookshelves.

"What?" Anna said.

Dijon held up a letter, obviously mass-produced with lawyerly letterhead and a to-whom-it-may-concern look to it. "They recalled the Lewin electron microscopes. Major flaw. The readings are warped on about ten percent of them."

"Put. It. Down."

Schlessinger's voice was so deadly cold Anna backed a couple steps toward the door. The biologist was standing, her white hair, free of its braids, falling over her breasts like spiderwebs.

Frozen in his tracks, Dijon continued to hold on to the paper.

"You barge into my home"—Schlessinger stepped over the mess of the coffee table with the speed and grace of a young athlete— "you badger me with bullshit"—she stalked across the narrow room toward the paralyzed firefighter—"and you snoop through my mail." With that, she snatched the letter from Dijon's fingers. "Out. Get out. Out of my house."

Anna turned and fled, the unsubtle pounding of Dijon's boots half a step behind her.

"Holy shit, what was that?" Dijon asked when they'd completed their ignominious retreat and sat again in the sanctuary of the pumper truck. "She's crazy as a loon. Mrs. Ted Bundy. Like I'd want to read her frigging mail. It was laying there. Christ, a blind man would have been able to read it. What is her problem?" Dijon was babbling, creepy laughter mixed with his words.

"She was higher than a kite," Anna said.

"On Nestea? That's all it was. I've got a nose like a bloodhound."

"Not alcohol. Cocaine, maybe. Crack. Could be meth or just old-fashioned speed. Something. Her pupils were almost invisible and she was wired so tight she hummed."

"Damn," Dijon said. "I didn't think old people did drugs."

"Old people invented drugs."

"Witches and shit." Dijon shuddered.

Anna crossed herself. "Just in case you're right," she said when he looked surprised. She fired up the truck and backed out the fifty yards of driveway. There was room to turn around but she wasn't comfortable with her back to Marty Schlessinger.

Only once before had she had such a sense of malignancy. It was when she worked in Texas at Guadalupe Mountains National Park. She'd pulled over a blue sedan for speeding. The sun was high, the road public, and Anna well armed. The sedan had two occupants. The driver was a woman in her late thirties, weighing close to three hundred pounds, with small, very dark eyes. The passenger was a wisp of a woman somewhere between seventy-five and a thousand years old. Her eyes were the same beetle-back black.

As Anna approached the driver's-side door, she'd gotten a real bad feeling, as if some odor of pure evil poured out the open window. She didn't even ask the woman for her driver's license. All she said was: "Slow it down please," and, "Have a nice day." God knew what was in their trunk and Anna didn't want to.

Whether it was ESP or PMS, she never found out, but she'd never been sorry she turned tail and ran. Today she'd gotten a whiff of that same scent in Schlessinger's shack.

17

IGNORING the blaring headline, "POLICE CAPTURE SUSPECT IN BABY KILLING" shouting up from the paper on the table in front of him and nearly every other rag in the room, Frederick sat in the pub on Ninth Avenue waiting for Molly. In the three days he'd been in New York it had become "their" place. At least in his mind. Along with titillating excitement was a rising tide of self-contempt.

He'd found a reason to lunch with Dr. Pigeon Saturday, meet her for dinner Saturday night and brunch Sunday. Today he'd called the Chicago office pleading the flu and, to the tune of $220 a pop, reserved another couple of nights at the Parker Meridien. He'd worked harder than a roomful of hot new recruits tracking down the leads he had on the threatening letters.

In seventy-two hours he'd lost control. It started over drinks the first night. Sometime between salad and coffee at Saturday's lunch he'd slid over the edge. Love at first sight? He scoffed, making a small noise he passed off as a cough, not wanting to call attention to himself. As if talking to oneself were cause for comment in Manhattan. There was an apt definition of love at first sight floating around the E-mail circuit: when two horny but not particularly choosy people meet for the first time.

Chemistry? Biology? Maybe simple neurosis. Anna was getting too close—and at his ardent behest. Promises had been, if not made, certainly implied: letters written, laughter shared, a future together strongly hinted at. Was this just panic, this sudden infatuation that gripped him as if he were a boy of fifteen? And not merely over a Jean or a Janet or a Judy, but with Anna's sole and beloved sister.

Not aware he did it, Frederick buried his face in his hands, a parody of the tortured soul. Though he was aware logic—not to mention everyone he knew—would see this dramatic shift of affections as a psychological blip on his aging radar, in his heart there was a romantic arrogance demanding it be True Love.

He was ashamed. On some level he was aware of that. The telltale sign was secrecy. Like a lovesick coed, he wanted to talk about Molly but kept her name a mystery, even when he talked with his daughter, Candice.

Frederick lifted his head and took a long pull on his Scotch, then checked his reflection in the mirror over the fireplace to see if his histrionics had made his hair clownish. He downed the rest of his drink and signaled the waiter to bring him another.

Soon, he knew, the process of his exoneration would begin. Bit by bit he would change what needed changing. Each time he told himself the story he would come out looking a little cleaner. Frederick's judgments were cruel, damning. Years before, he'd learned how to keep them from turning and cutting him. After the process was complete and he was once again whole, there would be only a scar.

Anna would hate him.

Endangered Species

She was proud. She'd never let on. Like Mary Tyrone in *A Long Day's Journey into Night,* she would forgive but she would never forget. Respect would die. Touched by betrayal, memories would be transmuted from gold to lead.

With something akin to desperation, he pawed beneath the paper he'd been pretending to read to find the folder. When self-analysis came close to an unpleasant truth, Frederick turned his mind to his work. It was what he was good at.

None of the leads Molly provided him with went anywhere. James Lubbock, the man angling for disability, had sued and won, this time claiming a back injury. His hostile wife, Portia, had been happy to tell Frederick more than he'd ever wanted to know about the Lubbock union. The money, not surprisingly, was still not enough, but the Lubbocks were on to other scams and had forgotten Molly Pigeon's unprofitable sense of ethics.

Sheila Thomas, the not so gay divorcée, was head over heels in love with the lawyer who had gotten her such a lousy settlement, and quoted Dr. Pigeon the way the newly converted quote Jesus.

Thomas bored him. The page tired his eyes. His concentration splintered. Though his head didn't ache, Frederick rubbed his temples. His train of thought was derailing, Molly Pigeon, or his sudden attraction to her, filling his mind.

When emotional lightning strikes once, it's easily passed off as the real thing. By the third or fourth hit, the possibility it's a neurotic pattern and not love had to be considered.

There'd been a woman in California, a married woman, he'd made a fool of himself over. Much, he suspected later, to her great if adamantly denied delight. A lawyer in Oregon he'd thrown himself at, only to run like a scalded cat when she began to talk commitment. Then Anna: Anna had been slow and sure. Time had passed, they knew one another. It had been, he'd told himself, Real.

And it had been blown away over lunch by this new wind that

Molly breathed through his soul. Frederick laughed aloud, no longer concerned that others might stare. Maybe the Scotch was kicking in. "Soul" might be a little less specific a part of the anatomy than that which was acting as lightning rod. Intellectually, he knew Molly might be another symptom of whatever: a choice between the tedium of having and the endless potential in wanting. What saddened him was that he didn't give a damn.

Anna was fading. Just like that, dissipating into a vague fog the way a dream will on waking. A memory that ached only occasionally, like a bad tooth when he bit down on it.

The light Frederick saw himself in was rapidly becoming less than flattering. Forcing himself to sit up straight, he fixed his mind on the work before him.

Nancy Bradshaw, the smasher of lamps, had proven a bit more of a challenge, but the end result was no more promising. She'd moved to Vermont. Assuming correctly that someone as volatile as Molly had said Bradshaw was would have little patience with posted speed limits, Frederick had traced her through outstanding traffic tickets.

Miss Bradshaw's new employer told him she had been vacationing in Ireland for three weeks and wasn't due back till Thursday. That effectively let her out of the picture unless the plot was ridiculously convoluted, which was seldom the case.

Nancy Bradshaw's defection left Frederick fresh out of ideas. In his mind's eye he'd seen himself hauling the perpetrator off in chains after a suitably Schwarzeneggeresque rescue of the imperiled heroine. Failing that, he'd hoped to have a *fait accompli* to lay at Molly's feet.

The pub door opened and Dr. Pigeon walked in. Frederick saw her through a haze of Scotch and rose-colored glasses. Her suit was perfect, cool white linen with a salmon blouse of what was undoubtedly silk, soft to the touch. Despite the heat and the time of day, she looked fresh. In the moment that she paused, scanning the tables for his face, he noticed how pale she was, the slight crumpling of her features. Molly Pigeon looked afraid.

Frederick's first rush of feeling wasn't compassion, it was satisfaction: she needed him.

18

ANNA WAS FEELING bereft. The guys, including the usually ra-
tional Al, had gone jogging. Anna had escaped, though not un-
scathed. Gender and age had been touched upon with good-natured
ridicule. Rick had been closest to the mark; Anna wasn't so much
lazy as genetically skinny and congenitally opposed to profitless exertion. Dijon had offered to chase her with a girl-hating reptile of
some sort to give the exercise a point. Anna had declined his generous offer and slipped away to the ranger station for an uninterrupted
evening with AT&T.

Neither Molly nor Frederick was home.

She'd called both three times over the past hour and three times
had hung up without leaving a message. A message was a commitment. If she called again afterward it would prove she was desper-
ate, or worse, pathetic. The etiquette of phone tag had grown more
complex with the advent of the answering machine.

Endangered Species

Anna broke off another chunk of a Nestlé Crunch and chewed it slowly. Lights off, she sat in the chief ranger's office, her feet on his agonizingly tidy desk. It wasn't merely cleared of debris; everything was lined up in precise rows, like men on a chessboard: tape dispenser, stapler, electric pencil sharpener, each a careful two inches apart and square with the blotter. Lined up on the opposite side of the desk, the opponents faced off in the same two-inch formation: stamp dispenser, pencil holder, paper clip magnet.

Alone in the center of a rectangle of unmarked green, Anna's candy wrapper looked craven, a malicious act of vandalism. Finishing the last of the chocolate, she folded the leftover paper neatly and set it two inches from the pencil sharpener.

Squat and colorless in a faint spill of moonlight, the phone sat like a malevolent toad at the edge of the desk. Years of isolation, of distance from family, friends, and lovers, had created in Anna a love/hate relationship with telephones. They were often her only contact with the people she cared about, and at the same time not only pointed up how fragile that connection was but, she was sure, in some arcane way managed to warp the very relationships it made possible.

Perhaps the plastic contained some dormant virus that came to life when pressed long enough against the warmth of human flesh. Once revived it would be in a unique position to penetrate the brain orally or aurally, causing a chemical imbalance that brought on obsessive calls to empty houses, fights with sweethearts, and long silences costing more than ten cents a minute.

The clock over the door insisted it was just nine p.m. She would wait another half hour. If nobody was home by then she'd give it up as a lost cause.

Tilting back in Norman's chair, she cast about for something with which to amuse herself. Tidy men were not particularly entertaining, no flotsam or jetsam to fiddle about in. Normal men, men who didn't clean out their wallets but transferred the whole mess every few years when a new wallet appeared under the Christmas tree, carried their history in their back pockets.

Desks served the same purpose, if on a more businesslike plane. Hills Dutton, Anna's district ranger in Mesa Verde, had a magnificent desk. His professional past could be read in geological strata as one worked down through the accumulated canyons of paper.

Hull was either indescribably tedious or had something to hide. Anna clicked on the desk lamp. Just passing the time, she jiggled the drawers. They'd been locked. A sense of challenge crept into her idle snooping. Rangers were the most trusting creatures on the planet. They habitually left wads of money, candy, hollow-point bullets, house keys, car keys, and confiscated alcohol littered around the office. Amazingly enough, with the exception of the candy, none of it ever disappeared.

The only people Anna had known to lock their desks—all two of them—both turned out to be chronic litigators, always embroiled in one lawsuit or another against the NPS. Their secret-squirrel tendencies sprang from paranoia that the information they'd gathered was actually worth something. With a renewed sense of purpose, she searched all the standard key hiding places but came up empty-handed.

A quick search of Renee's drawers proved more satisfying. A key tagged "Norman's Desk" lay prominently in the pencil tray. Like any task, once undertaken the search took on a life of its own, becoming important by the simple fact it had proven difficult. Anna carried the key back to the chief ranger's office with a pleasant feeling of accomplishment.

After all her suspicious surmisings and stealthy machinations, the prize wasn't worth the game. The desk's interior was as sterile as the surface. Files were carefully marked and each folder contained what it advertised. Stationery and envelopes filled wooden racks. In the center drawer, the one usually doomed to catch life's precious litter, there was precious little.

Anna flipped through Hull's desk calendar. On the day of the airplane crash he'd written, "Slattery, Stafford meadow—10 a.m.," as if he'd intended to keep the appointment. The other entries were what might be found in any day planner, notes of meetings and times. "Cheryl" was dotted here and there and "Ellen" made a number of appearances along with personal hieroglyphics—PU and PO, asterisks and underlinings. Cheryl and Ellen, Anna knew from the general scuttlebutt, were Hull's wife and daughter.

The only thing of interest was an envelope with a handwritten address and a Pennsylvania postmark. In for a penny, in for a pound, Anna thought, and shook out a single sheet of paper covered with the same loopy writing as on the envelope, and a snapshot.

"Dear Norm, I don't think the change has done Ellen—"

Anna refolded the paper and stuffed it back into the envelope unread. The letter was clearly personal and there were limits to the rules she would break without probable cause. Somehow looking at a picture was different. Pictures, by their nature, seemed in the public domain. The photograph was of a young girl. Anna would have guessed she was eighteen or nineteen but loopy letters in pencil read, "Ellen on her 13th birthday." Norman's only daughter. There was a family resemblance in the watery blue eyes and narrow, squared-off chin. Heavy makeup and what looked to be very expensive, if tasteless, teen-tart clothes hugged the chunky frame of a body not yet out of childhood.

Engrossed as she was in meddling, when the phone rang Anna reacted so violently she cracked her kneecap on the underside of the desk. The pain was intense but would be short-lived. Breathing deeply and counting backward from twenty, she glowered at the phone as if it had attacked once and might try it again. By the fourth ring she'd recovered and decided to answer it. There wasn't a chance in hell it was for her but at this time of night it was possibly urgent.

"Cumberland Island National Seashore," she said.

"Yeah. Hey. This is Charley Riggs. Who am I talking to?"

Anna was momentarily starstruck. Riggs was the Southeast's regional director. Silently she closed and locked the desk drawer lest he sense her transgressions. "Anna Pigeon, presuppression, fire crew," she answered formally.

"Drought's pretty bad there, Anna?"

She recognized the use of her name for what it was—a politician's trick—but she didn't resent it. Government agencies were highly political. It was, if not good, at least expedient to have a politician in charge.

Dutifully she prattled on about what they'd been doing on Cumberland, until Riggs signaled her to stop with an indrawn breath. "Well, hey, Anna, that's terrific—"

Anna rolled her eyes and wished she had another chocolate bar.

"Is Norm around? He said he might be working late tonight."

No, Anna told him, and could she take a message? Well, hey, Anna, she could.

"I just got out of a backcountry management retreat in Big Cypress and need to talk to him about the airplane wreck. Tell him to give me a call as soon as he gets in tomorrow, would you, Anna?"

"Yes, sir." She wrote the message down on a notepad placed precisely two inches from the phone. A stray thought jarred her as she watched the regional director's words draining from her pen. "Hey, Charley, how long was that retreat?" Maybe in her next life she'd go into politics.

"Five days. No fax, no phone, no running water. We got a lot accomplished but I'm getting too old to sleep on the ground."

Anna laughed politely and hung up.

The thirty minutes she'd designated had passed. She had permission to try Molly and Frederick again, but she didn't reach for the telephone.

For some reason Norman Hull had lied. He'd not been on the phone with the regional director when the ill-fated Beechcraft left the ground. Anna had little doubt that if she nosed around she'd find that Renee was under the impression Hull had received the lifesaving call on the mainland and the woman in St. Marys believed just the opposite. Two lies, each tailored to support the other. Deceit of that caliber usually sprang from a more than casual motivation.

She unlocked the chief ranger's desk. Having been handed probable cause on the proverbial silver platter, she took out the handwritten letter and read it through. It was family news. From the context, she gathered it was from a sister of Norman's. Ellen had been sent to Pennsylvania for a visit with the cousins, had proven to be a major pain in the butt, and was being put on the next bus back to Georgia. Anna refolded the letter carefully and placed it precisely where she'd found it. A man as anal-retentive as Norman Hull would notice any disruption.

Again she went through the files, this time with greater interest. The bottom right-hand drawer held confidential personnel folders— the record of each employee, including letters of commendation and censures, their personal information, and the numbers that Americans carry from cradle to grave.

Anna pulled Slattery Hammond's folder from the neat arrangement of hanging files. There wasn't much to it; he'd worked for the parks only sporadically, and as he was strictly seasonal, the service didn't much care how he made ends meet in the off months.

She looked through the sheets quickly. All of it was standard— memos, evaluations. When she reached the page containing his personal data, she stopped. Hammond's life insurance was handled by a company in Washington State. Dead he was worth $125,000.

Dead by accident on the job: $250,000. Double indemnity. Given what Slattery did for a living, that codicil wasn't surprising. Pilots tended to believe the fool killer would call them home long before they had a chance to die peacefully in bed; a romantic notion and most often wrong. The insurance companies bet on that. This time they lost. Anna scanned the rest of the document to see who had won. The beneficiary was Linda Hammond, a resident of Hope, Canada, wife of the deceased. Should she predecease him the moneys would be put in trust for his son, Dylan.

Hammond was married. Had Lynette known? Certainly no one else seemed aware of it. Would a self-professed Christian commit murder to revenge a broken heart and a damaged ego? Absolutely. Human beings weren't linear creatures, cut from one piece of cloth. They routinely harbored moral dichotomies that would short-circuit the most sophisticated robot. And most did it effortlessly. Maybe Lynette was not only Christian but Catholic. Fornication, murder, a quick confession, and she'd be back on the Lord's good side.

Nothing in Mitch Hanson's history called attention to itself and Anna went on to Lynette's. Her only claim to fame was having started out in the Park Service as a GS-1. Anna hadn't known that low a designation existed. The stamp on her pay envelopes must have been worth nearly as much as the check itself.

There was no folder on Schlessinger. She was attached to the NPS but not of it. Turtle-research funding was obtained from other sources. Whoever was head of Resource Management kept the files on the marine biologist.

Renee, Norman's secretary, had held more jobs than looked good on a résumé and hadn't the sense to disguise that fact. She'd been with Cumberland Island National Seashore for fifteen months. A personal best.

Dot and Mona were not represented. As VIPs, the chief ranger would not be in charge of them.

Todd Belfore's folder provided a couple of tidbits of information. He had health insurance through the NPS but no life. After the baby was born they might have bought some. Now it was too late. Of greater interest was the fact that he'd been a district ranger in North Cascades. He had transferred to Cumberland on a lateral— no promotion, no raise in pay. Though Cumberland had undeniable charms, one could argue it was a step down in status. North Cascades was considerably bigger and had that certain cachet unique to the western wilderness parks.

Todd and Slattery had been in Washington, working for the NPS, at the same time. Within several months of one another, they'd moved clear across the continent, where they died together in a planned plane wreck. It was possible they'd had dealings in the past, that someone wanted both of them dead and found a way to kill two birds with a single actuator rod.

Meticulously, Anna replaced the files and double-checked to see all was as it should be. Having closed and locked the desk, she pulled the sleeve of her fire shirt down over her hand and polished her fingerprints from the drawers and the key. Not for a moment did she think Norman would have the desk dusted for prints. She was just killing time.

Ten o'clock rolled around and she tried her phone calls again. Molly didn't answer. Frederick's machine in Chicago picked up and Anna left a message. No face lost—she wouldn't call again tonight.

From habit she rattled the doors and windows before she let herself out of the ranger station. At Mesa Verde it was what the late ranger did each night.

The moon was high, the air warm and sweet with the scent of mimosa and the tang of the sea. Tonight Anna wasn't drawn into the southern dream; tonight it felt cloying, unclean, as if the air clung to her skin, clogged her throat and mind. The sandblasting of lies and counterlies, drug addiction, clinical depression, heat, broken hearts, and ticks was beginning to get to her and she longed for the cool arid mesa she'd come to think of as home.

And, she admitted reluctantly, she was lonely. Before Frederick, lonely was a state of mind she'd grown accustomed to, risen above, and finally, come to find peace in. Now there was a hollow place behind her breastbone when he didn't answer the phone.

Absurd, considering that two nights before, this very intimacy gave her the heebie-jeebies. When next she talked to Molly she'd ask her for a magic incantation, a rite where the word "codependent" figured prominently. Smiling at the idea of modern witchdoctoring, she felt better.

Tabby was still up when Anna got back to Plum Orchard, and the good feeling evaporated. Grief was wrapped around her, blurring her features. Color was gone from her skin and even her hair looked closer to gray than blond. She'd lost weight, the flesh melted from her face and bones showing through in a death mask. Thin and brittle-looking, her arms and legs poked out around her belly. She more closely resembled a refugee on the six o'clock news than a pregnant American.

Anna made a pot of hot tea—a concept she'd picked up from reading dead English authors—and arranged it prettily on a tray with two ornate teacups and a plate of eternally fresh Ho Hos.

Tabby was in the tiny living room sitting on one end of the sofa where Anna slept. Maternity fashions don't lend themselves well to mourning. The bright red and black horizontal stripes on Tabby's smock made her look even more ethereal in contrast. The lights were off but for a lamp on an end table. Its forty watts didn't make a dent in the darkness shrouding Tabby Belfore.

Near the entrance to the hall, scattered across the hardwood floor between two cheap new area rugs, were brown pebbles the size of marbles: deer scat.

Endangered Species

"Where are Dot and Mona?" Anna asked as she set the tray on the coffee table and began pouring. The VIPs had the evening shift, as they termed it, and had promised to sit with Tabby. This enforced lack of privacy would have driven Anna insane; the constant pressure of eyes on her skin, voices in her ears. With Tabby it had been deemed necessary, at least for a while.

Tabby sat immobile, her hands folded on what was left of her lap. If she heard Anna, she lacked the energy to respond. Anna repeated the question and forced a cup of Grandma's Tummy Mint into the woman's lax fingers.

"Gone home," Tabby replied in a monotone.

"When?"

Tabby shook her head. The question was too complex.

"Drink your tea," Anna ordered, and watched as the girl sipped mechanically. The bandages were torn from her forearm and the puncture wounds scratched open. Spots of blood had smeared but Anna could read the letters they formed: *T O D* and what was probably part of another *D*. Todd. Anna remembered girls in high school making crude tattoos of their boyfriends' initials with sewing needles and ink from fountain pens. Tabby seemed so painfully young. Compassion fought with irritation in Anna's breast.

Tabby Belfore was beyond the palliative effects of either, so Anna opted for shock therapy. "You and Todd knew Slattery. You met him when you worked in North Cascades," she stated flatly. "What was between Todd and Slattery?"

Tabby blinked several times, then focused on Anna's face. Her mouth opened, closed, and opened again but no words came. Tears filled her eyes and spilled down her drawn cheeks. Tabby put the teacup and saucer down on the table and pushed the tears into her hair with the heels of her hands. A string of pronouns dribbled brokenly from her lips: "I . . . He . . . We . . ." Her hands fell to her belly, clutching it protectively. More tears, unchecked this time, then she said in a whisper Anna had to strain to hear, "No. No. No. I can't."

Anna was casting about for words of reassurance or a mild form of blackmail she might use to pry out the woman's secrets, when Tabby stood abruptly. With her altered center of gravity, the movement threatened to overbalance her and Anna sprang to her feet to steady her.

"Leave me alone!" Tabby choked on the words.

Anna let go and watched till she closed the bedroom door between them.

Sitting back down, she eyed the untouched Ho Hos suspiciously. Real chocolate was never that shiny, that compliant. Sipping tea, she tried to let the frustrations of the day drift away and failed. Unable to reach anyone by phone or in person, her sense of isolation had grown more acute.

"Fuck you all," she grumbled after a while, and crawled into her sleeping bag. *Lost Horizons* was where she'd left it on the end table. She couldn't remember how many times she'd read it, three or four. Old stories were the best stories.

19

TIRED AS SHE WAS, sleep wasn't going to happen. As with all insomniacs, Anna's body refused to fit into the contours of her couch. On firelines she'd slept the sleep of the innocent on crude beds hacked from earth and stone. It was the mind-prodding that kept her awake. Constantly rearranging limbs and pillows was merely a distraction.

Perhaps she was getting too old to be a field ranger. On her next birthday she'd be forty-two. Maybe it was time to move into management. In the climate of equal opportunity that pervaded the NPS it shouldn't be too difficult. She was qualified and she was female—worth a lot of points on somebody's register.

Theoretically, hiring was color- and gender-blind but managers were evaluated on how many "minority" people they brought on board. Once Anna had confronted a personnel officer on this seeming dichotomy. The message was clear: There Were Ways. Last names. Voices on the phone. Accents. And if worse came to worst, word would filter down from higher up disclosing a coveted "quality" of a certain applicant.

Anna had no compunction whatsoever about cashing in on this fortuitous turn of events, she just didn't care for management. She didn't like to lead and she wasn't much of a follower. Fieldwork suited her. Till her body betrayed her, she'd go on doing it. It was the transience that was beginning to weigh heavily.

Frederick Stanton came to mind—not cloaked in a fantasy of home and hearth but surrounded by an ambiguity that brought with it a sense of malaise. Lately he'd pressed her to move to Chicago; make a geographical if not an emotional commitment. Anna was cynical enough to wonder if love and hope spawned his desire or if he too felt a little lost, in need of an anchor. They'd known each other long enough that heartthrobbing romance was no longer a factor. That was the problem; without the narcotic of being "in love" the pain of change was too great.

Anna opened her eyes and let thoughts of Frederick go. The top pane of the window behind the sofa framed a moon, dime-sized and distorted. In Georgia even the moonlight was warm.

Striving for physical if not spiritual ease, she wriggled out of her pajamas and dumped them on the floor. When a guest, she tried to sleep clothed lest she offend her host's delicate sensibilities, but it was absurd, like suits for swimming, panty hose under trousers, and underwear with dresses.

Rearranging her sleeping bag against the draft from the air conditioner, she contemplated life on the island. Though motorboats daily ferried visitors to and from St. Marys and cars traveled the inland lanes and residents came and went by plane, the island fostered a sense of separateness—a people different as the animals were different—altered by the unique demands of the environment. Like mountaintops and desert strongholds, human beings sought out islands for a lot of reasons. Some washed ashore, cast up by the storms of their lives. Some were running, some hiding, some chasing a dream.

And, on Cumberland, some were committing murder.

Rather generous of them, Anna thought. It gave her something to do at night besides count sheep. An image of Tabby, widowed and scared in the other room, flashed through her mind trailing a comet's tail of guilt. She refused to grab on. "I didn't kill the guy, for Chrissake," she whispered to the shadows lace and moonlight painted across her chest, and began ruminating on possible murderers.

Todd Belfore and Slattery Hammond were dead, one or both targeted for murder. Todd and Slattery had known each other at North Cascades and Tabby wouldn't—couldn't?—say why.

Anna heard Tabby say Todd would leave her. Slattery flew drug interdiction, was suing Alice Utterback and wooing Lynette. Lynette thought Hammond loved her and wanted to marry her. Hammond had a wife. An Austrian had a ruined leg from a shotgun shell. Schlessinger had a habit and an attitude and lied about hearing the shot. Mitch Hanson was a goldbrick and a double-dipper, roundly disliked by Schlessinger. According to Dijon, he had been inordinately cheerful, pottering around the crash site cracking jokes before the corpses were cold. A blond and a brunette were featured on Slattery's wall and three used tampons inhabited his freezer.

Separating the clues from the flotsam of human idiosyncrasy was a bitch. How, if at all, Hanson, Schlessinger, and the shotgun wound fit into the Beechcraft sabotage, Anna couldn't fathom.

She resurrected her dead pillow and settled into a new position. Fragments of ideas continued to jump docilely over her mental fence: baby alligators hooked on bologna sandwiches, plastic bags in the outboards, volunteers with orphaned fawns, separated actuator rods, chipmunk piglets. Still sleep eluded her. Giving it up as a lost cause, she threw back the sleeping bag and padded out through the kitchen, snatching up a dish towel to protect her bare behind from the splintered steps that led down from the apartment.

In her current role as incubator, Tabby kept the air conditioner on high and Anna welcomed the moist warmth of the night. With the heat came a twinge behind her left ear. She fingered the diminishing lump. She'd forgotten to include that incident in her inventory of significant happenings. She wrote it off to brain damage and revised her mental list. An unknown assailant, hiding like a bogeyman in Hammond's bedroom closet, had bashed her over the head with the butt of a twelve-gauge shotgun.

List complete, Anna's mind became empty. The exquisite balm of the South wrapped around her. Though she loved the high deserts, felt renewed by the harsh vistas of the West, there was no denying the sultry pleasures of Georgia. Breathing deep and evenly, she closed her eyes to better let the night soothe her.

Through the music of frogs came the shattering crunch of shod feet on gravel. Peace was canceled. With the noise a sudden realization came to Anna: she was naked, or in local vernacular, buck nekkid. Night crawlers seldom separated art from pornography. All at once she felt vulnerable; a wrinkling white-skinned woman on a peeling white-painted step.

For the past quarter of an hour she'd sat without moving. If she continued as still, the odds were good she would remain undetected. Slowing her breaths, aware now of the myriad sounds of a body sustaining life, she froze.

Reacting to a seldom-used instinct, her bare skin was prickling. Sensations were clear and sustained in their detail. Rough wood pressed into her buttocks with a mild ache, warning her not to sit too long, not to compromise mobility. The soles of her feet stuck damply to the step below, her own sweat providing traction should it be needed. A breath of air touched her left cheek, teasing the fine guard hairs.

Undoubtedly there was a time in man's evolution when these things combined to warn and prepare, to help survive. Years indoors, feet on concrete, had forced the intellect to try and compensate for the sensate and Anna found the alarms of her body to be a distraction. Fervently she wished she'd dressed. Even a T-shirt and panties would have helped.

The crunching stopped. In the thick silence she became aware that the song of the frogs had stopped as well. A minute ticked by, cataloguing the discomforts of a body in stasis. Reveling in her captive state, a mosquito whined bloodthirsty threats in her ear.

A frog peeped, then another. They'd gotten over their panic. Anna had not. Without the crunch she couldn't locate the interloper. Perched naked as a jaybird on the top step, it was possible that she'd been seen and the prowler had fled in unseemly—and unflattering—haste.

The theory died as it was born: no racket of retreating steps. Left behind was the disquieting knowledge that in the inky shadows on the drive someone stood watching or waiting or both.

A shriek of metal ripped the darkness. Anna's senses were stretched, a web of nerves. They caught the knife-edged noise in their silken strands and Anna twitched as if she'd been struck. The urge to leap up and bolt indoors quivered through her. She breathed shallowly, like a woman having contractions, till the terror passed. All this transpired in a Jack Robinson minute and she found herself thinking of Einstein, wondering if there was an untapped internal correlation to his theory of relativity.

With the passage of knee-jerk panic, the source of the noise became clear. It was the familiar rasp of the passenger door on the pumper truck being forced open over a rusted wrinkle acquired in a past encounter with another vehicle. A soft thump followed; the seat back being pulled forward, hitting the steering wheel.

Anna stared until her eyes watered. She'd parked the truck beneath a venerable magnolia. Light-reflecting waxy leaves kept the midnight beneath safe from the moon and her prying eyes.

Faint rustlings and bumpings painted a picture on the black screen of her vision. Someone was rummaging through the truck, stirring the rusted mess of tools behind the seat, rearranging water bottles and insect repellent cans.

Dressed, Anna would have confronted the intruder and gotten at least an ID. Sans clothes she felt too vulnerable. She was annoyed to note the protective magic with which modern women imbued a layer of cotton. Surely, unencumbered by flapping fabric, one could fight harder, run faster, escape with more agility. Not to mention the possibility of distraction to one's opponent. Still, she didn't move.

Heavy and low, the sound of ripping rose through the darkness. Seats being slashed. Nothing else in the aging vehicle was made of fabric.

Metal squawked again, announcing the end of the assault on the truck's interior. Anna watched the sharp edges of the shadows to see if the night visitor would expose himself. A moment of silence reigned, the crunch of gravel began, then faded in the direction opposite the mansion. After a moment it stopped and was replaced by the delicate crushing of leaves. Whoever it was had left the drive, keeping to the shadows. Within moments the faint sound of leaves underfoot was gone as well.

To be on the safe side, Anna waited another long minute before easing to her feet and slinking back indoors.

Armored in NoMex and armed with a flashlight, she emerged five minutes later and clattered down the wooden stairs. Attempts at stealth would have been fruitless given her footwear, but Anna wasn't interested in sneaking. Knife-wielding night creepers were best scared far away before any investigation was undertaken.

Following the selective eye of the flashlight, she traced the marauder's progress through the cab of the truck. The seat was again upright, the glove compartment gutted, its eclectic innards strewn across the floor. A motley collection of tools and litter had been raked from beneath the bench seat. Chaos being its usual state, the clutter behind the seat looked much as it always did.

On the back of the seat on the driver's side, approximately where a small woman's shoulder blades would rest, were two deep slashes, short and vertical, the way old medical texts illustrated the proper cut for sucking poison from a pit viper's bite. The neat slits struck Anna as a violent form of shorthand.

The content of the message was unclear but the blind malice made her scalp crawl. A twinge was frightened from the tender spot behind her ear. This was personal, though for the life of her Anna couldn't guess why.

20

BY THE TIME Anna climbed the stairs once more, dawn was drowning the stars over the Atlantic. She showered, dressed again, and made coffee to create the illusion she'd enjoyed a night's sleep. A report would have to be filed on the vandalism done to the truck's upholstery, but no one would care. It wasn't as if the slashes lowered the relic's trade-in value. By the light of day she would do a more comprehensive inventory, but she was sure nothing had been stolen. There wasn't anything of value in the truck to steal: no car phone, no radar detector, not even an AM radio.

There was an outside chance the vandalism was random. Even paradisiacal islands had their share of malcontents. Or the attack could have been politically motivated, aimed at fire policy, the National Park Service, or even the United States government in general. The aftershocks of Waco, Texas, the Oklahoma bombing, and assorted lesser calamities were being continually resuscitated by the hot breath of publicity-hungry groups. Mostly down-at-the-heel men with too many guns and too few brains who'd taken it upon themselves to tarnish the memory of the American militia by embracing the name and not the ideal.

Random vandalism appealed most strongly to Anna. Mindless, without purpose, it struck and was gone. Like lightning, it often did strike the same place twice, but one entertained the reassuring delusion that it would not. Organized political vandalism had its merits as well. The caricatured macho of feral militias was a villain Anna loved to hate. She'd been surprised a spate of movies and television shows hadn't sprung up around the concept. Hollywood had been in search of a serviceable evil since the end of the Cold War.

Restoring order to the toolbox and the disemboweled glove compartment, she turned these temptations over in her mind. In the end she had to abandon both. Plum Orchard was too isolated for violence of the random variety, particularly the sort that customarily fell to disgruntled teens. Political groups tended to leave a calling card—those that were literate, Anna in all prejudice felt obliged to add. That left her where she'd begun, with the uncomfortable knowledge that it was universal malice, malice toward fire crew in general or her in particular.

Near the gravel drive a portable water tank of rubber held up by metal piping was kept full. The tap ran slowly but steadily, and over time, would fill the man-made reservoir. As part of her morning's chores, Anna unrolled and spliced together two hundred feet of cloth hose and ran the line from the tank by the spigot to one of the two tanks situated on the open green area where helicopters could get access. Evaporation sucked up nearly a fifth of a tank every twelve hours. Topping them daily was one of the duties of the fire crews.

That done, she tested her patience and the muscles in her right shoulder pull-starting a Mark IV portable pump. When it was up and running, smashing the tranquillity of the morning and hardening the hose with moving water, she took shelter under an oak and mapped out a plan for the day.

Dijon would be with her again. He was up for pretty nearly anything that broke the monotony and was not yet old enough to worry about getting caught. As long as they covered the island at least once, Guy wouldn't much care how they spent their time. On an island eighteen miles long and three wide it wasn't as if they were going to wander off. Their job was mainly to be around just in case.

Both tanks were topped. Absently, she followed the hose back toward the pump. Sweat beaded on her upper lip and her shirt stuck to her back between her shoulder blades. It was 6:35 in the morning.

Parked behind the pumper truck was a battered orange Volkswagen bug, the chassis turned to burnt metal lace around fenders and door from the incursion of rust. The din of the Mark IV had covered the sound of its arrival and, lost in her thoughts, Anna had not seen it. Inattention made her nervous. Dreamers were easy marks. Muggers, rapists, pickpockets, could cut them out of a crowd. Purse snatchers made a living off of them. The frank delirium of a southern August carried away sharpness on zephyrs of scented air, softened reality with a brush of Spanish moss. The South was famous for vivid eccentricity. Anna could see why. Anger flared in the heat; reality became tenuous.

The Volkswagen belonged to Lynette. A cross dangled from the rearview mirror and the Virgin Mary rode in regal splendor on the narrow dash. Brochures of Cumberland Island and field guides to the Southeast were scattered over the back seat and the floor. A box of files filled the passenger side.

It was Tuesday. Probably Lynette's lieu days were midweek. Anna hoped so. It would be a relief to know there was someone to sit with Tabby. She regained the stairs and climbed to the apartment. The door was open but the screen closed and latched. From within came the murmur of prayers. A faint clicking accompanied them and at first Anna thought someone was telling the rosary through her fingers, but the sound was coming from a flat green insect the size of her thumbnail clinging to the screen.

"God can forgive anything." Lynette's low voice trickled out through the wire mesh. She spoke in a monotone, the intensity of her personality rather than changes in pitch adding color to her words.

"Not this he can't. Not me," Tabby returned. Her voice was choked with tears. Her voice was always choked with tears. Though Anna understood and even empathized, it was beginning to get on her nerves. Sliding down, fanny on the steps, back against the railing, she settled in for some unabashed eavesdropping. If she was caught she could pretend she simply didn't want to disturb their devotions.

What a prince, Anna thought of herself dryly. Tilting her head back against an upright, she closed her eyes the better to listen.

"That's kind of arrogant in a way," Lynette said gently. "It's like saying, 'My sin is *so magnificent* not even God can forgive it.' "

"You don't understand," wailed the eternally drowned voice of the widow.

"Try me."

Anna's ears pricked up, or felt as if they did, but the hoped-for revelation was not forthcoming. Tabby cried out, "I can't!" and dissolved again.

Anna liked Tabby well enough but the woman had a bit of the invertebrate about her. It was hard to picture her under an airplane, her pregnant belly thrust up like a fecund shark fin, unscrewing the panel to the actuator arm. Nor could she picture her offing her husband.

What about offing Slattery?

Twisted soap opera plots gamboled through Anna's brain. The baby was Hammond's, Hammond was going to tell Todd. Tabby had been jilted by Hammond. Or jilted by Todd. Todd and Hammond were secret lovers. Everybody was related and separated at birth.

She laughed and pulled herself up from the warm wood. Prayer service was over. She wanted to make herself a peanut butter and jelly sandwich and get on with the day. Banging on the screen she yelled, "Somebody let me in."

Lynette unlocked the screen. Round without in any way being fat, her face was a soft oval, eyes wise and blue. In the 1930s she would have been considered a beauty. Lynette was in her late twenties and, if one saw with the eyes only, she looked it. Fine lines were forming around her mouth, and her forehead was creased from years of raising her eyebrows in concerned interest. To the other senses, Lynette registered as considerably younger. Innocence, trust, a wit that was sharp but never cutting, gave her a childlike quality that somehow missed being treacly.

"Off today?" Anna asked, to have something to say.

Lynette shook her head, her permed curls quivering charmingly. "I don't go on till ten-thirty."

Anna nodded. Boatloads of tourists from St. Marys would be arriving. Lynette gave them a tour of the splendid ruin of Dungeness mansion, the impressive bones of what had been one of the premier homes in the 1880s. Fire and time had reduced it to memories evoked by steps, stone patios, partial walls, and cold fireplaces. For Anna's money it was as inspiring in its own way as the ruins of the Anasazi in Mesa Verde National Park. Dungeness had yet to acquire the patina of centuries but already it spoke of a unique human history, a nostalgia for better days.

"Tabby is making herself sick over something," Lynette said as Anna spread a meticulously even layer of peanut butter on a slice of raisin bread.

"Other than death and impending birth, what do you figure?"

Lynette flicked up a bit of peanut butter from the side of the jar and put it in her mouth. Her fingers were tapered, almost pointy, her teeth small and even. "A fight?" she hazarded. "That would be a drag, wouldn't it? To tell your sweetie he's a real son of a bitch and then have him die thinking you meant it? Even if you did?"

"A drag," Anna agreed. "Was Todd a son of a bitch?"

"Who ever knows, but I don't think so. He seemed sweet and sweet on his wife. No eyeballing-the-naked-ladies sort of thing."

"Does Tabby have anyplace to go? The NPS isn't going to toss her out on her ear anytime soon, but she can't stay here forever. Whoever replaces Todd is going to need a place to live."

"Tabby's from money," Lynette told her. "Old lumber money out of Seattle. Her folks will take care of her and the baby."

"Now would be a good time to start," Anna said sourly, and wriggled her PB&J into a sandwich bag stolen from the Belfores' cupboard.

"They're somewhere in the Far East on a Stanford University tour to see primitive peoples." Lynette spoke as if she were reading the words from a snooty brochure. "Incommunicado for another week or so. Then they'll come."

Relief hit Anna harder than she would have expected. Being even peripherally responsible for the weeping, gestating girl was tiring. "At least she'll be financially secure." The meager lunch complete, she turned her back to the counter so she could watch Lynette. "Both widows are," she said. Nothing but polite confusion crossed Lynette's smooth face. "Slattery's wife will be taken care of by his life insurance."

"Slattery wasn't married," Lynette said. It didn't sound as if she believed it, at least not a hundred percent.

"A wife and a little boy in Washington State." Anna knew she was being cruel. She needed the truth and didn't know any other way to get at it. Fleetingly, she wondered if biologists testing pain response in animals forgave their actions with the same rationale.

"A little boy?" Lynette echoed, her voice small and stunned.

She might have suspected Slattery was married but Anna was willing to bet the farm on the fact that he had a child was new information. Lynette turned and left the kitchen without a word.

Anna had delivered the blow, made the world a slightly more miserable place, and gotten virtually nothing for it but the sense that maybe, just maybe, Lynette was lying about not knowing Hammond had a wife. Not much to pin a murder indictment on.

Heat and the dusty jolt of the truck brought on a wave of fatigue. Had there been a time she could stay awake all night, eat cold pizza for breakfast, and bound out to take on a new day? She remembered there had. Of course she did; one of the wonderful things about youth was attaining a respectable distance from it. In retrospect, all things became possible: endurance greater, grades improved, romance polished to a fine shine.

Slowing the truck to a crawl, she began a mental list of things to do. It was not yet eight a.m. The office would be empty. There'd be a phone she could use and the necessary privacy to make the most of it. Frieda would have had time to cull, charm, and weasel information from all available sources. Between the computer, the phone, and her wide-ranging, if eclectic, contacts, there was little she couldn't ferret out of a federal agency. With luck she would have gotten the dirt on Hammond's suit against Utterback and his connection with the Belfores.

This murder was not unlike the Deep South itself, intricate, slow-moving, relationships unclear, each aspect draped or veiled by something else. Facts married to their first cousins producing information that was slightly out of whack.

A silver pickup appeared in the lane ahead and politely pulled to the side so Anna would have room to pass. Peeking from behind palmetto fronds, the little truck looked almost coy and Anna smiled as she slowed to squeeze by. Dot was driving, wild gray curls half-captured beneath a red ball cap, hands in the ten and two position. Anna glimpsed Mona nearly hidden behind a stack of antiquated turtle files. The fawn was on her lap, his head out the open window like a dog's.

As the pumper truck edged by, both women waved and both grimaced identical grimaces as they pointed to the pile of paperwork between them. On Mesa Verde there were two trees that had joined together late in life. Pushed over by a storm, they became one rather than die. Anna wondered how many years it took human beings to grow together like that.

When she reached the fire dorm she found Dijon balancing on a four-by-four that had been laid on the ground to delineate parking lot from "lawn." A subtle distinction the sand did not recognize.

"Where the hell have you been?" he asked as the truck rolled to a stop. Before she could answer, had she indeed intended to, he tossed his yellow pack into the truck bed and was jerking open the damaged door. "You're late," he accused, and looked at his watch. "Taxpayers' dollars at work and all that. At my salary you've just upped the gross national debt by a buck and a quarter."

The other truck was gone, as was the ATV. Dijon had been left all alone. Entertaining himself was not his strong suit. To make amends, Anna told him of the vandalism of the truck. She omitted her nudity, preferring to seem a coward than a prude.

Dijon indulged in a favorite law enforcement pastime: Monday morning quarterbacking. A minute or so after he'd finished telling Anna what he would have done—and with the guaranteed success rate of hindsight—he settled into a brief silence, fidgeted, then moved on. "So, what have we got on the agenda for today, Mata?"

Anna raised an eyebrow.

"Like in Hari. Mrs. Sherlock."

Anna nodded to keep him from further analogy. "Mata" was better for the self-image than "Marple" and he was headed in that direction. "Ranger station," she said. "I'm going to call Frieda. See if she's turned up anything more. Maybe you could call what's her name, that girl—"

"*Woman.*"

"*Woman*—of tender years—who works the Visitors' Center on St. Marys."

"The pudgy blonde or the lanky one with the nice set of . . ."

Anna counted to three waiting for the inevitable punch line.

". . . teeth?"

"Whoever." Though she'd probably seen and talked to each of them at least once in passing, Anna had noticed neither of the young women. "Which one was on duty on Thursday morning?"

"Blond pudgy," Dijon answered without hesitation. Hormones had temporarily given him an almost superhuman memory for gender details.

"Okay. Her. Call and find out what the deal is with Hull. She's got the idea he was on the phone with the regional office. Not true. Maybe she'll tell us something we can use."

"Right. And why am I supposed to be calling Ms. Georgia Peach?"

"I don't know. Boy meets girl. Boy calls girl. Be creative."

A silence stumbled between them that was so unlike Dijon that Anna looked over at him. "What?" she demanded.

"She's white. Don't look so offended. White's not innately disgusting. But this is Georgia. PC ain't happening. What if Daddy's a good ol' boy with a shotgun and a sheet?"

Anna hadn't thought of that. "Pretend you're Rick," she said after a moment.

Dijon laughed. "You're frigging weird, you know that?"

He'd do it. "Good," Anna said, and having rolled one fender into the single scrap of shade the lot afforded, she turned off the ignition.

Frieda had been busy. In her mind's eye, Anna saw a map of the United States lit up by telephone calls as was sometimes depicted in old movies. The lawsuit against Alice Utterback was more than just a nuisance suit. Slattery had a strong case. According to Frieda, in Alice's zealousness to bring women pilots on board, she'd pulled strings in personnel. When the job descriptions were published, they were explicit almost down to bra size, making it virtually impossible for any but the four targeted women to obtain the positions.

Utterback was working with the knowledge of her superiors. The United States Forest Service had come under contempt of court a few years earlier for failing to hire women in sufficient numbers. Alice had been instructed to see it didn't happen a second time. But though the Forest Service would presumably cover any financial losses incurred had Hammond pressed his suit, Utterback would have paid for it with her career. Every public relations disaster required a sacrificial lamb. Sometimes the lambs were innocent and sometimes not, but the chosen took the hit for the rest of the flock.

Alice Utterback didn't strike Anna as the type to go like the proverbial to the slaughter. Neither did she seem the sort to commit murder to avoid it. There was that about the woman that led one to believe she would fight her battles in the open and by Queensberry rules.

The dispatcher had less luck in her inquiry into the Belfores' connection with Slattery Hammond. North Cascades was a big park and wild; the districts didn't overlap socially as much as in smaller parks. Hammond had flown out of Redmond and lived in Hope, Canada. Todd was district ranger in the Cascades. The Belfores kept an apartment in Hope, where Tabby spent most of her time. Evidently Tabby was frightened by the wildness and isolation of the Cascades. Todd came to town on his weekends. There was not even a whisper of anything between Mrs. Belfore and the pilot. In a town the size of Hope, unless Tabby was infinitely more resourceful than Anna gave her credit for, there would have been gossip had the two been seen together.

Frieda had tracked down the particulars on Hammond's marriage. They were separated and had been since the birth of their son two years before. Mrs. Hammond had filed for divorce on several occasions but never went through with it. According to what Frieda had been able to gather, she wasn't terribly broken up over her husband's demise. Disposing of the inconvenient remains and getting her hands on the insurance money were the goals an ungenerous co-worker attributed to her. There wasn't as much judgment in that as the bare words implied, Frieda told Anna. The Hammond marriage had not been crafted inside the pearly gates. For the past twenty-three months, the Mrs. had a restraining order against Slattery and was fighting a dogged court battle to keep him from unsupervised visitations with his son. Near as Frieda could tell, the restraining order wasn't a onetime, divorce-spawned action. Hammond had two previous orders filed against him in the past three years. With the exception of the last, all had been withdrawn.

"That might explain the police visits to his apartment," Anna said.

"That would be my guess," Frieda replied.

Anna thanked her for her work, and after a minute or two of pleasantries, she rang off.

"Anything?" she asked as Dijon let himself into the chief ranger's office and sprawled in the straight-backed visitor's chair by the door.

"God, I'm good," he said cheerfully. "Rick's got a date for the day after we get off this desert isle, and if he follows my lead, he might even get lucky."

"He's married," Anna said flatly.

Dijon made an exaggerated face depicting horror. "Well, gee, that changes *everything*."

So much for family values. It was a moot point anyway. As soon as their tour of duty was over, they'd all be flown out of Georgia on the first available plane.

"What I got," Dijon said, and ticked the points off on fingers so free of calluses that Anna guessed to date he'd done little but read and write about fieldwork, "our Norman was on the mainland at the time the plane went down. Ms. Pudge saw him come off the dock in St. Marys around nine-thirty that morning. After the news of the crash reached him he came back by helicopter. It was the chief his own self who told her he'd been on the phone with whosis in the regional office at the magical moment he was supposed to be rendezvousing with Hammond. Ms. P. said Hull told her he'd taken the call over here. It didn't seem to bother her that he'd have to break half a dozen laws of physics to pull that off. I didn't push her, her being blond and all. Didn't want to tax her brain."

Anna nodded. "Hull told Renee he'd taken the call in St. Marys." Briefly she pondered in silence. "Lies are good," she said at last. "Gives us something to go on."

"So we work it out backwards," Dijon said, as they motored sedately up the lane toward the north end of the island, burning petrol and being available. "The Beechcraft is tied down in an open field in the dead center of the island for two and a half days and two nights. Sometime during that—what?—sixty-two hours, person or persons unknown sabotage it. That pretty much counts everybody in. No one that's not in jail can account for that long a stretch of time. Anybody off the island?"

"Not that I know of," Anna replied. "Easy enough to check."

"Screw alibis?"

"Pretty much."

"Witnesses?"

"Maybe," Anna granted. "Dot and Mona live right off the end of the airstrip. They may have seen something. If they did, I can't imagine they wouldn't have come forward. There's no such thing as a secret on this island. I doubt there's a soul who doesn't know the plane was wrecked on purpose. All we've managed to keep under wraps is how that sabotage was accomplished."

"Maybe the old ladies don't know it could've happened over a three-day period. Maybe they only thought about who was hanging around an hour or two before the plane took off," Dijon said.

"Worth a stop," Anna conceded.

Dijon whooped. "Hot on the trail," he said, and: "Can I interview the old broads? I thought of 'em."

Inwardly, Anna groaned. At least she thought it was inward until Dijon said: "Stop making noises like a buffalo in heat. I won't fu— foul up. Jesus. Give me a break."

Anna said nothing. She was cursing the buddy system a paucity of vehicles had saddled them with.

"Come on," Dijon wheedled with transparent charm. "Old ladies respond well to godlike young men. Take you for example."

Anna laughed. "I'll watch and learn."

The meadow near Stafford House and Dot and Mona's cottage was set on a neck of the island not much more than a mile wide. The field was good-sized; enough space to house a dirt airstrip with room on either end to climb clear of the ubiquitous live oaks and pines. Ribbons of shell-and-sand cut the meadow from the surrounding woods. Stafford was at the eastern edge of the airstrip. An eerie spot called appropriately the Chimneys bordered it to the north where a settlement of slave cabins had been burned to the ground after the Civil War, leaving a grove of brick-and-mortar monuments: chimneys designed to harness fire and left as a testament to its final victory. To the east, pines cut off the view of the Atlantic. Left over from the days they were grown for harvest, the trees marched away in orderly rows.

Dijon and Anna emerged on the southern edge of the rough rectangle to find the place bustling—or as close to a bustle as the heat would allow. The blue truck Alice Utterback had been given was parked beside the airstrip. Three figures clad in the pale green of the United States Forest Service were creeping along, heads down, eight or ten feet apart. Along the shaded tabby wall at Stafford, a peanut gallery had formed. Guy was there, spread over his ATV like a blanket. Lynette Wagner sat on the wall, her legs dangling down near the crew boss's shoulders. She was laughing at something Guy said. In the unguarded moment, his face glowed with pride and pleasure. His defenses down, joy stripped his worn face of years. Anna was surprised she hadn't noticed before. He was sweet on Lynette. But then everybody was sweet on Lynette; Marshall had gotten lost in the crowd. A scrawny band of gold on the left hand was not proof against the girl's charms. Anna made no judgment calls. Given life in the nineties, it was a wonder anyone's marriage survived. For a brief moment, one that passed so quickly she didn't even need to hold herself accountable for it, Anna was glad she'd been widowed. The untimely death of her beloved Zachary had left her heart broken but her dreams intact. For Anna Pigeon and Juliet Capulet True Love would always exist.

Oblivious of fire ants and the ubiquitous ticks, Dot and Mona sat nearby on the ground, Flicka butting first one, then the other in successful bids for attention.

"Quite a crowd," Anna remarked as she and Dijon pulled over into the shade.

"Best show in town," Guy drawled. "Where are the two of you headed? Al and Rick have gone north along the beach." It wasn't really a question. Guy had a laid-back management style. He was merely checking his troop deployment.

"We thought we'd do the same but stay inland," Anna answered dutifully.

"Sounds good." He loosed a stream of tobacco juice politely downwind of the ladies.

"Where's Tabby?" Anna asked Lynette.

"At the apartment. Marty's helping her pack up some of Todd's stuff."

Dijon made face; a mime depicting comedic surprise. The helpful domestic scene struck Anna as unlikely too but she didn't say anything.

A minute or two was ticked off by the incessant clack of cicadas.

"I wish something would break," Guy said. "Rain, wind, fire, any damn thing. I swear ain't nothing changed since we got here but me. I'm a damn sight older, I can tell you that."

"You don't want wind or rain," Lynette teased him. "You want fire. You're such an old fire horse, you'll die and go to hell and think you've landed in heaven."

"If it's burnin' I'll put it out," Guy bragged inoffensively, and won another laugh from the young interpretive ranger.

"Have you guys worked together before?" Anna asked on impulse.

"Three project fires," Guy said. "Okefenokee once, and Big Cypress twice. Lynette here's one of the best fire dispatchers in the business."

Anna filed that bit of information away. Because they were transitory, not connected to the island in any visceral sense, she hadn't considered anyone on fire crew to be a suspect in the sabotage of the Beechcraft. Naive: all worlds were small worlds, circling their own tiny suns and evolving their own forms of intelligent life. "Did you ever work a fire with Slattery Hammond?" she asked abruptly.

As heavy-handed as the question was, Guy didn't seem alarmed by it. Either he was ready and had rehearsed his answer or the idea of his being connected to the man's death was as far from his mind as it had been from Anna's.

"I don't think I have. He may've flown bird dog on some fire I worked out west. That'd make sense if he's been in the business long. Pilots don't mix with grunts. Liable to get those snazzy orange flight suits dirty."

Anna sighed. If every man who'd ever fought fire or had a crush on Lynette Wagner had to be questioned, her life's work was cut out for her. Time to narrow down the possibilities at least by one.

"Be back in a minute," she said to no one in particular, and wandered across the dusty road toward the airstrip. The instant she stepped out of the shade, the sun slapped across her shoulders, pressing hot fabric against her skin. Plowing through the miasma of heat, eyes to the ground, Wayne and Shorty were showing the effects of it. Both had sweat pouring from beneath their caps and Shorty's face was a lovely heatstroke red.

Alice Utterback was as cool and unperturbed as ever. Anna fell in step beside her and stared at the ground just as if she knew what they were looking for.

"*Clews,* dontcha know, *clews,*" Alice volunteered without being asked. "The odds are a zillion to one we'll turn up anything useful, but this has got to be the place our buddy detached the actuator rod. I figured we'd better give it the once-over on principle. Who knows, maybe the guy dropped his wallet."

"Why do you say 'guy'?"

"Just a figure of speech. An equal-opportunity guy."

It wasn't much of an opening but Anna decided to push her way in. "Speaking of which, rumor has it Hammond had a case filed against you."

"Among others."

Silence, embarrassed on Anna's part, fell between them. "Could it have ruined your career?" she asked finally.

Alice stopped and looked up. The patch on her lower lip that she'd been fingering during the investigation of the wreck had blossomed into the promised cold sore. "Probably the sun," she said, as if she felt Anna's eyes on the unsightly blister. "It tends to bring the horrid things out." Mirrored aviator's glasses obscured Utterback's eyes and Anna was uncomfortably aware she could be staring at her, reading her face.

"Hammond ruin my career?" Utterback said thoughtfully. "He'd've had to hurry. I retire next January. I've got a ranch to run. Could he have left a bad taste in my mouth if he'd gotten as ugly as I think he had the potential to? Sure. Nobody likes to lose. I wouldn't wish death on anybody, but if somebody had to go, I can't say as I'm sorry it was Slattery Hammond."

"Besides"—she smiled and returned to her survey of the sere grasses beneath their feet—"I've got an alibi. Me and Shorty and Wayne are the only ones who weren't on the island when the Beech was tampered with."

"Am I that transparent?"

"Like glass. I could have sent some flunky down to do it. There are people for that," Alice offered.

"That would be thoughtful. You were my favorite suspect. I liked the vigilante justice of it."

"Me kill Hammond . . . I must say there's an appeal there. Killing a government employee has got to be less complicated than firing one. Nah," she concluded after a moment's deliberation. "I don't think I could bring myself to screw up a perfectly good airplane. Were I to embark on a life of crime, I'd do it for cash, not revenge. I'd hire only women and only those of a certain age—somewhere between forty and ninety—women with sedans, credit cards, and salon-styled hair. Drugs, white slavery, gunrunning—you name it—we could take over the market. Nobody would suspect us of a thing. Least of all of having initiative and a brain in our heads."

"It's something to think about if the ranching doesn't work out," Anna said.

"Mmm. I did get some info back from the lab," Alice went on. "Not that it sheds any light on the matter. They analyzed the contents of the plastic bags we found in the outboard fuel tanks. Now here's a question for a trained investigator: They were sandwich bags. What do you figure they were found to have contained at one time?"

"Sandwiches?"

"On the nose." Alice tapped the end of that feature with a stubby finger. "Traces of a substance that was probably mayonnaise and a bread crumb or two."

"Weird." If silence tokens agreement, Alice Utterback agreed. "Your end of the investigation is about finished," Anna said. "How much longer will you be staying on?"

"Not much if I'm reading the signs right. I was over to the Hulls' for dinner last night. Unspoken rule: Lesser brass has greater brass home to dinner the first and last nights of detail. Maybe he knows something I don't. Nice wife. His kid's a piece of work, though."

"Alice!"

The women looked up. It was Shorty who'd hollered. Looking apoplectic from the heat, he was mopping his brow with a blue handkerchief. "We about done?"

"All done," Alice said. "We're beating our heads against a brick wall here."

Alice stuck out her hand to Anna. "In case I don't see you again," she explained. "It's been good working with you."

"Likewise." Anna shook hands briefly, feeling less ridiculous than usual performing the ritual.

"I'm sorry I didn't kill Slattery."

"That's all right," Anna said generously. "It was just a thought."

Plum Orchard was on their way to the north end. Anna said she needed to stop and pick up something she'd forgotten, but it was just an excuse to check on Tabby.

The widow was comfortably ensconced on the sofa under the icy blast of the air conditioner, directing the marine biologist's efforts. Marty, dressed this time in khaki shorts and a black tank top, her white braids loose around her face, was boxing books. Both seemed sane, sober, and constructively occupied, so Anna left them to it.

"Maybe Schlessinger's got a heart of gold under all that dead meat," Dijon said when they'd left.

Anna just grunted. She wasn't in the mood to give anyone the benefit of the doubt.

"At least she wasn't fucked up," Dijon said, and: "Excuse my French."

Anna nodded an acceptance of the apology.

"You sure she was last time?" Dijon asked.

"I'm sure. But what the hell? It was her day off."

"Want to take another look at the wreck?" he asked hopefully. Anna shook her head. "Be that way," he said. Pulling a Walkman from his yellow pack, he effectively entered another dimension.

Anna was glad to be left alone with her thoughts, though they were scarcely entertaining. Vague disquiet was the underlying theme regardless of whether she contemplated her personal life or the tangled web somebody was weaving on Cumberland Island. If the knot on her head and the slashes behind her shoulder blades were any indication, a web she'd stumbled into.

When Anna was in her teens and Molly in her early twenties, they'd been addicted to true crime stories and would while away long car trips trying to plan the perfect murder. There was always a hitch. With this one Anna couldn't find that hitch. The murder weapon—the separated actuator rod—could have been put in place at any time over a sixty-two-hour period. The Beech was tied down in the open in a relatively secluded field. Practically everybody had opportunity. Two men were killed, so motive was stretched thin. Means was a little narrower. Not everyone was possessed of the know-how to disable a twin-engine airplane. But given enough effort, most information is available. There was pathetically little to go on. Norman Hull had called in the county sheriff and he and a local FBI agent had visited the site, but nothing had come of it. They could add nothing to what Utterback had already discovered.

Had the deaths been the end of it, Anna suspected whoever had done it would get off scot-free. Statistics were in their favor. A majority of murders went unsolved. The attack on herself and the truck suggested removing Hammond and Belfore hadn't proven the final solution the perpetrator had hoped for. Somewhere on the island was a loose end. If she could find it before it was tied off, she would find her man—or woman, she reminded herself. Equal opportunity.

A break in the flickering tunnel of trees brought her out of her reverie. Mitch Hanson's grader was pulled off the road, the driver nowhere in sight. Concentrating on the configurations of clearing and trees, Anna reoriented herself. They'd been on the road a quarter of an hour or more. That would put them just north of where the plane went in, east of the loggerheads' nesting area. She stopped the truck, tapped Dijon, and pointed. When he removed his headset, she said: "Hanson's grader."

"So? Maybe he's taking a piss."

"Want to mess with him?"

She didn't have to ask twice. Hey, it was something to do. Having completed the ritual toxification of boots and trouser cuffs against social-climbing ticks, they walked into the woods on the opposite side of the road from where the grader was parked. This far north, the road ran along the edge of navigable land. To the west, hidden by dense undergrowth and trees, Brickhill River meandered through the salt marshes that formed the western half of Cumberland Island National Seashore. Eastward, toward open ocean, were two miles of maritime woods, a designated wilderness area uncut by roads or trails.

Pleasurably aware of the soft duff beneath her feet and the simple joy of her own body's motion, Anna walked with Dijon under the canopy of live oaks. They walked without talking. It lent the exercise a needed touch of tension, and if they actually hoped to catch Hanson in a more compromising activity than merely zipping his fly, it would help to come upon him unawares.

Much of the way was blocked by undergrowth. They could have pushed through the copses had they chosen to, but a knowledge of the creatures dwelling therein dissuaded them. In addition to the Golden Orb spiders, the protected thickets were rich with the scurrying of rodents and hence a favorite haunt of the island's rattlesnake population. Anna didn't mind the enforced circuitousness of the route. If Mitch had half the cunning and sloth his fellows attributed to him, he would also have followed the path of least resistance.

Temperatures climbed to close to a hundred degrees. Even their slow and easy progress brought on a sweat. The trickle under her hair felt like the creep of six-legged beasties and, for the first time in years, Anna contemplated cutting her hair off. The heat, the work, and the washing were getting to be less of a trade-off for the occasional compliment. For a second or two she dared hope vanity, like puberty, was something one eventually outgrew.

"Here's our pal," Dijon whispered. Anna stopped at his shoulder and listened to the crunch of approaching footsteps. They'd been walking for twenty minutes. At a rough estimate it would put them just less than a mile into the woods. No great distance in the scheme of things, but a trifle ambitious for a man of Hanson's age and girth.

"Long ways to go for a pee." Dijon echoed her thoughts.

The whisper of crushed leaves that heralded the man's approach gave way to the man himself. He pushed clear of the grabby fronds of a palmetto and started across the clearing in their general direction.

"Gun," Anna murmured. Dijon tensed beside her. It was the magic word at FLETC, the Federal Law Enforcement Training Center, located an hour or so away in Glynco, Georgia.

"Got it," Dijon breathed.

Hanson carried a Marlin 30-30 on his right shoulder, his elbow crooked familiarly over the stock. Maybe Marty hadn't been lying about hearing the shot that wounded the Austrian, but simply suffered confusion as to when and how many. This would be about where Shawna, the Austrian's girlfriend, had placed them—between Lake Whitney and the road. A 30-30 wouldn't have done as much damage as a shotgun but most hunters owned and used more than one weapon.

Slung over Hanson's left shoulder was a burlap bag filled with lumps. Poking out from the tied-up neck of the sack was the handle of a small folding shovel.

"Saint Nick's evil twin," Dijon said, and Anna smiled.

In a moment Hanson would see them. To dispel the idea they were lurking and spying, Anna stepped out of the brush and hollered. Mitch looked up at the sound of his name. What could have been furtiveness—or just the alarm of being hailed when it wasn't expected—flickered across his face. A suffusing of bonhomie replaced it almost instantaneously. He changed course, stumping toward them waggling the fingers of the hand balancing the rifle as if seeing them was the biggest treat he could imagine.

"Nice gun," Dijon said.

"Rifle," Hanson amended. "This is my rifle, this is my gun." He gestured toward his crotch. "One is for fighting, one is for fun."

Ex-military. Anna had forgotten.

"Hunting?" Dijon asked.

Hanson raised both palms—a neat trick considering his burdens—in mock surrender. "You got me. Don't shoot." He winked at Anna. "You can cuff me though, if you promise to frisk me afterward."

Their lack of response didn't dampen his spirits one whit. "I've got a permit to shoot pigs," he said. "They eat pygmy oaks. One of Norman's pet-endangered weeds. Don't noise it about. You'll have every bleeding heart in the country screaming we're murdering Wilbur."

Dijon looked confused.

"Like Babe but older," Anna explained.

Dijon shook his head disgustedly. "What's the younger generation coming to?" he said for her.

"Any luck?" Anna asked, eyeing the sack he carried. There were no signs of blood on the burlap and the lumps were distinctly unpiglike.

"Not today," he said.

"What have you got in the bag?" she asked casually.

Hanson laid a finger alongside his nose and winked in a practiced manner. "Things to make little girls ask questions."

Anna winced. "You want I should kill him?" Dijon asked.

"Yes please. What do you have in the bag?" she asked again.

"For me to know and you to find out," he said. Again the wink. Anna was beginning to think it was a habitual disarmament technique. It set her teeth on edge.

"Can I look?"

"Got a warrant?" Hanson lost none of his good humor but the joke was over. He wasn't going to share the secrets of the sack and there wasn't a damn thing Anna could do about it. Not legally, anyway. "Where y'all headed?" Hanson's bright blue eyes flitted from Dijon's face to Anna's. "You're a ways back. Spot a smoke?"

"No such luck," Anna said. "I'm beginning to think Cumberland is fireproof."

"Hot day for taking in the sights," Hanson pressed. "But I'd take it as an honor to show you around."

For whatever reason, he was determined not to leave them on their own in what was apparently his neck of the woods.

"Anna had to pee," Dijon announced.

Mitch raised his eyebrows. A mile-and-a-half round trip was a long ways to find a ladies' room.

"Shy bladder," Anna said, and: "If you'll excuse me . . ." She walked purposefully in the direction the sack-wielding Hanson had come from. Behind her she heard a brief splutter but there was no way he could follow. Ladies' rooms, even when comprised of palmetto and pine, were sacrosanct.

What she expected to find—especially in the few minutes a respectable bathroom visit allowed—she wasn't sure. Something in the combination of gun, sack, shovel, and winks made her want to take a look at where Hanson had been, before he had a chance to retrace his steps and erase any tracks he might have left behind.

Walking rapidly, she scanned the earth and surrounding foliage for any signs of activity. Hanson had made no effort to disguise his trail; there was no need to. In the deep and shifting leaf litter, so dry that puffs of dust settled over footprints minutes after they were made, Davy Crockett would have had trouble tracking a moose.

Anna followed her earlier theory of taking the easy way. After five minutes of searching she was rewarded by signs of fresh digging around the base of a pine. A patch of ground a foot square and several inches deep had been disturbed, the soil overturned onto the needles. The edges of the dig were square and clean, marks smooth and six to seven inches across: the size of the spade on a folding shovel. Three feet from the first dig was a second. This one was almost hidden under the rotting remnants of a fungus-encrusted log. Beyond the crumbling trunk lay a broken piece of one-by-twelve. Partway up, on the bark of the pine, was a cut. Fresh sap oozed from a gash an inch wide and half an inch deep where a chip had been hacked out.

"Did you fall in?" A hearty voice pushed through the tangle of woods between Anna and the men.

She ignored it. Running, she zigzagged through live oaks and skirted undergrowth, looking for other disturbances to the ground or the surrounding plant life. Thirty yards further in, just where the way opened through a daunting wall of palmetto, she found the marks of another dig, this one long and narrow, a trench four feet long, three inches wide, and about that deep.

"Are you okay?" came a bluff shout. Dijon had failed to curb Hanson's rescue—or survival—instincts any longer. The two men were shouting after her. Soon they would follow if they hadn't already started.

Anna didn't want Mitch to know what she'd found until she figured out just what it was she *had* found. Running as swiftly and lightly as she could in the heavy boots, she made her way back past the place she'd first discovered turned earth. Rebuckling her belt as if she'd recently doffed her trousers, she emerged in the path of Dijon and Mitch only slightly out of breath.

"We were coming in to pull you out," Mitch said jovially.

The routinely scatological turn of his humor left Anna unamused. Coy crudities, like bad puns, created a conversational vacuum. Luckily little was required of her. A noncommittal grunt seemed to fill the bill and the three of them walked out of the woods, Hanson's chatter clearing the way of all indigenous fauna.

Back at their vehicles, the maintenance man carefully stowed his burlap sack and rifle in a locking toolbox behind the seat of the grader. Then, elbows on the tailgate of the pumper truck, settled in to chat till the rains came. A subtle form of filibuster. Hanson had no intention of leaving the area till Anna and Dijon were safely on their way.

There was nothing for it but to concede. Mouthing the usual platitudes—"Better get back to work. Be seeing you. Take it easy"— Anna climbed behind the wheel. In the side-view mirror she noted that Hanson watched them till a turn in the road took them from view.

"So what did you find?" Dijon asked.

"Digging," Anna said succinctly.

Dijon thought about it for a moment. "Morels?"

"Not mushroom country or morel season. Besides, there's no law against gathering mushrooms. He would have shown them to us."

"I knew that. Just testing you."

"Ginseng?" Anna ventured. Ginseng root was highly prized by the Chinese and had a growing consumer base among herbalists in the United States. At present market value it sold for about four hundred dollars a pound. The humble root was reputed to cure most ailments and serve as a preventative for the rest. Digging ginseng in the wildlands of the South and East had been a means of income for generations of locals. The national parks were dedicated to protecting the fast-vanishing plant, but because of the wealth of plants and the easy access, park lands were favorite targets of the gatherers.

"Does ginseng grow on Cumberland?" Anna asked.

"Soil's wrong," Dijon replied. "And pygmy oaks don't grow within two thousand miles. Only place I know of is on the coast of California. Whatever Hanson was hunting, it wasn't pigs."

21

"Is EVERYBODY here frigging weird or is it just me?" Dijon asked.

"It's just you," Anna reassured him.

They'd left Mitch standing guard over his grader, passed Al and Rick near The Settlement—a cluster of houses, including Marty's, that were still privately owned—and driven out to Lake Whitney to eat their sandwiches. It was a bit of a challenge to drive to Whitney. A road existed but it was rough at best and guaranteed to mire a heavy vehicle like the pumper axle-deep in sand at worst. Today they'd avoided the worst. Adopting Rick's beach-driving techniques, Anna had roared through the soft spots like a bat out of hell to the accompaniment of colorful rodeo-inspired epithets from Dijon Smith.

Now they sat in the perfect white sand of a dune that was creeping inland, threatening the little freshwater lake's existence.

"What did you get from Dot and Mona?" Anna asked.

"Zip. Or more accurately, too much zip. Pretty nearly everybody, including us, had been around that meadow in the last three days. Near as the old ladies can remember, the only people who actually messed with the airplane itself were Hammond of course, Norman Hull—"

"Makes sense, especially since he flew with the guy off and on."

"Todd on his security rounds, and Hanson with the gas truck."

"Everybody and nobody."

"Back where we started?"

"Back where we started," Anna agreed. "Want to go for a walk?"

"Do I have a choice?" Dijon pushed himself to his feet and stuffed the remainder of his lunch into his yellow pack.

Circumnavigating the lake to the northwest, Anna led the way. The edges of Whitney were rich in plant life, glistening cattails and lily pads the size of dinner plates. The maritime forest pushed back from its shores to higher, drier land. There was little cover. Letting the heat dictate a languid pace, Anna walked slowly. A beautiful young alligator, not more than four feet long and still bearing the yellow hash marks of childhood on its tail, stared emotionlessly at them from a cool lair of mud beneath the water grasses.

"Hey," Anna said, pointing, "company."

"God, I hate those things."

"You're going to hurt his feelings," Anna warned.

"They don't have feelings," Dijon returned. "That's what makes them so creepy."

Looking at the dead reptilian eyes, Anna tended to agree but chose not to give Dijon the satisfaction. "You never know."

"Let's just hope he prefers white meat," Dijon said, and made her laugh by giving the alligator an absurdly wide berth.

On the opposite side of the lake, Anna found what she was looking for: Shawna and Guenther's camp. The two were responsible, if not law-abiding, campers. They'd had a small fire but they'd doused the embers with water, then stirred the ashes and doused it again in the prescribed manner. No litter marred the sand and Anna found the remains of the fire only by careful searching. They'd taken the time to bury the asn and spread the charred wood so those next on the site could enjoy the illusion of pristine discovery.

"Well, that was edifying," Dijon said sarcastically when she had finished. "More than worth an alligator-infested hike in the noonday sun. What are we looking for, exactly?"

"Beats me." Anna shoved her ball cap back and scratched at the roots of her hair where sweat and sand combined to torment her scalp. As hot as it was and as destructive to the skin, she loved the feel of the sun on her face. For a moment she reveled in the sybaritic blast before replacing her hat. "Guenther getting shot the same day as the crash; he and Shawna camping out here where nobody's supposed to be not more than a mile or two from where the plane went in. It seems too cozy for coincidence."

"Coincidence is cozy where cozy ain't supposed to be."

Anna didn't dignify that with a reply.

"Ooh, I get it, international conspiracy," Dijon said. "He's Austrian, she's what . . . Cheyenne?"

"Navajo, I think," Anna said absently.

"Mafia drug cartels," Dijon said with certainty. "Exporting ceremonial peyote. Hey, lookit here." He jumped back from, then sneaked back up upon, a mark he found in the soft soil at the lake's edge. "Snake track. Jesus, I'd hate to meet up with him in a dark alley."

They had continued around Lake Whitney to the south rather than retrace their steps. Anna caught up to him. A stick-straight trail cut from the waterline across the sand to disappear into a rugged stand of high grass. She squatted down on her heels and examined the mark. It wasn't a snake's trail or the drag of an alligator's tail. The line was drawn too straight to have been made by any animal other than man.

"Hopscotch? I dare you to cross this line?" Dijon suggested when she voiced her thoughts.

"Your guess is as good as mine."

Once into the coarse grasses, the line disappeared. After a few minutes' search, they chalked it up to one more question in the growing catalogue of unanswered questions they'd been compiling.

Depressed, Tabby had retired early, barely finding the strength to murmur a goodnight in Anna's direction. After the vandalism to her truck Anna had taken note of the fact that Tabby had access to the fire escape from her bedroom window by way of a narrow wooden catwalk that ran the length of the apartment. Because of the woman's condition and her emotional frailty, it hadn't crossed Anna's mind till too late that Tabby could well have been the vandal. In her blind assumption of Mrs. Belfore's helplessness, she hadn't bothered to check her room to see if she was still in bed. Just to be fair, Anna put a mental mark in her sleuth's debit column but didn't take it very seriously. Her belief in Tabby's ineptitude was rooted too deep.

She returned the tepid goodnight and was glad to see the door close behind the girl. The day's adventures had earned her a headache and two ticks, one lodged at the nape of her neck, the other under the waistband of her trousers. Even a head-to-toe inspection with a hand mirror and combing her hair with a fine-toothed comb didn't rid her of the feeling that bloodsucking insects were crawling all over her.

Near nine o'clock, with Tabby presumably safe in bed, it was dark enough for decency. She drove the three miles down through the Chimneys and out to the beach. Floating on the tide, she began at last to feel free of wildlife.

Away from home, the daily routines of life, and the people she'd come to know over the years she'd been at Mesa Verde, time came unhinged. A peculiar sense of having always been gone, of all other lives being just a memory of a dream, closed over her. Over others as well, near as she could tell. This disconnection allowed for behaviors that wouldn't be considered in the familiar matrix of real life. Without the checks and balances provided by friends, family, and the eyes of one's neighbors, risks were taken and rules forgotten. Anna wondered what would happen to Flicka when Dot and Mona left the island, if Guy was having—or hoping for—an affair with Lynette, what Slattery Hammond had done to deserve a restraining order, why he kept used tampons in his freezer.

Letting the waves nudge her toward shore, she touched bottom with her hands and felt her body bob sweetly on the sea. A stray statistic about a majority of shark attacks occurring in less than three feet of water rose in her mind. She banished it.

Eye level with the night beach, she let the disparate images of the past several days flutter through her brain in no particular order: Guenther, Shawna, the shotgun wound, Hanson, the shovel, the sack, the digs, Lake Whitney, the camp, the ruler-straight snake trail, the basement of Stafford, the fawn, the fertilizer, the weed killer. The pieces came together; a pattern once seen suddenly so obvious she cursed herself for a fool.

She rolled over on her back. Sand being pulled from beneath her fanny and heels gave a disconcerting sense of movement. Full of stars, the surface of the sea glowed. On the horizon there was the hint of a moon yet to rise.

If she was right—and she was certain she was—there wasn't anyone she dared tell. With the exception of Alice Utterback, no one on the island was off the hook as a suspect. Should she do "the right thing" and confide her suspicions to the local sheriff, his first call would be to Chief Ranger Hull. Anna wasn't convinced that would be such a good idea.

Sliding from the Atlantic on elbows and knees, much as she imagined the first sea beast had made its way onto land, she enjoyed a last wave across her backside, then stood to let the kind night air dry her skin. Hair slimed down her back nearly to bra strap level— had she not metaphorically burned that offensive garment two decades back. Water, feeling clammy now that she'd become a creature of the land, trickled from the sodden tresses. Again she thought of scissors, the freedom of shorn locks.

The moon pushed out of the ocean and laid a silver trail to shore. As the desert does, sea and sand collected each scrap of illumination, reflecting it back from shell, water, and salt till the air and land seemed alight from within. The magic of the night began working on Anna. Returning to the couch in the Belfores' grief-soaked apartment, exposing her flesh to the artificially chilled air, struck her as repugnant. This was a night to wander alone like a wolf or an owl, seeing, not seen, becoming part of darkness and shifting light. A deeply buried maxim of training warned her to wake Dijon, Al, Rick, or Guy and bring them along on her quest. Two things argued against it. Firstly, the adventure should take less than an hour. She had no intention of endangering herself. The second and more compelling argument was that she had been so much in the society of human beings, eating, drinking, and sleeping with the sound of others' breathing in her ears, that to give up her solitude was too great a sacrifice.

Dressed in running shoes, the baggy NoMex trousers, and a T-shirt she'd bought to commemorate the Jackknife fire before it had become national news, Anna drove slowly north along the oceanfront. She kept the vehicle near the water's edge where the sand was firm. Not only would any itinerant loggerheads be safe from her wheels, but her tire tracks would be erased by the incoming tide. The moonlight was such that she drove without headlights. In the directionless light the landscape was painted in a thousand shades of gray, silver, and gold.

When she'd first come to Cumberland all the beach looked the same; fourteen miles of white sand with dunes west and water east. The sameness had struck her as tedious. After countless forays up and down this stretch of coast, she'd come to know its ways: where the alligators liked to come down to fish the tide pools, the paths that snaked out from the woods where cabins or camps once existed, dunes that hid lush interdune meadows where horses and deer grazed, a rise of earth held in place by oat grass where the loggerheads had laid their eggs and where every day Marty Schlessinger checked her precious treasure, each hoard marked on a map and jealously guarded from harm.

South of the nesting ground a wrinkle of sand beckoned and Anna parked the pumper behind its sheltering crest, safe from view either by land or by sea. Keeping to the valleys between the dunes, she made her way toward the woods. In her pack she carried water and a flashlight. A compass was in her pocket. The need to stay close to the truck in case there was a fire call-out, coupled with heat, ticks, and general lethargy, had kept Anna from exploring this four-mile-square chunk of official wilderness in the heart of the park. From the maps, she knew it was free of private lands, roads, inholdings, campgrounds, trails, or any other form of "improvement" that might hamper its wilderness status. Having been religiously protected from the cleansing qualities of wildland fire, the area was dense with palmetto, oak, and pine. Robbed of sunlight by the forest canopy, it allowed little else to grow.

According to the topographical map Wayne and Shorty had used to plot the location of the wrecked Beech, the plane had gone in a mile south and 1.7 miles east of the loggerhead nesting ground. An educated guess put Hanson and his grader slightly further north, almost on a straight east-west line with the nest sites, near where Shawna estimated they were when Guenther was shot.

As soon as she reached the cover of the woods, Anna walked north along the tree line, keeping a practiced eye on the dunes. When she reached the place just inland from the turtles' nests, she pulled out her compass. The forest closed overhead and she waited for her eyes to adjust. Live oak branches, grown wide in their search for light and air, created a living ceiling, but such was the spread of the branches that enough light trickled down so that, with care, Anna could make her way with only occasional assistance from her flashlight.

Her estimate of an hour's outing had been overly optimistic. Burdened as she was by the need to move silently and without light, circumnavigating thickets of palmetto and stands of pine, the mile she had to walk took on the dimensions of a serious cross-country hike. Still, if it hadn't been for the mosquitoes, she would have enjoyed herself. The dark, the stealth, the knowledge that she was the hunter and not the hunted, gave her a sense of power and freedom. She thought of Hanson and his pig rifle, of hunters out for sheep and elk and deer, and wondered that they could find this same thrill with such helpless prey in their sights.

Complying as rigidly to her westward heading as the vagaries of nature would allow, she eventually reached the clearing she knew had to be there. When strung together, hints as to its existence had formed a compelling picture. Hanson had evicted Dot and Mona from Stafford's basement so he could store fertilizer, weed killer, and PVC pipe there. On the edge of Lake Whitney, the only reliable freshwater source on this end of the island, was a line straight as a die. Guenther had been shot but had neither seen nor heard his assailant. Days later Hanson was removing something from earth and trees in the same part of the forest.

A marijuana field was the only explanation that fit all the facts. The PVC pipe laid into Lake Whitney provided the needed water, the hapless U.S. taxpayers the fertilizer, the farmer's time, and undoubtedly much of the equipment used in the cultivation and the building of booby traps to scare off marauders—both accidental and those intent on stealing the illegal crop. It would have been one of these traps the Austrian had stumbled into: a shotgun shell rigged to a trigger device buried beneath the duff. With the plane crash and the shotgun incident focusing attention on this part of the island, Hanson must have decided to remove his booby traps, begin to fold his tents preparatory to slipping quietly into the night. That was what he'd been in the process of doing when Dijon and Anna had come upon him.

She secreted herself in shadow, a live oak between her and the moon, and studied the operation. "Clearing" was too grandiose a term. What lay before her was more accurately an opening in the woods. Trees were scattered throughout—enough for camouflage, but widely spaced so sunlight could make it down through the canopy to the plants. For the space of an irregular acre, planted in a hodgepodge so as not to call attention to themselves from the air as a man-made cultivation, were cannabis plants. It looked as if Hanson had begun prudently. There were only ten or twelve mature plants and they'd been placed in careful disarray, most snuggled up to a palmetto or tucked in a grove of immature pines to disguise their nature from casual eyes and their bolder green foliage from calling attention to itself from the air. Hanson hadn't built any telltale structures. He either carried the tools he needed in with him each time or had them cleverly cached—probably in a shallow underground bunker.

A plot this size—of sinsemilla, a prime strain—carefully husbanded and harvested, would augment one's salary considerably. At a guess, Anna put the profit at about thirty thousand dollars annually. If he kept it on a small scale, Hanson probably could have gotten away with it for the seven years until he could once again retire and pick up pension number two.

Fortunately for law enforcement officers, enough is seldom enough. Apparently Hanson was running true to form and getting greedy. Dozens of immature plants had been planted in the open areas between the mature cannabis, quadrupling the size of the original plot, calling for more pipe for water, more fertilizer, making booby traps a necessity, and soon becoming obvious to low-flying aircraft. When this many plants matured, all but the most brain-dead pilot would question the dark green cancer spreading beneath the dusty gray of oak leaves.

Until Slattery Hammond started flying drug interdiction, Mitch's little operation would have been fairly secure. Had Hammond seen the plot? Told Todd as the island's law enforcement ranger? Was their last flight the one in which he would show Todd the plants? That seemed likely enough. As Alice Utterback said in the beginning, the job of drug interdiction brought with it its own cadre of enemies.

Considering Slattery's less than spotless reputation, it wasn't too great a leap of logic to picture him demanding a slice of the profits in return for his silence. Hanson, just absorbing the cost of expanding his business, chose to add murder to his credit list rather than blackmail to the debit column. Or Hammond saw nothing, knew nothing, and Belfore was the victim, the blackmailer, or both.

As Anna's mind opened to the possibilities, the details of the clearing began to manifest themselves. In the open area, a grassy place around a single lightning-blasted oak, was a derelict hog pen, its weathered boards falling together to form a ramshackle lean-to. On either side of this structure, maybe twelve feet away, was a pile. At first glance Anna took them for branches and other forest litter that had been cleared away to make room for the new marijuana seedlings.

The careful way they'd been stacked, in neat bonfire cones, intrigued her. Ten minutes motionless in shadow, eyes and ears open, convinced her she was alone. Rising to the obnoxious cracking of knees and ankles, she ventured out into the dappling of moonlight. The cones were of marijuana plants, young plants, rudely pulled up by the roots and tossed on what looked for all the world to be burn piles. A drug war? Villain number two destroying villain number one's cash crop for spite or business? On a plot as small and inaccessible as this one, that struck Anna as highly unlikely, but stranger things had happened in the history of the war on drugs. A war the average American was losing and the politicians and drug dealers were winning. Fear buys votes and drugs are a politically correct evil to rail against.

Voices, low and murmuring but unmistakably human, rooted Anna to the spot. On the tail end of the sound came a slash of light, two flashlights probing her darkness like Darth Vader's sword.

Instinctively, she dropped to the ground. Footfalls and light approached rapidly. Whoever it was moved without any attempt at concealment, probably unaware they were not alone. Anna was determined to keep it that way.

Directly in front of her, offering its questionable refuge, was the derelict hog pen. Choosing not to think about what other life-forms might have taken up residence within, Anna crawled beneath the rotting boards. Inside, there was just room to sit up, her head brushing the lumber. The sticky touch of spiders' webs trailed across her left cheek and she steeled herself for visitations from many species.

Trapped in the close dark of a sty, the Golden Orb, for all her impressive proportions, was preferable to brown recluses or black widows.

Contemplation of arachnids was pushed aside by the arrival of potentially more injurious beasts. Anna arranged her legs in a half-lotus beneath her and folded her hands loosely in her lap, mimicking the attitude of meditating swamis. It was a position she could maintain for several hours if need be. In front of her was a triangle where the boards of her makeshift hiding place opened out onto the clearing. Though she felt exposed, she knew she sat far enough back in the shadow that, short of a direct beam of light shined in at ground level, she would remain invisible.

With a discipline born of long practice, she evened out her breathing and emptied her mind. In the forced calm the voices became recognizable. Hanson—as she had surmised—and one other, a woman. If she'd ever heard her voice before, she couldn't place it, and she settled down to listen.

"What a shame," the woman said.

"It was a crazy-ass thing to do anyway." Hanson. "Cost is no object when it's not you paying."

"Still and all—"

"Hand me that."

These fragments were accompanied by the crisscrossing beams of light and the noises of rummaging: something metal, a chunk of wood or hard plastic, shoes stomping through dead leaves. The pocket of noise moved from the edge of the clearing toward Anna's shelter. Bars of light fell through the rude wood as the beams scratched over the tumbled-down hog pen. Anna cringed as if the light burned, but the touch was fleeting. Discovering her hiding place was not the goal of this nocturnal excursion.

"Think anybody'll see it?" asked the woman.

"Not at night. By daylight nobody'll even know it happened."

Endangered Species

An odor, peculiar in the wilderness, assaulted Anna's nostrils. Lighter fluid. A gasp escaped her lungs and her heart began to pound. Forcing again an internal stillness, she felt the panic recede to a prickle on her scalp and a queasiness in her stomach. With a few deep breaths these symptoms, too, were banished.

The voices were ten feet away. The lighter fluid was not meant for her.

She heard the avaricious crackle of flame before she saw it. When orange splintered through the boards of the sty, Anna put her eye to the crack. Hanson, squatting, his back to her, had fired the pile of marijuana plants. The glow lit the face of the woman next to him. His wife, Louise; this was a family business. Anna remembered Alice Utterback's cynical plan of a crime ring of middle-aged ladies. Utterback had been dead on. No one, Anna included, would have suspected Mrs. Hanson of any crime more sinister than munching a few grapes before the bunch was weighed at the local Sack & Save. Even on a moonlit night, in the woods, burning an illegal drug crop, Mitch's wife looked innocent. She was in her fifties, slightly overweight, with chin-length brown hair tied back with a scarf. Big-rimmed plastic eyeglasses dominated her face, and her hands were protected by gardening gloves, the kind with elasticized cuffs and sprigs of little green-and-pink flowers.

Smoke from the burning pile drifted in Anna's direction. The light piercing her shelter became tangible as orange fog poured in. She pulled the neck of her T-shirt up over her mouth and nose. The gesture was largely futile; cotton knit had no proven capability for filtering out noxious gases, but old habits die hard. The smell of the smoke triggered a time warp in her brain. Other than the occasional whiff from around a campfire or the cab of a vehicle she'd pulled over, Anna had not breathed marijuana smoke in quantity since college. The odor was unmistakable and, for a goodly number of those in her generation, nostalgic. It swept her back to the days when the world's great evils were either unknown or considered combatable; a time when she was an immortal, invincible and all-powerful in the sublime ignorance of youth.

From habit long dead and, she'd thought, forgotten, she inhaled the smoke and held it trapped in her lungs. In less time than it took to think it through, Anna realized what she was doing and breathed out. Jesus Christ, am I out of my fucking mind? She rubbed her face to clear it of real and imagined cobwebs.

"It'll go," Hanson said. "We don't want a big fire anyway. Though I suppose if it got away it'd cover a lot of sins."

"Now, Mitch," the Mrs. said reprovingly, and Anna had an almost unbearable urge to laugh at the absurd domesticity of the scene.

"You know I wouldn't," Mitch defended himself. Anna bet he would the moment the apron strings were untied.

The two of them crunched together through the leaves, their feet and legs visible from the door of Anna's sty. Resisting the temptation to hold her breath—and so more smoke in her lungs—she focused on becoming at one with the spiders and the pig shit.

A couple of yards to her left, the Hansons stopped and repeated the ignition process on the second burn pile. Smoke from both sides now; Anna fought to keep from coughing and giving away her location. The next time she had to pee in a bottle for the federal government's drug-screening lab, she was going to have a lot of explaining to do. The image struck her as unsupportably funny and she felt the giggles mixing with the coughs till it seemed she must explode. At that thought anxiety, bordering on mindless panic, swept through her so suddenly her bowels grew watery.

She was getting stoned.

She'd not been high, at least not on dope, since she'd given it up twenty-one years before. To fight off the demons, she tried to remember what she could of those long-gone days. Much of it was a blur. She remembered the silly things: the munchies and the giggles, the lethargy of sitting in front of an old black-and-white television watching Marcus Welby reruns. The memory of the bad acid trip that had forever ended her drug days forced itself into her mind and for a moment it seemed as if the precarious walls of her shelter were closing in of their own accord, flapping slowly like the splintered wings of a wooden butterfly.

Don't go there, she told herself in the words of a current cliché. The cliché was one she particularly despised and the fact that she had used it sent another stab of irrational fear through her.

Fires on both sides were catching on well. The inside of the hog pen danced with the flames, an orange and black disco light-show without music. Anna closed her eyes against it and tried to think, tried not to breathe, and failed at both. Flickering red and orange played across her closed eyelids. Fight it as she would, she had the sense of falling—tilting first one way and then another as if she would topple from her sitting position. The crackling burned at her brain in a low-grade fever and her skin crawled with sweat and fear and God knew what else.

At length the busy noises abated and Anna dared to hope that the Hansons had gone away and she could do the same. Opening her eyes required more courage than she would have thought possible. Had keeping them closed not been the greater of the two evils, she doubted she could have managed it.

Directly in front of her, framed in the angle of rough lumber and illuminated by the light of the fires, the Hansons sat in folding lawn chairs. She in dark blue polyester pants and a sleeveless cotton shell that exposed too much flabby upper arm, he in faded uniform trousers and a worn polo shirt, each with a beer in hand: a Norman Rockwell vision of hell. Again laughter threatened to tear its way out of Anna's throat and again it was quelled by a wave of ice-cold fear.

Time ratcheted uncomfortably.

Anna had no idea how long she'd sat in the hovel breathing smoke. A minute, an hour, three? All seemed equally defensible. Breathing was easier but whether the fires had grown hot enough to draw the smoke upward or whether the dope was having an anesthetic effect on her lungs, she wasn't sure. The impulse to cough had left her and she made a point of starting a "small blessings" list.

To keep her mind from wandering to less auspicious climes, she forced herself to concentrate on the Hansons. From all appearances they were relaxed, happy even. If Anna had had to categorize the tone they'd set for this bizarre evening's entertainment, she would have called it relief. The Hansons acted relieved.

How on earth they could be so sanguine about torching their cash crop mystified her. Of course, the way things were going, how her head remained on her shoulders was beginning to mystify her. The time, effort, and risk that would have gone into farming the plot had to be considerable, but the sudden expansion to take care of the new plants and the demands they put on the cultivation didn't strike her as something to be so lightly—not to mention downright cheerfully—destroyed.

No answers suggested themselves. Time drifted. Anna drifted. Once, twice, maybe a hundred times—she couldn't recall, nor did it seem particularly important—one Hanson or the other would abandon the lawn chair to poke up the fire or get another beer.

More than once, Anna had come gently back to earth having totally forgotten where she was or why. Each time, she was called back from the brink by the reality of the pains that were beginning to take over her body: aches in her ankles, numbness in her hips, itching on her legs and arms. With the unpleasant clarity born of discomfort the why of her predicament returned and she was reminded not to crawl out of the sanctity of her hog pen and into the lit clearing. Then more smoke would be sucked into her brain and, for a while, life would be on hold.

Endangered Species

High was not what it used to be, she thought in a moment between the drifts. Too much paranoia had been added to the mix: fear of the consequences, of the years, but mostly of her own mind. In her twenties she'd trusted it to guide her, answer her questions, make the right choices. Somewhere in her thirties she'd lost faith. She saw her mind now as a moderately useful, if highly overrated, organ, one susceptible to chemical storms, hormonal droughts, and the phases of the moon. Gone were the days when she could alter her reality with impunity. Being stoned had become less a matter of flying than of hanging on to some ragged edge of sanity and waiting for the smoke to clear.

The last thing she remembered was a sudden flare of light and Mitch Hanson's voice crackling through the saw of the flames: "Well, there goes the last of Ellen's college tuition."

"She saved her daddy's life. That should be worth at least a year with the Seven Sisters."

"Orinsing—" and an echo.

22

MOLLY HAD REFUSED to cry. She'd sat across the table in the pub, arm's length from Frederick, her nerves so tight he could almost hear them hum. The face he'd come to think of as exquisite—a word he customarily reserved for sculpture and fine porcelain—was closed to him. Pain was written clearly in the too-wide eyes and the controlled line of her lips, but he was not invited to solace her.

Over a Scotch she did not drink, she told him the baby killer the headlines had shouted about was the man on whose behalf she'd testified several years previously; the last time she'd ever been lured to the witness stand. Her testimony, along with the obfuscatory powers of the defense attorney and the slow wits of the prosecutor, had gotten the man a light sentence on an insanity plea. He'd served just over three years. Two weeks after he was paroled he had sexually assaulted and killed the three-year-old boy the tourists from Ely, Nevada, had discovered in the shopping bag.

The psychiatrist was walking the thin line between guilt and responsibility. The subject cut too close to the bone for her to share it in detail with a stranger, she'd said, and Frederick had been stung. He temporarily put aside his bizarre courtship of Anna's sister. To give Molly back some semblance of control, he steered the conversation toward the concrete: suspects, clues, the possible connection to the threats she'd received.

Despite the emotional pressure Molly was under, she hadn't come unprepared. Just once, Frederick wished she would. Then you could fancy it a tryst, he mocked himself; still, it would have pleased him.

As it was, she pulled out her black briefcase. Her secretary had spent the morning in research. Lester Mack, the man arrested for the murder of the boy, and the man whom Dr. Pigeon had been instrumental in saving from life in prison, if not death row, was paroled the same week she received the first death threat.

The stakes had definitely been raised. Motive, should they now be on the right track, was no longer a mystery.

Though Lester Mack had been released and Molly threatened before anyone should have known who murdered the boy in the Bloomingdale's bag, Frederick tracked down the parents of the three-year-old victim the following morning. Through his contacts with the NYPD, he learned that the parents were young, both Puerto Rican, with very little understanding of English. The mother had been sixteen and the father eighteen when Lester Mack's trial was in the news. He doubted even now that they connected Molly Pigeon with the murder of their son. Frederick moved on to more promising territory.

Four years before, Mack had been accused and found guilty of the assault and killing of two other children, both boys, both Puerto Rican, and both from poor families. Either Lester Mack had a racial taste in victims or he was clever enough to realize the difficulty poor families, particularly those with no command of the English language, would have in pushing a successful investigation and prosecution through an already overburdened legal system.

In an attempt to avoid being racist himself—in the sense of writing off the families of the previous victims as suspects—Frederick uncovered their whereabouts. One family, shattered by the death of their son, had returned to Puerto Rico, where they lived with the husband's mother. Frederick called and spoke with a brother—whether of the wife or the husband, his understanding of Spanish wasn't good enough to discern. As near as he could tell, no one in that household was aware of Mack's release or of his rearrest on suspicion of the same charges that had so impacted their lives.

The parents of Mack's other early victim had long since divorced. No one knew where the father had gone but his ex-wife thought he might have moved to Los Angeles. She had remarried and lived in Jackson Heights, where she worked in her husband's dry-cleaning business. She had read of the recent murder of the little boy. It had brought back the nightmares, she said.

When Frederick questioned her about Dr. Pigeon, she seemed to have only a vague recollection of the name. There had been a number of forensics experts and expert witnesses at the Lester Mack trial. She spoke English well enough to converse, but she'd been unable to follow the technical questions and the answers from the witness stand.

Frederick hung up convinced she'd not linked Molly with the release of Mack, nor did she have the linguistic skills to pen the threatening notes and alter her accent sufficiently to leave the phone messages Molly had played for him.

Endangered Species

Having arrived at another dead end, maxed out his Visa and irritated his boss, Frederick could no longer justify staying in Manhattan and had reluctantly boarded a flight to O'Hare. They'd not yet entered the airspace over Ohio and already he was missing Molly, or more accurately, the way he felt when he was with her. "Young" about summed it up. Banal as it was, he suspected this was what was meant by midlife crisis. Had he seen it coming, he hoped he would have had the good sense to buy a sports car or indulge in some other harmless cliché.

A sudden memory made him laugh aloud, drawing an uncomfortable glance from the matronly woman in the seat next to him. Two years before, he'd very nearly bought that sports car. He'd lusted after a lurid purple Ford Probe he'd seen in a dealer's window. He would have bought it if it hadn't been for his daughter, Candice. One night he'd mentioned it and she'd said in a voice rich with the scorn left over from her recent adolescence: "Yeah, Dad, like a Probe is a *sports car* . . ."

On his lap, closed in a battered leather notebook he'd carried for fifteen years, were three half-written letters to Molly, all carefully crafted with wit and charm. It was just a mind game, he told himself. He'd never send them. Unless Molly wanted him to. There was the loophole. One come-hither look and Frederick knew he would betray Anna in actuality as he had already in his heart. Not without a backward glance. He'd scourge himself for a week or two but the heady narcotic of new romance would kill the pain.

The world was full of people doing as he did on various levels. Most of them were sublimely unaware of their actions, of the absurdity of their self-made tempests. He wished he were one of them.

Molly was attracted to him. Frederick was an old enough hand to smell the pheromones. Whether she'd give in to it, he had no idea. He looked at the letters he'd started and wondered if he dared send them.

It had been so long since he'd been rejected by a woman, he wondered how well he'd handle it. Would he sulk, get angry, scurry away with his tail between his legs, pretend it never happened? Even thinking about it made him feel defenseless and a bit of a boob. Often the worst things that happen are when someone important sees to it nothing happens at all; a refusal of love, friendship, or help when it is most needed.

Leaning back, he tilted the seat the allotted five degrees and let that thought rattle around in his head. There was something about it that had caught in his mind, the idea of rejection being the unkindest cut, indifference the greatest evil, the murder of what might have been.

Tray tables were being put up in preparation for landing by the time the thought came to rest. That first night he'd met with Molly he had asked her about publicity. She mentioned the Mack trial. She said that after Lester Mack's sentencing she'd refused to appear for the defense ever again but that, because of the success of the defense, she'd been—how did she put it? It seemed important to remember her exact words. She said she had people "beating down her door."

The flight attendant tapped Frederick and he obediently returned his seat back to the full upright position. Before stowing his notebook as requested, he scribbled down a line of inquiry to follow up.

A new direction and an excuse to call Molly. Not a bad two hours' work.

23

"Orinsing."

Anna was overwhelmed by the world's incomprehensibility. All was black as pitch and she couldn't move. She probably wasn't dead. Twice before she'd thought she was dead and had been mistaken. She'd come to believe assuming one was dead—or wishing one was—indicated one was still living. Only mildly reassuring under the circumstances.

"Why does everything have to be so fucking *mysterious*." Mouth and throat were dry and the words whispered out like wind over parched earth, but it was reassuring to know some portions of her anatomy still functioned. If she could speak, she was breathing. Always a good sign.

Emboldened by success, she reached up to see if her eyes were open. Her knuckles rasped painfully against splintered boards. As through a shifting mist, memories of the night came back. She was in the hog pen, her forehead pushed against the slanting lumber of the roof. At some point she'd slipped the surly bonds of earth and tipped over; the slanted sides of the narrow enclosure had kept her from falling. Both legs were folded under her and both were as insensate as the weathered wood, so deeply asleep they ignored her orders to move, not responding with so much as a tingle to indicate life. They felt as if they'd been packed with sand, but she could move her hands and arms. She used one to prop herself upright. Her head weighed a ton and pressure had built inside to an uncomfortable degree.

Directly in front of her the world appeared vaguely lighter. Somewhere along the line she must have opened her eyes. They burned and teared. The view didn't change but she could feel water running down her cheeks.

"Water," she croaked, testing her voice. Thirst bore down upon her with a vengeance and she clawed her yellow pack from where it lay behind her left hip. Fumbling off the cap of the bottle, she held it to her lips with both hands, spilling water down the sides of her face. The melodrama of the picture she presented made her laugh. Her lungs sore from processing smoke, the sound came out on a hacking cough.

For a tense moment she waited for the racket to bring down retribution. There wasn't a sound from without. In a way she was disappointed. The shed had become intolerable and she wasn't altogether sure she could get out of it without assistance. Feeling as she did, the thought of being murdered—if the dispatch was quick and painless—wasn't without its attractions.

In a past now obscured by cannabis smoke, she had folded her legs into a half-lotus. Her lap was lost in the darkness that wrapped cocoonlike around her. The puzzle of how to disentangle limbs she could neither see nor feel baffled her. Her brain too was cocooned in darkness and smoke. Idly she wondered how many more little gray cells had gone the way of the dodo.

A fuzzy thought made its appearance in her blasted mindscape: At least I won't get glaucoma for a while. That brought on the giggles and she knew she was still high. Paranoia made its familiar appearance on the tail end of the laughter and she waited, consciously breathing, till it passed.

Reality began reasserting itself in negatives: it was not light, she was not straight, she was not dead, no one was going to come and pull her out of the hog pen. Armed with knowledge of the parameters, she took action. Helen Keller learns yoga, she thought as she felt down the length of her calf till her hands closed around the ankle that rested on the inner thigh of the opposite leg. Grasping it firmly, she pulled it free and tossed it in the direction of the outside world. It fell with a clunk that sounded as if it had struck something solid. Easy, she reminded herself. In the not too distant future she would have to pay the price for any injuries inflicted.

The plan was a bust. One leg under her and one thrust out in front cemented her more firmly than ever onto the shed floor. Walking her hands back down the leg from the knee, she hauled the ankle up to its former resting place. After what seemed a long time in thought, she gave up trying to outsmart her body. She hurled the yellow pack out first, then, using the strength of her arms, pulled herself forward, rocking her torso over the useless legs. With hands and elbows, she dragged her body from the enclosure.

The smell of smoke had given way to the smell of wet ash. Anna rolled onto her back and sat up, her sleeping legs splayed like logs before her. *Shh,* she heard her grandmother's voice say in her head. *You'll wake them up* . . . And when she did, it would be excruciating; the unbearable tickle of sensation returning to a million oxygen-starved cells.

Not ready to face that, she left them unmolested and dug the flashlight from her pack. The lawn chairs were gone, the piles burned down to ash, the ash cooled with water and raked over with needles and debris. Shining the narrow beam as far as it would reach into the recesses between the thinly scattered oaks, Anna noted the mature plants were missing as well. Those plants had achieved the stature of small trees, twelve or fifteen feet high and carrying enough dope to retail for $1,500 to $2,500 a plant. They were gone as if they'd never been. Even the roots had been dug up, or the stems cut flush and covered with leaf litter. The Hansons had been busy little bees.

Confusion swirled, turning Anna's thoughts into a tornado that threatened to rip up what little equilibrium she'd regained. How long had she been down the rabbit hole? It was night. Which night? The ashes still gave off heat and she took comfort in that. She'd not lost a day. Screwing up her courage, she dug out her pocket watch and shined the flash on it: 2:42. Four or five hours had passed since she'd crawled into the hog pen. For at least three of that she'd been asleep. Lost time. It made her nervous. She put the watch and flashlight away and began to massage her legs.

Twenty minutes later she had her body back, such as it was. It was not pleased with her, nor she with it. During her protracted sabbatical from reality, she'd become home to a thriving colony of chiggers. Several times she tried to count the bites but always lost her place. She'd find herself, numbers gone from her mind, head hanging, trouser legs rolled, wondering what she'd been trying to prove. Conceding victory to the chiggers, she turned her limited attention span on ticks.

By the light of her flash she began detaching engorged insects from her person. One or ten or a hundred—she couldn't tell. At first she crushed them between her nails. The death penalty: not revenge, just discouraging recidivism. It wasn't long before the gore upset her stomach and she stopped, satisfying herself with flinging the bugs into the darkness and trusting she'd have moved before they had time to crawl back.

Like a tape loop on video, she saw herself taking the same action over and over again. Having no idea whether or not she was making any progress, she finally stopped but she doubted she'd gotten them all.

Minutes ticked by as she sat in the dark, trying to decide what to do next. Eyes and lungs burned, the pressure in her head had transmuted into a dull ache. There weren't three square inches of skin anywhere on her body that did not itch with such viciousness it took all her self-control not to claw the flesh from bone. Anna hated the South and everyone and everything crawling around in it.

A solution came to her: she had to get the hell out of there. When she tried to stand it came home to her how thoroughly ripped she was. Many sheets to the wind. Vertigo made the forest whirl. She fell to her knees and vomited up the water she'd consumed. Nausea: she didn't remember that from the good old days. Her body had outgrown its tolerance for recreational poisons.

Stomach empty, she felt marginally better and pushed herself to her feet, achieving the vertical on the second attempt. Around her, black trees were spinning, she could feel them, and dared not look. Eyes down, she fished out her compass and shined the flashlight on it. Looking only at the controlled world of the compass face, she began pushing determinedly east.

Distance was as relative as time had become. Anna followed the needle in her palm as a true believer would follow the star. Navigation around obstacles was beyond her mutant mental powers. Gone was her fear of noise or thickets. What was one more bite? Merely an addition to her already splendid collection. She bulled her way through the brush, trusting the rattlers had retired for the night and calling down curses on the head of any spider who wouldn't give her a fucking break.

An eternity of scratches and bumps and confused dreams later, she staggered out onto the dunes. Silver light bathed her and she dropped to all fours. "Thankyoubabyjesus," she whispered without thought of irreverence. Always before, away from the haunts of man she'd found solace. Fear of wild places had been alien to her. Control having been stripped away, the darkling woods took on a different face. Crumpled on the sand, the ocean at peace as far as she could see, she felt the soft light penetrate her soul, lift the darkness from within, and she understood at last why the ancients had condemned the wilderness as the walks of the devil.

Beauty, true and lasting beauty, was personified by the squatting bulk of the pumper truck. She'd come out of the woods just three hundred yards south of where she'd parked. She ran to it as to a long-lost love.

Before she left the denuded marijuana plantation, she'd finished the last of her water. It was with relief she downed half a liter from the canteen on the seat. Water cleared her head marginally. Motion had restored her muscles. She knew her lungs would hurt for a while. She'd consider herself lucky if she didn't come down with bronchitis. Of her myriad ills all were somewhat alleviated but for the ticks and the chiggers.

Having doffed only her boots and pocket watch, Anna waded fully clothed into the sea and let the ocean close over her head. Salt water purified, weightlessness calmed her spirit. Time warped again but this time she could live with it. She luxuriated in the warm surf. Bobbing like a bit of kelp on the tide, she lay at the surface, watching the panorama of beach.

The nesting sites of the loggerheads were invisible in front of oat grass, thrust up black and spiky, the light of the moon behind the blades. A trail, something dragged, cut between two of the nests, breaking down a lip of sand carved by high tide. The Hansons, Anna thought, dragging their harvest. Wind and water would obliterate the track by noon. An ideal setup: a couple on a houseboat known to anchor in different places to savor island views. A few nights a year they anchor just off the beach, drag their goods in, stow them aboard, and motor sedately away.

Dragging the booty over Marty Schlessinger's prize cache of turtle eggs: Anna pressed the heels of her hands to her temples and squeezed as if she could wring the dope smoke from her system and glimpse what flash of thought that image had engendered. Had Marty known of the marijuana plot, found it perhaps in her wanderings? Would she kill to protect the eggs? Possibly. But killing Todd or Slattery—or both—wouldn't stop the harvest, whereas one word in the right NPS ear would have shut the whole operation down. Besides, looked at realistically, assuming Schlessinger still retained that capacity, two people dragging a few bales of weed over the top of the nests would do them no harm.

If it occurred on a night the little loggerheads were hatching, making that first perilous journey to the ocean, interference might do some damage. The turtles were slated to hatch within the next week. Had Marty tried a preemptive strike to keep the traffic off the beach? Had the Hansons guessed and harvested early?

"Bullshit," Anna said, and splashed salt water in her face. Taking a deep breath, she submerged until a fit of coughing forced her to the surface. "Work, damn you, work," she said aloud, and smacked the side of her skull. The jolt seemed to do some good. The flaws in her line of thinking became apparent. The night the turtles came out was marked on calendars all over the island. The beach would be alive with rangers and volunteers come to assist and celebrate. That would be the last night the Hansons would choose for any illicit activity.

Nothing made sense.

Her ability to think was spent. Her brain unraveled and she floated, her clothing waving about her like Ophelia's shroud.

Anna reached Plum Orchard before sunrise and squished up the stairs. The door was unlocked as she had left it and no one stirred within. Another small blessing duly noted. What with one thing and another, she was out of patience. She doubted she could bear the whey-faced sorrow of Tabby Belfore with equanimity. And given the way she looked at the moment, Tabby's laying eyes on her couldn't be good for the baby.

Standing at the sink, she downed another sixteen ounces of water, loaded the electric coffee maker for eight cups and clicked it on. Its little electronic eye was scarcely redder than her own. On the way to the bathroom, she left a trail of soggy clothing.

Hot water, then cold; she switched back and forth, applying age-old remedies for sobering up. The passage of time was the only way to cleanse the body of drugs but the wives' tales were rooted in a modicum of fact. Cold showers and hot coffee could transmute a dopey, knee-walking drunk into a wide-awake, alert, knee-walking drunk if assiduously applied. Anna would settle for that.

Two more ticks were dislodged by repeated shampooing. Her legs from midthigh down were a mass of red bumps that itched like the devil. Chiggers. A little red bug that lived in the South and, not surprisingly, was a relative of the tick. According to Dijon, an expert on all things repulsive, the little buggers burrowed in and lived there. The thought gave Anna the willies, so though she suspected it was true, she pretended it wasn't.

Five-fifteen found her dressed in clean clothes—two cups of coffee roiling in her stomach, wet hair hanging in witchy ropes—pacing around the tiny living room trying not to scratch. The black fog that clogged her brain had yet to dissipate. Anxiousness bordering on panic licked around the edges of her awareness and she was consumed by irritability. At 5:17 a.m. she banged open the door to Tabby's bedroom.

"Who on this island cuts hair?" she demanded when the sleepy young woman peered over the bedclothes.

"Huh?" Tabby blinked, her eyes round and rabbity.

Everything about the woman so aggravated Anna's strained nerves that she had to fight down an urge to slap her.

"Cuts hair. Snip, snip. Every park I've ever worked in has some-body who cuts hair." Anna knew she was irrational. She knew she was growling. She didn't care.

"Cuts hair?" Tabby echoed stupidly.

Anna began to count to ten, silently, in her head. At seven Tabby managed: "Lynette. Lynette'll do it."

Anna closed the door with a bang and left.

Lynette was up. When Anna drove in she was out on her diminutive front porch in a gold and black kimono feeding the dog. If she was surprised to see Anna, red-eyed and chigger-gnawed, walking up her front steps before sunrise, she was too polite—or too wise—to say so.

"Tea?" she offered.

"Can you cut hair?" Anna asked without preamble.

Ten minutes later she was seated on a stool on the porch, a towel draped around her shoulders and a cup of sugared tea steam-ing in her hand. A light bulb, decorated with a folding paper shade the size and shape of a beach ball, cast a warm glow over a jungle of potted plants and ceramic animals.

Lynette's calm acceptance soothed Anna more than she would have admitted.

"Cut it off, all of it," Anna said as Lynette emerged from the cabin with comb and scissors. Her voice sounded far away, as if she was listening to herself on the radio, and she stopped speaking. Being stoned was an art form and she had long ago lost the knack. Piled on top of the night's adventures, the dissociation was disorienting, frightening, and she wanted little more than to be straight. Time, she promised herself. If memory served, by noon she should be completely down.

Had Lynette questioned or argued or pried, Anna had no doubt that she would have run screaming into the woods. As it was, the woman began gently brushing the tangles from her hair, taking great care not to tug or pull. While she worked she talked, her voice low and sweet and monotonous, like rain on the roof. The words themselves were unimportant. Occasionally Anna tuned in: "We used to have a corgi . . . The dress my sister wore was this awful tangerine . . . Mom said the cats couldn't sleep on the bed . . ." Pointless wonderful stories without drama, violence, or passion.

Knots inside Anna's head began to loosen and, as the planks beneath her became covered in hanks of hair, she felt as if a vise were being unscrewed from her skull; blood flowed, thoughts moved. She started to cry.

Lynette either didn't notice or kindly forbore comment. The snipping went on a long while, or so it seemed to Anna—time continued to do its petty-pace thing, skewed by drugs and distraction. When she eventually came back from the nowhere she'd gone to, Lynette no longer chattered but hummed a melody: "Amazing Grace." Religion, at least of the church-and-Sunday-school variety, had never made much sense to Anna but she'd always loved that hymn. This creaking morning it fell on her ears like the voice of fate itself. Once before, she'd reached religious epiphany through music. She was a sophomore at California Polytechnic State University. The song had been the Beatles' "Here Comes the Sun." She'd been stoned then as well, but having a considerably better time.

"Was blind but now I see." Lynette put words to the tune. Her voice was cool and soft. Anna liked hearing her sing.

Her sing.

The two words reverberated.

"Orinsing," Mitch Hanson said that, or something that sounded like it. Anna drained the last of her tea and set the cup on the porch rail between a blue glazed rabbit and an African violet.

Whispering on stockinged feet, Lynette picked up the mug and slipped through the screen door to make more tea. Anna scarcely noticed she'd gone. The old fat dog collapsed at her feet. She kicked off her moccasins and rubbed her toes along his back. He grunted, admitting to at least one porcine ancestor.

There goes Ellen's college tuition. Ellen Hull? Norman Hull's daughter?

A year with the Seven Sisters. Radcliffe? Barnard, et al?

Orinsing—and an echo. *Orinsing-sing.* Or in Sing Sing. Ellen would end up in college or in prison.

A bit of the letter Anna had found in the chief ranger's desk from Ellen's aunt in Pennsylvania made sense in this new light. "The change isn't helping Ellen. Things aren't working out." And a bus ticket back to Georgia. Alice Utterback: *Nice wife but that kid's a piece of work.* In Hull's calendar beside his daughter's name had been the initials "PO" on several of the dates. Parole officer.

"Ellen's selling dope," Anna said to the dog. "Her dad must get it from the Hansons. Ellen peddles it in the schoolyard." What could be better? The girl had just turned thirteen, according to the letter. Most definitely a minor and, so, hard to prosecute.

She saved her daddy's life. What was that about? Had Ellen, via the Hansons, told her dad not to be on that plane? Or had she known Todd or Slattery was onto the marijuana plot, told her dad, and Dad saw to it they were disposed of? Had the Hansons intended to kill Hull and Ellen told him and so saved his life? That would mean not only the chief ranger but his daughter could be in danger. If at first you don't succeed . . .

"Shit! I cannot, cannot think," Anna muttered, and found another cup of hot tea pressed into her hands. She sucked at it greedily. "God, but I'm thirsty," she said by way of thanks.

"Can you tell me what happened to you?" Lynette asked. She'd taken up the scissors again and was snipping near Anna's right ear. Anna set down her tea, turned, and took hold of the other woman's wrist, pointing the scissors away from her throat.

"That depends on whether or not you killed Slattery Hammond and Todd Belfore," she said bluntly.

Lynette's eyes widened and her breath was drawn in with a shush of sound. She looked shocked, not guilty, but over the past hours Anna had lost faith in the reliability of her perceptions.

"Why would I do that?" Lynette said. That wasn't an answer but it didn't strike Anna's ear as an evasion either. Lynette made no attempt to free her arm. It was beginning to shake.

"Woman scorned and all that," Anna hazarded. "You found out Slattery was married."

"I didn't know he was. Not till you told me."

An idiotic rhyme racketed through Anna's fogged brain and before she could stop herself she gave voice to it. "Liar, liar, pants on fire."

Lynette looked startled, laughed; then her face blanked and she stared into the darkness. "I guess I knew," she said.

Anna waited. After a moment the woman began to tell her story.

"The morning Slattery was killed I went by his house to pick up some things. There was a letter and I read it. She didn't mention the little boy."

Anna's grip tightened. "What time was it?"

"When I read the letter?"

"When you were at Hammond's house."

"Early. Eight or a little before."

Anna's attack had been later in the day. Lynette could have been lying about the time, but she didn't think so.

"I was there in the afternoon," Anna said, loosing Lynette's wrist and turning back on the stool. "There was no letter." From the corner of her eye she could see Lynette's hand come up, the sharp scissors pointing at a soft spot just below Anna's ear. For too long, Lynette neither moved nor spoke, and Anna wondered if she'd misjudged her quarry. She tensed, ready to grab the scissors if she had to.

A sigh so deep Anna felt the air puff in her hair gusted from Lynette's lungs. Their little tableau came to life. Lynette combed, snipped; Anna picked up her mug of tea. "I took it," Lynette admitted. "I was going to confront him with it the next time I saw him. First I wanted to pray about it."

"Any revelations?"

"Somebody should punch the SOB's fucking lights out."

Anna spewed a mouthful of Earl Grey into a Boston fern. "Don't do that," she spluttered. "You'll choke me to death."

"Someone did put his lights out," Lynette said soberly. "I've felt bad and not only for the deaths. I don't know that I was in love with Slattery—he wasn't the kind of man that is good for people—but I was very attracted to him. I thought maybe . . ."

"All he needed was a good woman's love?"

"Pretty stupid?"

"Not necessarily."

"I felt bad about him and Todd. Me praying and them dying. Not that I prayed for their death. I'd never do that. But God knows our hearts. There's a dark spot in mine. There was that day."

If Lynette's God couldn't reassure her he didn't down airplanes on a jilted girlfriend's whim, Anna certainly wasn't going to try. "What were you picking up at Hammond's house?" she asked instead.

"Some boxes Dot and Mona needed back for their updating project."

Because she needed to talk and Lynette was willing to listen, Anna told her about the night in the hog pen, the Hansons and their remark about Ellen's college tuition. She finished her story at the same time Lynette finished cutting her hair. Drugs, murder, and conspiracy were temporarily shelved for the important things in life. The two of them went into Lynette's crowded bathroom so Anna could see her new hairdo.

In the old and spotted glass, her face looked unfamiliar. Hazel irises were rimmed with bloodshot whites. Time's crows had left tracks around her eyes, and her forehead was creased with lines etched deep by the sun of the high deserts. She ran her fingers through the short hair, liking the feeling of lightness, cleanliness. "I look like a little boy," she said in some wonder.

"Or a pixie."

"A little old man is more like it." Anna riffled the short hairs on her left temple. All were white, standing out in a fan against the darker reddish brown over her ear. "My neck looks chickeny." Lynette didn't chime in with the expected compliment and Anna was mildly offended. "I like it," she said at last. "I like it a lot."

Third mug of tea in hand, sipping this time, satiation lending her a veneer of civilization, Anna sat out on the porch. Bare legs propped up on an overturned bucket, trousers hung over the rail, she waited for the dots of clear nail polish to dry. Southern wisdom—or a sinister bent toward practical jokes—had inspired Lynette to daub the lacquer on each and every chigger bite. The theory behind the practice was that, deprived of oxgen, the bugs would suffocate. Anna hoped it would be a slow and hideous death.

Lynette was curled in a hanging basket chair suspended over the dog. "Why would Mitch and Louise burn Norman's share of the crop—if it was Norman's?" she asked.

"Spite? Malice? Revenge?" Anna suggested. "Maybe they were gunning for Hull and got Todd by mistake."

"Norm might have asked them to burn it. You know, saw the light and wanted out of the business," said the kinder Lynette.

"Wouldn't the Hansons just say, 'Goody, more for us,' and keep the lot?"

"Too much work for the two of them?"

"The area getting too hot to wait for a second crop to mature?"

Both tired of the guessing game and relapsed into silence. Strains of "Be Careful of the Stones That You Throw" sounded from the stereo inside. "Good stuff," Anna said of the music. "Incredibly rich."

"Staple Singers. Black gospel."

"No white gospel?"

"We try," Lynette said, and Anna laughed at the disappointment and resignation in her voice. "I guess when for generations the Lord and music were the only outlets allowed for self-expression, you get really good at both."

Light was beginning to raise the night to the east. "I'm dry," Anna said, and stood to pull on her trousers.

"Are you straight?"

"As an arrow," Anna lied.

"What will you do now?"

"Go after the Hansons. See how involved Norman Hull is, then call in the cavalry."

"If you need any help, let me know. I'll pray for you or whatever you need."

"Praise God and pass the ammunition?"

Lynette's blue eyes twinkled mischievously. " 'An armed society is a polite society.' "

Anna couldn't but admire a woman who could quote Jesus and Al Capone.

24

"WHAT THE HELL happened to you? You look like you got run over by a bush hog."

"I think it makes me look kind of like Audrey Hepburn."

"Yeah," Dijon agreed. "She's been dead awhile."

"What's put you in such a good mood?"

"Ask me where everybody is," Dijon said. "They took the boat to St. Marys for groceries."

"Ahh." Fire crew's island sojourn was two-thirds through. The one big outing, one usually involving fast food and an opportunity to walk on honest-to-God pavement, was the shopping trip to the mainland for supplies. "Left holding the bag?" Anna asked unsympathetically.

"Pun intended?" Dijon grumbled as he arranged himself on the seat of the truck beside her.

Engine idling, Anna sat for a moment trying to remember what it was she needed to do. "Food," she announced at last, and clicked off the key. "I've got to make lunch. I've run out of the stuff I took to Tabby's."

"Now you tell me." Dijon groaned as if buckling and unbuckling his seat belt were the most onerous of tasks.

"You do need airing off."

"You're telling me. I'm getting sand on the brain on this rock."

For some reason, one she herself did not understand, Anna didn't tell Dijon of her night, or the Hansons. Several times, as she made her sandwiches, she started to, but something—caution, confusion, or simply mental fatigue—stopped her. With tendrils of dope smoke curling through the recesses of her brain, she felt a need to clarify a few things before she went public; opened herself up to the communal, and therefore picayune, scrutiny of the bureaucracy. Like any other government agency, the National Park Service lacked a bottom line. The buck stopped nowhere. Too many chiefs and not enough Indians.

"Too many cooks spoil the stew." Anna concluded her litany of aphorisms out loud. Dijon's look warned her to be more guarded in her actions, at least for a while.

Dijon drove, Anna rode shotgun, happy to be quiet, to gaze at the scenery unfurling beyond the windshield, and let time pass. They took the pumper north along the beach, following the same path she'd driven twelve hours before. In daylight the oceanfront lost much of its magic, flowing away as open and harmless as a Coppertone ad.

At the northern tip of Cumberland, Dijon stopped and Anna indulged in the voyeuristic pleasure of watching him break the law. As he dropped bits of Ritz crackers on the muddy bank, a flotilla of Maggie-Mary's offspring formed up in the pond they called home. A dozen or more sets of eyes, barely above the level of the murky waters, were propelled toward his feet by the flick of banded tails. Still no sign of Mama. Anna was not disappointed.

Though it was not yet ten in the morning she ate her peanut butter and honey sandwich and a banana. Soon she would be herself again. Normalcy was folding around her like an old bathrobe. The effect was enervating. As reality encroached, her experience of the previous night seemed the more unreal by contrast. Almost as if she had dreamed or hallucinated the entire incident. Such vagaries of thought did little to motivate her. Being thrown into the machinery of a law enforcement investigation inspired only by her drugged recollections was an unattractive notion. In a bit, she promised herself, she'd make those calls.

They reached Plum Orchard just after one o'clock. While they topped off the two water tanks on the expanse of lawn, Anna told Dijon what she knew and suspected, omitting only that she'd been trapped breathing marijuana smoke for four hours. She wasn't up for the jokes that was bound to generate—all with her as the butt.

"You've been keeping this a secret all morning?" Dijon asked accusingly.

"I needed to think," Anna defended herself.

"Yeah. Like that's something you do well all by yourself."

"I've got to think about that," Anna said, and Dijon sniffed.

Tabby was out and the apartment in disarray. Books were scattered across the floor and half a dozen cardboard boxes of papers and files covered the coffee table and one of the chairs. As from another life, Anna recalled that the clutter had been there that morning, she'd just been too distracted to take note of it.

Using the phone in Tabby's bedroom, she dialed the St. Marys Police Department and asked to speak with dispatch. "This is Beth Cuvelier in probation," she lied when a female voice came on the line. "I'm working on that juvenile case—Ellen Hull. I need the exact arrest times for my report." Deceit required more energy than the direct route but, out of her jurisdiction, trying to get information on a juvenile arrest, it struck Anna as the most efficacious approach.

"Oh, yeah," the woman said. "I got that. Hang on a sec."

Anna allowed herself a small sigh of relief. Her creative powers were at a low ebb. Having to elaborate would have taxed them.

"Okay," the woman said, to the accompanying sound of papers being shuffled. "Here we go. Thursday, at oh-nine-hundred-and-seven, Miss Ellen Rachelle Hull was taken into custody. Do you need the names of the arresting officers?"

"Give me what you've got," Anna said, and poised her pen over a scrap of envelope she'd salvaged for the purpose of taking notes.

"Officers Mangino and King arrested her a block from the school where she attends seventh grade. They booked her on Possession with Intent to Sell. Twelve ounces of a substance that field-tested as marijuana were confiscated from her book bag."

"What time were her parents notified?"

"I wasn't on duty but Janice has got it down here. Officer Mangino knew the girl. He asked Janice to notify her parents while still on scene. Jan's got a 'no answer' at the residence at nine-thirteen and the call to Norman Hull at his office on Cumberland Island down at nine-fifteen. I guess she caught him just as he was going out for an airplane ride. Too bad. A day in jail would be good for little Miss Ellen."

"Probably. You say Officer Mangino knows Ellen or her folks?" Anna left the question as open as she could, hoping some useful information might be forthcoming.

"Oh, yeah," the woman said. "We all know Ellen. She's been in and out of here since she was eleven years old. No one can figure out where a kid that age gets the stuff in quantity. Her folks are at their wits' end. Norman's been hoping that Citadel case will work out so he can ship the little twit off to military school." A suspicious silence followed; then the dispatcher's voice came back over the wires. "Your office should have all this," she said warily. "Isn't Felicity handling the Hull girl anymore?"

"I'm just helping out," Anna said. "I'm a temp. Thanks." And she got off the line. Taking the envelope with her into the living room, she slumped down onto the sofa. Chewing on a granola bar he'd liberated from Tabby's kitchen, Dijon sat cross-legged on the floor looking through the books.

"Ellen was arrested shortly after nine a.m. the morning Hammond and Belfore were killed. The police dispatcher called Norman on the island at nine-fifteen. That matches up with your pudgy inamorata's saying he arrived at St. Marys around nine-thirty. Up till then he was apparently planning on being on that plane with Slattery." She sat for a moment tapping the corner of the envelope against her front teeth and listening to Dijon crunch granola.

"Do you think he made up that bullshit about getting a call from the regional director so he wouldn't have to tell anybody his baby girl was a drug dealer?" Dijon asked.

It made sense to Anna. As often as it happened, whenever a law enforcement officer's child ran afoul of the law it was embarrassing. The public viewed it as proof of something rotten in the family. Worse, those who had more empathy subjected the parents to their pity.

"If this kid has been at it since she was eleven and the Hulls are talking military school, it doesn't sound as if Daddy is her supplier," Dijon said.

"Nope. Surely a chief ranger would do a whole lot better job of covering his tracks."

"And not use his own kid."

"That too. Louise Hanson," Anna said after a minute. "She was Ellen's 'special friend.' I remember Norman's secretary telling me that. She said they shared an interest in gardening. Didn't they just. What do you bet Louise is the one who got the girl involved?"

Dijon looked shocked. "Old Mrs. Hanson?" He shook his head. "No. You've got to be kidding. You're not kidding. No," he said, and shook again as if ridding himself of the idea. "Mrs. Claus filling the kiddies' stockings with dope? I don't believe it."

Anna reminded herself to call Alice Utterback and sign up for her crime ring. They'd make a killing. "Let's go by the office," she said, pushing herself out of the couch's embrace. Till she sat down, let herself relax, she'd not realized how bone weary she was. "It's time to bump this upstairs and get back to our own work."

"Tick watch," Dijon said, but he scrambled to his feet fast enough.

The chief ranger was not pleased with Anna. For over an hour she sat in his office, confined to the single straight-backed chair, enduring withering disapproval, while he made the necessary telephone calls.

Acting alone was not the Park Service way. There was the chain of command to be adhered to. That one link was dead and the other a suspect did not let Anna off Hull's hook. First, that he was the suspect did not endear her to him in the least, and second, she could have called somebody. *Anybody,* was the implication. That she, a lowly GS-9 field ranger, not even in her home park, had taken it upon herself to do something was, in Hull's view, untenable. A strong letter would be written to her supervisors. Had she been possessed of sword or stripes, Hull left no doubt in her mind, they would have been broken, thrown ceremoniously in the dust and she herself driven from the fort in ignominy.

Anna made a few feeble attempts to explain that her brainstorm to track down the Hansons' drug plot had come late at night, that she was merely going to take a peek, and that the impetus to go solo derived less from John Wayne than from Greta Garbo: she wanted to be alone. Each word only served as a little shovel, digging her deeper.

Regarding the delay in reporting that morning, the chief was even less understanding. In his fussy, gentlemanly way, he raked her over every coal he could find. More than once it occurred to Anna to tell him she'd failed to report in a timely manner because she was stoned out of her mind, but she had a feeling it would not improve her professional image.

While she sat in the nonlethal equivalent of the electric chair, he went on with his strategy making. He only spoke to Anna for the purpose of reprimand, but from his phone conversations she learned that it was Hanson's Friday. Their houseboat had been in its slip near the ranger station on Cumberland that morning at seven when maintenance came on duty. Unless he'd dumped the marijuana between four a.m. and seven, it was still on board. As usual on his weekends, he and Louise would be docking in St. Marys. After Anna assured Hull for the umpteenth time that neither Mitch nor his wife knew they'd been found out, he arranged for the Park Service and the Coast Guard to stake out Hanson's mainland berth in hopes they could find who his connection was.

The chief ranger informed whoever was on the other end of the line that the Hansons were also wanted on suspicion of murder; they were to be considered armed and dangerous.

As a result of Todd Belfore's death, Hull was shorthanded. He would take three members of fire crew, all commissioned law enforcement rangers, along on the bust. Part of Anna's punishment was that she would not be included in this elite. Under normal circumstances, the snub would have rankled more than it did. As it was, she was relieved to be given the night off.

Throughout the grilling, she'd been careful not to say anything about Dijon's involvement. The tactic worked and the young ranger was invited along on the stakeout. Rick would be left on the island with Anna to mind the store. Dijon was gleeful. Anna hoped she wouldn't be around when the news was broken to Rick.

Day drifted into night. The cloud of disfavor hanging over her grew darker with each passing hour. Guy was offended she hadn't come to him with her suspicions. Rick and Al sided with the crew boss. All of them were more or less pissed off because they'd missed out on the excitement, and covering it with overstated concerns for her personal safety. Guy and Al were mollified by their inclusion on the stakeout. Rick was not to be borne. To hear him tell it, he was the only one capable, trained, qualified, and spiritually prepared to make a major drug bust. Leaving him behind was tantamount to shackling Superman with kryptonite just as the busload of school-children plummeted off the cliff.

The whole performance made Anna tired. Her head throbbed with defenses she never bothered to put into words. The Hansons would be caught; Anna wasn't going to get fired. Theoretically all's well that ends well. She chose to leave it at that. Near nine she was finally able to slink away. The men, clustered happily on the dock playing with bulletproof vests and personal flotation devices, didn't even notice her departure.

For them the case was closed. For Anna it was merely over. Too many questions remained unanswered. Who had knocked her out with the butt of the shotgun and why? Who had slashed the truck seat?

Hanson could have done both. Maybe there'd been something in Slattery's house that incriminated him and he didn't want to be caught in the act of retrieving it. If he'd not found that something, he may have searched Anna's truck on the chance that she'd made away with it after she recovered from the knock to the head. That was a possible explanation for two of the questions but others remained for which she could devise no solution.

The Hansons' involvement in the marijuana cultivation was fairly straightforward; it tied Mitch solidly to the booby trap that lamed the Austrian, though no one would ever be able to prove it. Louise's connection with the crop was equally well established, as was her connection with Ellen Hull. From what Anna had heard of the girl, a combination of threats and bribes would probably be sufficient to get her to squeal on her special friend.

Damning as these bits and pieces were, they didn't prove either of the Hansons removed the actuator bolt and sabotaged the Beechcraft. Mitch very possibly was cold-blooded enough to do it. Anna always suspected overly jolly people of hiding black hearts. When she was a child, clowns had made her nervous. There was something sinister in the exaggeration of their features and in their unholy need to make short people laugh at them.

Burning the dope struck her as incongruous. Anyone with the greed and determination to take lives to further the business wouldn't be the type to cheerfully kiss off plants worth potentially a hundred grand or more. The assumption the plants had belonged to Hull had provided a weak rationale for torching them. Now even that was gone.

If Slattery was blackmailing the Hansons, and that was the motive for killing him, why burn the profits saved by hard-earned homicide?

Not her case, she reminded herself, not her park, and obviously, not her day. It was with relief she saw it drawing to a close. Two nights with little or no sleep were catching up to her. Her vision tunneled until all she could see beyond the battered olive green of the truck's hood was her sofa in the cool quiet of the Belfores' living room.

Tabby was home. She'd been to St. Marys for a checkup. The baby was fine, a boy. Tabby proudly announced she could see his "little tally whacker" on the ultrasound. Todd was to be the baby's name. No surprise there.

Lynette was with Tabby, and after the baby news was shared, both women went out of their way to compliment Anna on her hair. Tabby said a woman named Frieda had called. A Bella somebody had spilled something in Anna's house. Please call back. There was nothing Anna could do about a ruined rug or a stained chair from two thousand miles away, so she decided the call could wait.

A bottle of Chardonnay sat on the coffee table; both Lynette and the very pregnant Tabby held a glass. "The baby's pretty much fully baked or I wouldn't have any," Tabby explained, though Anna was too tired to notice and too indifferent to take the woman to task for it if she had.

They offered Anna a glass and she actually considered accepting. A year or more had passed since she'd last imbibed. Tonight she was saved from the temptation of alcohol by the reality of marijuana. She'd just been too high too long. Even a gentle white wine buzz wasn't appealing. Taking a cup of tea in its stead, she settled onto the uninhabited end of the sofa and answered all of their questions about Mitch and Louise and Anna's night out.

Oddly enough she found she enjoyed talking about it. The men had given her such short shrift. Angry they'd not been included, angry they'd not been given the decisions, the power; they were critical of every choice she'd made, every observation, concerned her actions had robbed them of glory in the present or would come back to bite them on the ass in the future. Giving this adventure to a "girl" was roughly the emotional equivalent of telling the dog one was going to give it to the cat.

Good to be among your own kind, Anna thought of the women, and smiled wearily. She felt her teacup being taken from her fingers and realized that for a while she'd been telling her story with her eyes closed.

Then she wasn't telling it at all.

25

THE VOICES of the women wrapped around Anna, made her feel safe, and she let herself sleep there in the chair. It was as if she floated on a velvet river. Now and then she'd drift close enough to the shores of consciousness to make out words from the gentle murmur of conversation. For once Tabby wasn't crying. Anna was immensely comforted by that. Having been assigned the girl's interim caretaker, she'd felt responsible for her happiness.

People can't make people happy, Anna thought drowsily. That's why animals are so beloved. The right person can make a cat happy. Anybody can make a dog happy. The vision evoked of joyous furbearing mammals made her want to laugh, but the weight of her languor was too great.

Words evaporated, Morpheus overwhelmed cannabis, and all was deliciously blank. When she was again aware, sleep was ebbing, but she did not yet want to return to the world of the living. In blissful somnolence, she stayed in her chair, eyes closed.

Talk had turned to outdoor sports as it often did when two or more Park Service people gathered. Fitting, she thought in pleasant confusion, that Wilderness should be present when two or more were gathered in Her name.

Tabby and Lynette were reliving favorite hikes, canoe trips, camping spots, and glorious climbs. As their voices lovingly recounted days of ice storms and sunsets, rapids and rappels, a niggling sense of disquiet built under Anna's breastbone and she wondered what triggered it. For several minutes more she lay as one dead, listening.

Tabby was telling of a splendid hike in the Cascades, a rare day when the sky was cloudless blue and mountain peaks had thrown off their customary shroud of virga, of seeing a bear with cubs in a meadow, two eagles high above fighting or flirting over the living prize of a hapless bunny.

Despite the pastoral—if somewhat graphic—scene, Anna felt the disquiet deepen. "I do so miss all of that," Tabby said, and Anna realized what was bothering her. Her eyes popped open. The women gaped at her like heroines in a melodrama when Dracula suddenly awakes in his coffin.

The Chardonnay was gone, a bottle of Chablis taking the place of its fallen comrade.

"You're awake," Lynette said unnecessarily.

"You lived in town, in Hope," Anna said to Tabby. Even to her own ears it sounded like an accusation.

"Not for the first year or so," Tabby replied, with the air of someone defending herself but not sure from what.

"I thought the wilderness scared you."

"I love the outdoors," Tabby said, bewildered. "It's one of the

things that brought Todd and me together. We both loved all of it."
The name of her dead husband having been invoked, tears flooded
her throat.

Anna wished she'd had the good sense to remain asleep. "Why
did you move to town?" she pressed.

"I . . . We . . . It just seemed better," Tabby finished lamely.

Anna struggled upright on the soft couch cushions and rubbed
her legs from the memory of their having failed her once before.
Friction stirred up half-smothered chiggers and they began to itch
fiercely. "I've got to go out," she announced.

Slattery Hammond's house was not difficult to break into. It was
merely a matter of prying off a screen that showed signs of having
been pried off numerous times before when previous occupants had
inadvertently locked themselves out. The latches on the aging sash
windows—where they remained attached—were willing to give up
their secrets when a little force was applied.

Once inside, Anna flipped on the overhead lights. Dense foliage
effectively screened the house from the road and she had the added
security of knowing that anyone who might take her to task for
unlawful entry—not to mention once again following up on an un-
authorized hunch—was well off the island staking out the Hansons.

The place was just as she'd left it, down to the dirty dishes on
the table and in the sink. The smell had escalated, a considerable
rankness enhancing the illusion that all the oxygen had been
leached out of the air.

Sitting at Hammond's desk near the front door, she studied the
five snapshots Scotch-taped to the wall. She took one down and
slipped it in her pocket, then jerked open the desk drawers. On her
previous visit she'd been looking only for Hammond's logbooks, had
opened only containers and envelopes that might have concealed a

long narrow ledger. The packets of color snapshots in their Wal-Mart envelopes had earned only a cursory glance.

Anna pulled them out and laid them on the desk. Sifting rapidly through, she looked at each photo, then checked the processing date on the envelope.

When she emerged from Hammond's quarters, stars prickled a perfect cloudless sky. The light was fragile but tenuous, revealing nothing yet refusing to give way to night. For a moment Anna stood trying to capture the essence of peace that solitude customarily afforded. On Cumberland it was not to be found. Though the island lacked the richness and verdancy of a jungle, the heat-soaked trees hiding behind veils of moss breathed out the same powerful secrecy she'd felt the few times she'd been in the tropics; a knowledge of things unseen, powerful and dark. It was no mystery to her that voodoo developed in a hot island climate, that witches preferred the darkling woods.

Shaking off thoughts of less than corporeal dangers, she sought the pragmatic sanctity of the truck. Making one brief stop at the fire dorm to collect the key from the nail where Guy kept it, she drove to the ranger station.

Frieda picked up on the sixth ring. Time zones were working in Anna's favor. In Colorado it was not yet nine o'clock. At the sound of the Mesa Verde dispatcher's voice Anna experienced a stab of homesickness. In that instant she was back on the high tableland, the delicate scent of pine and dust in the air, a memory of sunlight on the cliffs. "How's Piedmont?" she asked, one's cat being the living, breathing embodiment of all that was Home.

"Hey, that's what I called you about," Frieda said. "Well, not exactly but sort of related." She laughed. "Not related at all really, but funny. Oops. Maybe not. I guess you had to be there."

Frieda was a bit tipsy.

Anna envied her. They'd begun their relationship as drinking buddies. The friendship had endured through Anna's climb onto the wagon and was as strong as ever. Still, when booze called, it was usually in Frieda's warm tones. She had a knack for giving everyday things a festive air: filing, typing, drinking.

The dispatcher would hardly announce the death of Anna's orange tiger cat in such cheerful tones; still she forgot the reason for her call in her concern for Piedmont. "What happened?" she asked bluntly, cutting across the wine-tinted babble.

"It's a long story. Well, not that long." Anna waited through what she knew was a fortifying sip, probably of a hearty red. Frieda resumed: "Bella came with me to feed Piedmont—she takes care of the socializing end." Anna smiled to think of the little girl her fat tomcat had taken such a shine to. Bella Meyers suffered from dwarfism. With her fairy face and foreshortened legs, Piedmont looked the size of a mountain lion when he walked next to her.

"Anyway," Frieda went on. "They got to playing and one or the other of them—Bella says Piedmont, Piedmont insists it was Bella—knocked over the urn with Zach's ashes. You left it on the coffee table. I guess the top was loose."

Anna remembered. "I was going to sprinkle him," she said feebly. She'd been going to sprinkle her late husband's ashes for nearly nine years. Somehow she never quite got around to it.

"They scattered all over your Navajo rug."

"That's okay. Zach always liked that rug. It won't hurt if a little bit of him gets vacuumed up every now and then. I've been meaning to cast those ashes to the winds. Maybe this is an omen telling me it's time to get on with it."

"It's an omen, all right." Frieda laughed, then made an effort to get herself under control, but amusement percolated beneath her words. "I shouldn't laugh," she apologized. "You may not think this is all that funny. Bella cleaned them up like the good little girl she is. She thought they were cigarette ashes and she didn't want them to make your house 'all stinky.' She flushed them down the john."

Breath gusted from Anna's lungs. She remembered the paralysis and panic when she'd fallen from the horizontal ladder in second grade and landed on her back. Gulping fishlike, she managed to get enough air to speak. "She flushed Zach down the *toilet*?"

Frieda laughed. "Sorry," she said more soberly. "Yup. Right down the loo." Again she giggled.

So many years of toting a sacred icon, never finding a place holy enough to commit it to, then a seven-year-old girl consigns it to the sewers. "Jesus," Anna said. "That's that, I guess."

"That's all the news that's fit to print," Frieda said. "Jennifer's here. I ought to go make hostess noises. Are you okay?"

"I'm fine." Anna restored the phone receiver to its cradle and sat for a bit in Norman Hull's high-backed chair. Hollowness formed within her and she wasn't sure, but she thought she felt lighter, as if a burden carried so long its weight had become part of life had been lifted. Frieda was right: an omen. She would have preferred something classier: a burning bush or a host of angels singing on high, but as omens went this one got right to the point. Anna laughed. "Sorry, Zach," she said in the general direction of the ceiling. "We've all got to let go sometime."

Frederick's oft repeated invitation to move to Chicago and set up housekeeping came to mind. Forty-two; Anna counted up her years on earth. How many more chances would she get? According to the tabloids it was a buyer's market. Her stock wasn't slated to go up anytime soon.

"Get thee behind me, Satan," she said to ward off the fears of a generation.

Anna doubted she'd ever move back to a city. Not just to be with Frederick Stanton, at any rate. In her head she heard Molly's voice pitched in her best shrinky tones. "Listen to the qualifier, Anna: 'Not *just* to be with Frederick . . .'" Anna waved a hand in front of her face as if dispensing a crowd of angry mosquitoes.

Plunked untidily in the perfect order of the chief ranger's desk, the phone reminded her of why she'd come. "Precocious senility." She excused the lapse as she picked up the receiver and punched in Frieda's number a second time.

"That's not what I called about," she said when Frieda answered. "Remember you told me Slattery Hammond had two other restraining orders filed against him in addition to the latest one his wife filed?" Anna gave Frieda a second to assimilate the change of subject, then pushed on. "You said they were withdrawn. At the time, I just assumed they were filed by Mrs. Hammond. Feints before the actual battle so to speak. Do you remember if she filed all three?"

Frieda said nothing.

"Are you there?" Anna demanded.

"Keep your pants on," Frieda said mildly. "Give me about fifteen minutes and then call me at the office."

"Thanks," Anna said.

"Don't mention it. I was just relaxing after a ten-hour day. Abandoning my guests and rushing back to the office at the drop of a hint is my idea of a good time."

Anna laughed because it was true.

She passed the time by going over the photographs she'd confiscated from Slattery's desk. Laying them out like a hand of solitaire, she trained Hull's lamp on them and studied the figures. They were all very much alike; long shots, some obviously taken with a telephoto lens. The breathtaking scenery of the North Cascades served as a backdrop. In each was a figure, usually alone but sometimes in a group of two or three others. About a third of the pictures featured a slight, brown-haired woman dressed for hiking, most often in shorts but in full yellow rain gear in half a dozen of the shots. A baby in a backpack was strapped on her back. Because of the distance from the cameraman to his subject, Anna couldn't make out the woman's features, but from the straightness of her spine, the slender body, and the infant, Anna guessed she was young.

The pickup date on the Wal-Mart envelopes containing the photos of the woman and child was within the last eight months.

The second group of pictures, four rolls of film's worth, were older. The most recent was dated seven months previously. The others went back a year and a half. These followed the same pattern as the shots of the brunette: all long shots, all of the same woman, all against the dramatic scenery of the Cascades. The only difference was these were of a slight blond woman with shoulder-length hair. The same woman who'd sparked a sense of recognition in Anna when she'd first looked at the snaps taped to Hammond's wall.

The telephone rang and she jumped as if she'd been poked with a cattle prod.

"Frieda here," the dispatcher cut in, before Anna could finish the litany of Cumberland Island National Seashore. "Good news/ bad news joke. I found it faster than I thought I would and it has less information than I remember. The only restraining order that's got a name attached is the one that stuck, the one his wife filed against him. Since the other two were rescinded they've got a record of the action but not of who initiated it."

"What were the dates?" Anna grabbed the phone pad to scribble on. The top sheet held a note from Dot and Mona: "See us ASAP." Anna stuck it under the corner of the phone where Hull couldn't miss it and ripped off another sheet for herself.

"Let's see . . . The first was August of last year and the second was December, same year. Are you onto something?"

"I'm afraid so. I'll keep you posted. It's okay about the ashes."

Fried laughed. "Sorry," she said. "Something about it just gets to me."

"You didn't tell Bella?"

"Heck no, the kid's got enough to worry about as it is."

"Tell her thank you for me," Anna said. As she hung up she could hear Frieda was laughing again.

Headed north, back toward Plum Orchard, Anna drove slowly. Night had triumphed. With oak branches meeting overhead there were no stars. All that existed of the world was the narrow stripe of color brought to life by the truck's high beams.

The effects of the marijuana were gone but for lethargy and the occasional flash of disorientation, yet Anna couldn't seem to fix her mind on the problem at hand. She knew she should be mapping out a plan of action or, if she was to bow to the wishes of the Park Service in the person of Norman Hull, a plan of inaction until all the proper channels had been followed.

Rolling along at fifteen miles per hour, she was content to let the road hypnotize her. Had Hull or Guy or the implicated *anybody* been available, she might have called them. The Hanson stakeout had denuded the island of law enforcement for the next eight hours. It occurred to her to go by the fire dorm and get Rick but this wasn't his kind of bust. A black belt didn't qualify him for delicate situations and this was one china shop Anna wouldn't relish seeing a bull loosed in. With a sinking sadness she knew even her lightest touch was going to cause irreparable damage.

Pinpricks of light disturbed the black of the forest's ceiling. She had reached the meadow by Stafford House. The moon had yet to rise and the meadow slept. As she turned onto the lane, the truck's headlights raked the dry grass, sparking green fire from the eyes of a family of deer snuggled down for the night.

Endangered Species

Life, especially life in such a graceful and benign form as a doe and her fawn, raised Anna's spirits. She lifted her chin and willed the mesmerizing flicker of woods from her mind.

Dot and Mona's cottage was almost obscured by the tabby wall that protected it from the road. A window near the roof shone with yellow light, creating a portrait of a fairy tale house in the woods. Images of witches and ovens and murderous children arose to spoil the effect. "Stop that," Anna told herself.

In front of the gate a darker spot marred the dirt. A pothole, Anna guessed, though she didn't remember a crater of that magnitude on her drive south. She had gritted her teeth to take the jar when something about the shadow's configuration changed. As her headlights hit it, two glowing green eyes peered up from the tightly curled body of a fawn. Too late to brake, Anna jerked the wheel to the right and bounced out across the rough meadow.

The near miss left her shaken. Taken as a last straw dropped upon the back of a camel who'd been stoned literally and pilloried metaphorically, it weighed heavily. Tears threatened. Anna cursed them down. Anger followed, but one look at the animal, standing now, gazing trustingly in her direction, left it nowhere to bestow itself.

"Come on baby," she said, letting herself out of the vehicle. "It's time you were home in bed." The same could be said for her. The beneficial effects of her brief catnap were wearing off.

At the sound of her voice Flicka bleated and scampered over to butt his head against the palms of her hands. Unfailingly enchanted by the little creature, Anna folded herself down in the grass and lost herself in the wonder of his spotted back, the liquid eyes, the strong willowy neck and tiny perfect hooves.

"Miles to go before I sleep," she explained when she finally forced herself to rise. "And miles to go. Come on. Let's get you home. Your fairy godmothers will be worried."

The truck was well off the road, so Anna left it where it was and walked to the wall. The gate was an unlovely modern addition of welded pipe and sheep wire. Usually it stood open. Tonight it was shut, effectively penning Flicka out. Were Dot and Mona weaning the fawn, teaching him to go back to the wild? Anna abandoned the thought as soon as it surfaced. The VIPs were too sensible to shut an animal as young and unafraid as Flicka out on a public road at night.

"After you," she said, and shooed the fawn in ahead of her. He didn't take much urging. Like any child, at suppertime he wanted to be home and safe and fed. As she latched the gate behind her, she could hear his hooves clattering on the stones of the cottage's front walk.

Inside the wall, parked to one side where it was not visible from the road, was an ATV. She wondered who had come calling that was too hoity-toity to park in the street like everyone else.

Flicka was scraping at the door with sharp hooves, punctuating this polite request for admittance with rattling butts to the door-frame. Either the old ladies weren't at home or they were hard of hearing.

Having followed the fawn up the walk, Anna rapped on the door and hollered: "Anybody home? It's Anna from fire crew."

Muttering emanated from within and she realized how quiet the house had been. The cottage didn't have air-conditioning. Windows on either side of the door were open, the light and air shut inside by tightly closed mini-blinds. A voice carried through as if Anna were inside with them.

"Who is it?"

Mona: without the stalwart, clever woman in evidence to back up the voice, Anna heard the tremor of age. "Anna Pigeon from fire crew," she repeated.

More muttering, footsteps; then Dot came to the door. She didn't look pleased to have someone show up on her doorstep after eleven at night. Anna played her only card. "I found Flicka," she said, and unabashedly hid behind his adorable spots. Dot's face softened at once, so much so that Anna was afraid she was going to burst into tears.

Pushing open the screen, Dot knelt down, her fat knees filling the sill, and gathered Flicka into her arms. She buried her face against the fawn's neck, knocking her glasses askew. "Flicka, we've been so worried about you," she said into the silken hide.

"Was he lost?" Anna asked. "If he ran off, he must have decided which side his bread was buttered on. I found him curled up in the middle of the road out front." No response from Dot. Anna was somehow disappointed. "I nearly ran him over," she added. Even with the prod, the expected gush of thanks was not forthcoming.

Dot scooped Flicka up and carried him inside.

"Anna, come in," Mona called.

A sensitive individual might have been put off by Dot's snub, but Anna wasn't yet ready to go back to the apartment and do her duty, so she trailed the woman and fawn inside.

The cottage had pioneered the concept of a Great Room when it was an architectural convenience rather than a status symbol. A single multipurpose room was easier to build and heat than a house cobbled up into private areas. Dot and Mona had filled the compact space with the clutter of academia. Books, papers, boxes, teacups, and overfilled ashtrays spilled across the dining table and all but three of the chairs. Two of these were occupied. Mona sat upright in a ladder-back chair. A cigarette burned in her right hand. Her left rested on a Coke can on the table. She looked tired and distracted. It added years to her already considerable account.

Marty Schlessinger sat behind the table between Mona and the empty chair. One hand was on the table. The fingers trembled ever so slightly, like an aspen in a light breeze. Probably high, Anna thought.

Dot, Flicka captive in her arms, perched on the edge of the third chair. Anna was left standing. "Turtle stuff?" she asked, to fill the awkward silence she'd brought in with her.

"Always," Mona said.

Thick as a pea soup fog, silence descended again, the only sound Mona's fiddling with the pop-top on her coke. Clickclick-click.

"The files are a mess," Schlessinger said. Her voice was cool and even. If she'd been using for a while, she probably functioned better high than straight. As if on cue, Dot and Mona nodded sagely. Click. Click. Click.

Whatever they were up to, Anna was not needed to make a fourth. She took one more stab at an invitation. "An all-nighter?" she asked, reminded of college and speed and last-minute cramming.

"Surely not." Mona. Clickclickclick.

So much for fantasies of procrastination. Anna was forced to take the hint. "I've got to run," she said. "Places to go, people to meet, all that sort of thing." No one said a word. Three pairs of eyes followed her as she beat a hasty retreat to the door.

"Thanks for bringing Flicka in—" Dot hollered as the screen banged shut.

"But don't let the door slap your ass on the way out," Anna finished the sentence.

The Chablis had fallen, making two dead soldiers littering the coffee table. Fluorescent curls of Cheetos provided a surrealistic array of splattered intestines to further the theme. Tabby and Lynette, heads together, were giggling over a Victoria's Secret catalogue; a scene from a pajama party at a home for unwed mothers.

"Hey, Anna." Lynette's voice was delicately blurred by a wash of white wine. "Did you get what you needed done done? We missed you."

"Short hair makes you look ten years younger." Tabby repeated a compliment from earlier in the evening just to be personable. Wine had worked its spell on her. Her cheeks flushed prettily and the tight reins of tears had been loosed at the corners of her eyes, restoring her girlishness.

Here, at least, Anna was welcomed. Not for long, she reminded herself.

The phone rang, jarring Anna but apparently delighting the others. Tabby snatched it up, burbling a happy, "Hello!" Joy was slapped from her face by the vicious hand of memory. "Oh, it's you," she said coldly. Then to Anna: "It's for you."

"Was it something I said?" came Dijon's voice.

Anna remembered the cruel moments of forgetfulness after Zach had died. Tabby had thought it was Todd calling. "Nope. What's up?"

"Jesus. If I wasn't so bored, I'd hang up. Nothing's up. Zip. Nada. A bust of a bust. Captain whosis—the Coast Guard guy—got tired of waiting and we nabbed 'em. Two old farts grilling wieners on a houseboat full of weed. Talk about your adrenaline rush."

Anna smiled. "No fisticuffs?"

"Shit—shoot, no. Not even an interrogation under hot lights. Hull told the Hansons they're suspected of a double homicide as well as marijuana cultivation and they fell all over themselves to cooperate.

"Hammond was putting the squeeze on them. Louise swore he made them plant three times what they had. 'Just plain greedy' she called him." Dijon laughed. "According to her they were just poor pitiful servants. Since they burned Hammond's share of the crop, she seemed to think we should let them keep theirs out of pure gratitude. Both swore Hammond did the whole booby trap deal all by his self and they, like good citizens, removed the hazard as soon as they found out. Like there's anybody left alive to say different."

"How about the sabotage?" Anna was uncomfortably aware of Lynette and Tabby hanging on every word of her side of the conversation.

" 'Not guilty.' What did you think they'd say?"

A tiny irrational hope that had dared to stir in Anna's breast was quashed. "You guys coming back anytime soon?" she asked.

"You're kidding, right? We'll be filling out forms longer than the perps' jail sentences."

Fifteen seconds of silence ticked by while Anna shuffled her thoughts. A look at Tabby decided her. The girl was small, frail, drunk, pregnant, and unarmed. Piece of cake, Anna thought sourly.

"Thanks for calling, Dijon. I was worried about you all. Good talking to you, old buddy." Dijon's voice jolted in Anna's ear.

"Right. All that," she said absently, and hung up the phone.

Anna pulled up a kitchen chair and sat across the table from the women, where she could see them yet keep her distance and her mobility. "I've got some pictures I want you to look at." She cleared away the magazine and Cheetos, then dealt the snapshots out, right side up, to her audience on the couch. Tabby and Lynette put on faces depicting interest and enthusiasm, willing to be amused, happy to let Anna in on the fun.

"What a lovely place," Lynette said, absorbed in the photos as well as the role of girlfriend. "Northwest? Olympic maybe?"

Anna was watching Tabby. At first she'd looked at the snapshots with the same slightly bleary good cheer as the interpretive ranger. Slowly it dawned on her what the photos were of and where they'd come from. The party look drained from her eyes, then the blood from her cheeks. She became so pale Anna was afraid she'd faint. Her small swollen hands pulled away from the photographs and comforted one another on her lap. Her mouth contorted, ready to cry. Anna had prepared herself for waterworks but none came. Eventually even a river of tears must run dry.

Grabbing her belly, Tabby began to breathe in short, shallow gasps.

"Don't you even *think* about having that baby now," Anna said sharply. "Open your eyes." Tabby opened them. "Breathe in slowly and regularly." Tabby did.

"What's going on?" Lynette asked.

"Shh," Anna hushed her. "You breathing?" Tabby gulped and nodded. "Tell me what happened. I've mostly figured it out, but I want to hear it from you. Then we'll decide how best to handle it, okay?"

"Okay," Tabby whispered, and reached for her glass. It was empty.

"I've got more in the car," Lynette said. "It's warm, but—"

"We don't need more," Anna cut her off. "Tabby is going to be just fine. We're going to work this out." She let a stillness settle around them. Anna's rudeness had sufficed to cut through Lynette's alcohol haze and she sat meekly on the couch waiting for events to unfold.

"I'm . . . going to be sick," Tabby said.

"No you're not," Anna told her. "You'll feel better after you talk to me."

Tabby laid her head back and closed her eyes. All the tension went from her body. Her fingers ceased their stranglehold on one another and her hands opened like flowers, palm up on her thighs. "I wanted to tell," she whispered, and Anna hitched her chair closer to hear. "But if I told I'd go to jail. The baby would be born in jail. My little boy." She opened her eyes and looked at Anna. "They won't let you keep a baby in prison, will they?"

"I don't know," Anna said honestly.

"They'd take him. I know they would. Who'd leave a baby with a murderer? He'd know I killed his daddy." From a deeper well of grief, Tabby drew up tears thick as glycerine. They slid over her temples to disappear into her hair.

"There's the burning bed precedent," Anna said without much hope. "Extenuating circumstances. Hammond was stalking you, wasn't he?"

Tabby nodded, her fine hair scrunching into a halo against the back of the sofa. "He started not long after he came to the Cascades. At first I was flattered. He paid attention to me and gave me little things—a flower, a pretty rock, like that. I wouldn't ever go farther and he started being mean. Following me. Letting me know he could find me no matter where I went, that he could get into our house even if we locked it. He read my mail. Left things on the seat of my car when I'd locked all the doors. Showing me how easy it would be to get me. I talked to the police. The only real ones were in Hope and they had no say in the park. Hope's not even in the United States. Todd and his two seasonals were the only law enforcement in the district. Slattery never got seen doing anything by anybody but me and sometimes I'd say he'd been somewhere bothering me and he could find some girl to say he'd been with her. The Park Service was kind of wanting Todd to keep out of it, being as he was my husband and all, but there was nobody else. I don't think they believed me anyway.

"Todd got pretty crazy. I was scared he'd get hurt or kill Slattery and go to jail. We got an apartment in town where there'd be people around—people who could help me if anything . . . happened. Slattery started doing the same things in town. I filed a restraining order a couple of times. The police thought I was just trying to get attention because my husband was in the park and stuff. Then I'd tell them about Slattery bothering me in the park but that wasn't even in Canada. Finally they talked to Slattery but he sounded so good and I sounded so stupid. And we were Americans and everything was just screwed up. Slattery said the restraining orders didn't mean anything. And he was right—he still found me no matter how hard I tried never to be alone. He threatened to hurt Todd so I withdrew my complaints.

"I got pregnant and Todd put in for a transfer. Slattery won, we ran. I thought that would be the end of it. Then he showed up here. He'd followed us. Everything started over. But now there was the baby. Slattery said things about the baby. That I was pregnant made him mad. He said he'd kill the baby if I didn't do certain things. You know . . . things."

"I get the picture," Anna said.

"Now I think *I'm* going to be sick," Lynette said.

"Be my guest. Go on," Anna told Tabby.

"Todd was losing it. That's what we were fighting about that night you broke us up."

"He said he'd leave you."

Tabby jerked her head up. It bobbed independently from the slack body as if a puppeteer had pulled but one string. "No sir," she said childishly.

" 'You would leave me.' " Anna quoted her words back at her.

"Did he think you'd encouraged Slattery?" Lynette asked gently.

"No. No. Nothing like that." Looking both alarmed and mystified, Tabby fought her way upright on the sofa. A cloud moved away from her sun and she smiled in the midst of this grisly recital. Obviously the threat of Todd's leaving was a greater evil than stalking or being stalked. "I remember why I said that," she said with relief. "Todd said he was going to kill Slattery and I said he'd go to jail and he said that was okay and I said it wasn't, because then he'd leave me."

"Why was he on the plane with Hammond?" Anna asked.

Tabby dropped her face in her hands and rocked herself forward and back around the embryonic Todd junior. "I don't know. Maybe he wanted a place to talk to him in private. I don't know. I swear to God I didn't know Slattery wasn't going by himself. I never would have done it, never, if I knew somebody else might be hurt. I was just scared. Then Todd got in . . ." Her voice trailed off. Anna and Lynette exchanged looks. Anna was half afraid Lynette's beliefs were going to lure her into saying something inane about God teaching lessons in his Old Testament persona. The look of empathy on Lynette's face made Anna ashamed of the thought. Kindness and Christianity were equally revered—or synonymous—in Lynette's heart.

"So you sabotaged the Beechcraft," Anna summed up for Tabby.

"Yes."

"Do you know who the brown-haired woman is, the one in the other pictures?"

Tabby shook her head.

"No matter," Anna said. "If she was another of Hammond's victims, he won't be bothering her anymore."

"Can I get a drink of water?" Tabby pleaded.

"Go with her," Anna said to Lynette.

A self-confessed murderess and a drunken lover of the deceased left the scene. Anna couldn't dredge up an iota of concern. She couldn't picture Tabby taking it on the lam in a stolen VW bug. Trusting in her judgment of human nature was born more of habit than experience. She'd written Tabby off as a suspect, deeming her too ineffectual to ruin the Beech. Who knows, Anna thought indifferently, maybe she was wrong again and Tabby would come charging back through the kitchen door wielding a bread knife à la *Psycho*.

Inept fumbling noises emanated from that general direction.

"Let me do it," she heard Lynette say, then ice cubes falling into a glass, clickclickclick.

"Dammit." Anna jumped up from the chair. "Tabby!" she hollered as she bounded toward the kitchen. "Tabby!" By the second shout she was almost on top of the girl. Big-eyed and miserable, Tabby leaned against the counter clutching her water glass with both hands like a little kid.

"How did you do it?" Anna demanded, taking hold of the narrow shoulders.

Tabby folded in on herself, shrinking from Anna's touch. "I was scared," Tabby cried with a convincingly terrified quaver in her voice.

"Stop it," Lynette said, and laid her hand on Anna's wrist.

"No," Anna said. "This is good news. How did you do it, Tabby? How did you know how to break the airplane so it would crash?"

"I was doing the dishes and a sandwich bag fell in the sink. It went down and settled over the drain so the water wouldn't go out."

"You put sandwich bags in the gas tanks so they'd stop the flow of fuel and the airplane would crash. Have I got it right?"

Tabby nodded.

"Hallelujah." Anna dropped her hands from the girl's shoulders. She hadn't misguessed. Tabby was a lovely little idiot, albeit one with murderous intent. "You didn't kill Todd and you didn't kill Slattery. Those bags didn't do a damn thing but float around in there. Even if by some freakish chance both bags floated over both outlets and stayed there long enough to make a difference, the Beech still had its inboard tanks. We know what wrecked the airplane," Anna said, trying to get through the tragic glaze over Tabby's eyes. "It wasn't you. You failed. You didn't hurt anybody. The baby won't be born in jail. Nobody will take him away from you."

Tabby was unmoved, face pinched, shoulders hunched.

"Jesus," Anna said in desperation. "You do it, Lynette. It's all true. Swear to God. I've got to go." She stopped at the door and turned back. "Better yet, take Tabby with you. Get Rick. Tell him I need backup. Stafford House. Soon as he can get there."

"Rick. Stafford. ASAP," Lynette repeated.

"Seat belts," Anna reminded the interpreter, and ran down the wooden stairs hoping it wasn't already too late.

26

CLICKCLICKCLICK.

Click. Click. Click.

Clickclickclick.

Remembering, Anna was stunned by her own boneheadedness. Dot and Mona were vintage World War II stock: B-52s, cigarettes, red lipstick. And Morse code. SOS. Distress signals had been plentiful: the nerves, the snubs, the tension, the silences. Preoccupied with Tabby Belfore, Anna had failed to realize their import.

As she fired up the pumper truck, Tabby and Lynette came out of the upstairs apartment. Legally Lynette was too drunk to drive but at this hour of the night she would be the only vehicle on the road and, given the surface of the lanes, Anna doubted the VW could get up enough speed to do too much damage if she did stack it. "Wear your seat belts," she reminded them again. She cinched her own so tight it bruised the thin layer of flesh over her hipbones, but it would keep her behind the steering wheel during what was promising to be a wild ride. "Take care, take care," she whispered to herself. Dead or injured she would be no good to anyone. *Better to be late to Golden Gate than to arrive in hell on time;* a piece of rhyming wisdom handed down from her father played through her mind. Raised in California, she and Molly had missed the point of the lesson when they were children. They thought "Golden Gate" referred to the bridge in San Francisco.

Under the present circumstances, the poem was too apt to be comforting. A few minutes might make the difference between who lived and who died. Anna's foot grew heavy on the gas pedal and she held on to the steering wheel with all her might, keeping control of the fire truck as it leaped and bucked over the rutted road.

Everyday life was full of unanswered questions, small mysteries that one took no note of. However bizarre any given fact, any unexplained occurrence, unless it could be tied into the problem, it wasn't useful information. That was a sticking point in murder investigations; what to factor in and what to ignore.

Anna had chosen to ignore a smattering of disparate pieces on the assumption they were unrelated to the puzzle she was working on. During the jolting ride from Plum Orchard to Stafford, some of those pieces began to fit in the holes left by the Hansons-as-killers theory.

Marty had thrown Anna and Dijon out of her home after Dijon had read the memo recalling the Lewin electron microscopes. Dot and Mona complained that they were to have two paid assistants, neither of whom had materialized. Slattery Hammond had taken an uncharacteristic interest in the loggerheads nesting on Cumberland Island. Lynette had gone by Hammond's the morning of the crash to pick up something the VIPs had lent him and needed returned for their turtle project. That afternoon Anna had been coldcocked by someone searching for something they didn't want anyone else to

find. Later Anna's truck was searched and vandalized but nothing
was taken, presumably because whatever the thief had been looking
for wasn't there. Later that same day, in a sudden act of charity that
went against the grain, Marty Schlessinger offered to help Tabby
sort and organize the files Todd left behind. The job had been abandoned halfway through, leaving the apartment and the widow in
greater confusion than before. Tonight Anna found a message on the
chief ranger's desk from the VIPs: "See us ASAP." Then Dot and
Mona's home awash in files, Flicka shut out in the road, and a Coke
can used to tap out SOS.

Anna was willing to bet there never had been an electron microscope—or Schlessinger had sold it. The money for assistants listed
had gone into her pocket, then up her nose. Discrepancies in the
files might have been able to prove it. Slattery's sudden interest in
endangered species must have been sparked by some suspicion of
Schlessinger's activities. He'd studied the files, obtained proof, and
threatened to expose the biologist.

Given this new slant, even the lie about hearing shots the day
the Austrian was injured was explained. Possibly Marty, with her
knowledge of the island, had stumbled across Hanson's operation.
For whatever reasons—indifference, power, or free dope—she had
kept quiet about it. When things started heating up after the wreck,
she needed to point the investigation in a safe direction. What better than a marijuana plot? Judges, police, and the American public
were more than willing to believe cannabis farmers capable of any
sort of ghastly crime.

"Damn," Anna muttered through clenched teeth, afraid if she
loosed her jaws she'd bite off her tongue. Murders bore a disap-
pointing relationship to magic tricks—once one knew how they
were done they bordered on the banal, leaving one feeling, instead
of awestruck, thoroughly foolish for having been taken in.

Stafford was just over three miles from Plum Orchard. Anna

made it in four minutes, possibly a land speed record for that stretch of road. After she rolled to a stop by the wall, she could feel her viscera quivering from the bombardment. Having armed herself with a flashlight and a tire iron, she slipped from the truck and, keeping to the darkest stretch of night near the wall, put twenty feet between herself and her vehicle. Crouching down in a corner formed of wall and palmetto, she waited. Bursting upon a crime in progress with no weapon and no backup was not appealing. She wanted to get the lay of the land before she made any decisions; see if the clanking arrival of the truck stirred anyone from the cottage grounds.

A minute, then two, of forced inactivity passed. Nothing moved, nothing sounded but for the creak of the cooling truck engine and the stirring of a summer night. Convinced she was alone or out-smarted, Anna came quietly to her feet. The tire iron, a heavy cross suitable for dispatching felons and warding off vampires, she shoved through her belt to free up her right hand. Her left clutched a flashlight with a beam so brown and myopic she tossed it away in disgust. Such a light would serve only to pinpoint her whereabouts.

The gate remained closed, Schlessinger's ATV parked in the lee of the wall near the VIPs' truck. Noiselessly Anna let herself in and, following the darkness where it flowed deepest, moved to the cottage and pressed herself against the wall beneath the single high window. The light had been extinguished and there was no sound from within. Again she waited for two interminable minutes but nothing called attention to itself, not a footfall, a word, or the telltale shush of fabric against wood.

Fear dug taloned fingers into her stomach at the thought she had come too late, that Dot and Mona lay inside, forever quiet, their knowledge and their files expunged from the face of the earth. How hard could it be to kill two old ladies? Depended on the ladies, Anna thought. Dot, Mona, Alice—these were not women who'd go gentle into that good night. She took comfort from that and from the presence of the vehicles. If Marty had finished her work, her ATV would have been gone.

Continued silence reassuring her, Anna crept around the corner of the house to stand to one side of the front door. Darkness mixed with the heat, filling the cottage's interior. The barest breath of air came from behind and she thrilled to feel it ruffle her newly shorn locks. A sudden bleating and a clatter followed it. Flicka had caught her scent and skittered across the hardwood toward the door.

Anna swallowed her heart down to its usual resting place and stepped away from the screen. The noise of the little animal had startled her but she took it as one more sign the cottage was empty. With Dot and Mona available, Flicka tended to ignore mere mortals.

Reaching inside, she felt for the light switch. Flicka pushed out as soon as the latch was free and jumped up like an ill-mannered puppy, his sharp hooves awakening the chiggers in her thighs. Protected by the lath and plaster of the wall, Anna switched on the interior light, then bobbed quickly, one eye over the windowsill, one eye low around the doorframe, trying not to provide a target where a target was expected or leave it there long enough to be blown away.

The great room was empty. Papers were everywhere, the file boxes overturned. Half-burned pages smoldered on the hearthstones. A bath and bedroom opened off a stubby hallway to the rear of the house. Had Anna been armed she might have felt duty-bound to go in. Building searches gave her a bad feeling. In training she'd only been killed twice, both times during a building search. She was not sorry to be excused from this one, and heartily relieved there were no dead bodies cluttering up the front room.

Leaving the light burning, she ran lightly around the small dwelling. Afraid of being abandoned for a third time in a single night, Flicka hesitated for a moment, making short runs back and forth, then trotted off, sticking close to Anna's heels.

Playing at Wee Willie Winkie, she peered in the windows and spied through the lock on a back door that looked as if it hadn't been opened in fifty years. Enough light spilled into the back rooms that Anna was satisfied that, unless the three women were crowded together under the bed, the cottage was empty.

Relief didn't live long enough to blossom before it was replaced by alarm and frustration. Dot and Mona had been taken somewhere. First rule of self-preservation: Never let yourself be taken to the second scene of the crime. Regardless of promises made, evildoers don't move the party for the greater comfort of the victim. Anna remembered a defensive-tactics instructor shouting at a timid young woman student, "These guys will rape you, kill you, and leave your body in a ditch. Why is it you don't think they'd lie to you?"

Having returned to the front of the cottage, she stepped inside hoping to find something to indicate where Marty had taken them. They'd gone on foot, that much was clear by the vehicles left behind. It had been less than an hour since Anna had seen the VIPs. The sorting and destroying of files must have taken up some of that time. They couldn't have gotten too far. Anna had 360 degrees to choose from, all equally dark and uninviting. To the east lay forest, the Chimneys, and the sea. To the south was the sound, the marshes, and an old cemetery. Westward the sound snuggled up to Stafford's grounds. North was the designated wilderness area with both forest and saltwater marsh. A wealth of places to hide a body or two. With care and tides and fiddler crabs, a learned biologist could probably manage it so they'd never be found; not by dogs and not by time.

Standing in the mess, Anna noticed she'd lost her shadow. Flicka had been with her when she came back from the rear of the cottage but hadn't followed her inside.

First the fawn was shut outside the grounds. Possibly it had been an accident. Maybe an act of intimidation, adding anxiety about their pet to Dot and Mona's mental stress. Or the fawn was a distraction Marty didn't need. With coke and adrenaline calling the shots, the woman was undoubtedly operating on the edge.

Then Flicka was shut inside.

Because he'd tried to follow, was Anna's guess.

"Flicka, here baby," she called softly, hurrying out into the yard. *Hey, Lassie, Timmy's in the well,* came a mocking thought, but it was the only hope she had to go on and she clung to it.

A brief search located the fawn. He was standing at the edge of the cleared ground behind Stafford House. On seeing Anna, he bleated once, then stared into the black wall of woods. Afraid she would distract him, she fell back and hid in the shadows of what once had served Stafford as a servants' wing. For maybe a minute the animal trotted back and forth at the tree line bleating; then he stepped delicately into the foliage and was gone.

Anna followed as fast as she dared, entering the woods where he had vanished. A fatted moon had deigned to rise and fragments of light littered the forest floor. Relying on hope as much as hearing, she trailed the little beast. Once he'd established his direction, he moved along at a good pace. Near the salt marshes that skirted the sound, the woods thinned.

The tide was in. Only the tips of the grasses showed above the water. They ebbed and flowed with the currents. In the unrevealing light of the moon, it was impossible to tell where grass ended and water began. The shoreline was equally uncertain. Land and marsh and sea blended seamlessly into one another. Fireflies added their stars and brought the sky into this confluence of elements.

Trusting to the fawn's sense of smell, Anna followed in his wake. Several times he stopped and wandered aimlessly along the edge of land and marsh bleating plaintively. At each stop Anna found herself holding her breath, afraid both that he'd lost the trail and that he'd found its end. Bodies, weighted and submerged in the high saltwater grasses beyond the low-tide mark would be effectively hidden from the world. The natural action of the sea would wash away all signs of interference. Carrion eaters would take care of the rest.

Flicka stopped a final time. Anna waited for him to pick up the scent. Time dragged. The fawn paced and cried. Twice he lay down and curled nose to tail as if he'd given up. He was as nervy as Anna and the respites were short-lived. After a restless moment he'd leap up again to run along the water's edge. At length he trotted back toward Anna, stopped dead in the path, and sitting on his haunches, bleated at the moon in a gentle parody of the wolf. Flicka was lost. Then so were Dot and Mona.

That's what you get for trusting prey to track predator, Anna thought acidly.

For lack of a better idea, she stayed where she was, eyes and ears waiting for the night to tell her something. The moon had pushed above the trees to the west. In this wan light, she noticed a scrap of white suspended several feet above the ground. A piece of paper had fallen and been caught on the spines of an oak seedling.

Wishing she had a flashlight and cursing whoever was responsible for maintaining Cumberland Island's fire cache equipment, she lifted the paper to her eyes. Of itself it told her nothing, but excited at the possibilities it suggested, she walked along at a snail's pace, searching each bush and blade of grass. Ten feet further on she was rewarded for her diligence. A second bit of paper was trampled into the wet earth in a footprint—it was too dark to see it without a flashlight but Anna could feel the edges with the tips of her fingers. By turning the paper this way and that she could discern what could have been the marks of a sneaker tread.

Four yards further she found another. Eyes opened by this discovery, she began looking for other signs, and despite the poor light, found them. Dot and Mona had dragged their feet, broken off twigs, dropped bits of paper and, once, a button from a blouse. Crafty old women, Anna thought, and smiled. With a more durable form of bread crumbs, they'd left a trail a blind woman could follow. Cast in the role of that blind woman, Anna inched along the narrow stretch of land between woods and water noting unsmoked cigarettes, a pocketknife, Mona's Timex, Dot's pinky ring, and three more buttons. She left the items where she found them. If Rick had better luck with his flashlight, he was sure to stumble across the trail more quickly than she had. She could use the company.

Heartened by Anna's taking the lead, Flicka gave up mourning and trotted at her side, poking at each new piece of information with a cool dry nose.

Twenty minutes were marked off in butts and buttons, then thirty; still Anna's ears picked up no sign of the other women. Going was slow, but at a guess, she and the fawn had been following the trail for a mile to a mile and a half. Schlessinger was walking Dot and Mona up the waterline into the designated wilderness area of the park where, though less than pristine or untrammeled, there was less likely to be any future disturbance of her makeshift graveyard. In wilderness areas no power equipment was allowed: no cars, ATVs, chain saws, bulldozers. The less readily accessible an area, the less it was used by visitors. Over the years Anna noticed even a modest walk—a half or three quarters of a mile from the parking lot—and the tourist component was reduced by ninety percent. People were lazy, people loved their cars, felt insecure away from them. Law enforcement officers—even federal law enforcement officers, contrary to some opinions—were people. Without compelling evidence, the further one had to walk from his patrol car, the less likely a search of that area became.

To Anna's right the bank grew steep. Currents eddying through the sound had undercut the soil and it had fallen away, exposing roots the size of a man's thigh. In places trees had all but toppled into the marsh. Clinging tenaciously to life, they hung over the sea grasses at right angles. In the dark, with what appeared to be a vast meadow undulating to her left, Anna found it unnerving. Her faith that she knew up from down had been severely challenged over the previous thirty-six hours.

Navigable land narrowed between the crumbling bank and the muddy commencement of the marsh. Losing options put Anna on edge but this was where the VIPs' trail was to be found and she had no choice but to follow it.

When she and the ever-faithful Flicka had traveled another mile or more, her ears picked up the sounds they'd been straining for. Voices, muted, distant, and suddenly stifled, hit her senses with the impact of an air horn in a closed room. She stopped so suddenly Flicka stumbled against her. The fawn, her admirable compatriot, had just become a liability. When he caught the scent of his bene-factresses he'd trot bleating into their midst, effectively announcing that he'd been freed and possibly followed. Anna's memory flashed back to a night in west Texas when she'd nearly laid down her life for a mountain lion. For those who'd seen the light, animals made good hostages. Anna could easily see Schlessinger, a knife at Flicka's throat, saying: "Nobody moves or Bambi gets it." Chances were Dot, Mona, even she, would do as they were told rather than see that perfect life cut down.

Sitting on a fallen log, Anna unlaced her boots. Beneath she wore two pairs of socks, thin knee-highs next to her skin to wick away the sweat, and thick cotton midcalf socks over those to cush-ion her feet from the rude leather of her Red Wings. Having pulled off both pairs, she laced her bare feet back into the boots, then fashioned a collar and leash for Flicka by tying all four socks to-gether. The end of this stretchy line she jammed down over a stub of broken branch that stuck up from the log where she sat.

"I'll be back," she whispered, and cupped his face between her hands. "Please, please be quiet or I'll make you into a venison sand-wich."

Flicka licked her hand.

"Stay," she whispered, and moved quickly away, afraid to look back lest eye contact inspire a spate of hopeful bleating.

The collapsed bank reached to the edge of the sound, blocking her path and providing cover. She stopped and listened. Flicka was blessedly quiet. From beyond the irregular wall of soil and roots she could hear Mona.

"I can't walk anymore." Mona's voice was too high, too loud. A thud, the recognizable sound of metal striking flesh, followed.

"Quiet." Schlessinger.

Moaning as directionless as that of the wind in the mountains undercut the command.

"You didn't have to—" Dot.

"Quiet!"

Quiet followed. Mona's bones were old, growing thin and brit-tle. Did one's skull grow thin and brittle as well? Anna couldn't remember reading anywhere that it did. Pressing her belly into the dirt, she wriggled her way upward. The ridge was ten or twelve feet high on the landward side and exposed the reaching claws of live oak root. Seaward it dwindled to nothing where the current took and redistributed the soil. Where Anna was it was maybe six feet high, and soft from its recent separation from the island proper. Loose dirt served her well, covering the noise of her ascent. Lizardlike, she reached the top of the berm and lifted herself up on her arms to peek over the crest. A lizard measuring distance, she thought as she bobbed on her short front legs. Laughter, as unbidden as when she was stoned, built in her lungs and she wondered if she'd become humor-impaired from her recent adventures.

On the far side of her hiding place Dot, Mona, and Marty Schlessinger were crowded onto a narrow neck of beach, squeezed between bank and marsh. Schlessinger stood, her shoulders and butt resting against the vertical wall of dirt. She held a six-cell flashlight in her left hand, its powerful beam trained on the two VIPs. In her right was a handgun. Not the simple cowboy six-cylinder wheel gun, but a Glock or a Sig-Sauer. Anna wasn't enough of a weapons aficionado to know the difference in the dark, but she could tell it was a semiauto with a magazine holding ten to thirteen rounds and one in the chamber. Looking at the familiar chunk of iron, she felt soft and naked. It wasn't at all pleasant.

Mona was crumpled in a heap, hugging her left knee the way Anna had seen injured hikers do. Dot knelt behind her in the mud, cradling her head against her chest. From beneath her fingers, near Mona's temple, a line of blood or slime crawled downward. By the indirect spill from the flashlight, Anna couldn't be sure which it was. It just looked black and viscous.

"She can't walk any further," Dot said firmly. "Your hitting her is just going to make it worse."

"I told you, I've got a bad knee," Mona said in a reedy voice. "It's gone out on me before. I can't walk on it."

"An old football injury," Dot said.

Anna caught the wry and startled glance Mona shot her friend.

"Two choices," Schlessinger said. "You get up and walk or I shoot you where you sit." Her body never changed position nor did the expression on her face alter in any way. Because she held the light, Anna couldn't see her as well as the others, but by the reflection of the moon off the water, Schlessinger looked too tightly strung, a guitar string about to snap. The skin of her face was rigid beneath her eyes and over her cheekbones. In the brief silence that followed the ultimatum, Anna became aware of the faintest of sounds, like distant rocks clashing together in the surf. Marty was grinding her teeth. The barrel of the gun hanging down by her thigh twitched spasmodically. The fingers of her left hand drummed on the barrel of the flashlight.

If her drug of choice was cocaine and she'd bolstered her courage with a line or two more than she was accustomed to, Marty Schlessinger was in a volatile state. Fear was not a factor, but paranoia was. Pain wouldn't figure into her equation till the drug wore off. Freedom from fear and pain gave her more courage than Anna cared to think about. Consequences, squeamishness, ethics, morality—all the leverage human beings use to keep themselves and one another from tearing society apart would have no effect.

"Shoot me then," Mona said, and dug a cigarette from the pocket of her trousers.

"I thought you used those to leave a trail," Dot said accusingly.

"Held one back to smoke before the execution. I'm a sucker for tradition." The words were brave and Anna was impressed, but she noticed Mona's hand shook so badly she could scarcely light her cigarette.

Their captor seemed not to hear or not to process the information. With a visible effort to keep the quaver from her lips, Dot went on with forced nonchalance. "We left quite a trail, Marty. There's no way you can erase it all. We left enough clues to send you to the gas chamber. Why don't you just let us go? Mona and I don't care a fig about this turtle thing. We never really understood how it worked. We're just a couple of senile old schoolteachers. Let us go and this never happened." Her voice grew stronger as she spoke. Years of compelling children to learn were not wasted.

With a glimmer of optimism, Anna waited for Marty to see reason.

Unmoved and unmoveable by humor, logic, or pathos, Schlessinger raised the semiauto with the unstoppable glide of a machine; preprogrammed and soulless.

"Holy shit," Anna whispered. All the weapons she didn't have flashed before her eyes. The tire iron still hung from her belt but it only worked when applied up close and personally.

The pistol was reaching the end of its arc. No sign of humanity yet sparked in Schlessinger's pupilless eyes. Dot and Mona, closed in a circle of hard light, Dot's hands on Mona's shoulders, watched the barrel with frozen fascination. In a supreme act of courage and defiance, Mona raised the cigarette to her lips and took in a lungful of smoke.

Time was up.

Without thought, Anna snatched up a rock the size of a Ping-Pong ball and hurled it at Schlessinger. Gender had robbed Anna of a childhood spent throwing and catching spherical objects. The rock hit the biologist in the hip. Light and gun rotated toward the embankment. Three rapid shots were fired into the woods. Schlessinger thought Anna was above her.

"Run!" Anna shouted. Dot and Mona sprang up, Mona's knee miraculously healed. The shout brought Schlessinger's gun and flashlight back around. She caught the VIPs in the beam. They had bolted north, away from the fall of dirt that hid Anna. Land gave way to marsh and they plowed only a yard or two through the knee-high muck and grass.

Screaming like a banshee, Anna began throwing everything she could lay her hands on: rocks, sticks, dirt clods, and something that felt suspiciously like a frog. Her shrieks were guttural, visceral, everything she could remember from training, monster movies, and PBS snuff films. She hoped she sounded like an army of lunatics.

Forgetting Dot and Mona, Schlessinger turned on Anna, this time firing in the right direction. Anna saw the muzzle flash at the same instant she felt a slug pound into the dirt by her elbow. Loose dirt was no match for bullets fired at close range. At best it would slow them down just enough so the hole they blasted through her body would be bigger and she'd die with less time for suffering. Balling up like a pill bug, she rolled to the bottom of the hill.

Three more shots slammed into the bank in rapid succession, sending down a rain of dirt. Now would be a good time for backup, Anna thought, though to be rescued in such an ignominious position would be galling.

She wanted to uncurl herself and move to better cover. The original barrage of rocks would have tipped anyone off—even someone slightly mad and seriously high—that their attacker was unarmed. Any minute Schlessinger would be coming over the ramparts of Anna's fort. For what seemed a deadly eternity but was less than a second or two, Anna's body refused to uncoil, to expose more of itself to danger. Then she was on elbows and knees snaking south through the mud. As she crawled, she hollered for Rick, Al, Dijon, and Guy; like Beau Geste, calling up a phantom army to keep Schlessinger off balance long enough for Dot and Mona to get out of the line of fire.

Given the efficiency of the island grapevine, Anna didn't hold out much hope the ruse would work for long. That the Hansons were to be staked out for a drug bust wasn't common knowledge, but everyone knew fire crew had been called off Cumberland for some law enforcement cloak-and-daggering.

A broken beam of light snapped over the berm. Anna logrolled into deeper water. Stretched full-length, she presented an irresistible target. The water was close to body temperature, making it hard to tell where she was wet and where she was dry. She could feel her hands sinking into the ooze that nourished the salt meadow. Grass, terribly sparse for the duties she required of it, rose a foot or so over her head. Disturbed slime gave off the rich smell of death and new life intermingling.

Distressingly buoyant, Anna's legs wanted to float, her shirt and trousers ballooning with air. Grasping the grass down near the roots, she anchored her boots in the muck and forced her body beneath the surface.

Marty Schlessinger reared up on top of the tumble of earth. Either she was crazy or she'd figured out Anna had nothing but rocks in her arsenal. Anna suspected both.

"Aaannaaa." The call was long and eerie, like that of an evil child. "Olly olly oxen free."

Despite the tropical temperature of the water, Anna felt an icy current running down her spine. Crazy people made her nervous. Politically correct or not, crazy people made everybody nervous. In madmen one couldn't help but see one's own potential slippage from sanity. All rules were suspended. The game changed. Not even the board remained the same.

"Your little old ladies are dead."

Sadness seasoned by a bitter sense of failure welled up within Anna. A repulsive gush of self-interest carried it away. Marty didn't dare leave Dot and Mona alive. If she'd already succeeded in killing them, Anna's responsibilities were at an end. She could lie low. She could run away. She could save her precious little hide. Inch by inch she began easing backward through the marsh grass toward the open sound. A quarter-mile's slither would bring her to swimmable water. After her long intimacy with chiggers and ticks, leeches struck her as almost family.

Pathetic bleating halted her progress. Flicka, tied to his stump, had been alarmed by the shots. Sorry, Anna thought cravenly. You're on your own.

"Flicka!"

Anna winced. It was Mona. Schlessinger had lied—or been mistaken. At least one little old lady was still alive.

His mistress's voice excited the fawn and he began to cry frantically, as if he were being disemboweled with a dull knife.

"Flicka!" Mona called again, closer this time. The fawn, unwitting, yet as effective as a Judas goat, was leading Anna's lambs to the slaughter. Cowardice begged her to stay in the marsh, her arms and legs and heart were heavy with it. Warm enfolding mud was her dearest companion. Eyes above the waterline no more than a self-respecting alligator's, Anna watched the events on shore unfold. Things slowed. A creature of the marsh, she watched the human drama with something approaching disinterest.

Grimly, methodically, reminiscent of the wooden men in clocks who raise their mallets day in and day out to strike off the hours, Marty Schlessinger's gaze was pulled from the south where Anna hid. The semiauto began to swing up. Pivoting smoothly on her uphill foot, she turned toward the fawn's guardian angel.

Necessity overcame self-preservation. With a shout, Anna came up out of the mud like a creature in a horror film. Less than twenty feet separated her from Schlessinger, but it stretched as distance will stretch in a dream. Pulling the tire iron from her belt, Anna pushed though air thick as the mud she'd come from. Roaring filled her ears. Some of it she recognized as her own, some a higher-pitched staccato. Mona and maybe Dot shouting.

Her back to the bank, the ocean in front of her, besieged from two sides, Schlessinger screamed like a cornered animal. The flash-light fell away, its beam spiraling down the side of the mound. Marty had the pistol in both hands. Fire flashed. Anna saw the ten inches of blue and knew the shot had gone in the direction of the VIPs. She yelled again. Time and distance collapsed. Suddenly she was at the bottom of Marty's mountain. Black of metal, of roots, of human limbs ran together. An explosion, so close Anna was deaf with it, struck at the same time as a numbing blow to her inner thigh.

Anna had been punched, rolled in toxic waste, tumbled off cliffs, and once, a woman had tried to drown her. But never had she been shot. Outrage flooded her veins. "You shot me!" she heard herself screaming. "You fucking *shot* me." Fury swept her up. She'd never been so angry; she was amazed her hair didn't catch on fire.

She hit Schlessinger in the knees and the woman fell back, head down the far side of the berm. Her feet came up; the toe of one boot caught Anna under the chin. Maybe it hurt, maybe it didn't. Anna was beyond pain.

Grasping Marty's ankles, she clawed her way up her body. Dirt mixed with the water streaming from her clothes and she stuck like glue. A fleeting question: How much of it was blood? She was alive, so the femoral artery hadn't been severed. That would have to be good enough.

Hands hammered at her head. Anna fought back, smashing the tire iron into what she hoped was fallible human flesh and not the unfeeling dirt of the bank. Locked in tightly, there wasn't much leverage and the blows did little harm. Stiff, clawlike fingers tore at her cheek. One ripped the corner of her mouth. She bit it and hung on like a terrier. Blood trickled down her throat, choking her. Her teeth were stopped by Schlessinger's bones.

Reduced to hand-to-hand: Schlessinger had lost her gun. Optimism lent Anna strength. Eyes were useless, the world was black. Her nose was clogged with the smell of dirt and sweat and fear. Kicking hard, she launched herself over the top of the crumbled earth to land on the biologist's chest. Shoving the tire iron down on Marty's throat, she held on.

The finger was wrenched from her jaws. Arms, strong as cable, wrapped around her. Together she and Schlessinger rolled down the far side of the bank. The cross of iron caught on something and was ripped from Anna's fist. She felt the tail end of it rake across the side of her neck. The fight had been going on less than half a minute but already Anna could feel her energy peaking and knew that before long she'd be out of gas. Fueled by drugs, Schlessinger had the upper hand.

Endangered Species

The world twisted. Schlessinger was on top, her weight pinning Anna to the muddy earth, her knee planted in the middle of Anna's chest. Fingers closed around her throat. Air was cut off. Muscles were burning up their reserves. Anna could feel her limbs growing heavy, her chest swelling. Grabbing one small finger, hopefully the one she'd bitten half through, she bent it back with all the force she could muster.

Schlessinger shrieked, high and wild like a wounded cat, and Anna sucked oxygen in through a bruised throat. Shouting and curses battered the air above her. Schlessinger still had one hand locked on the soft flesh of Anna's neck. Her fist began to pound into Anna's face. By whipping her head from side to side, Anna kept the blows glancing off. One landed true and she felt her eyeball explode under Marty's knuckles.

Anna jerked the knee of her uninjured leg up and arched her back. Unseated, the biologist fell away. Anna was stunned. She'd practiced that move a hundred times in self-defense classes all over the country. It never worked. But then she'd never been matched with someone her own size. The men she'd sparred with usually outweighed her by forty pounds or more.

Rolling to her stomach, she pushed up on all fours in time to catch a boot to her right ear. Down again; night closed around her in black bat wings, all the hurts heretofore unregistered clamoring for revenge; revolutionaries at long last loosed from under the thumb of the tyrant.

Doggedly she tried to think how she'd parry the killing blow.

It never came.

Shouts rained down instead, and light scraped across her face. Anna lifted her head. A great shadowy hulk that could only be Rick Spencer clutched a windmill of arms and legs to his chest. In the agitated strobe of a flashlight held in unsteady hands, Anna could see he'd caught Marty.

"Don't move or I'll break your arm."

"He will," Anna mumbled through rapidly swelling lips. "I'd do as he says if I were you."

Schlessinger continued to struggle. There was a sickening snap, a scream, then silence.

"You okay, Anna?" Rick asked.

"I was winning."

"Right."

Anna tried to rise and her left leg collapsed under her. "I'm shot," she remembered aloud. "She shot me. My leg."

"Shit." The flashlight beam had steadied. By its light Anna could see Rick threading two pairs of flexi-cuffs from the band of his hat and securing Schlessinger's wrist. "How bad are you?"

Anna shook her head, remembered she was in the dark, and said: "I don't know. Maybe bad."

"Shine the light on her," Rick ordered.

Anna cringed as the beam struck her eyes, then swept down her body.

"God damn," Rick said, and Anna was scared.

"Bad?" Anna tried to keep the fear from her voice and failed.

"I found it." Dot came into the circle of light, the butt of Marty's gun pinched between her thumb and forefinger.

Rick jerked down on the flexi-cuffs. Marty cried out and crumpled to the ground. "Move and I'll break your other arm," he warned. This time she believed him. Rick was causing Schlessinger unnecessary pain. Police brutality. Anna was all for it.

Rick took the gun from Dot and ejected the magazine into his hand. "Glock. Two rounds left. And one in the chamber. Safety is off. Just point and shoot. Anna, can you handle it?"

"For now."

Rick handed her the Glock and said to the VIPs, "If Anna passes out or whatever, you take it and keep the suspect covered till

I get back. If she does anything you don't like, just shoot her. Can you do that?"

"Yes indeed," Mona said, with a clarity that satisfied him.

"I'll get the paramedics out here. I won't be long. You hang on, Anna." Taking the flashlight, he set off back toward Stafford at a run.

By the light of the moon, Anna could see Dot and Mona staring at her with concern. Schlessinger had neither moved nor spoken since Rick sat her down. Most of Anna's body hurt. Her face felt like hamburger. Her left leg ached from groin to knee. Her head swam and nausea, brought on by blows to her belly or the blood she'd swallowed, threatened to boil up out of her throat.

Anna was scared.

"Can I hold Flicka while we wait?" she asked.

27

THE KEY to finding was looking in the right places; an absurd truth that negated the value of the search. Frederick was feeling let down. Success had rendered him of no further use to Molly Pigeon and he dreaded the call he must make telling her the good news, yet looked forward to it with the feverish optimism of a young lady in a Jane Austen novel.

He'd been home in Chicago for several days. The clutter of his apartment, once a comfortable refuge, felt claustrophobic. The chirpy attention of Danny and Taters, his two budgies, merely reminded him of how pathetic his social life had become. Anna had called twice and he'd let the machine answer. Before they spoke again, he needed to talk with Molly. Tonight was the night.

Chicago was in the clutches of August, his window-mounted air conditioner unequal to the task of making the house livable. Clad in underpants and a T-shirt, he sat in the living room feeling he should dress for the phone call and condemning himself as an idiot for the thought. Idiocy won out. He slipped a worn pair of khakis over his Fruit-of-the-Looms and sat down again facing the telephone.

Putting off knowing the inevitable for a few more minutes, he picked up the folder from the coffee table. Molly had given him hers at their last meeting and he smiled at the skull and crossbones, the dripping dagger. He'd saved it like a memento; he drank Scotch neat to feel close to her. In short, he clung to all the trite signs and symbols of romance. "Can't help myself," he said to Danny. The little bird hopped to the phone receiver and looked up at him expectantly. "I've never had the time to devise any symbols for myself."

The folder contained notes from the work he'd pursued on Molly's case. He'd used government time and equipment but didn't feel a shred of guilt. In the past twenty-five years he'd donated more hours of his life to the federal government than he'd ever tallied up.

His instinct on the plane had been right; Molly's was a sin of omission. He'd traced the three people who'd pressed her hardest to represent them or theirs in the wake of the Lester Mack defense. Second time out he hit pay dirt. One of the supplicants was a woman, a well-educated divorcée, with one son. At eighteen, that son had been arrested for the rape and torture of a sixteen-year-old high school girl who later died of injuries inflicted. Dr. Pigeon had refused to testify on the boy's behalf. He'd been sentenced to life, had served three years, then died in a knife fight in the prison cafeteria. Six days later Lester Mack was released, alive, well, and walking the streets a free man.

To the bereaved mother, this chain of events was cause and effect; proof Molly Pigeon could have freed her child and had chosen, instead, to be instrumental in his murder.

Frederick hadn't been able to interview the woman himself. NYPD detectives had done the honors. Given an audience of apparently sympathetic men in suits, she had confessed to the notes and messages. What she would be charged with remained to be seen. Nice upper-middle-class lady under the strain of grief—odds were she'd be given a slap on the wrist and Molly would be left looking over her shoulder for a while.

Not altogether satisfying in Frederick's opinion but par for the course. Bureaucrats made lousy heroes. There were too many Occupational Safety and Health Administration rules to allow for riding in on white horses and rescuing damsels in distress. Not to mention the civil suits the average superhero would leave himself open to.

He put down the file, lured Danny off the phone, and lifted the receiver. Molly answered just as he was about to hang up, not willing to face her answering machine. It was good to hear her voice. He let himself relax enough to lean back in the chair as he told her of the dead convict and his mother's confession. Molly listened without interruption, and when he finished, she waited a moment, letting the information soak in.

"Well," she said finally, "speaking as a citizen, I can't say I'm overwhelmed with relief. Professionally, I expect this will be the end of it. The first crush of grief is past. She frightened me, she got some attention. She knows I know she knows, so to speak, and should my body turn up in an alley, the police will know where to start asking questions."

"That's about it," Frederick said; then because he wanted to comfort, he added: "I don't think you'll hear from her again."

"No," Molly agreed.

Silence crept between them.

"Have you heard from Anna?" Frederick asked.

More silence, then: "I've been out most evenings."

"Neither have I." He wondered if he was telling the same lie as Molly. "You know I have feelings for you," he said awkwardly.

"I know."

No help there. He waited with growing discomfort. "And you?" he asked when he couldn't take it anymore.

"It doesn't matter," Molly said flatly. He knew it was true. Molly was Anna's sister. He'd expected nothing less. Still, he'd hoped, been intoxicated by the fantasy.

"Will you tell her?"

"Tell her what?" Molly was being intentionally obtuse. He waited and she relented. "No. And neither will you. Ever."

Frederick stirred his Scotch with his finger. The ice cubes had melted in record time. Like my love life, he thought with a dose of self-pity. It was time to hang up, but as he knew there'd never be another call, he procrastinated.

"Somebody should tell her something before she moves to Chicago," he said, because he was angry and to keep Molly with him a little longer.

A short bark of laughter struck across the phone line. "I wouldn't worry about it. Anna will never leave the wilderness."

28

RICK HAD GONE, and with him the noise and surrealistic horror of the fistfight. Marty lay like a broken doll where he'd left her, neither speaking nor responding when spoken to. Her arm must have been hurting but stubbornness or the anesthetic qualities of cocaine kept her from alluding to it.

Clasped in the loving arms of Dot, Flicka had been returned to the circle, and Anna found comfort in stroking the soft hide. Mona, her head seeping blood where Schlessinger's gun barrel had struck, was slightly dazed but insisted she was uninjured in any serious sense.

The dust settled and their minds began working again. Dot took the Glock and stood guard over the prisoner while Mona helped Anna peel off her mud-encrusted trousers. There was no blood and no wound, only an area of discolored flesh halfway between knee and crotch.

Endangered Species

"Wonderwoman," Mona said, and Anna laughed shakily. Schlessinger's bullet had struck some solid object—wood or stone—and a piece of nature's own shrapnel hit Anna in the leg with the force of a fast-pitched hardball. The belief that she was shot had been nearly as debilitating as the blow.

Tears prickled behind her eyes and she snorted to frighten them away. "I'd've felt pretty doggone silly if I'd died of this," she said as she zipped her pants. The power of the mind was an awesome thing. She was reminded of a woman who died from a king snake's bite. She was so sure it was a rattler, and so afraid, she'd gone into shock and died before she reached the hospital.

After a few tries, Anna found she could walk. The pain was bad enough that she guessed there might be a hairline fracture of the femur, but nothing that wouldn't heal itself in time.

Waiting for a lights-and-sirens rescue with hot and cold running paramedics anxious to get in on a bona fide gunshot wound was too loathsome to contemplate. Having prodded the resolutely mute biologist to her feet, Anna leaned on Dot and they began a slow limping trek the two miles back to Stafford House.

To help pass the time and take their minds off their injuries, Dot and Mona filled in some of the blanks left in Anna's picture of events. Schlessinger, believing Dot and Mona to be dead women, had indulged in boasting of her own cleverness.

Anna had been right about the microscope and the assistants. Both had been billed to the loggerhead account and the money taken by Schlessinger, but it went deeper than that. The ten-year turtle study was funded by a $112,000 grant to be paid in two installments, half on commencement and half two years into the study. Schlessinger had embezzled and spent the first half very quickly. In September she was to receive the second half. Hammond figured out the scam and wanted fifty percent as his price for silence. Marty hit upon a less expensive guarantee.

Schlessinger had been given carte blanche more or less, and had been the only one to take an interest in the loggerhead project files until Chief Ranger Hull decided to have them updated and put on the new computer system. Evidence of the embezzlement was there to a trained eye. Suddenly it became imperative that Schlessinger locate and destroy the old files.

And, Dot added, the old file clerks as well.

While they talked, Marty shambled along ahead of them, her eyes on the ground, picking her path with great care, looking for the smoothest trail, one that wouldn't jar her broken bones.

Anna asked her how she'd known to sabotage the actuator rod and whether she'd lied about hearing the shotgun blast that took the Austrian's leg, but she wasn't talking.

"Oh, so now the cat's got your tongue," Mona said unkindly. No one begrudged her this minute breach of manners. "I seem to recall hearing that Old Number One died in a wreck. Want to bet it crashed for the same reason Slattery's crashed?"

A plane wreck; the answer had been in front of them all along. Anna remembered being told Marty's husband had been killed in a crash. Everyone on the island knew that. Like Anna, they'd probably assumed it was a car crash, America's favorite way to die. Perhaps Schlessinger knew how to ruin the actuator rod because she'd done it before.

Less than a mile from the cottage Rick came back to them. This time he was armed with a red jump kit of first-aid supplies, extra flashlights, and Lynette Wagner. A helicopter with emergency medical personnel was on its way from the mainland and would be landing at the Stafford meadow. Already the faint chuff-chuff of the blades could be heard in the distance.

Rick's admiration for Anna's fortitude turned to ribbing as soon as she admitted that she had not, in fact, taken a bullet.

"I'm shot! It's bad," he mimicked in a falsetto.

"It looks like it's going to leave a real nasty bruise," Mona said in Anna's defense.

"Oh, no! Not a bruise!" Rick squealed.

Anna groaned inwardly. She was never going to live this one down. Her only hope was to dye her hair, change her name, and leave town.

Lynette was, as Anna had come to expect, sympathetic and helpful. She was even reasonably sober considering the quantity of wine she and Tabby had consumed. Anna found Rick's teasing easier to bear up under than Lynette's kindness. It was part of an unwritten code. Bravery was possible when one's companions made light of one's predicament. Sympathy could unman the most stalwart.

Paramedics descended on them in a flurry of efficiency just as they reached Stafford's grounds. They did a decent job of hiding their disappointment at Anna's relative good health, settling for one broken arm (Schlessinger's), a possible concussion (Mona's), and assorted cuts and contusions.

As the last of the on-scene ministrations were being finished up, the sheriff from St. Marys docked at Stafford pier. Marty would be transported to the hospital, placed under guard, and removed to the jail once the doctors released her. Mona was also going to the hospital to get her head wound checked.

Anna dug in her heels and refused transport, even to the extent of signing the obnoxious form she'd shoved under countless park visitors' noses; a form swearing they'd been told what idiots they were and absolving the medical personnel of any liability should they get what they deserved for refusing treatment.

As they carried a compliant—almost to the point of being catatonic—Marty Schlessinger toward the waiting helicopter, Rick looked longingly after them. "This is really your collar, Anna. You want to go?"

"I'm already in enough trouble," she said. "Do you want it?"

"Is this a trick question?" Rick was so eager, she was tempted to torture him for a moment. Fatigue rather than a good heart stopped her.

"Be my guest."

Happy as a hound on a hunt, he loped off after the paramedics.

The sheriff took statements and drank instant coffee till Anna thought either her head or his bladder would burst under the strain. Four hours on the wrong side of midnight he finally left. Dot, Anna, and Lynette sat around the kitchen table in the cottage staring blankly at one another. Tabby snored daintily from amid the ruin of files on the sofa.

"Hey, some girls' night out, huh?" Lynette said after a while. "On top of everything else, my period started."

Anna tried to smile but it hurt.

"Don't let any of these southern boys find out," Dot warned her. "They'll steal your used tampons for deer bait. Ugh."

The packages of meat in Slattery's freezer; the frozen tampons. Anna thought she'd laughed, but all that came out was a strangled croak.

"You should have gone to the hospital," Dot scolded. "You're in worse shape than you think. You'd better stay here tonight."

"No," Anna said. "Thanks." Thoughts were hard to string together; movement struck her as wildly improbable. Yet, more than anything, she longed to be by herself, responsible for nothing and no one. "You'll stay with Tabby?" she asked Lynette when she managed to piece together what she needed and how to get it.

"Aren't you going back to Plum Orchard?"

"I want to go home." Dot and Lynette looked at her with alarm and Anna realized she was sounding a little off-the-wall. "Back to the fire dorm, I mean. My own room."

"I don't think you should be alone," Dot said.

Anna sat in mulish silence. A minute's war of wills, then Lynette sighed. "If that's what you want, I'll drive you over."

"I'll take the truck," Anna said. The need to be alone had mushroomed until she craved it as intensely as Marty Schlessinger must have craved cocaine. In her present mood she could easily understand killing for it. Solitude was a drug harder to come by in the modern world than most.

She tried to stand but couldn't do it without help. Her injured leg throbbed, the large muscle outraged at recent abuse. She ran her fingers lightly over it. The flesh was raised half to three quarters of an inch in an area twice the size of her palm. Frightening visions of blood clots and internal hemorrhaging made her wish for an instant that she'd gone to St. Marys. But only for an instant. *In hospitals everybody messes with you.* "I can walk," she growled. But she couldn't.

At a loss, Dot and Lynette just watched her clinging to the edge of the table. Finally Dot put her fists on her hips and puffed out her exasperation. "Anna, you're acting like a dog with a sore paw. We try and help you and you bite us." Her eyes bored into Anna's and, shamed back into third grade, Anna mumbled an apology.

"Much better. Mona's got an old cane from when she broke her foot. I'll get you that. Lynette will take you to the dorm. One of the boys can get your truck tomorrow. That's all there is to it. Are you going to be a pill?"

"No, ma'am."

As ordered, Lynette took her back to the dorm. Over protests, she drew Anna a bath, settled her in it, then used Guy's key to unlock the fire cache and brought her a clean pair of pants, a shirt, and a sleeping bag. "You can return them tomorrow," she said. "Who'll know?"

After the interpretive ranger left, Anna meant to shampoo her hair, wash her battered face and take stock of the damage. She fell asleep in the tub before she could begin.

A troubled dream was shattered by the bathroom door banging open. Anna's heart responded with a bang of its own and she started to get out of the bath. The water had grown cold. Her skin was puckered and white. She looked as if she were dead and wished it were true.

A shout of "Rick!" followed the crash and a shocked, "Who the fuck— My God, it's you," and a hasty retreat. Safe with the door between them, Dijon talked to her through the wood. "What are you doing here, Anna?" he demanded. "What happened to your face? Have you been having fun without me?"

Nearly a week had passed and Anna had gratefully settled back into the dull routine of presuppression. Her leg still hurt her but she kept it covered and never complained. She even kept her limping to a minimum except when she was around Rick. Then she let it show, hoping to keep her credit good.

Tabby had had her baby. A healthy seven-and-a-half-pound boy. Her parents were there for the birth and would fly her home to Seattle. Tomorrow they would all be flying home and Anna was relieved. Cumberland Island had taken its toll.

Zach was gone. As was Frederick. The night after Schlessinger's arrest Anna had finally gotten through to him by phone. She'd told him she was not coming to Chicago. He'd been understanding. So much so it had annoyed her, but she knew it was just her ego that was hurting. In time she'd be glad there were no hard feelings. Passion was a two-edged sword. It had cut neither of them too deeply.

Tonight she felt nothing but weariness and a sense of peace she'd not enjoyed in a while.

Stretching her injured leg out in front of her, she looked down the long expanse of beach. Everyone had turned out for the hatching, including the moon, full and ripe and inviting. On this one night human lights were banished and people were allowed to truly be a part of the night.

The nests they watched over were not the ones Anna had seen laid her first week on Cumberland. She and the others would be long gone when those turtles made their dash to the ocean. These were on the northern end of the island, out from the alligators' pond, where sound hooked into sea.

Lynette, Dot, Mona, and the rest of fire crew were spread along the dunes, each with a site to monitor. Air was warm and stirred with an offshore breeze. Sand and sea vied to see who had the most hues of silver in her gown. Stars burned low and steady. Schlessinger had traded this for a drug-induced high and, now, four walls.

Down the dune from where Anna perched, hugging her knees, the sand began to quiver. The movement was so minute it could have been a trick of the light, but she felt her breath catch in her throat. They were coming. Grains shifted, slid, formed tiny whorls and sinks as if the earth itself came to life. Sliding down as near as she dared, Anna watched the emergence of a new generation. The first miniature flipper pushed above the silver and she laughed aloud. A wee head followed. A mighty struggle contained in two inches of amphibian ensued. Anna wanted to help, to free it, to scoop it up and caress it, but man was its main predator. Her touch would be as soothing to the loggerhead as the lick of a pit bull to a newborn kitten.

Soon a dozen flippers had forced their way through the sand, exciting wavelets in a dry sea of their own making. When the first started its resolute march to an ocean it had never seen, Anna thought she would burst with pride.

Limping ahead and back, jousting with ghost crabs and shooing away gulls, she gloried in the progress of the turtles across the expanse of beach and laughed to see the waves pick them up for the first time, bobbing them about like awkward ships built by the hands of children.

The last three had reached the threshold of their new home, felt the wash of their new element, when Anna heard the shout.

"Maggie-Mary—she's after my turtles!"

"Take care of yourselves," Anna whispered to the last of the little loggerheads. "Duty calls."

When Death Comes Stealing

A Tamara Hayle Mystery
'A riveting, emotional page-turner of an
ending. An excellent debut novel' *Booklist*

Valerie Wilson Wesley

'Wesley is one of very few black women writers writing in
this genre ... a welcome new voice and a fresh point of
view'   *USA Today*

Tamara Hayle fell in love with DeWayne Curtis when she
was too young to know any better. The result was a
disastrous marriage and Jamal, now fourteen. A private
investigator, the last thing single mother Tamara wants
back in her life is her shady ex-husband, but when he begs
her to help him through some serious trouble she can
barely refuse. For his eldest son has died a violent death
and DeWayne's sons are the only humans he seems
genuinely to care about, apart from himself. Then five days
later there's another killing. And Tamara realises that
unless she does something, and quick, her own son is next
on a killer's list ...

'Quick and often funny ... reads like a successful
collaboration between Terry McMillan and Sue Grafton'
                                              Kirkus Reviews

'Grips you by the throat and never lets go until the last
spine-tingling word ... a well-created novel with a poignant
message that resonates long after the mystery is solved'
                                        Bebe Moore Campbell

0 7472 4759 5

HEADLINE